ALSO BY LUCY GILMORE

The Lonely Hearts Book Club
The Library of Borrowed Hearts

A THOUSAND LITTLE GOODBYES

LUCY GILMORE

sourcebooks casablanca

Published by Sourcebooks Casablanca, an imprint of Sourcebooks
1935 Brookdale RD, Naperville, IL 60563-2773
(630) 961-3900
sourcebooks.com

Library of Congress Cataloging-in-Publication Data

Names: Gilmore, Lucy (Romance fiction writer) author
Title: A thousand little goodbyes / Lucy Gilmore.
Description: Naperville, IL : Sourcebooks Casablanca, 2026.
Identifiers: LCCN 2026000934 | trade paperback | epub
Subjects: LCGFT: Romance fiction | Novels
Classification: LCC PS3607.I45258 T46 2026 | DDC 813/.6--dc23/eng/20260121
LC record available at https://lccn.loc.gov/2026000934

Printed and bound in Canada.
MBP 10 9 8 7 6 5 4 3 2 1

For Alex

Boba tea is way too sweet, but I'll drink it with you anytime.

CONTENT NOTE

A Thousand Little Goodbyes is, ultimately, a love story. Not necessarily *romantic* love but the love that exists between childhood friends, between a mother and her child, and between all the people who make life worthwhile.

It's also a story about death.

We've always been a divided and complicated society, but some of our starkest differences come from belief systems related to birth and death. In this book, I'm inviting you to take a journey through the entire process with me. You'll encounter children being born and other children (off-page) dying. You'll witness the toll that cancer takes on entire families. You'll also discover that not everyone approaches the process of saying goodbye in the same way, particularly when there is a choice in the matter through death-with-dignity services.

I am in no way an expert on terminal illnesses or end-of-life care, and there is still so much research that needs to be done on the subject, but I have always believed that the best judge for what is right for you is *you*—whether that means hospice care surrounded by those you love, a fight to stay alive using all available resources, or physician-assisted suicide in a safe and legal environment.

So proceed with caution, Dear Reader, and proceed with compassion. And always, always know that you are loved.

Additional content warnings include: parental neglect, emotional abuse, child abandonment, childhood cancer, teen pregnancy, teen runaway, referenced statutory rape, stroke, hospitalization, and grief and loss.

Chapter One

MEDFORD, OR

Present Day

"ARE YOU OKAY STOPPING TO SEE a two-headed calf, or does that hit a little too close to home?"

Chrissie Thomas glanced up from the map spread out in front of her, the pucker in her brow deepening as the May sunrise smacked her straight in the face.

"A two-headed calf?" she echoed. She dropped her finger to the route she'd been studying so she could return to it once Scarlett finished explaining this bizarre new conversational thread. Based on personal experience—twenty-seven years of it, in fact—this could take anywhere from a few minutes to several days. When it came to talking, Scarlett Sanderson was queen, king, and royal consort all in one.

"Yeah. According to this website, one head is named Peter and the other is Paul. For twenty bucks, you can get your picture taken with them. That sounds fun, right? Very P. T. Barnum. Unless you think it might upset you, in which case we'll skip it. There's a giant ball of twine in Minnesota that should scratch the same itch."

Chrissie gave up on holding her place and folded the map—a

throwback Scarlett had wheedled out of the gas station attendant to create a "more authentic road-trip experience." If *Chrissie* had been working at that gas station, she'd have taken one look at the RAV4 Hybrid they'd rented for the trip, plus the exquisite camel-colored cashmere sweat suit Scarlett was wearing, and demanded every penny.

But Scarlett had flirted and laughed and told her entire life's story to the poor man until he'd had no other choice. Charmed against his will—as people often were when the petite, lively brunette entered their orbit—he'd hand-selected the most useful maps, offered them free of charge, and even threw in a pack of meat sticks for good measure.

"I guess it depends on how well the calf—calves?—are being treated," Chrissie said. "Is it a nice place, or are their living conditions just going to make me sad?"

"The calf's not *alive*, Chrissie. He's taxidermied. In fact, this place has been around for like sixty years, so there's a good chance someone's great-grandpa just sewed the head of one animal onto another and has been using it to make money off tourists ever since." Scarlett paused, her lips forming a thoughtful moue. Scarlett was the only person Chrissie had ever met whose every action demanded a French description. She made moues and fell into bouts of ennui. She drank aperitifs and flaunted her décolletage at every opportunity.

The only French thing Chrissie could claim coming into contact with recently was of the toast variety.

"If he's stuffed, it's probably okay," Chrissie said, confused. "But I don't understand..."

Scarlett turned to face her. They were parked outside a gas station in Medford, Oregon, where their two-week cross-country journey was slated to begin. Since Scarlett had insisted they start early—which, as a morning radio personality, meant somewhere in the region of four o'clock in the wee hours—they had the whole place to themselves.

"You know what I mean. With your whole thing." Scarlett waved a vague hand in Chrissie's direction.

Chrissie glanced down. She was also dressed in oversized sweats, though hers were a much more affordable Walmart set, her brown hair swept up in a messy knot at the top of her head. It would have been easy to read censure into her friend's gesture, especially considering the outrage Scarlett had shown when Chrissie arrived at the door with her feet in a pair of oversized rainbow Crocs, but Chrissie didn't think her studied lack of fashion was the punch line this time.

"My thing," she echoed slowly.

Scarlett gestured again, even more vaguely than before. "Yeah. You know. Your whole *devoured my twin in utero* thing."

"Wait. Are you serious?" She almost believed Scarlett *was* serious for half a second before common sense caught up with her. "You wretch. Stop trying to rile me up. You don't honestly believe I'm walking around with my unborn twin's head sprouting out of my body."

"I mean, I don't know how it works." Scarlett blinked innocently at her across the console, but the twinkle in her dark brown eyes was unmistakable. "You *have* always been weird about wearing a bathing suit in public."

Chrissie gave in with a laugh. That, more than anything, confirmed her belief that this road trip was a good thing—a *necessary* thing. She couldn't remember the last time she'd laughed out loud, let alone at this hour. For the past few months, most of her mornings had been spent in the cold, stony silence of a teenager's wrath.

"I'm carrying around a tiny bit of extra DNA, Scarlett. It's not like I'm not walking around with random body parts in unladylike places."

"Huh." Scarlett made a face. "Is it bad I'm disappointed by that?"

"Yes," came Chrissie's quick reply. "But bless your heart for asking. I can't believe it took you this long to work up the nerve."

"Well, I didn't want to seem *intrusive*." Scarlett's sudden peal of laughter matched Chrissie's own. "Though I did used to sneak a peek whenever you changed into pajamas when we were kids. You were always so secretive about it, like showing a flash of stomach would put you on the straight path to hell. Which is a shame, because you've always had the most amazing body."

Chrissie rolled her eyes and started up the car. If she knew Scarlett—and she did—the two-headed calf would only be the first of many such stops. They had fourteen entire days to make their way from Chrissie's home in Oregon to the tiny village in Vermont where Scarlett promised a "mystery surprise" awaited them. Scarlett would want to visit every roadside attraction and hole-in-the-wall diner along the way, making the most of a vacation they'd spent the better part of their late teens and twenties promising they'd take before they reached the ripe age of thirty.

They'd reached thirty over four years ago without so much as a weekend girl's trip to take the edge off, but that was more Chrissie's fault than Scarlett's. Scarlett might have been a recognizable name in the talk-radio circuit, living her glamorous life in a sugary confection of a condo in downtown San Francisco, but Chrissie was the one with dentist appointments to schedule and volleyball tournaments to chaperone, not to mention an elderly cat with cystitis that caused him to pee on literally every rug in the house.

Despite Rufio's advanced years—the cat had to be, what, twenty by now?—he showed no desire to cross the rainbow bridge. The dratted animal would end up outliving them all, and since Chrissie had faithfully promised the previous owners of her house that she'd take care of him after they moved to Hawaii, she had no choice but to see him through to the end.

"If you had to humanely dispose of a cat, how would you do it?" Chrissie asked as she pulled the car out of the parking lot and headed in the direction of the freeway.

"Drown him," Scarlett responded without hesitation. She slipped a pair of oversized Gucci sunglasses over her eyes and settled back against the seat.

"Scarlett!"

Her friend's rich chuckle sounded again, filling the whole car with its warmth. That laugh was the main reason why her radio show, *Scarlett Sunrise*, was so popular. Five million listeners a week plugged in to that sound—no small feat when radio had been on the decline for years.

"What? You forget I've been to your house. I don't care how many candles and air fresheners you use. Nothing short of burning the whole thing down will get rid of that smell."

"I know." Chrissie heaved a sigh. "But Rufio can't seem to help himself."

Scarlett slipped the sunglasses down, piercing Chrissie with the rich chocolate of her gaze. "You know the people who sold you that house didn't actually move to Hawaii, right?"

"What?" Chrissie touched the brakes a little too hard, sending them both lurching against their seat belts. "What are you talking about? Of course they did. It's why they left Rufio behind. They said it would be cruel to make him go through all the state quarantine requirements at his age."

Scarlett's response to this was a slow shake of her head. "You poor, deluded fool. I'm pretty sure they only went as far as Ashland. They took one look at you, read your full measure, and saw a chance of escape. I bet their new house smells amazing—nary a whiff of ammonia anywhere."

Chrissie opened her mouth and closed it again, not so much at a loss for words as she was coming to the realization that Scarlett was right.

"So *that's* why they blocked my Facebook friend request. And here I thought I must've done something to upset them."

Scarlett clucked her tongue the way she always did when she was annoyed with Chrissie. But then she softened it by reaching over and patting Chrissie's gray-sweats-clad knee.

She always did that, too. Sweet with the sour. Pleasure with the pain.

"If ever I have a cat that needs killing, you're the last person on earth I'd turn to." Scarlett winked. "But if I want someone to drop everything for two weeks and come with me on the trip of a lifetime, then you're exactly my gal."

Peter and Paul weren't sewn together, but they were preserved in an enormous formaldehyde jar, which somehow seemed worse.

"Well, that was a bust," Scarlett said as she handed over the twenty bucks and accepted the glossy photo the proprietor printed out from his home computer. They'd been forced to sit and make idle chitchat with his wife while the image took shape. "You look cute, though, so that's something. You should set this as your Tinder profile and see what happens."

Chrissie peeked at the picture and immediately wrinkled her nose. "I don't even want to think about what kind of men would be attracted by two floating cow heads. Look. No matter which way you move, it feels like their eyes are following you."

"It's called trompe l'œil," Scarlett said matter-of-factly. One year abroad in Paris, and she could have moonlighted as a tour guide at the Louvre. "And believe me when I say those aren't the two things men will be focusing on in that picture."

They'd agreed to switch places for the next leg of the trip, so Chrissie opened the passenger door while Scarlett adjusted the driver's seat to accommodate her shorter stature.

"Admit it," Scarlett added as the pair of them settled in. "You haven't been on a date in the last decade, have you?"

Chrissie's response came with knee-jerk speed. "Yes, I have! I went on one a few weeks ago."

Scarlett coughed.

"Okay, a few months ago."

She coughed again.

Chrissie gave in by flinging up her hands. "Fine. It's been years. Are you happy now?"

"Not really, no. That's the most pathetic thing I've ever heard." Then, "How *many* years?"

Chrissie had to do some quick mental math. "Three, I think? I remember it was right before Kat had her tonsils out. The poor thing. She refused to let me leave her side even to sleep because she was so uncomfortable. We ended up bunking in her bed and watching every single episode of *Supernatural* back-to-back."

She still carried with her the memories of that week—up to and including the sickly sweet smell of her then-thirteen-year-old daughter's breath as her throat healed from the surgery—but she didn't regret them. If anything, she missed them. Kat hadn't needed her like that in very long time.

She hadn't *wanted* her in even longer.

As if reading her mind, Scarlett cast her a sideways glance. "You're a good mom, Chrissie. A great one, in fact."

"Say that to the text I got from her a few minutes ago."

"Uh-oh. Was it all in caps?"

"No. It was lowercase, which is worse." Chrissie dug out her phone and flashed the screen at her friend.

lily didn't kill me in my sleep but she did give me every bottle of acne cream she owns. she says i obviously need them more than her. hope your little trip is worth the future therapy bills.

Scarlett's signature laugh filled the car again. "Uh-oh. Lily is the frenemy?"

"Just enemy. No *f-r*." Chrissie tucked the phone away again, but not before texting back a GIF of a wide-eyed puppy looking remorseful. According to her daughter's superior wisdom, GIFs were woefully outdated and cringey in the highest degree, but Chrissie liked them. They made her feel fun. "Lily's the volleyball coach's daughter, and I can't say that I blame Kat for hating her. She looks like a young Tyra Banks and spikes like a doped-up Misty May."

Scarlett had yet to start the car, opting instead to turn toward Chrissie with the full force of her attention. That trait had always been both one of the best and the worst things about Scarlett. She *cared*, but she did it in such a way that it made Chrissie feel like she was standing naked on an empty stage.

"I'm assuming that second one is some kind of volleyball reference?"

Chrissie splayed her hands helplessly. "Welcome to my world."

"And this Lily girl... She's who Kat is staying with while you're away? You gave your only daughter into the care and keeping of a person she hates?"

An acidic pang of guilt took up residence in Chrissie's gut. It cozied up well with the nausea she was feeling from one of Scarlett's free gas station meat sticks. She shouldn't have eaten the thing so early in the day, but she'd never been one to let food go to waste. When her daughter had been a toddler, most of Chrissie's meals had been the last vestiges of macaroni and cheese or dinosaur chicken nuggets, the discarded crusts of sandwiches long gone stale. In fact, she *still* ate like that—hunched over the sink, picking the mushrooms and onions out of takeout containers so Kat wouldn't have to be confronted with their horrors.

"Technically speaking, she's being cared for by Walsh. The coach. His daughter is just an unfortunate side effect."

"Hmm," Scarlett said. Just that—just *hmm.*

"Look, it's not like I had a ton of options. Two weeks is a long time to ask anyone to take care of a sixteen-year-old. Her best friend is on the trip to New York, so staying with her isn't an option, and it's not like I can leave Kat on her own with Rufio the whole time. And my mom and dad—"

But here she cut herself off. If there was one person in the world she didn't need to explain her parents to, it was Scarlett.

The rest of it Chrissie *had* explained—or attempted to, anyway—though she doubted Scarlett understood just how much her daughter hated her right now. The only reason Chrissie had agreed to this road trip in the first place was because Kat had been invited on a tour of the United Nations in Manhattan with her history class for the same two-week period, an aligning of the stars that had seemed so fortuitous at the time that she almost suspected a trap.

There *hadn't* been a trap, but there had been a fall.

A vaping incident in the bathroom at school and the principal's strict no-smoking policy had ruined all of Chrissie's carefully laid plans. She'd had no choice but to ground her daughter, both literally and figuratively. Her airplane privileges had been revoked, the trip refunded, and alternate arrangements made. And Chrissie, with a conscience pricked so many times over it felt like a sieve, had done nothing to change her own plans except to beg Kat's volleyball coach to take her in while she was gone.

"I'm doing the best I can," she said, though she wasn't sure if she was convincing Scarlett or herself.

"Whoa, babe." Scarlett threw up her hands in a gesture of surrender. "You know I'm not judging your parenting choices. I'm just trying to figure out how I can bring this Lily girl down a peg or two. Do you think Kat would be willing to switch out her shampoo with Nair?"

Chrissie laughed, but that was quickly replaced by a frisson of alarm. With Scarlett, you never knew how far she'd push things.

"Please don't encourage Kat down that path. There's already a mean-girl streak in her a mile wide. It's so strange. I was prepared for every other aspect of adolescence—the heartbreak and the struggles, the cruelty of kids that age and how it can break you down inside—but no one ever told me that *Kat* might be the one to make everyone around her miserable."

"Maybe you should schedule her for another minor surgery," Scarlett suggested in a tone that indicated she was only half joking. "No one really *needs* an appendix these days, do they?"

"No way. A hospital is the last place I'm taking her for bonding time."

"Why not? It worked for us, didn't it?"

At this, Scarlett triumphantly started the car. That was another one of the best and worst things about her. Once she won an argument—or at the very least, *assumed* she had—nothing could drag her back into it again.

"Your problem, Chrissie, is that you're not willing to think outside the box. You never have been. You like it too much in there, all cramped and beige."

"I'm not beige," Chrissie protested, but in vain. Her friend might be the one dressed in head-to-toe camel and sporting a Burberry scarf over her pixie-cut hair, but they both knew that Scarlett was the one who brought color into the world.

Color and laughter and life.

Life most of all.

Chapter Two

PORTLAND, OR

1999

SCARLETT SAW THE NEW GIRL THREE times before she got up the nerve to speak to her.

At seven years of age, Scarlett should have been absolutely *drowning* in friends. She was funny, she was nice, and even though people said she talked too much, she didn't say even close to all the things that were bursting inside her heart.

Unfortunately, just about her whole life had been spent inside this stupid hospital, being poked and prodded and stabbed with so many needles that she had a favorite one. (The 24-gauge was the nicest, but only if Nurse Penny was the one putting it in. She always sang a little song that made it slide in like butter.) That was Scarlett's excuse, anyway, for why she took one look at the new girl and fell hard.

For one thing, the girl was probably the most beautiful person Scarlett had ever seen, all big blue eyes and long, silky hair. Scarlett coveted that hair more than anything else in the world, even more than the pretty flower scarves some of the other kids wrapped around their heads when they came in for treatment.

For another thing, the girl was sad. Not the usual kind of sad, like when people watched movies where everyone died in the end or got a tour of the pediatric cancer ward for the first time, but a different kind of sad—one that she tried to hide in the way she shuffled her feet and kept her eyes fixed on the floor.

Scarlett knew everything there was to know about people trying to hide their sadness. When you were a kid who had cancer-with-a-capital-C, that was all anyone did.

Getting stabbed with a needle? *What a big, brave girl you are!* (Smile.)

Puking your guts out from your recent bout of chemo? *There, now. Doesn't that feel better?* (Smile.)

Wheeling past the empty bed in the room next to yours, where just yesterday your friend Paco was playing checkers with his dad? *Don't cry, love. He's in a better place now. He wouldn't want you to be sad.* (Smile.)

"Psst!" Scarlett called from her position on her bed. She longed to spring up and chase the girl down the hall, but she was trapped by her IV. This was the good part of chemo, when the bad drugs hadn't hit yet but the good ones had. Scarlett always had a few hours where she longed to climb out the window and scale the hospital walls, certain that if she didn't make it to the rooftop, she could at least fly back down to the ground again.

"You!" she called again. "Girl with the hair! C'mere!"

The girl with the hair stopped in the middle of her slow shuffle down the hall. "Are you talking to me?" she asked in a soft voice.

She blinked at Scarlett without any of the usual embarrassment the other kids showed when they visited. People who weren't used to hospitals didn't know where to look, so their eyes darted around like the whole room was on fire—and like Scarlett was on fire, too. This girl's straightforward gaze was the opposite of that, like a splash of cool water on her heated skin.

In that instant, Scarlett decided this girl was her new best friend.

"Yes. You have the longest hair of anyone I've ever seen. Can I touch it?"

The girl found nothing odd in this request. She came closer to the bed and bent her head, letting the beautiful strands tumble like a waterfall over Scarlett's hand.

"Oh, it's perfect," Scarlett breathed as she ran her fingers through without hitting a single snag. "Even before all mine fell out, it was short and brown and boring. When I grow new hair, I'm gonna get some exactly like this."

"I'm growing it out so I can donate it," the girl said. "My brother's nurse said it's a nice way to help."

Now her eyes were doing that avoiding thing, only not in the way that meant she was uncomfortable with the dripping IVs and beeping monitors. She was back to looking at her toes in that sad way.

"Your brother is the one with leukemia, right?" Scarlett asked. The girl shifted her body toward the door like she was getting ready to leave, so Scarlett rushed, "I've seen him a few times, but only from far away. They keep him pretty isolated. There was a boy in here once who could only be visited from behind a plastic curtain, but we all kinda liked it. If you wanted to touch him or play with him, you had to stick your hands in these huge, blue alien gloves. He used to challenge people to Lego-building races, only of course no one else had a chance against him with those big ol' gloves. I don't really like Legos—they hurt my fingernails—but I always played anyway. He knew all kinds of weird facts about tortoises. Did you know that the oldest tortoise in the world is a hundred and sixty-seven? His name is Jonathan, which seems like a silly name for an animal, but that's grown-ups for you. They have no imagination."

The girl relaxed as Scarlett's chatter continued, which was the *exact* thing she was hoping for.

"What would you name a hundred-and-sixty-seven-year-old tortoise?" the girl asked.

If Scarlett hadn't been chained to her bed with all these stupid needles and cords, she'd have jumped up in excitement.

"Ooh, I never really thought about it before. Reginald von Otterwinks, maybe? Or Mr. Higgypiggles? Ol' Stompyfoots?"

"Sir Hides-a-Lot?" the girl suggested.

Scarlett giggled. "Yes! That's the one. You must be really smart, huh?"

The girl's cheeks turned pink. "I don't know. No one's ever asked me that before."

"Probably because they can already tell," Scarlett said with all the confidence of her seven years of life on earth. "Can I share a secret with you?"

"Oh, um." The girl looked around, her blue eyes wide. "Are you sure you should?"

Of course she was. All the secrets and hopes and fears that bubbled up inside her had been *waiting* for this chance to break free. She clasped her hands in front of her and, forgetting the machines hooked up to her veins, sat up straight in bed.

It was a mistake.

Before she could say even a little bit of what was in her heart, a swarm of nurses and techs came running into the small, one-window room that was both her jail and her home. All of a sudden, voices were demanding to know what she'd done to her port and was this girl bothering Scarlett and would they like them to remove her so she could take a nap—

"I'm not a *baby*," Scarlett said, fearful lest her new friend get the wrong idea.

"No, you're not. But your vital signs are all over the place, so I think it's best if we let Chrissie get on with her visit to her brother, don't you?"

Chrissie. Even the girl's name was perfect, like a whisper that slipped off the end of the tongue.

"Please don't take her away," Scarlett begged. She cast her biggest, saddest eyes up at Nurse Penny, but it was no use. The girl—perfect Chrissie with her perfect hair—was already retreating toward the door.

"You'll come back," Scarlett said—not as a question but a plea. She clawed like a wild animal to get out of bed, but Nurse Penny had already put something into her IV to make her sleepy. "Tomorrow, Chrissie. Promise me. Promise me you'll visit."

She couldn't hear Chrissie's response, but the girl nodded so seriously that Scarlett felt sure she could count on her.

People who looked that serious *always* kept their word. They had to. After all the cancer and pain and goodbyes, promises were the only thing they had left.

Chapter Three

BURNS, OR

Present Day

THEY DROVE LESS THAN THREE HUNDRED miles before stopping for the day.

"At this rate, it's going to take us two *months* to get to Vermont, not two weeks," Chrissie grumbled. She slung her duffel bag over her shoulder and prepared to help Scarlett hoist her eighty-pound luggage out of the back. She had no idea what her friend had packed to make her vintage Louis Vuitton trunk so heavy, but she suspected bricks.

"Hopefully the masonry kind instead of the cocaine variety," she muttered to herself as she took one end of the suitcase and lifted. Scarlett, never one to break a sweat if she could possibly help it, immediately dropped her own end. It was only through the quick reflexes borne of hours of butterfly drills with Kat's volleyball team that Chrissie managed to avoid toppling over.

"What's that about cocaine?" Scarlett asked. She looked wholly unconcerned with the bulbous dent now gracing the bottom corner of a piece of luggage Chrissie suspected was worth more than her first car.

Scarlett glanced around the unpaved parking lot of a town that looked like the setting for a low-budget horror movie and frowned. "If it's party drugs you're after, I think we might want to look elsewhere. I doubt you can even buy full-strength aspirin in a place like this."

"Scarlett, your beautiful trunk!" Chrissie cried.

"Forget it." Scarlett waved a negligent hand over the destruction. "It was always a bulky, pretentious piece of luggage anyway. I only bought it because I had grand visions of the two of us boarding a steam packet in our old age and traveling across all four oceans, sipping martinis as we flirted outrageously with men young enough to be our grandsons."

"That's a weirdly specific dream." Chrissie gripped the handle and started dragging the suitcase toward their roadside motel. In the same map-navigation-only spirit of adventure, Scarlett had made her promise they'd stay at non-chain lodgings—the more authentic and dilapidated, the better. "What changed your mind?"

The negligent hand became an airy one. "Oh, you know. By that time, we'll be teleporting ourselves places and printing clothes from kiosks on the street corner. No one will carry any bags at all."

Scarlett planted her hands on her narrow hips and scoured the streets for signs of life. Other than a murder of crows picking at the corpse of what appeared to be a raccoon, they had the town to themselves.

"Hmm," she said. "If we can't have street drugs or illicit liaisons with young men, what else do you think there is to do around here?"

For once, Chrissie had an answer ready to go. "There was a sign for hot springs a few miles back. Crane something?" She rubbed the back of her neck with a rueful grimace. "I hate to seem like a poor spirit on day one, but I could use a long, hot soak right about now. This trip would have been a lot easier when we were young."

"Chrissie, we're thirty-four, not eighty-four."

"It's not my fault. I'm not used to sitting in one place all day." She hesitated only briefly before adding, "Besides, heat helps dilate vessels and promote blood flow. It's very good for you—for *us*, I mean."

"Fine. I'll go sit in an old person's bathtub with you, but only if we smuggle in a few bottles of red wine."

In a perfect world, the debate would have stopped right there. Unfortunately, Scarlett didn't believe in a perfect world. She didn't even believe in the *possibility* of one—a heathenish outlook that her grandmother would have eschewed at the outset.

"You know you don't have to take care of me, right?" she said. "Turn off whatever's doing all the worrying and enjoy yourself."

Chrissie sighed. Sometimes—just sometimes—she wished Scarlett didn't know her quite so well. "It's my natural mom instinct. Sorry. I've been gone less than one day, and I already miss Kat. I didn't mean to take it out on you."

Scarlett had her arms around Chrissie before either one of them knew what had happened. The soft cashmere of her embrace was nothing compared to the warmth of her. Scarlett hugged the same way she gave attention—with the full force of her personality.

She also didn't hesitate to pull any punches.

"If you were at home with Kat right now, what would she be doing?" Scarlett asked. She clucked her tongue in a warning before Chrissie could reply. "And don't tell me she'd be doing something saintly like her homework or helping you make dinner. *Truthfully.*"

Truthfully, Kat was probably still at volleyball practice, but that wasn't what Scarlett wanted to hear.

"Belittling my every life choice and making me feel guilty for existing," Chrissie said obediently.

"In other words…"

"Struggling to survive as a sixteen-year-old whose head is full of social media and whose body is full of hormones."

"So close, and yet so very far away."

"Trying to exist in a world that's slowly disintegrating into a xerothermic ball of climate change."

Scarlett made the sound of buzzer with her mouth. Chrissie didn't want to *think* the next part, let alone say it out loud, but she had the feeling her friend wouldn't relent until she did.

"She'd be acting like an entitled brat," she admitted, her guilt its own xerothermic ball lodged deep in her gut. "And she wouldn't let up until one of us was in tears. Probably me. It's usually me."

Scarlett beamed at her friend as though she'd just won the final round of *Jeopardy*. "That's my girl! I would've just said the word 'bitch' and been done with it, but you've never been one to cut corners. Either way, consider this your break from responsibility and put that mom instinct away. I think I see a gas station next to the motel. Let's check it out before we head to the hot springs. What are the chances they have any bottles of wine that cost more than eight dollars a pop?"

Chrissie gave in the same way she always did: inevitably.

"Slim to none," she said as she followed her friend and continued dragging the dented trunk across the parking lot. "But we both know long odds have never stopped you before."

To Chrissie's relief, the Crane Hot Springs were a quiet, rustic set of pools set far enough outside town that you could see the entire night sky twinkling off in the distance.

"Hmm," Scarlett said, her nose wrinkled as she stood taking it all in. "Not very glamorous, is it?"

"You're at a hot spring in southeastern Oregon, not the Turkish thermal pools. I don't know what you were expecting." Chrissie led the way down the path to where the entry tickets were sold. A huge sign warned them that no alcohol was allowed, but Scarlett had already transferred their wine—twelve bucks each, thank you very much—into a pair of brightly stickered water bottles, so she wasn't worried about getting caught. As a teenager, Scarlett had been the first to discover that you could steal about a quarter of your dad's whiskey and replace it with water before he got suspicious; as a twentysomething concertgoer, she'd basically pioneered the art of smuggling in liquor with tampon flasks.

Not that Chrissie had much experience with either of these things. Her late teens and early twenties had been spent up to her ears in diapers and baby formula, her days and nights so blurred together that she sometimes wondered how she'd managed to make it through in one piece.

"Y'all can change in those rooms over there, and then you're free to access either of the main pools," the woman behind the ticket counter said as she wrapped bands around their wrists and ushered them through. "We only ask that you pee in the toilets and stay hydrated."

"Ah, yes. The two cardinal rules of any activity worth doing," Scarlett said, winking at the woman as they passed into the damp, white-tiled changing room. "You should cross-stitch that and put in on a pillow, Chrissie."

Since it was Chrissie's invariable custom to cross-stitch pillows and give them as gifts for every holiday, celebration, or event, she didn't take any offense at this comment. People loved her pillows. Even Kat still used the one she'd made that read, *Wait a Sec, I'm Busy Overthinking Things.*

To Chrissie's surprise, Scarlett angled her steps toward one of the private stalls against the back wall.

"Where are you going? I thought for sure you'd try and look for my twin's head again," Chrissie teased as Scarlett locked the door behind her. Then, when Scarlett didn't respond except to start rummaging around in her bag, she asked, "Is everything okay?"

"I'm fine. My new suit is a little tricky to put on, that's all. I don't need you watching me bend and stretch my way into it."

Scarlett wasn't normally the type to be squeamish about her body—she always said that a childhood spent with medical professionals treating her like a sack of rotting meat rendered modesty superfluous—but Chrissie understood her friend's reservations once she strode out of the changing room in a formfitting black two-piece with a high halter neckline.

"Scarlett!" She practically squealed the two syllables of her friend's name. "Did you get a boob job and not tell me?"

Scarlett turned sideways, one hand on her stomach and the other on her back as she thrust her chest out. Now that the sweatshirt wasn't hiding her figure, Chrissie could see that what had once been a pair of what Scarlett called *A-minus cups* was now a heavily weighted *C plus.*

"Is it that obvious?" she asked.

"To me, yeah. I can't believe you got surgery and didn't tell me. Can I touch them?"

Scarlett jumped back as if burned. "No, you can't touch them." As if shocked by the harsh note in her own voice, she immediately dissolved into her rich peal of laughter. "Okay, maybe ask me again after we finish our water bottles. But when are we gonna talk about what's happening over on that side of the room? So much for not showing your stomach in public."

Chrissie felt her cheeks burn. The bright pink string bikini she wore left little to the imagination—and lots to the powers of gravity. "I couldn't find mine, so I had to pack one of Kat's. It was either this or a horrible white crocheted thing that I *definitely* didn't buy her."

Scarlett's laugh sounded again. "I know you didn't. I did."

"Scarlett!" Chrissie cried again, this time without either heat or surprise. Since Scarlett was also the source of Kat's septum piercing, a brush with purple hair in the seventh grade, and a promised tattoo the day her daughter turned eighteen, Chrissie should have known that her friend wouldn't balk at a buying a bikini that was literally holding on by a thread. "Do you have any idea what happens to white yarn when it gets wet?"

"Well, you're not supposed to get it *wet*. It's a lounging suit, not a swimming one. I bet she looks amazing in it."

She did, but that wasn't the point. *Everyone* looked good when they were sixteen. Their skin still had all its elasticity.

"Here. Stand next to that towel rack and give me a pouty look. I think we should send Kat a proof-of-life photo." Scarlett snagged Chrissie's phone and gestured toward a cedar panel with puffs of steam billowing out from a grate on the floor. "And if she happens to realize her mom is a serious smokeshow in the process, so much the better."

The last thing Chrissie wanted was to preen against the splintery side of the building wearing a bright pink piece of floss, but Scarlett started shouting out commands in a way that brooked no argument. As she also knew all the best ways to pose a half-naked body—Jut that hip! Show me a little cleavage! Run from the camera like it wants to bend you over the table!—Chrissie knew she'd get results. Especially since that last one made her laugh out loud.

"Oh, yeah. That's the one." Scarlett returned Chrissie's phone. "I wish you'd laugh in pictures more. Even if you're in your stupid sweatpants and Crocs, your laugh always makes you look like you belong on the cover of a fashion magazine."

Chrissie sucked in a sharp breath as she glanced at the picture in question. With her hand on her hip and her head tossed back in laughter, the steam wrapping around her as if she'd just popped out of a genie's magical lantern, she looked… What exactly? Confident? Beautiful? Sexy?

Happy, she realized with a start. *I look happy.*

"Uh-oh. What's wrong? Did I give you a double chin or something?" Scarlett made a motion as if to grab the phone, but Chrissie snatched it out of her reach.

"No, it's perfect," she said, her lower lip wobbling—not in a sexy pout, but with the sudden urge to burst into tears. If Scarlett had asked her, two hours ago, the last time she'd felt truly happy, she'd have had a half dozen replies ready to go.

Watching Kat's volleyball team sweep the semifinals last month had been exhilarating. The one—and only—time Rufio had willingly crawled into her lap in a bid for affection had delighted her so much that both of her legs had fallen asleep under the cat's reassuring weight. She'd even taken herself out to a movie last week when one of her regular massage therapy clients had canceled at the last minute.

But Scarlett would have roundly dismissed each of these claims as a paltry offering on the altar of self-sacrifice. And Chrissie, though prepared to defend her life choices in almost every other setting, would have eventually been forced to agree.

Here, however, was concrete proof that she still had joy inside her—and that with the right coaxing, joy was ready to come out and play.

"I'm sending it to Kat right now," Chrissie said as she typed into her phone. "She'll probably just text something back like, 'Ew, now I can never wear that suit again,' but that's what the wine is for."

No sooner had they gathered up their towels and headed out to the first of the hot-spring pools when her phone chimed back.

> I know I said you didn't have to pay me for taking care of Kat, but if this is how you plan to reimburse me, I take back every word.

"Oh-god. Oh-my-god. Oh-dear-god, what-have-I-done?" Each word came out of Chrissie in a staccato burst. Her hand shook as she shoved her hair out of her face and looked closer at the phone. Sure enough, the recipient of her photo wasn't her sarcastic and wholly unappreciative teenager, but the man she'd basically coerced into taking care of her.

"No, no, no," Chrissie moaned. Scarlett opened her mouth as if to demand enlightenment, but Chrissie beat her to it. She shoved the phone in her friend's face. "I can't believe this. I sent the photo to Walsh instead of Kat."

Scarlett's gaze flicked up along the rest of the text conversation, most of which included last-minute reminders about feeding Rufio and a profusion of thanks for Walsh's generosity—a thing Chrissie felt sure she'd never be able to repay, even if she were to send him a hundred semi-scandalous bikini photos.

"Wait. Walsh is the volleyball coach, right?" Scarlett asked.

"Yes. *Yes.* What do I do?"

Scarlett ignored her and scrolled higher up the conversation. "The one who has the crush on you?"

"He doesn't—I mean, that's not—Scarlett, you're not taking this seriously!"

"The one who said three days ago, and I'm quoting directly from the source here, 'I'm tempted to cast the girls to the wolves and drive across the country with you?'"

If Chrissie were a woman given over to acts of petulance, she'd have stomped her foot right then and there. As it was, all the petulance had been mortified right out of her.

"Ooh, wait," Scarlett breathed. "He's texting again."

Chrissie's hands were shaking too hard to take the phone back, so she leaned over Scarlett's shoulder as the three dancing dots gave way to text.

By the way, I stopped by your house to feed Rufio like you asked. He seems lonely. Are you sure you don't want me to move him in with us until you get back?

That got Chrissie moving again. She yanked the phone out of Scarlett's hands and prayed that autocorrect would make up for the tremors that rendered her typing incoherent.

Please don't bring him into your house. He'll pee on everything you own.

I don't mind.

I MIND. I MIND VERY MUCH.

"Well, really, Chrissie." Scarlett tsked lightly. "I don't see what yelling at the poor man is going to do. He just wants to take care of your pussycat."

"That is *not* funny. You have no idea how much I'm already asking of him. If you'd ever been in a room with Kat and Lily at the same time, you'd understand. It's like playing passive aggressive ping-pong with two world champions. Only instead of trying to hit the balls over a net, they're aiming death blows at each other's heads."

As if listening in, another text came through.

The girls are settling in great together, btw. I'm glad you're having fun. You deserve it.

"Oh, he *likes* you," Scarlett said as she read the words aloud. "And even better, he knows exactly how to handle you. I approve of this one."

Chrissie resented the implication that she could be handled by anyone, let alone a man, but she allowed herself to be led into the warm, sulfurous pool without putting up much of a fight. For one thing, the water felt heavenly, like a bath that had been poured out too hot and allowed the perfect amount of time to cool.

For another, well…

"I can't date Kat's volleyball coach, Scarlett."

"Why not?"

Chrissie dipped lower into the water, letting herself sink until the steaming heat swirled around her face and hid the worst of her blushes. Scarlett would take one look at them and start circling like a shark detecting blood.

"Because Kat hates his daughter with the passion of a thousand fiery suns. Because she's already mortified by my every word and action." Chrissie hesitated a moment before adding the last one. "And because he's the closest thing to a father figure she's ever had. Walsh has been her coach for over half a decade. If I mess up that relationship for her, she'll never forgive me—which would be fine, because I wouldn't be able to forgive myself. You know how hard it's been not having her dad in her life."

Scarlett groaned. "Ugh. *Grimshaw*. Don't even get me started on that walking heap of pretention."

Chrissie had no intention of doing so. The last time Scarlett had gotten started on Kat's biological father, Chrissie had been forced to turn off her Wi-Fi so the police wouldn't be able to trace the "how to hire a hit man" Google searches back to her.

"Besides, I think half the reason Walsh flirts with me is because he knows I won't take things too far," Chrissie explained. "I'm his safe space. The other single moms have been on the catch for him for years—and they're none too subtle about it, either."

"Hmm." Scarlett pursed her lips before settling into a seat built into the rocky wall of the pool.

Chrissie was instantly on the alert. "What's that supposed to mean? Why do you suddenly look so devious?"

"No reason," Scarlett said in a voice so musical that Chrissie didn't trust it for a second. "I was just thinking that if I hadn't pressured you every day for a month to be my best friend, the two of us wouldn't be sitting here right now. You're not an easy nut to crack, Chrissie Thomas, but you're well worth the effort once you do."

Scarlett's smile took on a decidedly self-satisfied air. "And I think this precious Walsh of yours might already know it."

Chapter Four

PORTLAND, OR

1999

CHRISSIE CAME BACK TO THE HOSPITAL every day for three weeks.

Not always to see Scarlett, of course. In fact, she almost *never* came to see Scarlett, but Scarlett would beg and plead until Chrissie had no choice but to pop into her room from the family center or cafeteria or, as was most often the case, her brother's room at the end of the hall.

"I saved you my Jell-O cup from lunch," she'd say as she handed over that day's offering—orange or lime most of the time, but sometimes strawberry, which was ultra rare and therefore everyone's favorite. "Wanna play checkers with me? Or you could climb into my bed and we could watch the Disney Channel together."

Most of the time, Scarlett's tricks worked. With her brother almost always asleep and her parents busy with his doctors, Chrissie was free to play as many games as she wanted, her face screwed up in concentration as she plotted out her next moves across the checkerboard. They rarely talked about anything—or at least, Chrissie rarely talked—but Scarlett was happy to fill in the gap. She was quick to learn which topics were safe (Chrissie played the piano and loved the ocean, her allegiance torn equally between the two) and which were dangerous (her parents, her brother, her brother, her *brother*).

"Is Chrissie coming to visit today?" she asked Nurse Penny after two long, boring days had passed without even a glimpse of her. "I'm going home soon, and I want to make sure I give her my phone number before I leave. We're gonna hang out and visit the ocean together once I'm all better."

That was when the worst possible thing happened. Nurse Penny *smiled.*

"I'm afraid she won't be coming back, Scarlett," the nurse said. She put one of her hands on Scarlett's leg and gave it a friendly squeeze. A lot of the other nurses had cold hands, but Penny was always warm, like her heart worked overtime.

Today, all Scarlett wanted to do was kick that hand away.

She didn't do it, but she was awfully close, her muscles bunched up and ready for action. So much about her life was unfair—the cancer, the loneliness, the fact that she only had a grandma instead of two parents like the rest of the kids—that she made a vow right then and there.

When she was grown up, she was only going to do the things she wanted.

"What do you mean, she's not coming back?" Scarlett demanded. A weird blip sounded from the machine attached to her bed, but she ignored it. "She has to. She promised."

"Why don't we focus on *you* for today?" Penny suggested, still with that smile full of lies. "You're going home, remember? Your Hodgkin's is in remission. You've been working so hard to get to here that it seems a shame not to celebrate a little. I might even be able to steal you an extra strawberry Jell-O cup from the cafeteria."

Scarlett recognized a bribe when she heard one.

"I'm not celebrating without her," Scarlett said, and then the worst possible thing happened. Her lower lip started to tremble. She didn't want to cry in front of Nurse Penny, but she could already feel the fat, hot tears starting to build up. "Call her mom. Call her dad. Give them my phone number. If you don't, I'll rip my IV out. Just watch, and you'll see."

Nurse Penny gave her a look that was so full of sympathy that Scarlett almost ripped out her IV anyway. She had no use for sympathy. It didn't play games with you or let you brush its long, silky hair. It didn't teach you to play 'Chopsticks' on a whining, half-broken game room keyboard with only half its working keys. It also didn't smile all lopsided-like at your jokes because it was trying hard not to laugh.

"I can leave a message with the front desk, but that's the best I have to offer," Penny said. "If she and her family want to reach you, they know where to look."

And that was it. Penny spent a few seconds updating Scarlett's records on the computer before promising to return with the Jell-O.

"Oh!"

Scarlett heard the squeak of Penny's shoes coming to a stop just outside her door.

"What on earth happened to your—Oh. Oh, I see." She paused. "Go on in, hon. And if you need anything—anything at all—you just ask. We're so sorry about your loss."

Scarlett barely registered this last part. She was too busy holding her breath, terrified to empty her lungs in case she was wrong about who was standing on the other side of that door. But when a shy, scared head poked in, the air came out in a glorious whoop.

"Chrissie! I knew you'd keep your promise. Penny said I'd have to leave a note for your parents, but—" She stopped short as Chrissie stepped into the room.

Although she always looked nice, Chrissie was especially dressed up today. She wore a beautifully ruffled black dress, a bow tied at her waist and a pair of glossy black Mary Janes on her feet. Scarlett was just about to say that she looked like one of those fancy porcelain dolls you could order on TV when she noticed that her friend's long, silky, toffee-colored hair had been chopped off—and not in a cute way. The jagged ends played around her ears, a little too long in some places and too short in others. Someone had attempted to make her look better by putting a pearl headband on top of the mess, but she still had the appearance of someone who had taken a pair of garden shears to her own head.

"Your hair! Your perfect hair!" Scarlett wailed. She swung her legs out of the bed and started to drag her IV with her toward the door, but Chrissie dashed in before she made it very far. "What happened? Were you kidnapped? Did someone steal it?"

Scarlett really did cry now—big, wet droplets that trailed down her cheeks like something out of one of her grandmother's soap operas. She also pulled Chrissie into the bed with her, her arms around her friend as she ran her hand over the scraggly ends of her hair.

"You still look beautiful to me," Scarlett said. "I don't care what anyone says."

A strange, muffled sound escaped Chrissie. Assuming it was a sob, Scarlett buried her head in her friend's neck. She smelled like vanilla and butterscotch and soap, a combination that made Chrissie seem both a hundred years old and just a baby.

"It'll grow back soon," Scarlett promised. "Just like mine will now that I'm done with the stupid chemo."

When Chrissie pulled away, it was to show a face that wasn't lined with tears, but something else. Something that seemed so far away Scarlett couldn't touch it even if she wanted to—and she didn't want to. She didn't know a lot of things about the world yet, but that one seemed important.

The things that hurt Chrissie are bigger and deeper than the things that hurt the rest of us.

Chrissie's sad smile proved it. "Here. This is for you." Before Scarlett could protest, Chrissie thrust a plastic bag into her hands. "I asked my mom to send it to the wig people, but she said she can't handle it right now. Your grandma or maybe Nurse Penny should be able to do it for you, though. And I can grow more if you need it, but it'll take a while."

Scarlett opened the bag and peeked inside to find a long ponytail bound up in a blue scrunchie. One end of it was just as jagged as Chrissie's hair, and Scarlett knew that if she held it up to her friend's head, the ends would match perfectly.

"You…chopped off all your hair? For me?"

Chrissie shrugged and started tracing the line of the seam along one edge of Scarlett's colorful hospital quilt. "I was only growing it out so I could help other kids," she said. "Or maybe even my brother. But there's no point anymore. He died."

She stated this as though talking about the oatmeal she'd had for breakfast or the fact that she'd seen a pigeon on her way into the hospital. Scarlett, however, felt her whole body go numb.

So *that* was why Chrissie hadn't been around for a few days. And why she was wearing such a beautiful old-timey dress.

And why, she realized, that sad, faraway look in her eyes seemed like it was here to stay.

"Oh, Chrissie." Scarlett kept running her hand over Chrissie's hair, the uneven ends now so much sharper than before. "You must miss him. I'm so sorry."

Chrissie sniffled once—and only once. "Can I tell you an awful secret?"

Scarlett nodded. She didn't trust herself to do anything else.

"I'm the reason he's dead. I was supposed to be the one to save him, but I couldn't." Chrissie scooted forward until her knees banged against Scarlett's, her voice suddenly so quiet that Scarlett practically had to duck down low to hear the rest. "And even though I know I'm supposed to be sad, I'm really just glad he's gone."

Chapter Five

BURNS, OR

Present Day

CHRISSIE SIGHED AS SHE LEANED BACK against the motel mattress, Scarlett's fingernails raking over her scalp in a way that *almost* made it possible for her to ignore the body-shaped stain on the ceiling of their room.

"Don't tell anyone, but this is the most intimate I've been with another person since..." Chrissie scrunched her nose as she tried to remember the last time she'd touched someone who wasn't one of her massage therapy clients. "Well, let's just say that Leonardo DiCaprio was dating a woman in her early twenties and leave it at that."

Scarlett's laugh shook the whole bed. "That narrows it down a whole lot, thanks." She switched from her fingernails to a brush that she ran down the length of Chrissie's hair over and over again. Since it went all the way to the middle of her back, this took some time. "I'll never understand how you get your hair to grow so fast. Do you just, like, suck collagen out of young virgins or something?"

"Yes. That's exactly what I do in my vast amount of free time. Then I bathe in their blood to keep things interesting." Chrissie twisted her neck to look up at her friend, but Scarlett only tsked and forced her head straight again. "It's just hair, Scarlett, and not even a very pretty color. I'll never understand why you're so obsessed with it."

"That's because you forgot how much it bothered me when mine fell out. I'd already lost so much by that point. It seemed unnecessarily cruel to take that, too. In fact, the first time I ever saw you in the hospital, those long braids wrapped around your head like a halo, I thought I was being visited by an angel."

Chrissie snorted. Only Scarlett could make the grim, fluorescent-tinged memory of those days seem like something out of a Hallmark Christmas movie. "I'm pretty sure my hair was down that day. Besides, I knew even then that I wasn't going to keep it. I'm not going to keep this batch either, so don't get emotionally attached. I have a donation appointment for when our road trip is over."

All of a sudden, Chrissie felt her head being yanked back. It took her a short, stinging moment to realize that Scarlett had wrapped the long, hot-spring-dampened strands around her fist and was holding them like a horse's reins until Chrissie was forced to look up.

"Absolutely not. I forbid you from going back to that chop shop and letting them loose with the scissors."

"It's not a chop shop," Chrissie protested.

"Fine. A butcher, then. A hack with no sense of taste or style."

Scarlett twisted her wrist to the right, pulling Chrissie's scalp even tighter. Chrissie wasted no time in reaching over and pinching Scarlett's calf. With a howl, her friend released her grip.

"Ouch, you beast! That hurt."

"Then don't call my hair stylist a butcher. I'll admit that Monica tends to make everyone look like a medieval page boy, but that's part of her charm."

Scarlett snorted and swung her legs off the bed. Chrissie was about to ask where Scarlett was going when she unplugged her phone from the wall charger and started typing furiously on it.

"Okay, according to Google Maps, we should get to Boise by lunchtime tomorrow," Scarlett said. She reached down and absentmindedly rubbed her calf, where a bruise was already starting to form. Chrissie hadn't *thought* she'd pinched her that hard, and was about to apologize for the excessive force when Scarlett continued. "It's not Milan or my own beloved Jacques in San Francisco, but it's the closest we're going to be to a metropolis for the next week. I'm booking you an appointment at the most expensive place I can find."

"Wait. What?" Chrissie scrambled off the bed and tried to snatch the phone away, but her friend had already anticipated her. Scarlett dashed around to the other side of the bed and kept typing.

"It's my treat, so don't pretend like you need the money for Kat's braces or new volleyball shoes or cleaning supplies for that dratted cat you refuse to drown." Scarlett pressed one last button and tossed her phone triumphantly to the bedside table. "There! It's done. They have a twenty-four-hour cancellation policy, so there's no backing out now."

"But I don't want to go to Boise," Chrissie said. Then, feebly, "And Kat hasn't worn braces since she was twelve."

"And *you* haven't had a decent haircut since way before that," Scarlett said. She pursed her lips and added, "You always look like you're either getting ready to join Joan of Arc at the stake or popping out a dozen kids on a fundie compound. There is a happy medium, you know."

Chrissie didn't want to laugh, but she did. "It's never that bad."

"It's *always* that bad," Scarlett countered. Her own expression was much more sober than Chrissie's—a thing Chrissie didn't understand until her friend spoke again. "You know you don't owe anyone your hair just because it grows quickly, right? Not your hair, not your platelets, not your internal organs…"

"I've never given anyone an internal organ," Chrissie protested.

"And donating platelets is really easy. They take your blood out one arm, and then—"

Scarlett held up a hand to stop her. "I know how platelet donation works, thanks."

"Besides, I've gotten a ton of reading done in those chairs," Chrissie added. "It's one of the only times I get to just sit and relax, you know? I read the whole of *Anna Karenina* that way."

Scarlett's sober expression didn't lighten. If anything, it darkened even more. In Kat, an expression like that would only look petulant and sullen, but Scarlett looked like a silent film star—a French one, naturally.

"I want you to write down what you just said."

"What? Why?"

Scarlett grabbed a pen and notepad from the bedside table. The logo of the motel—Royal Mills—was emblazoned across the top in bright green. "I'm serious. Put it in ink and read it back to yourself."

Chrissie knew from experience that no good would come of playing Scarlett's games. Since the day they'd become friends, she'd found herself constantly twisting and turning and tying herself in knots before they even made it to the starting line.

But this was supposed to be a vacation, after all.

"Fine." Chrissie grabbed the pen and started to write.

I like donating platelets because it gives me time to sit and read without interruption.

"Good girl." Scarlett took the pen from her and liberally scratched out half of what she'd written.

I like ~~donating platelets because it gives me time~~ to sit and read without interruption.

"I'm not sure I understand what you're getting at," Chrissie said. "Lots of people like to read. It's not an exciting pastime, I'll admit, but—"

"But nothing. If you want to read a book, then read a book. Don't bend over backwards to justify it to the world." Scarlett paused a beat. "And if you want a kick-ass haircut from a place that costs two hundred dollars just for a consultation—"

Now it was Chrissie's turn to interrupt. "It costs *what*?"

"Then you can get a kick-ass haircut from a place that costs two hundred dollars just for a consultation," Scarlett finished in a hard voice. "You can still do the hair donating and bloodletting if you want to, but as a separate thing. A *different* thing."

Chrissie swallowed, doing her best not to notice how bitter the taste of her own saliva was on her tongue. That bitterness could have been a figment of her imagination—or the aftereffects of a bottle of wine that seemed to have been delivered to the grocery store straight from a tannery—but she suspected its true source. It was easy for Scarlett to lecture her about how she used what precious little free time she had, and even easier for her to throw money around like it meant nothing.

But Chrissie had more than just herself to think about. She had a daughter and her massage therapy clients and a cat that liked to look her straight in the eye when he copped a squat and peed on her favorite throw. She had bills to pay and four years of college to plan for, not to mention the crushing guilt that was affixed to her like the second head of a freak-show cow.

"Sure, Scarlett. I'll read a book for you if it'll make you happy."

"Not for me. For *you*." Scarlett peeled the top page off the pad of paper and folded it neatly in half. Tucking it carefully in Chrissie's palm, she gave an exaggerated yawn and started to flip off all the lights. "Hold on to that, okay? I get the feeling we're going to need it."

"Scarlett," Chrissie began, but her friend had already clicked off the lamps and was preparing to slip between the sheets. The hour wasn't terribly late, but if they were going to make it to Boise tomorrow in time for her hair appointment, they'd need to get an early start.

Besides, knowing Scarlett, they'd be up well before the sun, one of them bright-eyed and ready to face the morning, and the other with a terrible red-wine hangover and even worse regret.

"Oh, geez. You weren't kidding about this place, were you?"

The moment Chrissie walked through the door to a hair salon that had a bona fide bouncer at the door, his meaty arms crossed against anyone who tried to slip inside without an appointment, she knew she was going to hate every minute of this experience.

A young man, who stood only a few inches over five feet and had one of the neatest pencil mustaches Chrissie had ever seen, came forward to greet them with a silver tray holding two glasses of champagne. Scarlett sighed happily and reached for one, but she was delayed by a soft *tsk* as the man plunked a raspberry into each one. The popping fizz of the bubbles only made Scarlett sigh louder.

"Of everything I'm going to miss, I'm going to miss champagne the most," she said as she lifted the stem between forefinger and thumb and drank half in one gulp.

"Are you giving up alcohol soon?" Chrissie asked as she accepted her own glass and tentatively sipped. "Never say so. Your poor liver won't know what to do with itself. It'll probably go into shock."

"Livers are replaceable," the petite Clark Gable said with a wink. "Which one of you is Christina?"

"I am," Chrissie said. Since it was her turn to drive after this, she set the glass of champagne back down on the tray. "But only my mother calls me Christina. I'm Chrissie to the rest of the world."

"Well, Chrissie. You're in for a treat. Bernice doesn't usually take new clients on such short notice." He winked in a way that felt like both an insult and a papal blessing. "If you'll follow me, one of the salon assistants will wash your hair while another preps the studio."

"Wait. There's more than one person involved in this process?" Chrissie shot Scarlett an agonized look. "There weren't this many people in the birthing suite when Kat was born."

"I know. I was there, remember?" Scarlett laughed. "But there's no comparison. That was just a soul entering the world for the first time. This is your *hair*."

Chrissie would have stuck her tongue out at her friend, but she was being ushered into a dark, red-curtained room that looked like it moonlighted as a bordello. The overwhelming scent of roses dropped on her like a robe—as well as a *literal* robe, which the man swept around her shoulders in one debonair swish.

"You're in good hands with River," he promised. He wrinkled his tiny mustache before adding, "Actually, she's terrifying, but as long as you don't show fear, you should be fine."

"Are you serious?" Chrissie whirled around, but the man had already slipped out to chat with Scarlett in the waiting room. She had no doubt that Scarlett would regale him with tales of Chrissie's terrible haircuts and even worse sartorial style, but there was no time to dwell on that as a teenage girl with enough piercings to set off every metal detector in a three-mile radius entered the room. Her black hair was cut at an angle that completely obscured one of her eyes. The eye left exposed was ringed with an expert flick of eyeliner and the kind of smoky smudge that magicians spent their whole lives perfecting.

"Are you gonna sit, or do you want me to get up on tiptoe to reach your head?" the girl asked. She snapped her gum and jabbed a chipped black fingernail at the sink. "I don't have all day."

All at once, Chrissie felt her anxiety and discomfort melting away. *Not* because she was taking petite Clark Gable's advice to heart and showing no fear, but because with River, she was facing the familiar: a sullen, annoyed teenager who wanted nothing to do with her.

"You have such lovely eyes," Chrissie said as she settled into the seat and let River adjust her robe. "It's a pity we can only see one of them."

This was the exact sort of thing that mothers had been saying to their children from time immemorial, and it never failed to irritate. River was no exception. She yanked Chrissie's head back and began mercilessly running her hands through her hair.

"Is that supposed to be a joke?" she asked.

"No. Just an observation. I bet your mother hates it."

River snorted. "Close but not quite. It's my *step*mother who used to throw a hissy fit every time I left the house. You'd think I was walking around naked the way she carried on." She squirted a handful of rose-scented shampoo into her hands and began ruthlessly working it into Chrissie's hair. "Ugh. You have, like, a *ton* of hair."

"I know. It's a pain to take care of. I only let it get this long so I can donate it." Chrissie tilted her chin to look up at the girl. "Do you guys do that here? Save the hair by request, I mean?"

The girl blinked, her hands suddenly unmoving. "Is that something you want to do?"

"Yes, please. I can give you the address of the charity I usually send it to, or if you don't have the right mailing supplies, you can just put in a ponytail for me and I can do it later."

River started washing again, her movements much gentler this time around. "It's fine," she said. "I can mail it for you."

They didn't speak again for the ten minutes it took to shampoo and condition Chrissie's hair. Unlike Scarlett, Chrissie had always been comfortable with long silences, so she was happy to let the quiet settle. She was, however, much less comfortable with the tipping guidelines in a place that boasted no fewer than four different staff members for a single haircut. As River clicked the chair to an upright position, her hands efficiently toweling off the drips from the nape of Chrissie's neck, she even found herself feeling a little of that terror she'd been warned about.

"Um, should I tip you separately or just include it in the final bill?" she asked, trying not to wince as she thought about how much cash was in her purse. Most of this trip was being financed by Scarlett—partly because the whole thing had been her idea to begin with, but mostly because Chrissie would never have been able to splurge on a two-week vacation otherwise.

She had a comfortable number of rotating massage therapy clients, and the flexibility the career allowed meant she could accommodate Kat's busy schedule, but the gig economy was a tough one for a single parent even with the child support deposited into her account on the first of every month.

"I don't want a tip from you," River said, the words terse. She caught Chrissie's startled expression and sighed. "Sorry. My bark's worse than my bite. I only meant that you donating your hair is enough. It's for cancer patients, right? For making wigs?"

Chrissie nodded.

River's face set into a mask as hard as her piercings. At first, Chrissie thought she'd somehow insulted the girl, but she realized her error a few seconds later.

"My mom got one of those. Before she died, I mean. I tried to get her to wear some cool cosplay ones—just for fun, you know, bright pink and glittery—but she said she only wanted to look like herself again."

The set lines of River's face didn't soften, and Chrissie recognized the struggles of a teenager who was doing her best not to cry. Kat did the same thing any time the emotions under their roof got too soft. Anger and annoyance and frustration were allowed to escape without a check, but the moment she felt anything that could be deemed as weakness, she shut down.

"I'm so sorry for your loss." Chrissie reached out and touched the girl's shoulder. Then she said the only thing that had ever helped her when in the throes of her own grief. Not platitudes about eternal life or promises that things would get better with time—not even an acknowledgment of the things she must have undergone. "It's not fair, is it? To lose someone before you're ready to say goodbye?"

A startled look flickered in River's visible eye, but another thing Chrissie was able to recognize at a glance was a teenager on the verge of flight.

"Do I go through here?" she asked, indicating a gap in the curtain wall. She spoke with studied nonchalance, determined to meet this girl on the safe, neutral ground she clearly preferred. "You can probably tell that I've never gotten my hair cut anywhere as nice as this before. I'm not even sure what I should ask for."

"You want a vintage horseshoe cut," River said, the relief at her escape almost palpable. "Just below the shoulders, I think. No bangs. Light on the layers. That way you can still pull it into a ponytail when you don't feel like doing anything with it, but you can glam it up super easily. Like Katharine Hepburn."

Very little of what River just said made sense to Chrissie, but she was willing to play along. Especially when she took a seat in the chair offered her and rattled off the directions like she knew what she was talking about. Bernice, who was equally terrifying in a six-foot-tall-and-built-like-a-linebacker sort of way, accepted Chrissie's instructions with a nod of approval.

"Yes. Yes, you're right. You must have an eye for this sort of thing."

Scarlett, who knew very well that Chrissie had no eyes for anything related to fashion, watched with an amused smile as Chrissie's hair was pulled, chopped, and stored in a Ziploc bag discreetly brought out by River.

"Okay, we're *definitely* sending Walsh another proof-of-life photo,"

Scarlett said as Chrissie was carried out of the salon on a cloud of hair spray. She didn't manage to get a look at the bill, but the disregard with which Scarlett had signed the slip indicated that it wasn't beyond her friend's means.

Scarlett snapped a few candid shots with Chrissie's phone before she could think to put up a fight.

"And don't argue with me, because I saw the way you conned that poor washing girl into sweeping up your hair when Bernice wasn't looking. Have you *ever* been able to get out of a room without doing at least one act of selflessness?"

"I didn't con her into anything!" Chrissie protested, but it was mistake. While she was distracted, Scarlett sent one of her photos off into the void. "Please tell me you didn't actually text my daughter's volleyball coach a picture of my new haircut. He's going to think I'm deranged."

"Um, what he's going to think is that he can't wait for you to get back from this trip." Scarlett flipped the phone around to show Chrissie the picture she'd sent. "Did you even look in the mirror before you walked out of there? You look like a hot, modern-day—"

"Katharine Hepburn," Chrissie finished for her. And it was true. Something about Scarlett always brought out the best in her, because she once again looked relaxed, carefree, and happy. She also looked like she'd just stepped off the set of a 1940s period drama—one of the really good ones where they replaced all the closed-door sex scenes with the full Bridgerton experience.

An incoming text had her heart leaping to her throat.

"It's him, isn't it?" Scarlett waggled her eyebrows. "I bet it's totally a dick pic this time."

"Of course it's not! Walsh would *never* do anything like that." Chrissie felt her cheeks flame as her phone notified her that an image was attached. "At least, I don't think he would. Not while he has Kat staying there with him. Besides, wouldn't it take him a few minutes to get things, uh, *prepped*?"

Scarlett's rich peal of laughter sounded. "Chrissie, men have at least a dozen saved dick pics on standby at all times—usually ones they took in bathrooms with generous lighting. They're not sending you a live play-by-play."

"Walsh doesn't have anything like that stored. He's not that kind of man." Chrissie's finger hovered over the phone, hesitation holding her back. In all honesty, she didn't know *what* kind of man Walsh was—a thing she was both ashamed and proud of.

For the past six years, Walsh Hampton and his daughter, Lily, had been a regular presence in her life—hers and Kat's both. Kat had originally tried out for the volleyball team on a whim, driven by Chrissie's determination to see her in some kind of structured activity. Remembering the long, lonely hours she'd spent trapped inside her own house, her private piano lessons her only real break from the monotony, Chrissie had given ten-year-old Kat her choice of hobbies. And Kat, who'd never once even picked up a volleyball, had decided that nothing else would do for her but to throw herself heart and soul into the sport.

To this day, Chrissie didn't know if it was the uniforms that had appealed to Kat, if the spirit of competition had seized her, or if it was Walsh himself who had sparked such a love for the game. In her more honest moments, she suspected it was Walsh. From the moment Kat had stepped onto the court, nervous and unsure of herself but determined not to show it, she'd taken to the tall, jocular coach. He was a natural athlete, his six-foot-three frame fleshed out but firm, and demanded the best of his team at all times.

He usually got it, too. Not by being blunt to the point of rudeness, like Scarlett, and not by being a pushover to the point of roadkill, like Chrissie, but because people took one look at him and decided they'd do anything to earn one of his wide, impulsive smiles.

Chrissie hadn't been kidding when she said that all the other volleyball moms were on the catch for the divorced father of one. Walsh wasn't a conventionally attractive man, his head bald while the rest of him was covered in dark tufts of hair, his beard starting to show telltale patches of gray, but that was a large part of his charm. He looked like the sort of man who could weather any kind of storm—and who made sure everyone else weathered it with him.

"Okay, I'm going in," Chrissie said as she clicked the text notification. As soon as she did, she felt all the air leaving her lungs.

There, instead of a photo of his more intimate anatomy, was Walsh with a chef's hat on his head and an apron that read *Kiss the Cook*. His grin was lopsided but genuine, crinkled lines of laughter extending out on both temples.

Vacation looks good on you. Wish I could say the same about these ribs I'm basting. I think I used too much paprika, but Kat says they're her favorite.

"What is it?" Scarlett demanded as she tried to peek at the phone. "Did he actually send you a nude? Can I see?"

"It's not a nude." Chrissie's fingers shook as she typed back. "He's just being ridiculously nice to me and Kat, as usual."

You don't have to do that for her. She can eat whatever you're used to serving.

It didn't take him long to respond.

I don't mind. It's a good excuse to get out the grill. Besides, I might use the extra meat to try and buy Rufio's affection. I brought him over this morning, but I think he's still a little wary of me.

"Omigod, I can't believe he actually moved that dratted cat into his house." Chrissie moaned as she thought of how much it would cost to have Walsh's entire carpet cleaned once she got home. Rufio was not a cat who did things by halves.

She switched over to texting her daughter, but the response didn't do anything to reassure her.

KAT, WHY DID YOU LET COACH MOVE RUFIO INTO HIS HOUSE? YOU KNOW HE'S GOING TO PEE ON EVERYTHING.

don't worry. i'm training rufio to only pee in lily's room. that'll teach her to "accidentally" bleach my best satin pillowcase.

KATHLEEN GENEVIEVE THOMAS, DON'T YOU DARE LET THAT CAT INTO LILY'S ROOM. I FORBID IT.

too late. he's already sniffing around her favorite vans.

Then, you wanted me to get a project, remember? behold. i'm projecting.

Chrissie would have kept going, but she could sense Scarlett's impatience. "Sorry," she said as she tucked the phone away. She'd have to do some serious damage control later, but that would have to wait. Long-distance teenage drama was a lot trickier issue to navigate than she'd anticipated. "I know we need to get going if we want to reach Pocatello by nightfall."

Scarlett tilted her head to one side, studying Chrissie with an unreadable expression. When most people looked at her that way—intense and scrutinizing, no sign of either approval or condemnation—she assumed it was due to a physical flaw. Broccoli in her teeth, maybe, or a sty starting to develop in her eye. When Scarlett did it, the situation tended to be a lot more dangerous.

"Actually, I think we should stay here tonight."

"What? Why?" Chrissie glanced up and down the street, expecting to see a surprise party pop out of any of the small shops lining the street. It wouldn't be the first time Scarlett sprang such a thing on her.

"Because it's a shame to waste that hair on the road between here and Pocatello," Scarlett said as she wound her arm through Chrissie's. She started dragging. "Because I want to hear more about Walsh and why you turn that particular shade of pink whenever his name is brought up. And because I think we should glam it up while we still have the chance. I don't think we're hitting another major city until we get past the Dakotas, and that's too long to wait for a proper girl's night."

As was always the case where Scarlett and a good time were involved, Chrissie gave in. Somewhere in the back of her mind, she suspected that this was just a distraction, and that Scarlett was attempting to divert her attention away from something else—some deeper, hidden plan that would be foisted on her when she least expected it—but that didn't matter. Her hair looked fantastic, Walsh was making Kat's favorite meal for dinner, and her best friend of twenty-seven years wanted to take her out for a good time.

There were worse ways to spend a day.

Or a lifetime.

Chapter Six

PORTLAND, OR

1999

"GRANDMA, YOU HAVE TO PROMISE NOT to cry at her."

Scarlett stood in the big front window of the apartment where she lived with her grandmother, the scent of cinnamon and sugar flooding the air and Chrissie's gorgeous wig atop her head.

"Well, really, Scarlett. I don't cry *at* people."

Scarlett turned away from her watch of the parking lot to glare at her grandma. Grandma might have *looked* like an innocent bystander, with her pink frilled apron and her best lipstick on, but Scarlett knew better than to be fooled. "Yes, you do. Whenever someone tells you something sad, you fold them up in your arms and squeeze until they turn blue. Then you cry all over them and make them eat cookies. Even the other church ladies talk about it."

"She won't want any cookies? Oh dear. Would she rather have apple slices, do you think?"

Scarlett almost stamped her foot in frustration. When snicker-doodles were on the menu, there was only one answer.

"*Of course* we want the cookies. But no squeezing. And no tears. You have to promise."

"I promise to try my best," Grandma lied, her eyes already starting to water behind their thick cat's-eye frames. "But that poor little thing, losing her brother at such a young age. I can't imagine what she must be going through. We'll have to do everything we can to make her visit a nice one."

That was when Scarlett knew there was no fixing it. Her grandmother was going to cry all over her new friend—and she was probably going to do it for most of the night. They'd rented three different Mary Kate and Ashley Olsen movies, set up a fort of pillows and sheets in the living room, and had enough junk food to last them a whole week.

It was just like all the sleepovers she'd seen on television and read about in books. She and Chrissie wouldn't be able to gossip about boys because, well, they didn't know any, and braiding their hair was out of the question because, well, Scarlett's hadn't grown back yet, but all the rest was lined up and ready to go. Grandma had even bought a cucumber to cut into slices and pink nail polish so they could pretend to go to the spa in the bathroom later.

"She's here!" Scarlett cried as a shiny blue car pulled into the parking lot. It didn't look like the other cars down there, which were as rusted and faded as the apartment building itself, but Scarlett didn't care. Those dark-tinted windows hid the best friend she'd ever had—or *would* have, if everything went the way she planned. "Can I go down and help her with her stuff?"

"We'll both go," her grandma promised as she took Scarlett by the hand and unlatched the door. "I'm sure her parents would like a cup of tea before they leave."

They didn't.

Scarlett and her grandma had reached the bottom step by the time

Chrissie's parents were out of the car and looking up at the apartment building, their smiles pulled flat. Chrissie's mom was an older, more weathered version of her daughter, her neck and arms so long that she looked like a swan about to turn into a princess. Her dad looked like pretty much all the dads on TV, with a tie tight around his neck and a phone pressed against his ear.

"Yeah, I'm on my way now," he said into the phone. "There shouldn't be any more setbacks to the timeline now that… Well, you know my circumstances. I'm more available now. As long as it takes."

His hand lightly touched Chrissie's head before he walked a few steps away to finish his call in private.

Chrissie's mom was a *little* better. "You're Ms. Sanderson?" she asked as she took in Grandma's too-big T-shirt and worn leggings, the weeds sprouting up from all the cracks in the parking lot. Her flat smile turned into a frown.

"Guilty as charged," Grandma said. "Thank you for sharing your daughter with us for the night. It means a lot, especially since I'm sure it's hard for you to let her go just now. We're all so sorry about your loss. Would you like to come in for—"

"We can't stay," Chrissie's mom cut her off.

Grandma looked the way Grandma *always* looked when someone turned down her tea—like someone had left a pile of garbage on the living room floor.

"Are you sure?" she asked. "I have a lovely chamomile that I grow myself on our little terrace."

Scarlett rolled her eyes in Chrissie's direction, sure that her friend would share in the mortification of adults who grew things like tea and then sat sipping it for hours and hours, but she only stood there clutching a pillow in one arm and a stuffed rabbit in the other, an enormous overnight backpack sagging halfway down her body.

"I'm sure," Chrissie's mom said. Scarlett hoped that would be the end of it, and they could all head back up to the apartment to get this party started, but Grandma wasn't done yet.

"Then I'll make a few sachets for you and send them home with Chrissie," she said. "I always found a good cup of herbal tea soothing on those nights when Scarlett was at the hospital without me. It's not a cure for a broken heart, but it's something."

"Please don't," Chrissie's mom said sharply. As if aware that she'd been rude, she forced herself to add, "You've already done enough."

She looked down at Chrissie then—Chrissie, who hadn't made a peep except the sound of her breathing; Chrissie, who was staring down at her shoes and looking so miserable that Scarlett wanted to take a cup of hot tea and throw it in her mother's tightly pinched face.

"Don't be any trouble," she said, and then she did the same thing Chrissie's dad had done—lightly touched the top of her daughter's head as though testing to make sure she was real.

But they didn't kiss her. Didn't hug her. Barely even looked at her, really. Even Scarlett, who couldn't remember her own mother, knew there was something wrong with that. Especially when they got in the car and peeled away without once looking back.

Scarlett groaned when her grandmother didn't even wait for the car to be all the way out of the parking lot before darting forward and pulling Chrissie into her arms. Her grandma was a good hugger—no one was denying that—all soft and pillowy with the smell of the baby powder she used to dry her skin, but it took her forever to let go. She hugged some of the kids at the hospital for so long that they actually fell asleep against her.

"Grandma, the cookies are gonna burn," Scarlett tried protesting, but her voice was swallowed up by the sound of her grandma murmuring some kind of nonsense in Chrissie's ear.

Scarlett knew what the nonsense contained. *You're all right. I've got you now. Aren't you the sweetest thing I ever met? I could just gobble you up*. None of it ever made any sense, and it almost always ended up including the snacking on children's bones as if Grandma lived in a gingerbread house with an oven built especially for the job, but none of the kids seemed to mind.

This was no different. By the time her grandma let Chrissie go, her new friend's face was streaked in tears, her whole body heaving as she tried not to sob all over the parking lot.

"It doesn't matter, love," her grandma was saying as she hoisted the girl on her hip and started carrying her toward the stairs. "You just come on inside and have a little snack. We'll take good care of you."

Scarlett wanted to protest that Chrissie was *way* too old to be carried like a baby, but one look at the way Chrissie clung to her grandma's neck had her clamping her mouth shut tight. She also grabbed the backpack and stuffed rabbit, which had fallen to the pavement during the painfully long hug.

The backpack was too heavy for her chemo-wasted muscles, but she didn't complain as she marched up the steps in her grandmother's wake. Scarlett wasn't a very good hugger, and she didn't want to gobble anyone up, but for once, she and her grandmother were on the same page.

As long as Chrissie was inside *her* house, with her lopsided hair on a pillow next to hers and that look of sad, miserable heartbreak on her face, Scarlett was going to take good care of her.

That was a promise she planned to keep for the rest of her life.

"In this one, Mary Kate and Ashley go to the Eiffel Tower *and* Notre-Dame *and* a special French dance." Scarlett pushed the play button and settled in beside Chrissie to watch the third movie in their marathon. "Someday, I'm going to Paris, too. And New York, and London, and Hawaii, and maybe even San Francisco. What about you?"

The night was well advanced by this time, the pair of them settled in their blanket fort and the plate of cookies sitting empty on the floor. Even though Scarlett was barely able to keep her eyes open, she was determined to eke out every minute before sleep robbed her of her friend.

She'd always hated that sleep had the power to do that—not just to steal people, but to steal *time*. When she was grown up, she wasn't going to sleep any more than she absolutely had to.

"You can come with me to France if you want," she said when Chrissie didn't respond except to yawn loudly into her fist. "We can be just like Mary Kate and Ashley. In fact, in a few months, *both* our hair will be long enough to cut like theirs. We'll look like sisters."

Her use of that word—*sisters*—made Chrissie wince and hug her knees to her chest. Too late, Scarlett realized what she'd said.

So far, both of them had been careful to avoid the subject of Chrissie's brother. They also hadn't talked about the hospital, Chrissie's parents, or the fact that they'd practically pushed a seven-year-old-kid out of the car before driving away.

But Scarlett wanted to know. She *needed* it.

"I never had a sister," she said, hoping that would do the trick. "Or a brother. Just my grandma. My mom left me with her the first time I got sick. I was only three years old at the time, but she said the cancer was too much for her to handle on her own."

She sat and blinked expectantly at Chrissie. On the TV, Mary Kate and Ashley were running to greet their grandpa in France, but neither girl was paying them much attention.

"My brother's name was Malcolm," Chrissie said, and Scarlett felt a ripple of alarm at hearing the name spoken aloud. In all the weeks she'd been getting chemotherapy and trying to worm her way into Chrissie's heart, she'd never once heard her speak her brother's name. "He was a few years older than me. But I had a sister once—sort of. She was my twin. I ate her."

That made all of Scarlett's sleepiness disappear in a flash. She bolted upright and hugged her knees to her chest in the same posture as Chrissie. "You *ate* her? Why? What did she taste like?"

Chrissie giggled. Scarlett didn't know why, but that choking gurgle suddenly made her feel like everything in the world was going to be okay.

"I didn't *eat* her, eat her. It happened when I was a baby. When we were in my mom's stomach."

"Ohhh," Scarlett said as if that made perfect sense. Which it didn't. "But, like, *how* did you do it? Babies don't even have teeth."

At that, Chrissie launched into a halting explanation of events, most of which continued to make no sense to Scarlett and sounded totally made up. Apparently, the eating of a twin involved lots of hard-to-pronounce medical words and sucking things into your body like a sponge. Which, if you asked her, was both very strange and very, very cool.

"My mom says she didn't even know she was in there," Chrissie confessed. "My twin, I mean. Most people don't. It's just a thing that happens sometimes, and then you go on with your normal life."

"How come you know about it then?"

"Because I had all kinds of tests done," Chrissie said. She drew her stuffed rabbit closer, rubbing the ratty ends of his ears between her forefinger and thumb. "For Malcolm. My parents thought—What I mean is, they hoped—"

Scarlett interrupted with all the wisdom of her seven years of life on a planet that had dealt her an unfair hand.

"They wanted to use your bones, didn't they? To save him." She knew all about bone marrow transplants. Several of the kids who'd come through the cancer ward had to get one of those. Sometimes, they got better and she never saw them again.

Other times, they didn't.

Chrissie nodded and used the rabbit's ears to wipe away a stray tear. "They said they couldn't use mine because of how weird all my DNA is. They had to put him on a donor list instead, only no one else matched up."

For what had to be the first time in Scarlett's life, she couldn't find anything to say. To her, the tale was an ordinary one. Sad, yes, but no worse than any other Friday night. She sometimes wondered if that was what the doctors meant when they said chemo killed the good parts of your body as well as the bad ones.

Not cells, but something different. Something you could never get back.

"Now you know why I'm glad he's dead," Chrissie said, her face half-hidden behind the stuffed rabbit. "My parents can't blame me for not helping him anymore—for not being able to take away his pain."

Scarlett felt her lungs growing tight. Her parents didn't really blame Chrissie for that, did they? She was just a kid.

As if she'd heard Scarlett's thoughts out loud, a sad, crooked smile touched Chrissie's lips. "Besides, my parents never would've let me have a sleepover at your house before. Everything they did was for Malcolm, so everything I did had to be, too. Only now that he's gone..."

Scarlett knew what Chrissie was going to say and didn't want to hear it, didn't want this sadness to intrude on her first perfect sleepover with her first perfect friend, but there didn't seem any way to stop her.

"They never loved me the way they loved him," she said simply. "And now that he's gone, they don't have to try anymore."

Scarlett's hand shot out and touched Chrissie's knee, all bones and knobs. "I bet they're just sad, and that's why they didn't want any of my grandma's tea," she said. "Grown-ups don't always do nice things when they're hurting."

The look Chrissie gave Scarlett was one she knew she'd never forget. It wasn't one of those Band-Aid smiles she hated so much, but it wasn't a frown, either. Chrissie's face was just a flat, careful *knowing*.

"Is it okay if we go to sleep now?" Chrissie asked. "I'm pretty tired."

"Sure," Scarlett said as she clicked off the television and flipped down all the lights. Grandma worried about bills a lot, so she was always careful not to waste electricity. "But maybe we can finish the movie in the morning? I really am going to Paris someday, so I need to be prepared."

"I know you are," Chrissie said without a scrap of disbelief. "You're going to be rich and famous. I can tell."

As they settled into their side-by-side sleeping bags, Scarlett took a second to unzip hers and lock it in with Chrissie's. Chrissie felt cold to the touch, but Scarlett's temperature always ran hot. Giving her some of her body heat seemed like the least she could do.

"What about you?" Scarlett asked as she snuggled up next to Chrissie, Mr. Bunny wedged comfortably between them. "Are you going to be rich and famous when you grow up, too?"

"No," Chrissie said and closed her eyes. "I already know what I want to be when I'm an adult."

"What, a teacher? A doctor? An astronaut? I bet you'd be a great astronaut."

"None of those things." Chrissie let out a sleepy yawn and burrowed closer. "All I really want is a chance to be me."

Chapter Seven

BOISE, ID

Present Day

THE NIGHTLIFE OF BOISE ON A Tuesday night, while better than what Medford had to offer, wasn't much to write home about.

Scarlett led Chrissie into a classy, black-and-white themed piano bar within walking distance of their hotel. Proximity, Scarlett had maintained, was the only real prerequisite she had for their evening's entertainment. She said she wanted a place to show off Chrissie's haircut that wouldn't require them to spend any more time in the car—and if live music was a part of the deal, even better.

"I'm sure this place picks up after dark," Scarlett promised as she plucked a happy hour menu off the table. "The only people here this early in the evening are the olds and the cheapskates."

"And which ones are we supposed to be?" Chrissie asked. Despite her hesitation, she wasn't displeased to find that they were only two of a handful of people inside the bar. As much as she was enjoying her new look—including the sequined tank top Scarlett had forced her to buy from a pricey boutique, she didn't particularly want to shout to be heard all night.

"Neither. We're women who refuse to let society dictate our actions."

Scarlett set the menu down with a grimace. Although Chrissie was dressed to the hilt, Scarlett wasn't looking her best. Her face was pale against the cropped black turtleneck she wore, dark circles starting to form under her eyes.

"Is that why you're wearing a turtleneck?" Chrissie asked. "I thought for sure I was going to be treated to an obscene display of the new girls tonight."

"Nah, I didn't want to overshadow you. That's why I'm also going to start my night by ordering a hot chocolate instead of a martini. I wonder if they'll let me bring one in from the café next door."

It was on the tip of Chrissie's tongue to say that they could just as easily *go* to the café next door—or better yet, crawl into their pajamas and call it an early night—but she was stopped when a familiar face started moving toward them.

"Hello and welcome to—Oh!" River stopped a few feet short of the table, her one visible eye even more made up than before. "It's you."

"Chrissie," she reminded the girl in a friendly voice. She pointed at her hair, which swished around her shoulders like a curtain of silk. "Thanks for the suggestion, by the way. I've been getting compliments all afternoon."

"It looks great," River agreed. Then, with a nervous glance over her shoulder, "What can I get you two to drink? Pretty please don't order anything blended or smoked. The bartender's in a foul mood. If I have to ask him to make piña coladas all night, I'm not sure I'll get paid."

"Just water for me," Scarlett said.

Chrissie couldn't remember the last time Scarlett had ordered *water* at a bar, but she figured her friend was taking it easy on the girl.

"And I'll take a glass of house white," she said. "But you know it's illegal for you to work without getting paid, right?"

The look River cast her was so much like her daughter that she almost laughed out loud. She managed to hold herself in check until the girl took herself off to put their orders in with a bowlegged bear of a man who did, in fact, look to be in a terrible mood.

"The poor thing," Chrissie said as she watched River start to wipe down tables and light candles on the several dozen tables surrounding a glossy grand piano on a raised platform in the center of the bar. "She had to work all morning at the hair salon, and now this? I wonder if I should—"

"No."

Chrissie swiveled her gaze back toward her friend. "But you didn't even know what I was going to say!"

Scarlett held up her hand and started ticking off the possibilities. "You're either going to talk to the manager, call up the workers' rights complaint hotline, write her a check for several hundred dollars, and/or adopt her as your second child. *Third* child if you count Rufio—which I don't. That cat is a menace."

"The workers' rights complaint hotline exists for a reason."

Scarlett snorted. "This is our *vacation*, Chrissie. Our chance to kick back and spend some much-needed time together. I absolutely forbid you from bringing in strays. There's a lot of stuff I haven't had a chance to tell you yet."

A frown tugged at Chrissie's lips as she watched River start to carry away a tray of dirty glasses that weighed almost as much she did. That last bit—about the things Scarlett wanted to tell her—seemed important, but not nearly as important as the girl's plight. "She looks barely older than Kat."

"And I'm sure she has a perfectly adequate mother of her own to worry about her." Scarlett rapped her knuckles on the table. "Now. Tell me about Walsh. I want to hear all about his unrequited love for you."

Chrissie allowed herself to be distracted, but not without first remembering what River had said about her mother and the cancer that had taken her life. There was no age at which losing a parent was easy, but she must have been awfully young.

"'Unrequited' is a strong a word to describe our situation." Chrissie shrugged as she did her best to push the thought of a small, tear-streaked girl clutching a pink cosplay wig out of her mind. "Walsh asked me out a few years ago. I was tempted, but I pointed out how inappropriate it would be while Kat was one of his athletes, and he agreed. Ever since then, he's been a good friend."

"Friends don't ask friends to send bikini pictures."

Chrissie's cheeks flamed. "*You* do."

"Yeah, but only because someone has to remind you what a hot piece of ass you are. Have you guys ever chaperoned a volleyball tournament together?"

"Of course. Why?"

"Did he make any moves? Buy you a few strong drinks at the hotel bar? Ask you to put on those tiny volleyball shorts and do a dance for him?"

"Scarlett, there are like twenty girls on the team! Whenever we're at tournaments, we're so exhausted from trying to feed them and drive them around and make sure they aren't sneaking vodka into their hotel rooms that it's all we can do to keep our eyes open."

"Hmm," Scarlett said, her lips pursed as she absorbed this. She was still absorbing it when River returned with their drinks.

"I'm s'posed to tell you that your first drink is half off," she said as she set the glasses down in front of them. "The piano player called out sick, so wine is all the entertainment we have tonight. Bottoms up."

"No piano player?" Chrissie echoed. She stretched her fingers in an unconscious motion, a few of her knuckles cracking lightly as she did. "Is that why the bartender is being so mean to you?"

"No," River said. She clamped her mouth shut as though unwilling to say more, but then she sighed and dragged a hand through her hair, flashing Chrissie a sight of both her eyes at once. "He's mad because we broke up last week and I haven't been able to find a new place to crash. He says he can't bring any other girls home until I'm out of his hair. For some reason, he thinks me sitting on the couch watching old Buffy episodes is ruining his vibe." River snorted. "His *vibe*. Please. Before I moved in, his coffee table was literally a stack of pizza boxes."

Chrissie stole another glance at the bartender, who was cutting limes as though each one had offered him a personal insult. She wasn't adept at guessing people's ages, but his short buzz cut and abundance of tattoos aged him in a way that made her think he'd never again see thirty.

"How old are you?" Chrissie asked suddenly.

"Omigod, Chrissie, you can't ask people that." Scarlett rolled her eyes up at River. "You'll have to forgive my friend. She's basically an old woman in sheep's clothing. Do you know what she had for breakfast this morning? Oatmeal. With raisins and nonfat milk and some weird packet of seeds that she brought from home."

"They're chia seeds, and they're very good for you. It's like snacking on crunchy vitamins."

Scarlett and River exchanged a look that made Chrissie flush to the roots of her hair.

"Lots of people eat chia seeds. They're very hip right now. And I'll have you know that oatmeal is delicious. With enough brown sugar, it tastes just like a wet cookie."

"Yummy." A grin curled River's lips, making her look very much her age. "Wet cookies."

Chrissie laid a gentle hand on the girl's forearm, unable to suppress the maternal instincts that arose from the sight of that youthful smile. "Do you have people you can rely on, River?" she asked. "Do you need anything?"

River's whole body stopped in a way that spoke magnitudes, and in a volume that carried with it the force of a hurricane. Chrissie recognized the signs at a glance. She'd long ago cultivated a similar habit of stillness—of taking up as little space as possible, of making sure each action, each word, each breath would be welcome before she let it out.

Scarlett was never still. Kat wasn't, either. It was one of the things she loved about them both. They moved through the world as though they belonged in it—or, if they didn't, as though making space for themselves was only a matter of pushing out a few elbows until everything fell into place.

But not River. Not this girl who'd lost her mother and who worked two jobs to make ends meet, who was living with a man who was much too old for her because she had nowhere else to go.

"I'm eighteen," River said in a voice Chrissie had to strain to hear. "I turned eighteen yesterday."

Instead of the pang of sympathy this confession should have elicited, Chrissie found herself sinking into a red-hot quagmire of emotion. At first, she wasn't sure of the exact cause. Because that bartender had *definitely* broken the law by dating River? Because the girl should have been out celebrating her birthday instead of waiting tables? Or because Chrissie understood the significance of that number—of what it meant to be thrust into sudden adulthood without any kind of safety net in place?

By the time she finished asking herself the questions, she'd reached her answer. It was the last one for sure. Chrissie remembered all too well that feeling of being unmoored—of being eighteen and on her own, of knowing that the entire weight of her future rested on her shoulders and her shoulders alone.

In a word, it *sucked.*

"Happy birthday," she said as she lifted her hand from the girl's arm. River stared at her for a long, curious moment before nodding and slipping back into the kitchen.

A silence fell over the table as Chrissie tried to process what had just happened, but Scarlett broke it with a sigh so marked it practically had a pulse.

"Okay, *fine*," she said. "You win. Get it out."

"Get what out?"

Scarlett gestured at Chrissie's purse. "The piece of paper from the motel. Go ahead and write it down—the thing you're going to do. The thing you can't help but do."

Chrissie was tempted to pretend she didn't understand what Scarlett meant, but the sharp edges of her anger were still there, poking and prodding her into action. Most of the time, she was able to dull those edges with errands and to-do lists, the busy nothings that kept her day-to-day life on track, but Scarlett was right. She was already formulating a plan.

The folded piece of paper was in the front pocket of her purse where she'd left it. Underneath the first line, now reading I like to sit and read without interruption, she added another.

I want to help that girl out of her troubles, only you're being mean. Sorry, Scarlett, but if you love me, you'll let me. I have to do something. Don't be extra about it.

Scarlett took the pen from her and frowned over the words. After a few cross-outs, she handed the paper back.

~~I want to~~ help ~~that girl out of her troubles,~~ only ~~you're being mean. Sorry, Scarlett, but~~ if ~~you love me, you'll let me.~~ I ~~have to~~ do something~~. Don't be~~ extra ~~about it~~.

Chrissie read the changes aloud. "*Help only if I do something extra.*" She frowned over the words. "What do you mean? What kind of extra? You think I should call the police and have them arrest that man for statutory rape?"

Scarlett released a soft laugh. "No, Chrissie. I mean that if you want to help that girl out, you need to do something for yourself first. Something extra. Something daring. Something you promised yourself you'd never do again."

All of a sudden, the bar felt half its size. The piano, which had seemed fun and glamorous when they'd first walked in, grew to monumental proportions.

"Why are you doing this?" Chrissie asked as a sharp prick of anxiety started to tingle at the back of her throat. "With the haircut and the list and all this Walsh stuff, I mean? You haven't been this emotionally invested in my life in a long time. Something's up."

Scarlett sat back in her seat and took a sip of her water, her head tilted as she studied Chrissie in the dim lights of the bar. "I just think it's time, that's all. You're always so busy taking care of everyone else that you forget to consider your own needs."

The anxiety, which had been growing steadily with each word Scarlett said, transformed into a lump.

"So I'm proposing a deal," Scarlett continued, oblivious to how close Chrissie was to getting up and leaving the bar altogether. "You're welcome to help that girl or any other random passerby we meet, and I'll give you my full support while you do it, but only if you do something selfish first."

Chrissie couldn't pretend to misunderstand her. "Sitting down and playing that piano isn't selfish."

"You sure about that? You've been trying not to stare at it since the moment we walked in here. I'm guessing your fingers are itching to give those ivories a tickle."

"They're really not."

She glanced down at her hands and flexed them again, but this time, the reaction was a conscious one—conscious *and* annoyed.

Did Scarlett honestly think that this was the first time Chrissie had been in the same room as a piano since before Kat was born? Or that she hadn't toyed with—and discarded—the notion of taking up the instrument again on her own terms?

"You feel it, don't you?" Scarlett asked gently. "You *hear* it?"

Once again, Chrissie's anger was coming back full force. And once again, she found herself welcoming its warm glow.

"I haven't touched a piano in over a decade for a reason," she snapped. "And you know very well what that reason is. The last time I played was at your grandmother's—"

But here she cut herself off.

"My grandmother's funeral," Scarlett finished for her. She spoke in the flat, even tone of a woman who didn't dare step off the path for fear of being unable to get back on it again. "Grandma would've hated to think she had something to do with you quitting. You should play her song. Or not. Tonight is supposed to be for you, so dealer's choice."

Chrissie knew she was being emotionally manipulated. It was one of the many things Scarlett excelled at—pulling strings to get people on her side, using charm and sentiment when reason had no chance of success. At her most persuasive, Scarlett Sanderson could make driving a car off a cliff sound like a completely rational way to spend an afternoon, like taking afternoon tea with the queen or crashing a piano bar with all of six patrons inside.

And if she couldn't, she'd just keep talking and rationalizing until you gave in anyway.

"You don't think they'll kick me out if I sit down and start blasting out show tunes?" Chrissie asked without bothering to hide her sarcasm.

"If they do, I'll take a page from your book and tell that bartender I'm having him arrested for statutory rape." Scarlett crossed her arms over her newly buxom chest, confident now that she'd once again gotten her way. "Besides, you heard for yourself that their piano player is out sick. They'll probably jump at the chance to get free labor. Especially since you look every inch the part with that hair. People will think they've traveled back in time to a 1940s jazz club. Either that or a Looney Tunes episode. It all depends on whether or not you can sell it."

Chrissie pushed back her chair and got to her feet, her shoulders as set as they were resigned. She'd never admit it to Scarlett, but that hint of a challenge was more persuasive than all the other emotional acrobatics she was attempting.

In this mood—with this anger—she felt capable of *anything*.

Chrissie would have liked to say that the first touch of her fingers on the keys was like coming home again—that all the corrosion of disuse sloughed away, the notes coming back to her in a flash of insight from somewhere deep inside. In reality, she fumbled at least a dozen times, her opening of "Over the Rainbow" so disoriented that the song was unrecognizable until she reached the chorus.

But as she finished, a scattering of applause sounded and no one came forward to escort her off the premises, so that was something.

"Play us another!" a voice shouted—one that didn't belong to Scarlett. It was impossible to see anything under the bright overhead lights, so Chrissie closed her eyes and touched her fingers to the keys once again.

All of a sudden, she was transported back in time to one of the hazy memories she'd spent a lifetime trying to suppress. In it, Malcolm was dead, that much she knew for sure. In the before times, when Malcolm's wan face and labored breathing set the tone for her every waking hour, she'd almost never touched their family piano. Those long white keys had belonged to her brother's even longer, whiter fingers. *A prodigy*, she remembered hearing him called. *A natural talent seen only once in a lifetime.*

Chrissie could only take those people at their word. For as long as she'd been alive—the parts of it she could remember, anyway—Malcolm had been kept in a separate wing of the enormous house they'd called home. Away from the germs, away from the noise, away from the younger sister who woke up most mornings curled up at the foot of his bed like a stray cat.

The instrument had sat on a platform much like this one, dusted every day by the housekeeper hired to ensure Malcolm had a fighting chance against the cancer that seemed to return twice as much as it went. Chrissie had only tried to plunk at the keys once before the fallboard had been shut against her as firmly as Malcolm's bedroom door.

Your brother needs peace and quiet, Christina. We don't ask much of you, but that much isn't negotiable. Peace. And. Quiet.

She'd understood them perfectly. Her HLA markers didn't match her brother's, so she couldn't give him her bone marrow. All she had to offer in its place was her silence.

Imagine her surprise when, a few months after Malcolm's funeral, she'd been allowed to take formal lessons on the same instrument that had sat sacrosanct for so long. Not because her parents longed to hear the bright sound of music in the house again, and not because they thought she might enjoy a chance to share something with her brother, but because they simply had no idea what else to give her.

Not their attention. Not their time. Not their *love.*

She pushed the memory firmly aside, but the feelings lingered as she began playing the last song she'd ever put her hands to. The old Leonard Cohen standard, "Hallelujah," had been done and redone so many times that almost everyone knew the chords—secret or not. She was still faltering over the opening when a low, beautifully raw female voice joined her at the piano. She might have faltered even more once she realized that the voice belonged to River, but the girl nodded so encouragingly that she pushed through the clumsiness to what lay beyond.

Chrissie would never have Malcolm's natural talent—that fact had been borne in on her from the start—but she'd always loved the feeling of getting lost in the music. Practicing was brutal on her hands and recitals had been devastating to her sense of self-worth, but sometimes, just sometimes, she'd managed to convey her feelings in a way that even her parents had understood.

Pain. Anger. Fear. Loneliness.

Hope.

This time, when the song came to a close, the bar exploded in applause—or as much applause as half a dozen half-drunk patrons could muster when the clock hadn't yet reached five in the evening.

"Oh, wow. You're really good," River said, showing none of the self-consciousness that made Chrissie's whole body shake. "Do you know anything else?"

She did, but there was no way on earth she was making the attempt. "You're not so bad yourself," she said as she rose on wobbly knees and managed a smile. "Do you usually sing along with the piano player?"

"No way. Carlito would never allow anyone to outshine him." River tucked a strand of hair behind her ear, looking closer to eight years old than her supposed eighteen. "In fact, once he hears about this, he'll probably have me fired. So much for my ticket out of this city."

Chrissie darted out a hand and clutched River's forearm. It was the second time she'd done that—touched the girl without permission—but she couldn't seem to help herself. Scarlett's impulsivity must be rubbing off on her.

"Don't leave tonight without stopping by my table, okay? I'd like to help you if I can. What time are you off shift?"

River looked down at her arm and back up at Chrissie, her expression muted. "Not until midnight. You'll probably be in your hotel and asleep by then."

"I won't."

River hooked a thumb over her shoulder. "Maybe not, but your friend will. She doesn't look so good."

All thoughts of rescuing the girl fled at once, replaced by the even stronger need to rescue her best friend. Chrissie jumped down from the platform and marched over to the table.

"Scarlett, you wretch. If you're tired, you have to tell me. Are you feeling okay? Are we pushing too hard on this trip? We can always hop on a plane and go somewhere with beaches and a dangerously high UV index."

Although she *was* looking pretty tired, Scarlett didn't glance up, her phone in hand as her fingers flew over the keys.

"Thank you, Mommie dearest, but I'm fine. And you're already a huge hit with my listeners. Look." She showed Chrissie a clip from the song. Chrissie had to admit that the glittering tank top she wore looked good under so much illumination—especially once River joined her, her own black waitress uniform seeming to absorb both the light and the sound. "TikTok is gonna eat this up. They love a public sing-along like you wouldn't believe. It's the new flash mob."

"You put us on TikTok?" Chrissie asked, disregarding the bulk of this commentary. "Scarlett, what if River doesn't want to be filmed? What if *I* don't want to be?"

Scarlett kicked out Chrissie's chair and gestured for her to sit in it. Sometime in the past half hour, a second glass of white wine had made it to her side of the table. "Then I guess you shouldn't be so freaking talented."

As Chrissie sat and refreshed herself with most—okay, *all*—of the wine, Scarlett added, "How did it feel, by the way? Playing the piano again? Letting yourself go?"

Chrissie glared at her friend over the top of her glass. Drat Scarlett for putting her in this position. Drat her for always being right. And drat her for knowing exactly how hard to push before letting Chrissie's nature take its course.

"It wasn't as awful as I thought," she admitted before pointing a warning finger. "But don't think that means you can manipulate me into doing it again. I'm not a little kid anymore, willing to do your bidding at every turn."

Scarlett snorted. "You were never *willing*, Chrissie. In case you don't remember, every daring thing I got out of you, I had to get by force."

Chapter Eight

PORTLAND, OR

2002

SCARLETT HAD NEVER SEEN SUCH A fancy house in her life.

She'd also never seen Chrissie in such a state of worry—which was saying a lot, because Chrissie worried about *everything*.

At the ripe old age of ten, Scarlett's worries revolved mostly around how to score an audition to become a cast member of *Even Stevens* (she'd already written Shia LaBeouf eighteen letters, but he never answered), whether or not she could continue using her now-in-remission cancer as an excuse to get out of math class (outlook not so good), and what monstrosity her grandmother was making for dinner (she'd recently decided that going full vegan was the best way to keep Scarlett living until the even riper old age of eleven).

Chrissie, however, worried about Real Life. It wasn't enough for her to practice the piano for eleventy billion hours every day or to always eat everything Scarlett's grandma put in front of her, as if fish cakes made of seaweed and tofu were real food. Somewhere along the way, she'd decided that breaking into your own house in the full light of day would send them both to jail until they were grown-ups.

"All you have to do is give me a boost, and I know I can make it inside that window," Scarlett said as she stood peering up at the exterior bathroom wall. The small, square window was the only open one they could see, and since they'd already checked all the rocks in hopes of finding a fake key, it was also the only way inside. "Just make a little table with your hands. It'll be super easy."

Chrissie didn't make a little table. She didn't even try.

"We should go back to your apartment," Chrissie said. "I changed my mind. We're not supposed to be here."

She moved toward the bikes they'd parked on the side of the house. They hadn't even had to hide them. Chrissie's house was in Dunthorpe, one of those neighborhoods with houses so big you couldn't see who lived next door. There were tall bushes and fences and even a working fountain that kept trickling so loud it was making Scarlett have to pee.

Her own apartment, where the only fountain was the kitchen sink that drip-dripped all night long, was in Sellwood—close enough to bike, but only if they did part of it on the highway, which was why this trip was secret.

And important.

"I'm not going anywhere." Scarlett pushed up her sleeves and looked around until she landed on a pretty white garden bench made of scrolling bits of metal. "And neither are you. We came here to get Mr. Bunny, and we're not leaving without him. Help me push that bench over."

"But I'm supposed to be too old for stuffed animals," Chrissie protested. She tried grabbing Scarlett by the hand and dragging her away, but Scarlett was too strong for her. It was funny, when you thought about it. At ten years of age, Chrissie was six inches taller than she was and had never had any illnesses except for normal colds, but she was the most fragile person Scarlett had ever met. A strong wind could blow her over.

That, or a mean word. Those seemed to knock her down all the time.

"My mom's right," Chrissie said, almost tearful now. "I have to learn to live without him. Only babies need a crutch to fall asleep."

Scarlett pulled a gagging face. That was her usual reaction whenever Chrissie repeated one of the ten bazillion rules her mom and dad made. Grandma always reacted that way, too. Her face didn't gag, but it did get all pinched and mad. The only time Scarlett *ever* saw Grandma get angry was when Chrissie talked about her parents.

Not that Grandma said anything to Chrissie about it, of course. She just gave Chrissie extra hugs and cookies—the secret, nonvegan ones she kept hidden in her bedroom—before taking her mad, pinched face to church-basement bingo to blow off some steam.

"Your mom isn't here, so she doesn't get to tell you what to do," Scarlett said as she stomped over to the bench and tried pushing. The metal weighed a ton, so she didn't get very far. "C'mon, Chrissie. You can't go two whole weeks without Mr. Bunny. He'll get lonely in that big, empty house all by himself."

That seemed to do the trick—just like Scarlett knew it would, even though she'd never been inside Chrissie's house before. Chrissie never said exactly *why* she wasn't allowed to have friends over, but she did say that she could sometimes hear ghosts in the walls, begging to be let out.

That might not have sounded like much to anyone else, but Scarlett had lived almost her entire life in the apartment with Grandma, and she'd never heard anything even a little bit like a ghost. She heard toilets and cars and sirens. She heard babies crying and people shouting and the lady next door singing her kids to sleep. Even in the hospital, there'd always been beeps and squeaks and the hushed voices of nurses as they went about their business.

In order for it to be quiet enough to hear a ghost, well…it would have to be *very* quiet.

"Okay, but we're only popping in to grab Mr. Bunny. You can't snoop around or anything." Chrissie lifted her side of the bench and started to drag it over the decorative rocks. "I'm serious, Scarlett. I know you. You're gonna want to touch everything."

"I'm not!" Scarlett protested, but Chrissie was right, as usual.

The moment Scarlett slid through the bathroom window, her feet landing on the softest, whitest bath mat she'd ever seen, her fingers itched to skim over every available surface. The marble tiles, the shiny gold faucets, the way the little hand soap in the dish was shaped like a seashell—it was like something out of a magazine.

Since Scarlett's job was to slip to the back door and let Chrissie in that way, she got a chance to see the rest of the house just as up close and personal. Mindful of Chrissie's warning, she didn't snoop, but she did let her fingers trail over the wispy cream-colored curtains and the heavy-hanging paintings of things like old houses and even older castles. It wasn't until she opened the door and let Chrissie in that she realized she hadn't seen a single picture that didn't look like it belonged in a museum. Her own apartment had nothing but plastic-framed photographs and the silly macaroni art she'd made in the hospital years ago, which Grandma refused to throw away no matter how much Scarlett begged.

"Did you touch anything?" Chrissie asked, her face white with worry. "Because I know it seems like no one will notice, but—"

"I didn't," Scarlett promised, her fingers crossed behind her back. "Not really."

Chrissie narrowed her eyes as if able to see right through Scarlett's skin and bones. "If my parents know we broke in, they'll never let me stay at your house when they go on vacation again," she warned.

This was too much for Scarlett. She might have been terrible at math (it is decidedly so), and her grades at school were "understandable considering her developmental years," but she was no fool. She was also the kind of person who said the first thing that came to her mind.

A *spitfire*, they'd called her at the hospital. A *menace*, they called her at school. *The most daring girl I know*, Chrissie said—and that was the one Scarlett liked best.

"Yes, they will," Scarlett said. "They have to. They don't have anyone else to watch you, and we both know they'd never go on a vacation where they have to take you with them. That would mean they'd have to think about someone other than themselves for once."

She turned on her heel and started to walk through the house, this time letting her fingers land anywhere she wanted. She almost knocked over a huge blue-and-white vase holding a bunch of pussy willow branches, but she managed to catch it just in time. When she looked back to see if Chrissie had noticed, her friend was still standing by the back door, her face screwed up as if trying not to cry.

"Oh, Chrissie. I didn't mean it, I swear!"

She rushed back and threw her arms around Chrissie's shoulders. All at once, she remembered the other things the hospital and school said about her.

She doesn't think through the consequences of her actions.

Her heart's in the right place, but that impulsive nature of hers is going to be her undoing.

"I'm sorry I said that," she said, wishing she could eat the words—and, by extension, Chrissie's tears. "I'm sure they'll take you with them next time. I bet they're thinking of you and wishing they'd gone to Disneyland instead."

Chrissie sniffled and looked so sad that Scarlett could have bitten off her own tongue. "They're not thinking of me," she said. "All they can think about is Malcolm. They worried about him for so long that they don't know how to do anything else."

That was when Scarlett decided to take matters into her own hands. Chrissie almost never talked about her brother's death or how her parents had turned to stone because of it, about the hours she spent at the piano in hopes of getting them to pay even a *little* attention to her, but Scarlett knew. She knew down to her very bones.

"Which room is his?" she asked.

"Scarlett, no. We can't."

"Yes, we can. Who's gonna stop us?" Scarlett flung open the nearest door to show a dark green study with giant deer heads mounted on the walls. "Oh, ew. Did your dad shoot all those?"

Chrissie didn't allow herself to be distracted. "Let's just go get Mr. Bunny. I think my mom put him in the linen closet."

Scarlett marched forward to open the next door (a bathroom) and the next (another bathroom). "Why does your house have so many toilets? My grandma's church doesn't even have this many, and those old ladies take *forever* to pee."

Chrissie was betrayed into a giggle—just like Scarlett had hoped—but she resolutely shut all the doors. "It's upstairs, but I don't like to go in there. It's…"

"Creepy?" Scarlett suggested. "Sad? A place you're never allowed to go even if the whole house is on fire and it's the only way out?"

Chrissie nodded. "Yeah."

"Then we'll go there together. I want to see what all the fuss is about." Scarlett slid her hand in Chrissie's and stood there holding it. She knew it was only a matter of time before Chrissie gave in and led the way.

That was the thing about Chrissie—the thing that Scarlett liked most about her. She was terrified of everything and hesitant to step even an inch out of line, but that never seemed to stop her from living her life anyway.

"Okay," Chrissie said. "This way."

They tiptoed up the carpeted stairs to a dark, quiet hall that Scarlett could totally tell was haunted. Malcolm's room was the last one on the right, the only door in the whole house that was open a crack.

"They never close it," Chrissie whispered as she put a palm flat on the wood and pushed. "I don't know why. I think they're afraid that if they do, they'll have to admit that I'm all they have left."

Scarlett didn't scream all the things that were stuck in her throat. *Your mom is even worse than mine, and mine abandoned me to my grandmother the day I got sick. Why do they care so much about one stupid dead son when they have the best daughter in the world right here? Let's burn the whole house down and dance naked on the ashes!* Instead, she just nodded and allowed Chrissie to lead her inside.

The room was disappointing, to say the least. Scarlett had always thought that ghostly shrines were supposed to feel like stepping into church when all the lights were off or sitting in front of a television screen showing nothing but static. Instead, she found herself standing in a bedroom with dark blue old-fashioned wallpaper and a huge window overlooking the backyard. The bed was neatly made, the dresser free of everything except a single bronze trophy. True, there was a stack of Hardy Boys novels arranged on the bedside table and a framed poster of a bunch of piano keys on it, but even those felt bland in comparison with every other bedroom in the world.

"Huh," Scarlett said. She frowned as she whirled around, looking for a dirty sock or a stack of *Mad* magazines—*anything* to indicate that a living, breathing boy had once slept here. "It's not very interesting, is it?"

Chrissie shrugged. "My room is basically the same, only in pink and with Nancy Drew instead of the Hardy Boys."

For some reason, that made Scarlett feel even worse about what she was seeing. "Do you at least get a trophy, too?" she asked as she touched a fingertip to the bronze.

That was when she realized it wasn't a trophy at all. It was an urn.

Scarlett knew *all* about those. Once, one of the kids at the hospital had brought in a brochure from a funeral home. It had been full of silk-lined caskets and huge, fat-bellied urns, all of them promising a "fitting goodbye for your dearest loved ones." A bunch of the kids had sat on Scarlett's bed picking out their favorites. It hadn't been a *sad* day—she remembered them dog-earing the pages and laughing over things like special pockets for hiding their favorite treasures to carry with them into eternity—but one of the moms had come in and yelled so much that they'd all ended up in trouble with the nurses.

"I'm sorry. I didn't know." She peeked over her shoulder to make sure Chrissie wasn't breaking down or anything, but she only stood in the doorway with her arms crossed over her stomach, looking more guilty than upset. "Is it weird to know his ashes are sitting up here? Even when you, like, eat dinner?"

"A little." Chrissie paused. "Can we get Mr. Bunny now? I'm ready to go home."

Her use of that word—*home*—made something in Scarlett's chest give a lurch. Chrissie wasn't talking about this big, grand house where she wasn't allowed to touch anything or hang posters on the wall. She was talking about the cramped apartment where Scarlett and Grandma had to carry their laundry down the street to the laundromat and then sit for *hours* waiting for it to dry because if you left it there for even a minute, someone would take the pile out and leave it sopping wet on the floor.

"Not yet. First, I think you should steal something from this room."

"What?" Chrissie's arms fell from her stomach, her guilty look replaced by one of wide-eyed fear. "Scarlett, I can't do that! What if my parents found out?"

Scarlett cut her off with a sniff. "Who cares? It's not like they'll be able to prove it was you. Besides, they can't know *everything* that's in here. Let's look in the closet, maybe, or under the bed. That's where all the juicy stuff is."

"You don't understand," Chrissie said—pleaded, even. "They'll never forgive me if I mess this room up."

"So? Is their forgiveness even worth having?"

Scarlett knew the exact moment she got through—the exact moment the devil on Chrissie's shoulder pushed the angel off. It was in the way her wide eyes got even wider, with a sparkle in them that looked just like a shooting star.

"Actually, there is one thing I've always wanted." Chrissie slapped her hands over her mouth as if shocked by her own daring. Then, peeling first one hand and then the other away, she added, "It's in the closet. Top shelf. Near the back."

The fact that Chrissie knew exactly where to find her secret treasure—and that it was hidden away—was enough to assure Scarlett that she'd made the right decision.

She recognized the object the moment they lifted the plastic container from the top shelf. Everything in there was Tupperwared up and organized with a label—extra underwear, size medium; winter sweaters, WOOL ONLY; memory/keepsakes—but it was the one with the label of games and activities that Chrissie went to first.

"Ohh, Chrissie. It's *beautiful.*" Scarlett's voice turned reverent as she pulled out a paint-by-numbers kit that showed a pile of puppies spilling out of a basket. Each one had a big red bow around its neck, which matched an even bigger bow around the edge of the basket. "Malcolm never opened it?"

Chrissie shook her head as she accepted the painting kit, her hands gentle on the edges. "A neighbor gave it to him as a birthday present when he turned ten. He was too weak to do it by then, so he said I could have it and paint it for him. So he could hang it by his bed and think of me."

A red-hot emotion the same color as the bow took hold of Scarlett by the throat.

"But your parents wouldn't let you," she said, no hint of a question in her voice. "They'd rather it sit here in the closet forever than you have even a little bit of fun."

"No." Chrissie shook her head. "That's not it. Seeing it would just make my mom too sad, that's all."

"She's *always* sad," Scarlett said scathingly. "Sometimes, I think she likes it."

Chrissie nodded her agreement, which was all Scarlett needed to tuck the kit under one arm. Grandma had told her about a hundred times that everyone grieved differently, and that Chrissie's parents were doing the best they could with a bad situation, but when you loved someone—*really* loved them—you didn't drag them down with you. You used every bit of strength you had left to lift them up.

"Okay. You go get Mr. Bunny, and I'll find a way to tie this to the back of my bike. You can spend the next two weeks painting, and I promise not to interrupt you a single time. Not even if I'm so bored I want to scream."

Chrissie hesitated, but Scarlett refused to back down.

"It's what I'd want you to do if *I* was the one who'd died," she said. "I'd want you to paint and paint until the walls were covered with puppies. If it made you happy, I'd never stop you from doing anything. You know that, right?"

Scarlett knew the exact moment Chrissie gave in. Even more than the slow, careful smile or the way she reached over and gave Scarlett's arm a quick squeeze, it was in the way she got just a little bit taller.

Scarlett would always love Chrissie no matter what, but she loved her best when she took up as much space as possible.

"Okay," Chrissie finally said. "You're right. Thank you. I never would've had the guts to take it for myself."

"I know," Scarlett said, and she did—she really, truly did. "That's why I'm here to help you. And why I'll *keep* helping you until the day you don't need me anymore."

Chapter Nine

BOISE, ID

Present Day

THE KNOCK AT THE MOTEL DOOR came around four o'clock in the morning.

Chrissie, who'd only fallen asleep a few hours before, was startled into heart-pounding wakefulness, her every sense on alert as she leaped out of bed and reached for the nearest weapon. Since this was the bedside lamp, and the heavy metal base was screwed down to prevent theft, she didn't make it very far.

Not that it mattered when she found that Scarlett had already beaten her to the peephole. Scarlett was fully dressed and didn't seem at all disoriented as she glanced over her shoulder at Chrissie.

"It's your protégé," she said as she unlatched the chain and swung the door open. "River! What are you doing here at this hour?"

By this time, Chrissie had managed to orient herself to her surroundings. She also oriented herself to the fact that the girl's heavily studded face was streaked with tears, her hair dripping down her back as she stood clutching a faded yellow suitcase in the rain.

"Did you mean what you said before?" she asked, looking first at

Scarlett and then at Chrissie, oddly hesitant to cross the threshold into the room. "About wanting to help me?"

It was a good thing the lamp had all *four* screws because Chrissie managed to rip out two of them in her second reach for a weapon.

"What did he do to you?" she demanded. "Tell me where you live. Get me my pepper spray. Scarlett, call the police and warn them there's about to be a murder."

Instead of doing any of those things, River and Scarlett shared a knowing look.

"I'm serious." Chrissie shoved her feet into her Crocs and started reaching for her coat. The weather outside didn't look pleasant, but then, in this state of mind, neither was she. "Where are the car keys?"

"It's not my ex," River said. "I promise. Not in the way you're thinking."

River still stood on the other side of the door, so in the absence of a major felony to take the edge off, Chrissie drew the girl into the room and patted her down in an effort to examine her for injuries. Other than being soaked to the skin and trembling all over, she appeared to be okay.

"You'll have to excuse Chrissie for foaming at the mouth," Scarlett said as she shut the door behind them. "Her mama bear instincts are so deeply ingrained that if she took up residence in a zoo, people would come from around the world to catch a glimpse of her."

"My instincts aren't *that* bad," Chrissie said as she sank to the edge of the bed. When the adrenaline drained like that, ebbing out like the ocean at low tide, her knees were always the first to go. "People would only come from the next state, at most."

This earned her a watery chuckle from River, though the girl had her arms wrapped around her midsection and a look of increasing anxiety on her pinched face.

"Are you sure this is okay? I meant to come talk to you as soon as my shift got over, but I figured you were only being nice and—"

"It's okay," Scarlett said for both of them. "And I think I know what this is about. I'm sorry. I should've asked before I tagged the location."

"Wait." Chrissie looked back and forth between them. "What do you mean?"

Scarlett winced and handed Chrissie her phone. "You were right about posting that video. It's, uh, getting a lot more views than I was expecting."

Chrissie had to put on her glasses before she could look at the screen—without her contact lenses, she was basically a mole rat—but the sounds of piano music and River's raspy voice told her more than enough.

"Two hundred thousand likes?" Chrissie frowned down at the screen. "Is that a lot?"

"Is that…?" Scarlett's voice trailed off in disbelief. "In less than twelve hours? Are you serious?"

"It's a lot," River said quietly. She pushed her wet hair out of her face. "My stepmom—that is, my step*sisters*—saw the video right away. They, uh… That is, I didn't exactly…" She cast a look of such painful entreaty at Chrissie that it was all she could do not to pull the poor drowned child into her arms. "I didn't leave home on good terms. They've been looking for me for a while now."

Chrissie could have torn the lamp off the table for *real* this time—and for no reason other than to lob it at Scarlett's head. It was just like her friend to ignore all the warning signs and make a very public announcement of River's location without her permission.

Since brute force wasn't an option, and River was starting to look sick to her stomach, Chrissie did the only thing she could think of: She went to work.

"Okay, here's what we'll do. First of all, Scarlett will take down that video—"

"What's the point? This thing is a viral sensation. There's no un-ringing that bell."

"Scarlett," Chrissie warned.

"Chrissie," Scarlett warned right back.

"You had no right to post it in the first place."

"Technically, I had every right. You were performing in a public location."

They might have stood at this impasse for a while if not for River's quiet voice sliding into the conversation yet again. "It's fine. The damage is already done. There's no sense in deleting the video now."

Chrissie didn't like the idea of giving Scarlett a free pass, but if she'd learned one thing as the parent of a strong-willed teenager, it was when to choose her battles.

"Fine, it can stay up. River, is there somewhere safe we can take you? A relative you can stay with, or a friend maybe?"

She thought, but didn't add, a *female* friend. The idea of dumping this teenager with yet another man all too willing to take advantage of her situation was one that didn't sit well with her.

River looked down at her shoes, a clunky pair of boots that Chrissie noted for the first time were so battered that they were being held together with black duct tape.

"Well, I have this aunt—a *great*-aunt, really—but she lives all the way in Chicago." She glanced up again, a not-unhopeful gleam in her eyes. "You guys are on a road trip, right? Are you heading that way?"

The Windy City hadn't been on their list of places to visit, but it wasn't so far off the beaten path to make it an impossibility. It was also one of the many places Chrissie had never been before. Scarlett had lived there for a few years—fallen in love there, naturally—but that could be said of at least a dozen different global destinations. Something about big cities always put stars in her eyes and glitter in her pants.

"We are now." Chrissie did a quick mental calculation. "How much time do we have before they come looking for you?"

"I don't know. An hour? Two hours?" She shrugged in a way that both looked and felt wrong. "I didn't take anything valuable when I left, I swear. Just some stuff that belonged to my mom. My dad and stepmom don't even want it. Or me. They're just mad because my running away made them look bad in front of their friends."

"I'm ready to go whenever you are," Scarlett said. "Lead the way, oh captain."

Chrissie shot her friend a harassed look. For someone who had caused all this drama in the first place, she was being surprisingly blasé about it. "You could show a little remorse, you know."

"Why? This is exactly what you wanted. A chance to leap to the rescue." Scarlett paused, eyeing her carefully. "Aren't you even going to ask what River stole? Or why she left home in the first place?"

Chrissie was already shoving her clothes and toiletries into her bag by this point, but she had an answer ready to go. Not only did she understand what it was like to live with parents who cared only about the appearance of things, but the thought of her own daughter being in a similar situation—alone in the world and terrified half to death, in trouble of any kind, even that of her own making—was enough to make her throw caution off the nearest cliff.

"No," she said frankly. "None of that matters."

"Then there you go. What good would my feeling guilty do?"

Aware that River was watching this exchange in silent discomfort—and creeping toward the door in a way that presaged flight—Chrissie did her best to calm the girl.

"It's fine, River. I don't care what you did or why you did it. If you say you're in trouble and that there's a great-aunt in Chicago willing to help you out of it, that's enough for me."

"Th-thank you," the girl stammered in a subdued tone.

"We should all be so lucky," Scarlett muttered in an even more subdued one.

That was the end of the line as far as Chrissie was concerned. She wasn't sure what was coming over her lately, but something about spending all this time with Scarlett was bringing her buried girlhood emotions rushing to the surface.

"*Enough*, Scarlett," she snapped. "Have you forgotten what it's like to be that age? To have the safety net pulled out from under you and be thrust into the world without any kind of preparation?"

Chrissie stared at her friend, daring her to argue. Neither one of them could forget that particular summer of their adolescence, when life and death had become so intertwined that the two were forever linked inside her heart.

"I know you think I'm a pushover, and that I'm just a sitting duck for everyone to take advantage of, but this is what I do," Chrissie said. "When a fellow human being asks for my help, I give it. When they say they're in need, I take them at their word. I accept what the world gives me and do my best to bear it without complaint. Maybe that makes me weak or silly, and maybe I sometimes end up doing more harm than good, but it's the one thing—the *only thing*—I have. You know that better than anyone."

The silence in the room suddenly felt so heavy that it seemed she was going to be asked to bear *that*, as well. But even though Chrissie could feel her muscles thrumming with new energy, Scarlett did what she always did in situations like these.

She smiled.

"You're right, of course. You always are." Scarlett winked at River as though all of this was no more than a show for her entertainment. "You should thank your lucky stars, kid. The day Christina Thomas walked into your salon will end up being the best one of your life. You can trust me on this one."

And that was it. With an energy that matched her own, Scarlett swept through the room, packing up their things and making sure to look inside drawers and under the bed so they didn't forget anything. Within ten minutes, they were on the road and on their way.

"Is it okay if I sleep a little?" River asked from the back seat of the RAV4, where she sat with her battered yellow suitcase tucked carefully between her knees. "I haven't gone to bed yet, so I'm beat."

"You sleep as long and as hard as you want," Chrissie said from behind the wheel. She cast a sidelong look at Scarlett, whom she also suspected of not getting a single wink. It wouldn't be the first time. Many a childhood sleepover had turned into a horror show when she'd woken up to find Scarlett sitting upright, watching over her with an intensity usually reserved for serial killers and women who liked to take romance writers hostage in the woods. "In fact, I think you both should."

"I'll sleep when I'm dead," Scarlett said, the same way she had as a child. "For now, let's just enjoy the ride."

By the time they reached the Idaho-Wyoming border, Scarlett and River were the best of friends.

"I don't care what you say, Chrissie. We're stopping at Cokeville for lunch, and I won't take no for an answer." Scarlett glanced over her shoulder at River with a grin that could only be called conspiratorial. "The two of us made a rule before we started. We have to stop at every weird piece of Americana we come across on the road, and we *especially* have to stop if a town has a hilarious name. Cokeville demands its due."

Chrissie fought the urge to roll her eyes—and to release the fiftieth yawn that had overtaken her in the past hour. "Fine. We should probably switch drivers anyway. I don't understand how you aren't dead in your seat."

"I can take the next shift," River offered. When Chrissie's response to this was to lurch on the brakes, she added, "I'm a good driver, I promise. My dad used to take me out on his combine back when I could barely walk. I even drove one during the summer in middle school. They let you do that on farms, you know. It's one of the few places where they love child labor."

Scarlett snorted. "*All* places love child labor. Every corporation on earth would tap into the sweet well of innocence if they could find a way to do it without breaking the law. Is it true they hold demolition derbies on those combine things? I read about it in a book once—all the massive machines crashing and tearing into each other like mechanical dinosaurs. It seems fun, in a rugged-cowboy-without-a-shirt-on sort of way."

"Yeah, actually. The town where I grew up used to hold one every spring to kick off the planting season. Rural America is so weird. Drinking and breaking things are their two favorite pastimes."

Chrissie took the turnoff for the town of Cokeville—population 500—with mixed feelings. River might be unaware of what Scarlett was doing, but Chrissie had seen her friend do this kind of thing before. She was trying to figure out where River hailed from, and to do it in a way that lifted no red flags.

Because she was curious? Because she genuinely wanted to help? Or, as was most likely the case, because she knew it would annoy Chrissie?

"Well, it's not much to look at, is it?" Chrissie asked as she found a small outdoor café that appeared to be the only place short of a truck stop to find something to eat. It was only ten in the morning, but they'd been on the road for so long that her stomach was starting to cramp up with hunger. "Lemme check my messages real quick, and then we'll—Oh!"

Her phone started buzzing as she turned the notifications on. Then it kept buzzing until half the battery must have drained away.

Scarlett peeked over her shoulder. "What is it this time? More dick picks from Walsh?"

Chrissie didn't even bother to honor this with a response. She was already dialing Kat.

"Is everything okay, honey?" she asked the moment she heard her daughter's "Finally" on the other end of the line. "What's wrong? I've been driving so I had my phone on silent."

"You're *driving*?" came the hot retort.

Chrissie blinked at the vehemence in her daughter's tone. Kat was given to emotional extremes most of the time, but this seemed a bit much, even for her.

"Well, yes. Aunt Scarlett and I are on a road trip, remember?"

"I *know* you're on a road trip. One you said I wasn't invited to join. Even though I apologized for the stupid vaping—which wasn't even my fault, since I was only in the bathroom with the other girls for, like, two minutes—and begged you not to abandon me."

"Whoa, there," Chrissie interrupted before her daughter collapsed from asphyxiation. She hadn't taken a breath in the entirety of that tirade. "Slow down. What's this about? Did something happen between you and Lily? Or—Oh, no. It's Rufio, isn't it? What did he pee on? Was it *very* expensive?"

"Mom! Stop trying to change the subject. I saw the TikTok. The one of you playing piano."

"Oh. You did?" Her first feeling was one of delight that her daughter had seen the video and been moved enough to actually call—a thing teenagers only did on major holidays and when their bank accounts were low. Her second feeling was more anxious than anything else. "What did you think of it? I'm a little rusty, obviously, but—"

"*Who is that girl?*"

Chrissie glanced over at River and Scarlett before she even realized what she was doing. The pair of them were taking a selfie in front of a Welcome to Cokeville sign, a white substance powdered liberally under their noses. Her motherly instincts recognized it on sight as eye shadow, but that didn't make her appreciate the joke any more.

"Her name is River. She's quite the singer, isn't she?"

"*Mom*."

"Kat," she replied. It was the exact wrong thing to say.

"Do you have any idea how unfair this is?" Kat practically screeched. "I never get to go *anywhere*, especially with Aunt Scarlett. It's such a scam. All the other kids have dads and grandparents and hordes of fun relatives, but all I have is *you*."

As this was very much on trend with Kat's mood lately, and Chrissie had promised herself that she would give her daughter as much space as she needed to experience said moods, she let this remark pass.

At least, she let it pass on the phone. The truth of it still stung.

"I can tell you're upset, honey, but you have to understand my position—"

"No, Mom. *You* have to understand *my* position. You have no idea what it's like being your daughter. I swear, I sometimes think the only reason you had a kid was so you'd have one person in your life who couldn't leave you. Everyone else goes the second they can get free of you."

That one stung even more. "Kat—"

"I'm not done yet," Kat said through her teeth. "Not only did you refuse to take me on vacation with you the *one* time you actually do something interesting, but now you're playing the piano with some random girl. How do you think that makes me feel? When you basically abandoned me?"

Chrissie knew it behooved her to tread warily. Her relationship with Kat was already strained to the breaking point, their battles growing more and more pitched with every passing day. The fact that she'd invoked Chrissie's solitary state was clear proof of that. Those accusations only came out when she was *really* hurting, and when her mean-girl streak saw no recourse but to lash out in the one way she knew would hurt Chrissie the most.

Still. She couldn't help the next words from leaving her mouth. Apparently she was developing something of a mean streak herself.

"Sorry, kiddo, but you can't call me boring in one breath and then demand my company in the other. You're going to have to pick a lane."

The scream this elicited was cut short by a low, soothing murmur in the background that calmed Chrissie by proximity. And when a voice returned to the other end of the line, it didn't belong to her daughter.

"I tried to get her to wait and call you once she'd cooled down a little, but you know Kat," Walsh said with a chuckle. "She's fire and ice, that girl. I've never known anyone to throw herself wholeheartedly into life the way she does."

Chrissie glanced over at her friend again. Scarlett and River had given up on their cocaine photos and had moved on to ordering what looked to be every single item on the menu offered by the outdoor café.

"I know someone else *exactly* like that," she said, sighing. "I'm sorry. I could've handled that a lot better. My only excuse is that I'm operating on about three hours of sleep right now. Other than my daughter adding one more item to the list of things to hold against me for the rest of my life, how's it going? How are *you*?"

Walsh's rich chuckle sounded again. Chrissie wasn't sure why, but that sound was the only thing keeping her from breaking into exhausted, bitter tears right now.

"If you ignore the part where I share Kat's outrage about not knowing what a phenomenal piano player you are, I'm fine. I hope you don't mind, but I bought Rufio one of those little Astroturf rugs they sell at Costco. We're working on changing our bathroom preference from my living room rug to the plastic grass. So far, we're at about a negative 3 percent success rate."

There were several things in that statement requiring Chrissie's attention, but as was almost always the case where this man was concerned, she latched onto the wrong one.

"Oh, for crying out loud. *You* saw the video?"

He didn't seem to find anything odd in her reaction. "If you want my honest opinion, it was the shock of it that upset her the most. You don't even have a piano in your house. How did you learn to play like that?"

Chrissie closed her eyes and sank onto the seat of a peeling green picnic table. For some strange reason, she was shaking even more now than she had during last night's performance.

For an even stranger one, she found herself telling him the truth.

"A decade of private lessons. When I was little, I had an older brother who was amazing at the piano—a prodigy, really. He died when I was seven, so I sort of picked up where he left off."

"Based on what I heard, I'd say you were a prodigy, too."

Walsh's ability to throw out a compliment like it was the easiest thing in the world always warmed her from the inside out. It was the one thing both she and Kat couldn't seem to resist in him.

"That's nice of you to say, but you never heard Malcolm. For the longest time, I thought that if I just practiced hard enough, threw myself into lessons and recitals and got as good as he was, it might make my parents feel like we were still a family."

She couldn't recall the last time she'd admitted this out loud—or even to herself—but something about this trip and the Cokeville air and Walsh's ready sympathy compelled her to keep going.

"Unfortunately, it didn't work. I've had almost no contact with my parents since Kat was born, and I haven't had the heart to play any sort of music in the meantime."

"That's too bad," he said, still with that devastating combination of ease and sincerity. "I hope you find the joy in it again someday. Take it from a man who's seen his fair share of natural talent—it's a shame to let it go to waste."

As Chrissie struggled to hold back the emotions this remark elicited, Scarlett and River joined her at the table, each carrying an orange plastic tray loaded with food. Scarlett slid a particularly unappetizing basket of dried meat in front of her.

"Since you seemed so much in love with your meat sticks the other day, I got you the wild buffalo jerky," she said. "Apparently, it's a Wyoming delicacy. Here. You eat while I finish chatting with Kat."

Without giving Chrissie a chance to correct her assumption, she plucked the phone from her grasp.

"Hey, love!" she called. Then, with a smile, "Oopsies. Sorry. I just assumed Chrissie was talking to Kat." Then, smiling even bigger, "I know, right? It was even better watching them perform live. We're actually bringing River along with us for a while. She was in a spot of trouble, and Chrissie being Chrissie—"

Chrissie practically hissed as she tried to snatch the phone away from her friend. "Give that back."

Scarlett was, as always, too quick for her. She made a motion for Chrissie to eat and swiveled around to continue her conversation in peace.

Or turmoil, in Chrissie's case.

"Oh, don't worry. I'm doing my best to ensure she has as much fun as possible. Have you ever noticed that getting her to do *anything* for herself is like pulling a tiger's front teeth?"

River slid onto the bench next to her, busy unwrapping a grilled cheese sandwich that looked much more appetizing than Chrissie's endangered animal meat. "Is your friend always like this?" she asked.

"Yes, unfortunately. Be sure to hold any private phone conversations as far away from her reach as possible." Chrissie grimaced. "I really am sorry about this whole going-viral thing. I honestly didn't know she was going to post that video until it was already up."

"It's fine," River said through a mouthful of cheese and bread. "I never meant to stay in Boise for longer than a few months anyway."

"And your great-aunt in Chicago... She's a nice woman? You trust her? She'll take good care of you?"

"I hope so." River spoke in a doubtful way that did little to make Chrissie feel better about the girl's situation. She swallowed thickly and added, "Why are you being so nice to me? Scarlett's right, you know. I could be anyone. I might have a whole crew following behind us waiting to steal everything you have so we can run off with it in the night. We could rob you and leave you for dead."

That sounded so much like something Kat would say—sarcastic, smart, chip-on-her-shoulder Kat—that Chrissie almost laughed.

"If everyone in the world only offered to help those who'd proven themselves worthy of it ahead of time, what would be the point? No one should have to earn kindness. It should come standard."

Aware of how little she was taking her own advice, Chrissie plucked the phone from Scarlett—and right in time, too, since it sounded as though her questions were taking a *drastically* personal turn. No one who asked a man about what, exactly, had caused his ex-wife to run off was doing it out of the kindness of her heart.

"In case I haven't mentioned it enough yet, thank you for doing all this, Walsh." Chrissie spoke with only a trace of the embarrassment she might have felt a few minutes earlier. "I know you keep saying it's not a big deal—and to *you*, it probably isn't—but it is to me. I don't have a lot of people I can count on. Kat's lucky to have you in her life, and so am I."

She could tell she'd taken him by surprise by the way he coughed and then remained silent for a full twenty seconds.

"Sorry to put you on the spot like this," she said. "I won't thank you again unless you manage to get Rufio to actually *use* that Astroturf or if you somehow pull a miracle and get Lily and Kat to sit in a room together without clawing each other's eyes out."

He sighed in a way that managed to combine sympathy, exhaustion, and something that made her heart squeeze.

"I don't understand the two of them," he said. "On paper, they should be best friends. They both love volleyball and anime, eat way more peanut butter than any human being should, and act like feelings are a four-letter word. You'd think we wouldn't be able to keep them apart."

"Unfortunately, that's not how friendship works," Chrissie said as Scarlett started making kissy faces at the phone—ones that quickly turned pornographic. "When it comes to teenage girls, I've always found that it's the opposites who attract."

Chapter Ten

PORTLAND, OR

2004

THERE WERE ONLY SIXTY MINUTES IN an hour and twenty-four hours in a day. Seven days in a week and fifty-two weeks in a year.

Scarlett was starting to get seriously annoyed about all of it.

With that much time to call her own, she should have been able to spend a hefty chunk of her days with Chrissie. Even though they went to different schools, nightly chats on the phone helped take the edge off, and whenever Chrissie had an afternoon to spare, she pedaled her bike over to the apartment so they could watch *Charmed* together.

Unfortunately, afternoons to spare were becoming harder and harder to come by.

"I'm sorry, Scarlett, but I have piano practice" was the most common excuse, but there were other ones in there, too. About chores and homework, Chrissie's discomfort with bicycling on the highway after dark.

The solution to this problem seemed easy enough to Scarlett: Chrissie could just stay the night with her. Grandma was happy to make another school stop in the morning, and what was there waiting for Chrissie at her big, stupid house anyway?

A mom who couldn't look at her without seeing her dead son? A dad who worked and worked and worked until he could drink enough whiskey to collapse on his bed at night?

"I told you those things in secret," Chrissie said one day while the two of them sat on the beach of Powers Marine Park, their bare toes digging deep into the wet sand. The park was located almost exactly halfway between their houses, so they often found themselves meeting up there.

Today was overcast, so they were huddled under a blanket that Chrissie had packed in the little white basket affixed to the front of her bike. Scarlett would have been warm enough in her favorite oversized hoodie and the fluffy beige Uggs she'd had to beg and beg Grandma to buy her for her twelfth birthday, but thanks to her fancy private school's dress code, Chrissie was chronically undressed for the weather.

Chrissie always looked so pretty in her pleated khaki skirt and the fitted blue blazer, her (for now) long hair in two tight braids, but she also looked miserable, like she was wearing someone else's skin. In her most private thoughts, Scarlett coveted a similar dress code so she could do things like roll the waistband of the skirt up a daring six inches or sew her white blouse extra tight around the bosom the way the cool girls always did in the movies, but she'd never say so to Chrissie.

Chrissie would have been too scandalized. She didn't like anyone to see her knees, let alone the shape of her bosoms, which were *so* much bigger and better than her own.

"I'll ask if I can sleep over the Saturday after this one," Chrissie promised as she huddled closer to Scarlett for warmth. "Maybe I can even stay the whole weekend."

But that was a whole *nine* days away (two hundred and sixteen hours), and Scarlett was having none of it.

"Why not this weekend?" she asked. "Or both? You know I'm right about your parents. They won't care whether or not you're there."

She regretted the words the moment they left her mouth. Not because she was wrong—Chrissie's parents *wouldn't* care—but because Chrissie seemed to shrink into herself hearing them.

"I have a recital this weekend," she said as she traced swirls into the sand with her pointer finger. "And they both promised to be there."

Scarlett was forced to accept this. She didn't want to, and she didn't believe that Chrissie's parents cared two straws about the upcoming recital, but part of being the *Very Best Best Friend* was pretending to agree with something even it was the last thing you wanted to do.

She was proven right when she and Grandma entered the recital hall that weekend, Grandma all dressed up in her best church clothes and hat. The two of them sat in the front row so Chrissie would be sure to see them, so they missed it when Chrissie's parents came in.

They didn't miss it when the Thomases left, though. No one in the hall did.

"I have to get down to the job site," Chrissie's dad hissed after a drum solo that made the entire room shake. "I'm sorry, Moira, but this deal with the developers is too important. They're trying to pull one over on me with the import taxes."

"And what about my Junior League meeting? I had to move a lot of things to be here, and you know how long they draw out each performance to justify the costs of—"

The rest of the argument was cut short by the arrival of a short, cherub-faced violin player who screeched like a pair of cats in the alley behind the apartment, so Scarlett didn't hear the rest. She and Grandma peeked over their shoulders, though, to find that Chrissie's dad had made good on his threat to leave, leaving Chrissie's mom sitting next to an empty seat. She perched ramrod-straight in her own, her purse clutched in her lap and her face looking so bored at the thought of making it through another hour that Scarlett wanted to scream.

Today wasn't supposed to be about them. It was about their daughter—the daughter who did everything they asked and nothing they didn't, who had refused a sleepover of epic proportions in the vain hope that she might get their whole attention for all of five minutes.

In that moment, Scarlett came up with several excellent plans of action.

Plan number one involved pulling the fire alarm so that the entire recital crashed and burned around them. Plan number two achieved the same results without a fire alarm, but with Scarlett jumping up onto her chair and screaming all her fury and outrage until there wasn't any left inside her. Plan number three, however, was different. Smarter. Sneakier.

And much more difficult to put into action.

"Don't they know how much they're hurting her?" Scarlett asked her grandmother after the cherub-faced boy finished his violin song and Chrissie took the stage. She seemed so grown-up in a floor-length dress of dove gray, but the moment she scanned the crowd to find her mom sitting alone, she looked like she wanted the stage to open up and swallow her whole. "We have to do something, Grandma. We can't let this keep happening. They won't stop until she's as broken inside as they are."

But even though Grandma looked like she wanted to burst right out of her skin, she only pursed her lips and gave a light *tsk*.

"She doesn't need us to fight on her behalf," she said. "She only needs us to be here."

"But—"

"But nothing. That girl is stronger than you know. She's already been broken and put back together more times than most people five times her age. And what's more important—she's done it with grace and dignity every step of the way."

Scarlett assumed this was a commentary against her own nature, which contained nothing even approaching grace and dignity, but she didn't take it as an insult. Instead, she smiled and waved until Chrissie noticed her. She clapped harder than anyone else once the sad, beautiful song was over. And she decided right then and there that she'd stop at nothing—and she meant nothing—to ensure that Chrissie didn't suffer a second more than she had to.

"I know I'm not supposed to just stop by like this," Scarlett announced as she arrived, uninvited, at Chrissie's front door after school a few days later. "But I have terrible news. It's about my Hodgkin's."

Chrissie reacted to this news exactly as Scarlett expected—with a cry and a hug and the door thrown wide open.

"Come in," she said over the sound of the Thomas family housekeeper running a vacuum cleaner in the background. "You can stay as long as you need. My parents won't be back until late."

Then, with a peek over Scarlett's shoulder, "Don't tell me you *rode your bike* all the way here! Do you need a glass of water? To sit down?" Chrissie was already halfway through her house and pulling out a chair from the kitchen table. "I think my mom still has the tea your grandma gave her. It's probably super stale by now, but the smell might make you feel better."

Each suggestion was offered more and more urgently—and sounded more and more like torture. When Scarlett had pictured this conversation playing out inside her head, she'd forgotten just how much she hated being treated like an invalid.

"Can't we go outside and work on our tans or something?" she asked. But then she noticed the notebooks laid out across the table and hesitated. She hadn't pictured this part, either—the life Chrissie led that didn't involve her, this entire half of her she wasn't allowed to touch. "Oh. Um. Are you busy? Should I come back?"

"I was just studying." Chrissie waved the mountain of biology textbooks away. "I have a test tomorrow, but it's not important. Not anymore. Tell it to me straight. How bad is it?"

If she were to tell the truth, this answer would be an easy one: *Pretty good, all things considered.* At this point in Scarlett's life, she was an official six years in remission. She still had to go to the doctor an annoying number of times, and her grandma was still obsessed with "health-forward" food combinations like acai-and-spinach smoothies, but she'd managed to avoid the hushed and always lingering specter of relapse.

"Your long-term risk of a secondary malignant neoplasm is four times higher than average," the doctors would drone every chance they got. "Particularly in the breast and respiratory systems. And that's not counting the cardiovascular and gastrointestinal disorders that—"

But here she always tuned them out. She already knew all the terrible and painful things that might happen to her over the course of her lifetime, but what she was more interested in was what that life held for her beyond the doom and gloom. Why didn't they tell her what the chances were of her someday visiting Paris in the springtime? Or which of the Jonas brothers was most likely to see her across a crowded street and declare his everlasting love for her?

For once, however, Scarlett was grateful for all the medical jargon they threw at her head every time she set foot in that office.

"They think I might be exhibiting B symptoms," she said with a determined lift of her chin. "They're especially worried about my lymph nodes."

Chrissie didn't react as she nodded to the housekeeper and kept walking, her footsteps soft as she led the way down the hall toward the outdoor patio—the same patio they'd broken into a few years back. Scarlett hadn't been inside the house since then, but it seemed fitting that they'd return to the scene of their original crime.

But the moment she safely closed the door behind them, Chrissie's face started to crumple. "Oh, Scarlett. I'm so sorry. What does your grandma say? Is she okay? Does she need anything?"

Scarlett shrugged, feeling like Chrissie was stabbing her in the heart on purpose. *Of course* her first thought was for someone other than herself. Selflessness was baked into her DNA along with her weird rogue twin.

"You know Grandma. She's buying bone broth by the case and starting up the prayer circle again."

Since Scarlett had requested sun, sun was what Chrissie planned to give her. She started moving the furniture around to make space for them to spread out, soundly rejecting all Scarlett's attempts to help her.

"There. We should have a good twenty minutes before the shade will hit us." Chrissie stood appraising her work, her lower lip between her teeth as she struggled against tears. "Should I put on the new Kelly Clarkson album to distract us, or did you want to talk?"

"Talk," Scarlett said firmly.

This was her first mistake. Of all the people in the world who knew how little Scarlett liked talking about illness—particularly her own—Chrissie was at the top of the list. But she was a good friend and accepted this with a solemn nod as they settled onto the sun-warmed patio bricks.

"It sounds like they're just doing tests right now, yeah?" Chrissie asked. They lay side by side on their backs, their fingers clasped together as they looked up at the puffy white clouds. Chrissie's grip was so tight that it made Scarlett's heart squeeze just as much. "So it's not officially cancer yet? It could just be the bad flu that was going around last month."

Scarlett hesitated. "Yeah, just tests so far. But I'm scared, Chrissie. *Real* scared."

That was her second mistake. Fear wasn't an emotion that Scarlett Sanderson allowed herself to feel, let alone show.

"You're scared," Chrissie said slowly. "Of what, exactly? Being sent back to the hospital? The medical bills? Or—" She didn't say the word they both heard hovering on her lips: *dying*.

That was where the third—and final—mistake came in. Scarlett had armed herself ahead of time, preparing her speech in front of the bathroom mirror until big, fat crocodile tears streamed down her face, but she hadn't bargained on Chrissie looking at her like *that*.

It was the same look she'd worn at the hospital after her brother died. Like she wanted to shatter into all those broken pieces her grandma had warned her about...and like she'd fight to keep herself together with every breath she had.

"I'm afraid of falling behind in school." Scarlett blurted the words with none of the calculated despair she'd shown the mirror, an uneasy pang of guilt throwing all her carefully laid plans out the window. "I'm already failing English, and I don't want to be held back. Grandma and I were talking about it, and she thinks that if you tutored me—in the afternoons and evenings, I mean—I should be able to keep up with my classes."

Scarlett barely stopped to breathe before she kept going. "I know it's asking a lot, and your parents might not like it, but it would help me get through this so much easier and—"

Chrissie let go of Scarlett's hand and sat up. She was still dressed in her school uniform, now rumpled by the day and smudged with dirt from the patio, but it was her eyes that drew Scarlett in. Those big blue eyes were usually so soft and understanding, like a hidden pond you couldn't resist jumping into.

Now they were narrow and flashing, and Scarlett was registering that change in a big way—and she started panicking in an even bigger one.

"You think your cancer is back," Chrissie said flatly.

"The doctors think it *might* be back," Scarlett corrected her.

"And you aren't sure yet if that means you have to go through chemo and radiation again."

Bright red warning lights were starting to flash in the metaphorical distance, but Scarlett saw no way of backing down now. "It's too soon to say for sure, but I could be back on the drip any day now," she said. "You know how it goes... Everything is fine until it isn't." She soothed her conscience with the thought that she wasn't telling *complete* lies. These were all things she'd been told by medical professionals so many times that she could recite them in her sleep.

"But your grandma still let you hop on a bike and ride three miles—on the highway—to come ask me if I'll help you with diagramming sentences?"

In that moment, Scarlett knew she was done for. She *might* be able to convince Chrissie that her own personality had undergone a change by this devastating relapse, but they both knew that Grandma was the one part of her life that never failed to rise to the challenge.

Fully aware of the pitfalls now, she did her best to backtrack. "I snuck out without her knowing" and "Don't tell her or she'll just blame herself" worked for a few minutes, but the more animated Scarlett's attempts at persuasion got, the less she looked like a girl with one foot in the metaphorical grave. The sweat on her upper lip alone was a dead giveaway.

"Please, Chrissie," she tried in a last-ditch effort. She clutched her friend's hand as though her life depended on it—and in many ways, it *did*. "I can't do this alone. You're the only one I trust to take care of me."

Chrissie eyed Scarlett in a way that made her feel like both the worst and the best person in the world. The worst, because she was a liar and Chrissie knew it, and the best, because having a person who saw through you like that—without even having to try—was the most amazing feeling in the world.

Chrissie opened her mouth to speak, but the clicking of footsteps stopped her before she could make a sound.

"Oh, here you are. I've been looking everywhere for you." Chrissie's mom appeared in the doorway to the patio, looking both startled to find that her daughter was sunning herself when there was homework to be done and annoyed that she was doing it with a guest in tow. "Hello, Scarlett. I didn't realize we had you scheduled for a visit today."

This was said with such cold formality that Scarlett was tempted to hide behind Chrissie. She didn't know how her friend could stand it. Give her yelling and screaming any day—litter the floor with temper tantrums. *Anything* was better than this complete and total lack of emotion.

"We didn't have it scheduled," Chrissie said as she got to her feet. She brushed herself off and straightened her skirt, the movements as mechanical as her expression. "This is a surprise visit. Scarlett has some…news."

This was it. This was the end. Scarlett was about to buried alive under her own lies—and the worst part was, she *deserved* it. She'd dug this hole with her own selfish, greedy hands, and she had no choice but to crawl inside it until she smothered.

"Oh?" Chrissie's mother asked with a raised brow. Her gaze barely flicked over Scarlett. "Not bad news, I hope?"

Scarlett held her breath and waited to see how Chrissie would respond.

"The worst. Her Hodgkin's is back."

Scarlett wasn't sure which of them was more surprised by this sentence: her or Chrissie's mother. The woman's face went white before turning beet red, and she actually looked at Scarlett long enough to see that she was a living, breathing girl and not just an inconvenience in the quiet despair of her post-Malcolm life.

"Oh." The word came out like a shot, but it didn't feel like one. "Oh, dear. That's a shame."

On any other day, Scarlett would have been unable to contain her giggles at such a lackluster response. Today, she could only stare at Chrissie.

Chrissie, who was standing with perfectly erect posture as she faced her mother down. Chrissie, who was telling a bald-faced lie for what had to be the first time in her twelve years of life.

"Scarlett wants to know if I can come over after school to tutor her. She doesn't want to fall behind in her classes, but I told her I had to make sure it was okay with you and Dad first."

Chrissie's mother frowned. "I suppose that would be all right."

"I'll still do my chores and my own homework, of course. And I'll take the bus home if it gets too dark to ride my bike." Chrissie's sideways gaze slid toward Scarlett's. "Or I can just stay the night. Scarlett's grandma already said she can take me to school on those mornings."

"I see," Chrissie's mom said slowly, but Scarlett doubted it. That woman didn't see anything that was unpleasant or uncomfortable. It was like she'd had so much of it heaped on her at once that she'd decided it was easier to ignore reality from now on. "You're sure she doesn't mind, Scarlett?"

Scarlett jumped to attention. "No, ma'am," she said. Then, with all the panache she'd been lacking with Chrissie, she let her eyes fill with those big crocodile tears. "Thank you. I just know having Chrissie around will make all the difference in my recovery. She was such a help last time, and I barely knew her then."

Scarlett wasn't sorry when Chrissie's mom's face turned whiter. She wasn't even sorry when she turned abruptly away and went back into the house.

She was, however, *desperately* sorry when she looked at Chrissie again. In that moment, Chrissie looked exactly like her mom. Flat-eyed and cold, her emotions being squeezed smaller and smaller until they practically disappeared. It was more than Scarlett could bear—Scarlett, who'd been abandoned by her mother and survived cancer, who'd watched so many kids die that she literally couldn't even remember all their names.

I did that to her. I'm the one who made her disappear inside herself.

"Chrissie, I'm sorry!" Scarlett flung her arms around her friend, so frantic now that she was starting to feel sick for real. "I shouldn't have said that. I don't have cancer again. I'm totally fine. I just needed an excuse for you to come over every day, and this seemed like the easiest way to get what I wanted."

Chrissie held up a finger in warning, her head tilted toward the door as she listened to her mother's footsteps clicking slowly away. Only when they stopped did she drop her finger.

"Please don't be mad," Scarlett begged, still clinging to Chrissie's neck like they were both about to sink underneath the *Titanic*. "I won't lie about my cancer ever again. Pinkie promise."

Chrissie carefully untangled herself from Scarlett's grip. All that piano playing made her arms seriously strong, but Scarlett was starting to suspect that Grandma was right, and Chrissie's strength came from somewhere else entirely.

"Please," Scarlett said again. This time, the hot tears rushing to her eyes were real. "I take it back. I take it all back."

"It's too late for that," Chrissie said coldly. "I'm coming over to your house every day, and we're doing homework. *All* your homework."

A new feeling started to spring up inside Scarlett—not fear, but something else. Something scarier. The promise coming out of Chrissie's mouth was everything she'd wanted out of this plan, but nothing else about her best friend was.

"What do you mean?" she asked nervously.

"I mean you win. You got your way. You always do."

Scarlett's first instinct—to shout for joy—was quickly tamped down when Chrissie took a deep breath and spoke again, her mouth as hard and flat as the rest of her.

"But if you *ever* lie to me about this again, I won't forgive you. Not even if your cancer comes back for good."

"But I—"

"I mean it, Scarlett." Chrissie sounded so much like a grown-up—one of the good ones, the ones who held the world together for everyone else—that Scarlett felt like she was looking at a stranger. "I'll always love you, but that doesn't mean I have to always like you. And right now, I don't like you very much at all."

Chapter Eleven

CROOK COUNTY, WY

Present Day

"IT'S A ROCK," CHRISSIE ANNOUNCED.

"A *big* rock," Scarlett corrected her.

"A big, *famous* rock," was River's contribution.

Chrissie shielded her eyes against the glare of the setting sun as she stared up at—yes—a rock. Devils Tower had been touted in all the guides as a glory of nature, a geological phenomenon they'd have been foolish to miss, but she didn't see it.

"Sorry, guys, but I can't believe we pushed through a whole day of driving just to look at a rock pillar. Scarlett is so exhausted she can barely keep her head up, I smell like corn chips and stale coffee, and River, well…"

But here she stalled. River had spent most of the day in the deep and innocent sleep that only an eighteen-year-old stripped of all her worries could manage. No matter how rough the roads or how hard the wind had tried to blow them off course, she'd spent the entire drive curled up like a Labrador in the back seat, her gentle snores barely louder than the rumbling of the tires.

"River needs something to eat, or she's gonna die," River announced with a grin. "Sorry, Scarlett. I know this was on your bucket list, but my stomach's been growling since Casper."

As far as Chrissie was concerned, that settled it.

"I *knew* we brought you along for a reason," she said as she slung an arm around the girl's shoulders and started leading her back to the car. River's shoulders were too thin for her liking, but she was trying *very* hard not to make the girl feel like she'd just fallen into the hands of a neurotic mother hen—an insult Kat had flung at her head so many times that she suspected it was the truth. "We passed a cute log cabin bed-and-breakfast on the way in. I didn't see a vacancy sign, but I bet if we beg hard enough, they'll find a closet where we can stay."

Scarlett opened her mouth as if to argue, but she was starting to look like something Rufio had yakked up on the carpet—a thing he was prone to whenever he overate, which was every chance he got.

"Okay, fine," Scarlett said. "If you two want to thumb your nose at the majesty of nature, who am I to disagree?"

Even as Scarlett followed them to the car, she cast a longing look back at the butte. Since she wasn't normally one to be moved over the glories of the natural world—she was too much of a city girl at heart—Chrissie found this odd, but not odd enough to suggest they stay.

With Scarlett, the truth would eventually make its way out. Not because she was a person who did the right thing, and not because the guilt would eat her alive, but because she wasn't someone who could keep her feelings inside.

With Scarlett, what you saw was what you got—even if sometimes, just sometimes, it was the last thing in the world you wanted.

Chrissie knew she was in trouble the moment they set foot inside the bed-and-breakfast.

"Oh, my stars. It's you. It's really you. *Both* of you."

Chrissie wasn't a well-traveled person, so she'd always assumed that the state of Wyoming was one step removed from the Wild West. She'd read somewhere that there were only two escalators in the entire state, since any and all public buildings were either too old to have one or didn't bother with a second floor. She wasn't proud to admit it, but she'd always assumed this place was a backwater, a nowhere land, a place where the internet was a four-letter word.

Apparently, she'd been wrong.

"We've watched your video at least half a dozen times." The woman gushing at them from the living room, a soaring log-paneled room hung with a chandelier made of half a dozen moose skulls, turned and shouted at someone in the distance. "Harold, get out here. It's those piano girls."

"What?" came an irascible male voice.

"The. Piano. Girls. The ones who played that song that was banned at church—you know, the one we all thought was holy but that Pastor Tim says is actually about *s-e-x*."

Scarlett looked so delighted at this description—and by the woman, who was about ninety-five years old and was dressed in a red flannel nightgown layered over honest-to-goodness long underwear—that she clapped her hands.

"I don't believe this," Scarlett said. "You've actually seen the video?"

"We showed it on the big screen this morning," the woman said, puffing up her chest so much that her flannel ruffles fluttered. She pointed at a remarkably modern theater system in one corner of the living room. "Everyone was delighted. I don't suppose you'd be willing to tickle the ivories for us? We have a player piano in the dining room, but the only scroll we have is 'Ain't Misbehavin,' so it doesn't get much use. I'll throw in a 10 percent discount on the rooms."

If Chrissie had been asked her opinion, she'd have turned around and found somewhere else to sleep—up to and including the back seat of the rental car. But Scarlett was swaying on her feet, and River's expression wasn't one of alarm so much as a kind of childish delight.

"I guess I really am famous now," River said in a voice that held a hint of wonder.

"Fine. Twenty percent is as high as I can go, but you have to let us take your picture for our wall. The only other famous person we had stay here was the mayor's wife back in—oh, it must have been aught-nine or so." With another shout, she added, "Harold, was it oh-nine or oh-eight that we had the mayor's wife putting up in the Muskrat Suite?"

Chrissie was very careful not to catch Scarlett's eye for fear of bursting into laughter.

"That's generous of you, but we're happy to pay the full price," Chrissie said.

The woman's face fell to such a ludicrous degree that all three of them lurched forward as if afraid the rest of her was going to fall with it.

"You don't want to play? But you're both so talented, and we almost never make it out to concerts anymore. At our age, it's not easy getting around like we used to."

An uncomfortable silence fell. Every people-pleasing nerve in Chrissie's body—which, admittedly, was most of them—wanted to fulfill this sweet old lady's wishes and maybe even get bumped up to the Muskrat Suite. But there was more at stake here than just an impromptu concert, especially if the guests were going to be recording and uploading the performance.

"I don't mind," River said. Both she and Scarlett turned to face her, but her expression looked the same as it always did—a little sullen, a little bored, and as if her soul were a thousand years old. She caught their stares and shrugged. "I'm not, like, a *wanted criminal.* My family isn't sending bounty hunters after me."

"Of course they're not," Chrissie soothed, but there was no need.

"As long as you're okay with it, I'm happy to sing for my supper." Something like a smile touched the corner of River's highly pierced lip. "It's kinda cool, to be honest. I never thought anyone would care about my singing. A few more hundred thousand views, and I might even be able to turn into some kind of paying gig in Chicago. People do, you know. There are a ton of indie record labels based there. Can you imagine? It'd be nice not to have to work eight different part-time jobs to make ends meet."

"Uh-oh," Scarlett teased. "You're in for it now, Chrissie. River's figured out what makes you tick."

Chrissie didn't deign to give this remark a response. "It's not just you I'm worried about, River. It's my daughter, Kat. She was really upset by that video. We're going through a bit of a rough patch right now, and I don't want to make things worse than they already are."

She could hear Scarlett's teeth starting to grind in frustration, but River only shrugged again. "If you want, I could call and suss her out a little. If she's not into it, I won't say another word."

The old woman in flannel had long since given up on following the conversation, but at this, she pressed two large brass keys into Chrissie's hand and closed her fingers around them. "That's right, dear. You just let that nice young lady figure things out. Dinner's served at eight. You can play for us then. I hope you like antelope tenderloin. Harold does it up real nice, all slow-roasted and wrapped in bacon."

Chrissie visibly blanched at the prospect of such a dinner, but she was too polite to do more than murmur her thanks. She was also polite enough to unlock her phone and hand it to River.

To her surprise, River put it on speaker before dialing.

"*Ugh*, Mom. You don't have to call every three freaking hours. I'm fine. Rufio is fine. Lily might wake up to find a Sharpie mustache on her upper lip, but whatever you hear, it wasn't me."

"Actually, if you really want to get her, you should make a glitter bomb and rig it to explode in her underwear drawer," River said. "She'll be finding sparkles in her vagene for the next six months."

A strangled sound escaped Chrissie as she dove for her phone, but Scarlett was one step ahead of her. With a laugh that echoed off the moose skull chandelier, she wrapped her arms around Chrissie's waist and held on tight. "Oh, no you don't. Let the Zoomers handle this one. I'm starting to like this charity case of yours."

Chrissie wasn't. Chrissie was starting to regret every kind impulse she'd ever had.

"You're on speaker with your mom and Scarlett," River added. "So I'd avoid saying anything incriminating—at least until I turn it off again. I'm River, by the way. The one from the video."

"I know who you are," Kat said, her voice strained. "You're the girl scamming my mom."

"Scamming?" River snorted. "You're joking, right?"

"Um…you're the one hitching a ride across the country with someone else's mom and making her perform like a circus monkey to get views. What else am I supposed to think?"

Chrissie's eyes widened at her daughter's sudden lapse into territorial devotion. This was a new—and delightful—twist. She had no idea Kat cared this much.

"It's not a scam. She basically kidnapped me. I was just minding my own business at work and all of a sudden she pops up out of nowhere and starts, like, mothering me."

She said the word *mothering* like it filled her whole mouth. To Chrissie's surprise, Kat relented.

"Yeah, she does that to everyone, even if she's only known them for all of three seconds." A pause. "What do you want?"

"Other than to teach you *much* better ways of getting back at your nemesis? Just that I promised your mom I'd check in before we performed another duet. The place we're staying asked us to play at dinner, but your mom was worried you might not like it."

"Mom!" Kat practically screeched. "You're talking smack about me to strangers now? I thought you were, like, morally obligated to always take my side. It's supposed to be in the parental bylaws."

This, too, sounded more like possessiveness than anger. Chrissie leaned into it. "Sorry, kiddo, but I can't help talking about you. I'm too proud to keep quiet for long."

Chrissie could practically hear the eye roll from her distance of fifteen-hundred miles, but in the pause that followed, she could also detect her daughter's pleasure.

"Whatever," Kat muttered without any of her usual heat. "Go be famous. Don't be famous. But tell that girl if you start getting creepy online stalkers after this, I'm going to glitter-bomb *her* vagene."

"What'd she do to you anyway?" River asked as she shifted from one foot to the other. So far, she hadn't shown the least bit of discomposure at finding herself on the bitter end of a phone call that Chrissie was pretty sure they could hear at the top of Devils Tower.

"Um, other than abandon me to go on the adventure of a lifetime while I waste away in *Medford*? Let me see—"

River tsked impatiently. "No, not your mom. She's pretty cool, as far as old people go."

"*Old*?" Scarlett demanded. This time, it was Chrissie's turn to hold her friend at bay. "Who's she calling old?"

"I meant the girl," River said, ignoring them both. "The one whose underwear drawer you're going to rig tonight."

Kat giggled—actually *giggled* in a way that Chrissie hadn't heard in a very long time. "I can't do that. Walsh—he's my volleyball coach—would be the one who has to clean it up, and he's really nice. Besides, the cat would probably try to eat the glitter. He's certifiably stupid."

"Hmm. If you can get into her phone, you could change all

her contacts to the same name. That one always pisses people off—especially if you pick someone super random like Nicolas Cage."

Scarlett brought her lips to Chrissie's ear with a low chuckle. "That one's kinda funny, actually."

Chrissie waved her hand to shush her friend. She didn't want to miss whatever else Kat had to say. This was more personal information than she'd gotten out of her daughter in months.

"You know a weird amount about pranking people," Kat said.

"Yeah, well. We all have our strengths. Mine just happen to be pissing people off and occasionally singing a halfway decent song."

Chrissie held her breath, afraid that a return to the topic at hand would shut Kat down again, but all her daughter did was sigh and say, "Lily's not that bad. She's just one of those people who's good at everything, you know? Like, she never breaks out right before photo day or has a tampon string accidentally hanging out the side of her volleyball shorts. I've never seen her study for a test, but she somehow always gets the top grade, and she even reads for fun. Like, a lot." Louder this time, and clearly for Chrissie's benefit, she added, "Perfect people are *impossible* to live with—and the worst part is, they're always nice about it, which makes it that much worse."

Scarlett's chuckle sounded once more. "She's got you pegged, huh?"

"*Me*?" Chrissie returned, her brow puckered. "Since when has anyone ever accused me of being perfect?"

"Unless I'm mistaken, Kat just did. Poor kid. I never really thought about it, but sitting across from *that* over the breakfast table every morning must be rough." Scarlett swirled a finger in Chrissie's general direction. "Especially since I have no doubt you do things like make happy faces in the pancakes."

Chrissie didn't say anything. She *did* put happy faces in the pancakes, but that was because some days, it was the only time anyone in their house smiled. She also slipped notes into Kat's lunch with encouraging messages and kept her Starbucks app well supplied in case she wanted to stop by after school for a little treat. None of the things she did were earth-shattering—or, as Kat might say, *perfect*—but they were the sort of attentions that she'd always wished her own parents would show.

Hello. How are you? I'm thinking of you. I'm glad you exist.

She was so deep in her own reflections that she didn't realize River had finished up the call until she handed her back the phone and said, "There. Permission granted. That Lily girl sure sounds like a piece of work, doesn't she?"

"Wait." Chrissie blinked, taking in her surroundings as if seeing them for the first time. The golden-hued wood tones and scent of furniture polish, the animal heads staring down at them from almost every wall… It was as far from her cozy, floral house as possible, and it suddenly felt wrong. "That's it? She just…gave in?"

"I mean, I think she was serious when she said you were under no circumstances allowed to wear your 'In My Volleyball Mom Era' sweatshirt while you play the piano, and to be honest, I'd find that pretty uncomfortable myself, but yeah." River snapped her fingers. "Oh! And right after I turned off the speaker, she said to tell you that Rufio actually used the fake grass and that Walsh is taking them out to Wharf Fresh to celebrate. They're going to, like, order extra shrimp for the cat? I don't know. It all sounded random to me."

Chrissie could only stare as the words sank in, so it was probably for the best that Scarlett took the lead and directed them to grab their bags.

"Good. It's settled. Let's get changed and then head down for our next big showcase. By the time this road trip is done, we'll have you both on the path to superstardom."

When Chrissie emerged from the bathroom a half hour later, it was to find Scarlett seated on the edge of her log bed, considerably overdressed in a silky red blouse buttoned up to the top and a black leather miniskirt that left little to the imagination.

By comparison, her own clothes were…well. *Intentional.*

"You guys ready to head down?" River's head popped in through the adjoining door. There'd been quite a bit of arguing before they'd decided on the room assignments, but since Scarlett was the one picking up the bill, she'd had the ultimate say—and her ultimate say was that she and Chrissie would continue as planned, rooming together every step of the way to Vermont. This meant they were sleeping on narrow twins while River luxuriated on a California king, but Chrissie didn't mind. It was almost as if she was back in Scarlett and her grandmother's tiny apartment, where so many of her happiest memories resided.

River stepped into the room only to stop short when she noticed what Chrissie was wearing.

"Um…did you miss the part where your daughter said she hates that sweatshirt with the passion of a thousand burning suns?"

"No." Chrissie ran a layer of ChapStick over her lips and checked her hair in the mirror. Whatever magic had happened at that salon was carrying over into the next state because it still looked fantastic. "But it's my favorite, so I'm wearing it. Besides—I *am* in my volleyball mom era. Why should I hide my true self?"

Scarlett snorted as she rose to her feet and grabbed her bag. "Add a pair of linen coveralls and a pumpkin spice latte, and your basic-white-lady packaging is complete." She paused as she eyed the sweatshirt—which, yes, was oversized and tacky, but that was why Chrissie liked it. "Kat's going to be livid, you know."

"I know."

"But your whole approach to parenting is to tiptoe around her emotions like they're land mines. Since when do you deliberately provoke her?"

Chrissie drew a deep breath. The answer to that was easy: *Since about thirty minutes ago*. If someone had told her a week ago that she'd be purposefully antagonizing her daughter and throwing herself into the care and keeping of an entirely different teenage girl, she'd have locked them up and thrown away the key.

But Kat had sounded different on the phone. Playful, even. For the first time in a long time, Chrissie suspected that the thing that was broken between them wasn't unfixable. She could almost see the little girl who used to fling herself into her arms after school every day rippling underneath the surface, hear the pitter-patter of tiny bare feet as they tiptoed into her bed after a bad nightmare.

That girl was still in there; Chrissie was sure of it. She just had to find a way to breach the gap that time and hormones and their contrary natures seemed to be pushing open mile by mile.

"I don't have to explain myself to you," Chrissie said with a sniff.

"Atta girl." Scarlett started rummaging around in her bag. She had to work her way through half a dozen bottles of pills, three lipsticks, and a set of impossibly tangled headphones before she found the paper she was looking for.

"Oh, geez." Chrissie groaned. "Not again."

Scarlett tossed her both the paper and a pen. "You know the drill by now. Write it down."

Chrissie felt a little foolish doing this in front of River, but she knew her friend well enough to know that she wouldn't leave her alone until she added to her list.

I don't have to explain myself to you.

She also immediately handed the paper to Scarlett, knowing she would once again add her own improvements. She did, but with such quick efficiency that Chrissie was taken aback.

I don't have to explain myself to ~~you~~ ANYONE.

"*Now* you're getting the hang of it," Scarlett said. She started to scoop up her belongings to return them to her bag, but she noticed River eyeing her prescription bottles with intent, narrow-eyed scrutiny. "Can I help you? See something you like?"

"What? Um. No." River took a step back, her hands immediately shoved behind her back. Chrissie didn't miss the way she flushed, guilt in every line of her bearing. "What's all that stuff you're writing down?"

Scarlett accepted this change of topic, her insouciant air back in place as she explained the list they'd been writing together, but Chrissie wasn't so easily put off. She was only a massage therapist, not a doctor or nurse or anything, but she was required to take continuing education classes to keep her license current. A lot of the classes were about learning new techniques—she'd done Reiki last year—but others dealt with drug-seeking behaviors and other ethical red flags.

She *really* hoped that wasn't the case here. River was already dealing with so much hardship in her life. If she was an addict on top of everything else… Well, Scarlett wouldn't be happy.

Especially since Chrissie would feel herself honor bound to do something about it.

"Well, Volleyball Mom? Are you ready for the show of a lifetime?" Scarlett tucked her purse securely under one arm and practically pushed the pair of them out the door. "Because if bacon-wrapped antelope is all anyone has to look forward to, you two are about to be the highlight of the evening."

Chapter Twelve

PORTLAND, OR

2007

THE FIRST TIME SCARLETT AND CHRISSIE fell in love, it was with the exact same boy.

If Scarlett was honest with herself—*really* honest with herself, a thing she avoided whenever humanly possible—Chrissie technically had dibs. She'd been the first to spot him, standing bored and slumped over a book at the frozen yogurt shop where he worked. In true Chrissie form, she hadn't said a word to him other than a shy "hey," but then again, Chrissie only went to Creamy Dreamy to get plain yogurt in a cup with no toppings, so that tracked.

Anyone who stood facing a wall of chocolate chips, cookie dough lumps, and Marshmallow Fluff and then picked *none* of it was clearly a psychopath.

"You're a psychopath," Scarlett said as they slid into the red vinyl booth with their treats.

She dipped her spoon into her yogurt and licked at it in a way she hoped signaled her experience (third base, some heavy petting), but the boy, Grimshaw, wasn't looking at them. He was busy reading his book, as usual.

"All right, Chrissie," she announced as she considered the injustice of it all. How were her powers of seduction supposed to work if he never glanced her way? "The time is now. You've made us come here every day for a whole month, and you're dying to know what he's reading. Go ask him."

"Scar-lett!" Chrissie's cheeks flamed. "I can't do that. Look at him. He's gorgeous."

He was, in fact, gorgeous, and in an objective, unarguable way that appealed to teenage girls everywhere. His hair was a rich, mahogany swoop over his forehead, his dark eyes hidden behind a pair of thick glasses that made him look a decade older than his sixteen years. He carried his tall, wide-shouldered frame with an athlete's grace, and when he spoke, it was with a deep, velvety voice that was designed to haunt dreams.

If Scarlett, who had risen to her maximum height of five foot one years ago and *still* had to stuff her bra, looked even halfway as gorgeous as Chrissie, she'd have sauntered up there, batted her eyelashes at his brooding perfection, and offered to have his babies right there on the spot.

Only she couldn't have babies (thanks, cancer treatments) and was pretty sure she didn't want them anyway. Women who procreated went on to have boring Middle America lives, and Scarlett felt sure she was destined for greatness.

"I bet he's reading something super literary and deep." Scarlett angled her body to try and read the cover, but he was holding the book flat against the counter. "Or something dirty, and that's why he won't let us see what it is."

"It doesn't matter because there's no way he wants to be friends with us." Chrissie slumped low in her seat—or *tried* to, rather. All those years of piano lessons had given her posture like something out of a Jane Austen novel. "He has a job. He can drive. What would he want to do with a couple of freshmen?"

Scarlett snorted. For all that Chrissie was rich and beautiful, she had very little idea how the real world worked.

"We're not going to try and be his *friend*, Chrissie. You'd better go up there and ask him what he's reading, or I'll do it for you. And I can tell you right now that you won't like the way I go about it."

Chrissie heaved a sigh. "For once, can't you just let me do things my own way?"

"If you insist." Scarlett gave a casual—and carefully calculated—shrug. There was more than one method for getting Chrissie to do what she wanted, and as she'd learned the hard way, that method wasn't brute force. "I guess we'll just have to keep pining for him from afar. How Shakespearean of us. Should one of us carry a vial of poison just in case we end up in a star-crossed tomb together? I think my grandma has some antifreeze under the sink."

"Scarlett, I'm not doing it."

"I'm not going to make you *drink* the antifreeze. Just carry it for emergencies."

"You only want me to humiliate myself in front of him to clear your own path."

"As if any guy would pick me when you're offering yourself on a platter."

Whether because she agreed with this or—as was more likely the case—because she was tired of arguing, Chrissie pushed her half-eaten dessert across the table.

"Fine. I'll go ask him what he's reading, but if he laughs me out of the shop, then we'll have to find a new place to eat frozen yogurt. And you don't like the toppings from the Golden Spoon nearly as much."

This was a price Scarlett was willing to pay. Barely tamping down her squeal of excitement, she plucked a clip from her hair and used it to pin back the shaggy edges of Chrissie's. Chrissie had the unfortunate habit of chopping off literal feet of her hair once a year, and then doing *nothing* to style what was left, so the extra effort was necessary.

"There. Slap your cheeks to get your color up and you're good to go."

Chrissie didn't follow her advice. She merely cast Scarlett a look of patient resignation and slid out of the booth. From this distance, Scarlett couldn't hear the conversation unfold or even try to lip-read what Chrissie was saying, but she could see Grimshaw's reaction. He looked more surprised than pleased to be interrupted, but after about twenty seconds, he held up the book.

Dante's *Inferno* seemed like an incredibly boring choice to Scarlett, but from the way Chrissie's whole face lit up, she assumed her friend approved—and she approved hard.

Scarlett watched, a feeling of unease taking over as Grimshaw laughed at something Chrissie said, rubbed the side of his nose in an embarrassed way, and then handed Chrissie a used receipt and pen. Scarlett held her breath for the entire following sixty seconds until Chrissie returned to the table.

"Well?" she demanded as Chrissie slid back into her seat and began calmly eating her frozen yogurt again. "What did he say? Did you give him your phone number? Did he quote random book passages at you?"

Chrissie flushed slightly, but she answered the questions in the order in which they were received.

"He said he thinks the two of us eat an unhealthy amount of frozen yogurt. I gave him your number instead of mine because there's no way I'm letting him call my house. And I don't know if any of the things he said were a quote, but I wouldn't be surprised. He's read, like, a ton of books."

Her flush deepened, which was when Scarlett knew that she'd

pushed too far this time. Some people's lives changed when they got into college or lost a loved one. Others reached the point of no return when they were diagnosed with childhood cancer.

For Chrissie, the point of no return was right here, right now, with a boy who looked like a romance hero and read books as fervently as she did.

Why, oh why, did Scarlett let her impulsive nature call the shots? Why was she always testing Chrissie's boundaries when it was so obvious that life was already planning on putting them up for her?

"What else?" she asked, even though she was sure she didn't want to hear the answer.

"Oh, you know," Chrissie grinned around a mouthful of yogurt. "Just that I could borrow the book when he's done so we can chat about it over dinner sometime."

"Well, girls. I was hoping to hold this conversation off for a few more years, but it's high time we discussed the birds and the bees."

"Grandma, *no*." Scarlett looked up from the math homework she was decidedly not doing and slapped her hands over her ears. She gestured for Chrissie to do the same, but Chrissie was in the middle of calculating the perimeter of a trapezoid and didn't notice. "We're fifteen years old and have access to the internet. I promise we've seen what the bees get up to in their spare time."

There was only a 50 percent chance her grandmother would accept this, since she still viewed the internet as a newfangled blip in an otherwise analog world, so Scarlett added, "Besides, we've already taken like three human growth and development courses."

"Yes, but I've seen what passes for sex ed these days. The school boards are all so afraid of the PTA moms that they won't even suggest HPV vaccines." Her grandma cleared her throat and looked at

Chrissie. "Speaking of, dear, I don't know if your parents have taken you in for one yet, but—"

"Thanks, Nan, but I'm good. Medical checkups are the one thing my parents always remember."

Chrissie didn't look up from her page as she spoke, her relationship with Scarlett's grandmother so natural at this point that Scarlett sometimes felt as if Chrissie belonged more to her grandmother than to her. She'd never admit it to her friend—and barely even acknowledged it in her own heart—but she sometimes wished that she hadn't petitioned *quite* so hard for Chrissie to become her daily tutor/homework buddy. She loved seeing Chrissie every day, she really did. And the sleepovers that ended up happening more often than not were the highlight of her life. It was like she'd gotten the sweet, big-hearted sister that all girls secretly hoped for.

But there were times, like when Grandma bought huge bags of Chrissie's favorite candy (black licorice, of all horrible things) or stayed up late letting out the hem on Chrissie's recital dress instead of helping Scarlett with her science project, that she felt like she was being replaced.

Not in Grandma's *heart*, obviously, but in a different, secret place Scarlett couldn't access.

"I just want to make sure you girls are being careful." Her grandmother cleared her throat and leveled Scarlett with a knowing stare. "Your mother, Scarlett, bless her heart—"

"Nope. Absolutely not. We're not discussing this." Scarlett slammed her math book shut before doing the same to Chrissie's. Chrissie cried out at this—and at her broken pencil—but one look at Scarlett's face was enough to range her on the side of justice.

"Sorry, Nan," Chrissie said with a gurgle of laughter. "But you don't have to worry about me. Grimshaw is just a friend. We mostly read books together."

Scarlett lost no time in dragging her friend into the safety of her bedroom—or so she thought. The moment the door closed behind her, she'd hoped to shut out any and all conversations related to birth control, her mother, and her grandmother's attempt at instructing them, but Chrissie wasn't so easy to shake off.

"She's being protective," Chrissie said, so much kindness and understanding in her voice that Scarlett wanted to open the door again just so she could slam it. "It's cute, if you think about it."

Then Chrissie *did* think about it, which was the one thing Scarlett had been trying to avoid. Her mouth turned pensive. "Or maybe she just wants to talk about her. Your mom, I mean. I know you don't like it when anyone brings her up, but—"

"There's nothing to say." Scarlett flopped onto her twin-sized bed and lay flat on her back, her head propped on her hands. There was a damp patch in the ceiling from where the upstairs tenants had let their bathtub overflow a few months ago. She'd tried covering it up with a rainbow flag, but the pins kept coming loose so the ends fluttered over her head while she slept. "She had a baby before she was ready. That baby grew up into a sick kid. She decided the kid was too much for her, so she left."

"Scarlett..."

Scarlett's throat got tight in the way it did whenever she thought about her mother. She didn't remember anything about her, and even though Grandma had pictures—whole albums of them, actually—flipping through them felt like looking at the photos that came in frames from the store. In them, her mother was beautiful and dark-eyed and laughing, and almost always seemed to have her arms flung around the person next to her. As a kid, Scarlett had sometimes wrapped her own arms around her stomach and squeezed her eyes tight, imagining it was her who was locked in her mother's embrace, but by the time she opened her eyes again, she always felt worse.

Those pictures were someone else's life, someone else's memories, a Photoshopped version of a world she was never meant to inhabit.

Scarlett turned her head to glare at her friend, determined, as usual, to drag Chrissie in her wake. "Should we talk about *your* mom, too? About how she buys you the same sweater from the same store for your birthday every year? Or how you're still not allowed to hang posters or pictures in your room because it has to stay identical to Malcolm's even though you're five years older than he ever got to be?"

All the color flooded out of Chrissie's face, and she looked inadvertently to the wall, where the paint-by-number puppy picture they'd once stolen from Malcolm's room still hung. It was inexpertly finished and framed in a cheap black plastic frame from the dollar store, but not once, in all the years she'd had it, had Scarlett considered taking it down.

"It's okay to be mad at her," Chrissie said.

Even though Scarlett was in a nasty mood and they both knew it, Chrissie lay down next to her and found her hand. Their fingers intertwined with the ease of long practice.

"It's even okay to hate her," she continued. Then, after an agonizing pause, "But if you ask me, she did the right thing when she dropped you off here. She *knew* she didn't have it in her to take care of you, so she gave you to someone who could. That's more than mine's ever done for me."

Scarlett sighed. One of the worst things about Chrissie was that she knew just what to say to make Scarlett recognize all of her worst flaws. That was why terrible people always sought out other terrible people. To be friends with someone whose light always shone bright and good was to walk around with a constant spotlight on your sins.

"When I'm a mom, I'm never going to treat my kids that way," Chrissie said. Her cheek came to rest beside Scarlett's, the pillowy softness of it soothing her even more. "I don't care what happens to them or how hard life gets. Even if one of them dies and I'd rather turn myself off than go through the pain again, I'm going to be there for every minute. I'm going to care so much that they wake up every morning absolutely *smothered* by my love."

Scarlett gave a reluctant laugh. "That sounds awful. I pity your poor kids." Then, because this conversation was making her feel all the things she'd spent the last decade pushing down, she added, "I bet Grimshaw will be a good dad. He'll teach his kids how to put on eyeliner so it looks like they're not wearing any. Plus he's tall, so he'll probably throw out professional basketball players. Make sure you start them in sports early."

The cheek against Scarlett's grew suddenly warm.

"It's not like that between us. Not really. I think he mostly likes having someone who reads all his book recommendations without question." Chrissie paused as if considering her next words carefully. "You can have him, if you want. Well, he's not a possession, obviously, but you know what I mean. I don't know anything about boys or relationships, and you *definitely* have more of an idea about what goes on in beehives than I do."

"Yeah. You get stung." Scarlett followed this up with a laugh, but the sound was brittle around the edges.

The thing was, Chrissie was serious. She *would* step back and let Scarlett sweep the field. With just one word, she'd push down all her own feelings for the sake of what someone else wanted—and she'd do it without once counting the cost.

Scarlett might only be fifteen years old, but she was getting sick and freaking tired of people not counting the cost of things. When moms left or stopped caring, it was the kids who paid the price. When grandmothers gave up their golden years to care for their grandkids, it was a struggle all around. And when best friends let a hot yogurt guy who liked to read pretentious books slip through their fingers, Scarlett was the one who got mad about it.

"And don't even *think* about giving the things you like away," Scarlett said with a ferocity that she knew was misplaced. She snuggled deeper against Chrissie, her fingers curling like claws. "You take what you want from this world, Christina Thomas, and don't you apologize to anyone for it."

She thought, but did not add, *Not even to me.*

Chapter Thirteen

SOMEWHERE IN THE BADLANDS

Present Day

"IF I'D HAVE KNOWN YOU WERE going to go off and get world-famous, I'd have negotiated better terms and conditions."

Chrissie sat back in the passenger seat of the car, her feet up on the dashboard—very dangerous—and an arm hanging out the window—also dangerous. She was once again wearing the volleyball mom sweatshirt, her hair blowing in the wind and nary a scrap of makeup on her face.

She felt fantastic.

"Please don't remind me," she said into the phone. Both Scarlett and River had begged her to put the call through the car speakers so they could listen as she checked in with Walsh, but she'd shut that idea down right away. "I don't really understand why people are making a big deal out of this. There are thousands of musicians out there who are more talented than us."

Walsh's low, rich chuckle sounded. Even though it was ten o'clock in the morning and he was probably sitting at his desk crunching important accounting numbers, he'd picked up the call on the first ring.

That made her feel fantastic, too.

"It's the spontaneity, I think," he said, treating her playful question as though it required a not-so-playful answer. That had always been a trait she'd admired in him: his ability to cut through a joke with honesty. Few people could do that without sounding like a complete stick-in-the-mud. *She* certainly couldn't. "No one has any idea what kind of random location you're going to pop up in next. Lily and Kat showed me an online poll where people are trying to guess where the next video will come from. A lot of people seem to think you're fleeing to Canada."

Chrissie's feet dropped to the floor of the car. She was careful not to look over at where Scarlett sat behind the wheel of the car, but she could feel her friend's eyes on her.

"I'm sorry. Say that again?"

The other trait Chrissie admired in Walsh was that she didn't have to explain herself to him. Six years of tournaments and practices and carefully neutral flirtations had done wonders in getting them onto the same page.

"I know, right?" he said, his grin practically audible through the phone. "You could have knocked me over with a feather when I walked in to find them hunched over Lily's laptop together."

"No one was being strangled?"

"There was nary a ligature mark in sight."

"And everyone's hair was still attached to her head?"

"As far as I could tell, the claws were fully retracted. Mind you, I'm not promising the truce will last, but they seem to have offered a stalemate over, and I quote, 'the most embarrassing mother ever to walk the earth.'"

Chrissie gurgled on a laugh. Scarlett was so surprised by the sound that she touched the brakes too hard, sending them all lurching against their seat belts. Chrissie turned to glare at her but otherwise continued her phone call. There was no reason not to—the South Dakota Badlands offered sights of nothing but white clay and rocky desiccation in every direction. Some people might find the desolation pretty, but Chrissie had grown up in stark surroundings and refused to return to them.

Give her over-the-top florals or give her death.

"It was the sweatshirt, wasn't it?" Chrissie asked. She sighed happily. "I knew it was a good idea to wear it." Then, with a less happy sigh, "She didn't pick up my call this morning. I wonder if I should apologize."

"Don't you dare!"

The shout came at her from all angles—through the phone, from the driver's seat, and from the back.

Scarlett was the first to follow up. "So help me, Chrissie, if you apologize to that girl for wearing your own damn clothes on your own damn vacation, I'm dropping you off at the next mile marker and making you walk the rest of the way."

"I'm with Scarlett," Walsh said, still with the smile in his voice. "I don't condone leaving you to die on the side of the road, obviously, but Kat's not nearly as upset as she's pretending. I think she's proud of you, honestly. We all are."

Chrissie was quick to get off the phone after that. Not because she didn't want to hear more about how her daughter and Walsh felt about her, but because she didn't want to hear more about how her daughter and Walsh felt about her while Scarlett was weaving dangerously across the lanes.

"Would you please slow down and focus on your driving?" she said as she tucked her phone away and adjusted her seat belt to a more lifesaving position. "I refuse to die on a day when Kat and her nemesis bonded for the first time in their lives."

"I *am* focused," Scarlett responded. "I just wanted to hear what

Walsh was saying. Did he declare his everlasting love for you and your ugly sweatshirt?"

Chrissie snorted, but she'd have been lying if she didn't admit that her heart gave a small stutter at the thought. That stutter became more pronounced—dangerously so—when River leaned over the console and asked, "What's up with this Walsh guy, anyway? Are you guys, like, dating?"

"*No,*" Chrissie said at the same time Scarlett said, "*Yes.*"

River laughed and took Scarlett's side—which, given Chrissie's track record with teenagers, seemed par for the course. Nothing Chrissie ever did was good enough for her daughter, but in Kat's eyes, Scarlett could do no wrong. She was glamorous and worldly wise, the "fun aunt" who swept into town and swept her off her feet simultaneously. Even though Chrissie was the one who'd insisted they rescue River, this situation was turning out to be very much the same.

"Okay, Scarlett," River said. "Tell me everything."

"I wish I could. I don't know nearly as much as I want to. Chrissie has always been tight-lipped about her love life. Even as a teenager, she never kissed and told. But I do know that Walsh has been her daughter's volleyball coach for six years, and he's been pining after her *hard* for at least five of those."

"That's not true!" Chrissie protested, but she was about as involved in this conversation as the scrubby weeds they were passing in a blur.

"What's wrong with him?" River chewed on one of her fingernails. "Like, is he ugly or mean to animals or something?"

"Show him that picture, Chrissie."

The last thing Chrissie wanted to do was play one of Scarlett's mind games—especially one around such a barbed topic—but she pulled up Walsh's barbecue apron selfie all the same. She felt oddly nervous as she showed River, but she needn't have worried.

"Oh, he's *cute*. You know, in a middle-aged, Jordan Peele sort of way. Aren't you kind of young for him?"

Chrissie didn't point out the obvious fact that her age was *much* closer to Walsh's than River's had been to the bartender back in Boise. The high road had always been her preferred method of travel.

"I'm an old soul," was all she said.

"And not only is he nice to animals, but he's literally training Chrissie's elderly cat to pee on a patch of fake grass right now—even though she begged him not to." Scarlett laughed and swerved to avoid a tumbleweed. "*That's* how bad he wants in, but the poor guy has no idea how steep the climb is to reach her."

A hand slid between the seats and gently touched Chrissie's shoulder. "You mean because of your daughter?"

Chrissie opened her mouth to reply in a strong affirmative, but Scarlett beat her to the punch. "That's the reason she'll tell you, but it actually has more to do with her first love. Grimshaw Pemberly."

Chrissie's teenage boyfriend was the last topic she wanted to introduce into the conversation right now, but River only giggled. "No way. That can't be his real name. It sounds like something from a romance novel—one of those really good ones where the lady's dress is being yanked off by a naked Fabio."

"Oh, it's real, all right." Scarlett nudged Chrissie with her elbow. "Tell River the story of your torrid teenage love affair. I'm sure she'd enjoy it. We have to do *something* to pass the time between here and Minnesota, and a trip down memory lane seems as good as anything else."

"The situations with Grimshaw and Walsh are nothing alike," Chrissie said with a firm set of her jaw. "And I'm not talking about this. Not unless you're prepared to tell your part of the story."

She could have almost laughed at how quickly that shut the conversation down. Less amusing was how quiet River had grown in the back seat. Like any child of trauma, she'd caught the heavy, unpleasant undertones of the conversation and absorbed them as her own. Chrissie had spent so many years doing the same thing, eating her parents' long silences for dinner, curling up under the blanket of their unspoken loss, that she felt instantly ashamed.

She also backtracked the only way she knew how.

"I accidentally sent Walsh a bikini photo our first night on the road," she confessed. "I'm afraid he liked it a lot more than I expected him to."

"No way," River breathed, once again returned to the light, airy eighteen-year-old she deserved a chance to be. "Now *that's* a story I definitely want to hear."

The main benefit—if not the only one—of Scarlett's refusal to sleep past six o'clock in the morning was how much ground they could cover in any given day. Although it had been their original intention to enjoy the journey, stopping every few hours to take in the sights, rest, and spend time together, River's addition to the party had changed the tenor of things.

Now, instead of the laid-back atmosphere Chrissie had been hoping for, a sense of urgency swept over her at every gas station and bathroom pit stop, every convenience store where they stocked up on cheap snacks. Not because she thought they were being tailed, and not because she wasn't enjoying River's company, but because she couldn't rest until she knew the girl was where she belonged.

One of the few games she could remember playing with Malcolm as a child was a cracked plastic Connect 4 that had been stored in the hospital game room. At least half the pieces had been missing, so the odds were always stacked in red's favor, but that hadn't stopped her from carrying the flattened box reverently to Malcolm's room whenever her parents weren't looking.

She'd only been four or five at the time, barely old enough for solid memories to take shape, but she remembered how satisfying it had felt every time one of those circles fell into place. As an adult, she could look back and see that the thing Young Chrissie had liked was that no matter how the game was played, every piece fit perfectly. The colors and gameplay were secondary to the plunk-plunk of the world stacking up exactly as promised.

As an adult, she could see the same patterns dictating her life now. The world had *definitely* not worked out the way she'd expected, but she could still make sure that all the pieces—including River—ended up where they belonged.

"But I was promised a giant ball of twine, so a giant ball of twine I will see," Chrissie announced as she turned off the road for a town called Darwin, population 330.

"All the guides say you can't miss it," Scarlett said as she consulted one of the maps scattered throughout the vehicle. "It's pretty much the only thing this place has, and if you want to get inside the little gazebo where it's housed, you have to ask someone who lives here. Everyone has a key."

"Surely not *everyone*."

"Let's find out, shall we?" Scarlett rolled down her window and shouted at the closest passerby, a man of indeterminate age who was walking an overweight Yorkie along a side street. "Excuse me? Sir? Sir, can you help us settle a bet?"

The man turned toward them with a deep frown. The moment he saw the out-of-state license plates, his frown seemed to fold in on itself. Calling his new expression a *smile* would have been taking things too far, but it was close enough for Chrissie not to fear they were about to be murdered where they idled.

"If it's the Twine Ball Museum you're after, it's already closed," he shouted.

"Yeah, but I'll bet you have a key to the gazebo, don't you? And that all we have to do to borrow it is bat our eyes and smile nicely at you?"

River rolled down her window and added her entreaty to Scarlett's. "Please, mister? We've come all the way from Idaho—"

"Oregon," Scarlett corrected her.

"Thousands of miles, then," River said. "Or at least hundreds. Your dog is super cute, by the way. What's his name?"

That did the trick. Chrissie could only roll her eyes as the man informed them of his dog's name—Archibald—and lifted a piece of string from around his neck. Sure enough, a metal key dangled from the end.

"Just leave it in the lock when you're done," he said as he continued on his way. "I'll have my son pick it up later."

"You've got to hand it to small towns," Scarlett said as they drove the last few blocks to the ball of twine, the key secure in the palm of her hand. "If I had to live here, I'd be bored to tears by the second day, but there's something charming about how easily they trust people. For all that man knows, we're planning on setting the ball of twine on fire and ruining the only tourism income this place has. He reminds me of you, Chrissie."

If it had been up to Chrissie, she'd have refused to take the bait and left this conversation in the dust where it belonged, but River piped in with an eager, "Why? Because she trusts people too easily?"

"I don't trust them too easily—" Chrissie began, but it was no use.

"That, and because you could dump her in one of those little houses we passed on the way in, and she'd stay there until someone picked her up and moved her again." Scarlett feigned thoughtfulness with a purse of her lips. "And because in all the years that passed while she waited for it to happen, she'd *like* it."

Well, of course she'd like it. That was what rational people did.

They took the hand that life dealt them and sat down to play the game. They didn't flip the entire table upside down or force the player next to them to give up their hand. They didn't demand and prod and *needle* as though they weren't sitting right there trying to win just the same as everyone else.

"Ask her what her favorite place to go on vacation is," Scarlett added—maliciously, Chrissie thought. "Quick. Before she has a chance to think about it."

"I bet it's Disneyland," River said without giving *either* of them a chance to think about it. "And you probably love shopping at the mall on rainy Saturday afternoons, where you always order the biggest boba tea they have even though you hate how sweet it is. Oh, and you probably enjoy the heck out of Medieval Times whenever you go and would rather sit in a smelly school gym on a Friday night than go anywhere else on earth."

They'd reached the ball of twine by this time, but none of them were paying attention to it. As Chrissie put the car in park, they both turned to stare at River—Scarlett with genuine surprise and Chrissie with a dawning sense of just how much this girl had lost.

"How do you know all that?" Scarlett asked.

"Because," River said with a shrug. As she turned to look out the window, Chrissie thought she saw her wipe surreptitiously at a wayward tear. "Those are the things my mom loved. Or, I guess I should say the things she *pretended* to love for my sake."

"No." Chrissie shot a hand back and took River's in her own. The girl's palm felt sweaty to the touch, but Chrissie didn't pull away. She also kept looking into the back seat until River had no choice but to meet her gaze.

This River did, but slowly, carefully, as if afraid that moving too fast would unleash the emotions she was working so hard to keep concealed.

"She *did* love them, River," Chrissie said in a voice so soft they both had to strain to hear her words. "I didn't know your mom, but I'm telling you with absolute certainty that nothing brought her more joy than to see the world through your eyes. Every precious minute, every slimy boba, was like magic to her, and she wouldn't have given them up for a thousand luxury vacations without you."

Chrissie didn't hear the car door open or Scarlett slip out, so she had no idea how much of that she'd heard—if she'd heard anything at all. She found she didn't much care, however, when River squeezed her hand and sat holding it for a full minute. No words passed between them in the entirety of that time, but that was fine with Chrissie.

No words needed to.

Scarlett had already opened the door to the ball of twine by the time Chrissie and River joined her. The earthy scent of decades-old string was pungent but not overwhelming. So too was the ball itself. It was big, there was no doubt about it, but when all was said and done, it was just that. An oddity only of interest because of its size. A passing whim that had become one man's life passion until it took over an entire town.

Chrissie was the first to break the silence. "It's too bad we didn't bring Rufio. This is a cat's dream scenario."

Scarlett snorted. "To be crushed to death by seventeen-thousand-pound ball of twine? That's *your* dream scenario, not his."

"For the last time, Scarlett, I'm not going to murder an animal just because he's an inconvenience. Kat loves that cat—and so do I."

"Sometimes love means pulling the damn plug already." Even though Scarlett spoke lightly, there was an undercurrent to her words that only served to highlight the tension that had been building between the two of them. Chrissie had no idea how much all this dredging up of the past and scribbling commands on a piece of motel paper was due to the awkwardness of River's addition to their party and how much was the product of Scarlett's roller-coaster moods, but she didn't care for it either way.

There'd only been once in their shared history when a similar feeling of constraint had put a wedge between them. That particular time had resulted in Scarlett's year of art study in Paris, followed not too long thereafter by a ten-month stint in Bangkok—both of which had included radio silence on Scarlett's end.

At the time, Chrissie had been so hurt by her friend's defection that it had been a physical ache. *Especially* that first one, when Kat had only been a few weeks old and Chrissie was so overwhelmed that she sometimes cried through the night alongside her newborn daughter.

She wasn't sure if the same thing was happening now—if Scarlett was getting ready for a long, self-indulgent trip somewhere Chrissie wasn't allowed to follow—but she was starting to worry.

"The guidebook says we're allowed to touch it, but under no circumstances are we to cut off any of the twine and take it with us," Scarlett said as she toyed with one of the frayed bits nearest her head. "I think it's like taking obsidian from Hawaii. You'll be cursed for all time, hounded to the ends of the earth by Minnesota Nice."

Scarlett faltered over the last few words, her knees suddenly buckling as if under a massive weight—or a ball of tourist-trap twine. She staggered back two steps before both Chrissie and River caught her.

"Whoa, there," Chrissie said as she half dragged, half carried her friend out of the gazebo. "Slowly, Scarlett. *Slowly.*"

"I'm fine," Scarlett gasped, sounding anything but fine. She stiffened as if she wanted to cast Chrissie off but lacked the strength to go through with it. "Just put me down here. I'll be fine once I catch my breath."

From the look of it, Scarlett needed a lot more than a temporary infusion of oxygen. Her skin was pale, yes, but more than that, it was cold and clammy in a way that spoke of deeper and longer-lasting problems. When added to the pharmacy she was carrying around in her purse and how tired she'd been looking on this trip, Chrissie was ready to call it.

"That's it," she announced. "We're taking you to the doctor. Something's not right."

"I'm okay, Chrissie." Scarlett still spoke in that failing voice, but there was an underlayer of iron she recognized well. "I'm just having a dizzy spell, that's all. I think there's some kind of solvent in parts of that twine. I got too close and inhaled it."

Chrissie managed to drag Scarlett to a nearby bench. As she sagged gratefully and gracelessly down onto it, River and Chrissie shared a look that said everything they were both thinking—namely, that neither one of them had detected a hint of solvent.

"Scarlett, don't. You've always been a terrible liar."

Scarlett passed a hand over her eyes, but her breathing was already growing steadier. She even managed a shaky laugh, though it contained little humor. "That's not true. I'm an amazing liar. You're just the one person who always sees right through me."

"Should I call an ambulance or something?" River asked from where she stood back a few paces. She was watching the scene with a strange expression. "I didn't want to say anything earlier, but if you're taking—"

"*No.*" This time, there was nothing shaky about Scarlett's voice. "I don't need a doctor, and I definitely don't need an ambulance. For crying out loud, you two. From the way you're reacting, you'd think I cut out my own kidney. I'm just tired, that's all. I haven't been sleeping well."

This, Chrissie remembered with a twinge of guilt, was true. Part of it she ascribed to Scarlett's natural antipathy to sleep, but she also suspected sharing a room with her had something to do with it. Scarlett had been a lone, roving wolf for so long that she probably found it difficult to sleep next to the natural sounds of another human being.

"We're finding somewhere to park for the night, and that's non-negotiable," Chrissie said. "We've been pushing too hard. What we need is a real hotel—not one of your weird roadside attractions—with room service, a swimming pool, and with any luck, no sign of a piano anywhere."

"That should be easy enough." River pulled out her phone and, in the manner of tech-savvy teenagers everywhere, found what she was looking for in less than twenty seconds. "There's a chain hotel with spots available about fifteen minutes away. It's only got three stars, but—"

"It's perfect," Chrissie said as she took the phone and started to make the reservation. "Get the car and bring it as close as you can. The sooner we're in our pajamas and ordering an ungodly amount of french fries, the better."

Chapter Fourteen

PORTLAND, OR

2008

IF SCARLETT COULD GO THE REST of her life without seeing, talking to, or even *hearing* the name Grimshaw Pemberly, she'd have signed up on the spot.

"Grimshaw thinks we should skip his prom," Chrissie said as she sat at the piano in her living room, her fingers flying over the keys. Although Scarlett *liked* to listen to Chrissie practice, and would have been the first to defend her friend's massive talent to anyone who questioned it, this wasn't how she'd normally choose to spend a gorgeous day just a few weeks before school let out.

Being cooped inside with a piano was one thing. But a piano and talk of Grimshaw? *Hard pass.*

"Of course he does," Scarlett muttered. She was draped over the arm of a too-white couch, flipping through an architectural magazine that showcased dozens of houses identical to this one.

"I kind of wanted to go—dress-shopping and a fancy dinner and all that—but Grimshaw says it's just another example of society forcing us to focus on frivolity so we don't see the political dangers looming on the horizon."

Ugh. Was there *anything* fun that Grimshaw didn't consider a political ploy undertaken by the hands of a shadowy Man waiting in the wings?

Since it was impossible to keep the bitterness out of her tone, Scarlett waited for a particularly thunderous chord before asking, "And what do you think? You have just as much of a right to enjoy your life as he does."

Chrissie's playing didn't stop as she considered her response. Scarlett would have liked to point out that any sixteen-year-old who could play Stravinsky with her eyes closed deserved to go to a thousand proms with a thousand better boyfriends, but there was no point.

Chrissie was impervious to all of Grimshaw's affected, brooding flaws. When he got up on his libertarian soapbox, she stood by to listen to all the ways deregulation would save the world. When he wanted to skip Friday night football games to go to poetry readings or study the lyrics of indie folk records instead of doing, you know, literally anything else, she was right there in step with him.

It was enough to make a best friend scream.

"I think he'd have a lot more fun than he realizes, but it won't break my heart to skip prom as a junior." Chrissie glanced at Scarlett with a smile that made her stomach feel tight. "I'd much rather wait until next year when you and I can *both* go."

And there it was. The tightness in Scarlett's stomach turned to a lump.

When it came to boys, jealousy wasn't a good look on a best friend. In her heart of hearts, Scarlett *knew* that—and if Chrissie had fallen for anyone else on the planet, she'd have curled up next to her green-eyed monster and enjoyed a Friday night on her own without complaint.

But oh, how she *hated* that guy. Not because he was a pretentious sack of wind, and not because everything he said and did was a performative farce, but because the two of them were exactly the same.

They both wanted Chrissie's heart, and neither of them deserved to have it.

"There." Chrissie finished the piece she was practicing and stood up, stretching her arms above her head as silence once again descended upon the house. "I'm done for the day. Did you still want to check out that sketchy carnival in Ventura Park?"

Scarlett was on her feet in a flash. "Do you even have to ask? Sketchy carnivals are my favorite kind. I hope the Ferris wheel goes rogue like last time. We were spinning around on that thing for *hours*."

Chrissie laughed (a good sign) and then immediately pulled out her cell phone (a very, very bad sign). "Cool. I'll have Grimshaw meet us there. One of his cousins is in town this weekend, so..."

Scarlett bit back a groan. As far as she could tell, Grimshaw was related to no fewer than forty-five different male cousins, most of whom had tenacious body odor and even worse taste in literature than he did. He and Chrissie were constantly setting Scarlett up on blind dates with them, as if all that was needed to set the seal on their happiness was to ensure they always had a double date for the art-house movies Grimshaw favored.

"Don't tell me," Scarlett said, resigned to her fate. If she wanted to spend time with her best friend—and she did—she had to pay the price. "This one is different. A really great guy once you get to know him—and his acne will be sure to fade in a few years. All I have to do is be patient."

"I'm sure this one really is different," Chrissie promised as she closed the lid on the piano and started gathering up her things. "And if he's not, we can always abandon him inside the fun house."

Scarlett had to make do with that, but not before making sure she got one last dig in.

"Good idea," she said. "With any luck, he's so much like Grimshaw that he'll get lost admiring his own reflection in one of the crooked mirrors."

"You should ask Mitchell to go on the spinning teacups again. Now that his stomach is empty, he might actually enjoy himself."

Grimshaw was dangerously close to winking at Scarlett as he spoke, so of course she responded with a glare. Since she was holding two pink puffs of cotton candy and had a matching stuffed narwhal under one arm, she doubted her glare held much authority, but she kept it glued to her face anyway.

"These are—I mean *were*—my favorite sneakers," she said as she tried not to think about the bright blue splatter of vomit that now decorated the tops. Honestly, if you were prone to motion sickness, why on earth would you eat a blue raspberry slushie right before you got on a ride? "You made him sit next to me on purpose."

Grimshaw opened his eyes wide in an expression of innocence. It made his broodingly dark lashes look even less natural than usual. In all the time she'd known him, he continued to maintain that he'd never worn eyeliner a day in his life, but if that wasn't the work of an Urban Decay smudge stick, she'd eat this narwhal.

"Whatever can you mean, Scarlett?" he asked. "Of course Mitchell wanted to sit next to you. He's never been on a date with a beautiful older woman before."

His wide-eyed innocence turned to even wider-eyed malice. Scarlett wished there was a way for her to bottle up that look and share it with Chrissie, but of course Grimshaw would never let that happen. Around Chrissie, he was a perfect gentleman, content to hold her hand

and gaze adoringly into her eyes, generously sharing his cousins so her dear friend wouldn't end up a lonely spinster.

Around Scarlett, however, his true nature came out. It had no choice. That was what happened when like found like.

"You could have told us he's only fourteen *before* we got here," she muttered.

"What, and ruin the surprise?" He slung a heavy arm around her shoulders. "This is the most fun I've had with you in months."

Chrissie chose that moment to return to the group, her own arm around Mitchell as she led him away from the family bathrooms. The damp patch along the front of his shirt and the hangdog droop to his head indicated that her attempts to clean and cheer him up hadn't been a success.

In a few years—possibly ten—Mitchell had the potential to rival his cousin in terms of height, hair, and hotness. As it was, he stood only one bare inch taller than Scarlett, his hair cut in an unfortunate bowl shape, the gangly awkwardness of his fourteen years evident in every line of his bearing.

The fact that he'd taken one look at Scarlett and fallen into staring, speechless adoration didn't help matters any.

"See, Mitchell?" Chrissie gave the embarrassed boy's hand a comforting pat. "I told you she'd still be here when we got back. Scarlett doesn't care about things like getting sick on a ride. She's one of the nicest people in the world. Aren't you, Scarlett?"

Scarlett wasn't, and everyone here knew it, but there didn't seem to be any way to contradict the claim. When Chrissie Thomas looked at you with those soft, kind eyes and demanded that you be just as soft and kind in return, you did.

It was the one thing that made spending time with Grimshaw palatable—the one reason Scarlett hadn't secretly nanny-cammed her interactions with him and posted them online for all the world to see.

For some strange reason, Chrissie genuinely believed that Scarlett's heart beat the same way hers did—that if left to her own devices, her decisions would be right, honorable, and just. She believed the same thing about Grimshaw.

Scarlett Sanderson was a lot of unpleasant things, but a hypocrite wasn't one of them. If Chrissie could see something inside Scarlett that she didn't know existed, then it was possible that she could see it in other people, too. Maybe Scarlett focused on the manipulative weasel inside Grimshaw because that was the only part of him she shared.

"Here. I got you this." Scarlett shoved the cotton candy at the boy. "To clean the taste out of your mouth. Also because it was buy one, get one free."

"Really? For me?" Mitchell accepted the peace offering, looking at her with such pleased surprise that she was *almost* ready to rise to Chrissie's astronomical expectations. "Chrissie was right. You really are the best."

Scarlett flushed. She flushed even more when she caught Grimshaw's gaze, mocking her from beneath a pair of perfectly arched brows.

"Whatever. It's just cotton candy." She shoved the toy narwhal at Chrissie. "And this is for you. I beat Grimshaw at the water balloon race—and a good thing, too, because he was going to pick the vaguely racist burrito wearing a sombrero."

"It was a vaguely racist *avocado* wearing a sombrero," he corrected her with a grin. For some reason, he still had his arm around Scarlett's shoulders, the weight of it like a giant dead snake. He winked at Chrissie. "And I'll still win it for you if you want. But I should warn you—"

Scarlett's phone rang before he could warn them of anything. "Hang on," she said as she dug the phone out of her pocket. "It's probably just my grandma checking in."

But when she said hello, the voice on the other end was soft, professional, and not at all what she was expecting.

"Yes, hi. Is this Scarlett Sanderson, Laurel's granddaughter?"

At the sound of her grandmother's given name, Scarlett frowned. The only people who used that were scammers and bill collectors—usually the latter. "Yes, it is. But she's not here right now and I don't have anything to take a message. You'll have to call back."

"No, don't hang up! I'm calling from the hospital. I'm afraid I have some bad news."

Scarlett felt her knees grow weak, the cheerful chimes and shouts of the carnival receding into a low, distant hum. "What do you mean? What kind of bad news?"

She didn't hear the answer. The sounds of the carnival weren't the only things that were disappearing. Her whole body seemed to be moving down a long, dark tunnel that she remembered well.

Hospitals were bad. Hospitals were *always* bad.

Scarlett had no idea how or when Chrissie replaced Grimshaw, but she felt her friend's surprisingly strong arms wrap around her and hold her up. The phone was lifted from her hand before she could do more than sag gratefully against Chrissie's shoulder.

"Yes, go ahead. This is Chrissie Thomas. Uh-huh. Yep. At OHSU? We'll be there as soon as we can, thanks." Chrissie paused. "What was your name again? Oh, right. Thank you, Genie. We really appreciate you calling to let us know."

Scarlett wasn't sure why Chrissie's unfailing ability to act like a middle-aged woman who made good eye contact and always thanked her servers made her laugh, but it did. She was shaking all over and her heart was in a vise that didn't seem to have any intention of letting up, but she laughed all the same.

Chrissie understood the reaction without the need for explanation.

"Come on, Scarlett. Let's get you to the hospital. They weren't able to give me any details over the phone, but Nan is stable and awake, and that's enough for now."

It wasn't enough, not by a long shot, but Scarlett nodded and let Chrissie lead her away from the carnival rides. She stopped when she realized that both Grimshaw and Mitchell were right behind them.

"What are you doing? You can't come with us. My grandmother is... That is, she's not—" She looked to Chrissie in mute appeal, but her friend adopted that same middle-aged, capable air as before.

"It's okay, Scarlett. Let's just get you in the car and worry about the rest later."

Scarlett was tempted to pull rank and get rid of the two Pemberly boys with as little fanfare as possible, but she was being dragged in too many directions at once. Her heart was somewhere in her feet, her head was spinning like the teacups, and her muscles—they were shaking. Why were they shaking?

"Yeah, okay. Thanks." She passed her hand—also shaking—over her eyes and allowed herself to be led away. Somewhere in the back of her mind, she had the feeling she'd regret this relaxing of her guard, of allowing Grimshaw and his pukey cousin to slip through her defenses, but for now, all she wanted was to see her grandma.

No matter what the eventual cost.

Chapter Fifteen

HUTCHINSON, MINNESOTA

Present Day

THAT NIGHT AT THE BUDGET HOTEL, Scarlett slept like the dead.

If anything more had been needed to illustrate that all was not well with Scarlett, it was exactly that: She'd gone to bed at a reasonable hour, her plate of french fries largely untouched and one of Chrissie's shapeless sleep shirts covering her body. And then she'd *stayed* asleep. The sunrise had come and gone without Scarlett there to greet it, a breakfast of rubbery eggs and tepid coffee consumed without her commentary.

"Ten fourteen? Is that clock for real?" Scarlett sat bolt upright in the bed, her makeup so smudged that the dark bags under her eyes looked stenciled on. "Chrissie, please tell me you didn't let me sleep for twelve hours."

Chrissie and River both looked up from the foot of her bed, where they sat playing Go Fish with a deck of souvenir playing cards they'd found in one of the bedside tables. The game had been a lackluster one, and River had spent most of it looking increasingly uncomfortable with the length of time Scarlett was spending asleep, but none of that mattered as soon as Scarlett's rich brown eyes popped open.

"Good morning, Sleeping Beauty," Chrissie teased as she swept up a pair of threes. "We were starting to worry that we'd have to hit the pool without you."

"Why didn't you wake me up?" Scarlett tossed back the covers and bounded to her feet with an energy that made yesterday's near-faint seem like a faraway dream. "Half the day is gone already. And it's a nice day, too. Look. The sun is gorgeous."

"It'll still be gorgeous this afternoon," Chrissie promised, unperturbed. "The coffee is cold and the eggs are even colder, but you should probably eat something. You're looking way too thin, and you know how you get when your blood sugar is low."

Scarlett's only response to this was to scowl and shove a dry bite of toast in her mouth. She chased it with a gulp of cold coffee. "There. Happy now, Mommie dearest?"

"Not really. You should eat something with protein. I still have some of that buffalo jerky if your teeth are feeling up to the task."

River dispelled the growing tension with a laugh and a matching threesome of jacks. "You guys have known each other for a long time, huh? You remind me of the kids I grew up next to. There were three of them, all less than a year apart, and the way they used to aggressively tackle-hug each other is exactly how you two interact."

"I've never tackle-hugged anyone a day in my life," Chrissie protested, but Scarlett chose that moment to plow her into the bed with a hug that was *definitely* on the aggressive side. "Scarlett! *Ugh.* Stop kissing me. Your breath smells like death warmed over."

Instead of stopping, Scarlett nestled into her, the little spoon to Chrissie's bigger one. When they were younger, they used to sleep exactly like that, Scarlett's overheated body burrowing against Chrissie's until they both woke up in a sweaty tangle.

"If that's how you sweet-talk Walsh, it's no wonder you haven't gotten to second base yet," Scarlett said. Her breath was still awful, but Chrissie had to admit that it felt good to be like this again, with none of the reserve that being an adult seemed to impose on affection.

"What makes you think we've hit first base?" Chrissie asked without letting her friend go.

"Oh, that much was obvious when you got so flustered from the bikini pic. You wouldn't have been that ashamed of yourself if he hadn't tasted the inside of your mouth at least once."

"Scarlett, ew."

"What? It's a man's tongue, not a piece of gum you picked off the bottom of a chair." Scarlett turned to River and waggled her eyebrows. "Back me up here, River. How far down her throat do you think he got before she put a stop to things?"

River unfolded herself from the bed and scooped up the cards. She began backing away, but in a slow, smiling way that indicated how much she was enjoying this exchange. "I'm gonna go put my suit on. We're still doing a pool day today, yeah?"

Chrissie nodded before Scarlett could say anything to the contrary. "If you get down there before us, snag some of the good lounge chairs. I'll bring extra towels."

With that, River snicked the adjoining door closed, leaving Chrissie and Scarlett alone on the bed. Chrissie was almost always the first one to pull away in situations like these, so she forced herself to stay put.

She also forced herself to confront the elephant that was standing, clad in nothing but a pink bikini, in the middle of the room.

"Why are you suddenly all gung-ho about me and Kat's volleyball coach getting together?" she asked. Scarlett started to rear back, but Chrissie's massage-therapist arms were much stronger than Scarlett's radio-host ones. "No, don't. Walsh and I have been friends for *years*. And, yeah, we did kiss once, but that was a while ago—and it was less of a game of tonsil hockey and more of a slip when we both went the same direction for a greeting. It was awkward."

"That's exactly why. You need all the help you can get."

"Yeah, but you've never shown an interest in my personal life before this. Not since before Kat was born. It was like the moment she was put into my arms, you assumed my sex life would become forever null and void."

For the most part, it *was*, but what Scarlett didn't know wouldn't hurt her.

"I'm just being a good friend, that's all. I'm tired of seeing you shackled to that girl's moods and whims."

Those *moods and whims* were literally what got Chrissie out of bed in the morning, but she didn't bother trying to explain it. No matter how many times she told Scarlett that being a mother was the thing she loved most about her life, even when the difficulties dragged her down, she couldn't get her friend to believe her.

She disentangled herself from Scarlett's embrace and slid off the bed, no longer feeling the warm coziness from before.

"Is this the part where I ask you how your love life is going?" she countered. "Because if I remember correctly, your last boyfriend proposed to you on the Oracle Park Jumbotron before you soundly rejected him."

Instead of taking offense, Scarlett grinned. "Don't feel too bad for Hugh. He did it more for the PR than out of love for me. He was trying to get the people at iHeartRadio to bump his application to the top of the pile." She paused, considering. "It worked, too. I should've said yes just to teach him a lesson about using unsuspecting young women as professional springboards."

A now-familiar surge of annoyance replaced the warm, happy glow brought by the lazy morning.

"I'm just saying, Scarlett. It's not fair for you to stand there and judge all my life choices when your own aren't exactly ideal."

A frisson of something dangerous—something *real*—started to spark between them, but Scarlett brushed it off with a laugh. "Uh-oh. Sounds like someone wants me to pull out the list again. Do we need another lesson so soon after the last one?"

Chrissie's response was a grunt and to start rummaging in her bag for the pink bikini.

"That's what I thought." Scarlett tossed the words—and her head—as though she'd clinched the argument. "You only fight other people's battles. Never your own."

Chrissie wasn't sure why that particular jab was the one to make it through. She was well practiced in ignoring the things that Scarlett—and Kat—said to try and hurt her, and if the past few days had proved anything, it was that Scarlett was trying *very hard* to hurt her.

"And I'm getting seriously tired of it," she said, more to herself than to her friend.

"Then fight back," Scarlett suggested. "Right here. Right now. Show me what you've got."

But Chrissie only looked at Scarlett long and hard, taking in the exhausted lines of her face and the way she was curling her arms protectively over her stomach as though expecting an incoming blow. To strike at her now would only be cruel—and that was the one thing Chrissie refused to be, no matter how strong the provocation.

"I won't give you the satisfaction," she said as she headed for the door. "You forget how well I know you, Scarlett. And how much better I know myself."

Although the temperature was warm enough when they made it to the kidney-shaped pool, the sun decided it was tired of showing off. In May, this part of Minnesota was as mercurial as Scarlett, and the clouds blowing in from the west proved it.

Still, all three of them shimmied into their suits and flip-flopped out to the water's edge, determined to pretend, if only for a few hours, that they were basking in the tropics instead of a chlorinated concrete hole across the street from a strip mall.

"All I need now is a cabana boy and a wool cap, and I'm set for life," Scarlett said as she whisked off her towel and settled into the lounge chair. River had thoughtfully arranged them so they caught some of the steam rising from the hot tub. "Remind me again why we aren't taking a road trip to Mexico?"

Chrissie was too busy taking a book out of her bag—*I like to sit and read without interruption*—to answer. The choices at the take-a-book, leave-a-book shelf in the hotel lobby had been surprisingly robust, assuming you enjoyed eighties-era Danielle Steel novels.

Which, Chrissie was happy to admit, she did.

"Oh, how cute," River said as she watched Scarlett settle into her lounge chair. She was once again clad in her high-necked black halter bikini. "I love that suit. My mom had the exact same one. She said it cost a small fortune for a top like that, but it was worth every penny."

Scarlett didn't respond. Chrissie, afraid that her friend was taking her bad mood out on River instead of its true target—herself, stepped in to fill the breach.

"Good swimsuits always are. It took me a long time to realize that one should never skimp on socks, bras, or swimwear. I spent most of my twenties being stabbed by rogue underwire." Then, when Scarlett *still* didn't say anything, Chrissie turned toward her with her best warning scowl. Honestly, Scarlett had worse manners than Kat sometimes. "You're the one who taught me that. Remember the first time you took me to La Perla? I took one look at the price tags and—"

But here she cut herself off. Scarlett's own warning scowl was impossible to ignore, especially since it was being directed at River.

"What's wrong?" she asked, looking back and forth between the two. "What's happened?"

"Nothing is wrong," Scarlett said. "I'm totally fine."

To Chrissie's surprise, River clamped her mouth shut and nodded. She thought she heard the girl mutter something under her breath, but the words were impossible to make out over the sound of the hot-tub bubbles kicking into action.

Scarlett yanked the towel she was lying on and pulled it up over her chest. The action was a childish one, but it didn't make Chrissie soften. It only made her realize a thing she should have figured out days ago.

In the Scarlett Sanderson she knew, a boob job was an excuse to pull on skimpy tops and plunging necklines, to bend and twist until a nip slip was all but guaranteed. But, no. *This* Scarlett Sanderson had been drowning in high-necked shirts and flowy tops the entire trip, looking thinner and paler the more the miles wore on.

And the pills in her purse. Chrissie couldn't forget the pills in her purse.

That conniving, lying, sneaky little bitch. I can't believe she's doing this to me…again.

Chrissie sat bolt upright on the lounge and stared—not at Scarlett, but at River. "River, when you say that your mom had a suit like that, do you mean before or after her cancer diagnosis?"

"Um…"

"Don't answer that, River," Scarlett warned. "It's none of our business."

"Did she have breast cancer?" Chrissie persisted. "Is that what took her life? Do you recognize the pills Scarlett is taking?"

"River, I mean it." This time, Scarlett's words held less of a warning and more of a snarl. "Proceed at your own risk."

Unfortunately for Scarlett, River was made of sterner stuff—a thing Scarlett would have realized for herself if she'd taken any time to consider the girl's situation. An eighteen-year-old was practically a child, yes, but this was a child who'd been through hell and back again, who was even now trying to claw her way free of it. Vague threats from a woman wearing a mastectomy bikini top would hold very little sway over someone like that.

"Yeah, uh. I think I'm gonna go get dressed." River took one look at Scarlett's furious face and Chrissie's even more furious one and added, "And then I'm going for a walk. A *long* one."

Chrissie hated the thought of leaving that poor girl to her devices for the entire afternoon, but not as much as she hated Scarlett right now. They had one rule—*one freaking rule*. Months could pass without communication between them. One of them could get fake-proposed to at a baseball game without telling the other. Another one could spend every Saturday night in her pajamas binge-watching *Schitt's Creek* for the fifteenth time without judgment.

But when it came to the big stuff—the health stuff—they were supposed to be honest with each other. *Always.*

"When were you going to tell me?" Chrissie asked, her voice flat.

Scarlett was wearing her oversized sunglasses, so it was impossible to see her reaction, but Chrissie could guess how panicked her friend was right now. When trapped in a corner, Scarlett was the type to lash out as hard as she could. Kat wasn't the only one with a mean-girl streak in her.

"*When*, Scarlett?"

"I was working my way up to it, I swear. I just needed the right time—"

Chrissie flung up her hand. "Bullshit." The word snapped out of her like the crack of a whip. "The right time was the minute you got the diagnosis—no, the minute you started feeling under the weather. And you know it."

A feeling unlike anything she'd ever experienced before came over her. With as much radiation and chemotherapy as Scarlett had been subjected to as a child, they'd always known that another bout of cancer was a real possibility, but Chrissie had assumed it was a possibility they shared.

That was the whole point of them. Everything they did was supposed to be together. It wasn't just the two of them against cancer. It was the two of them against the *world*.

"Do you still want to touch them?" Scarlett asked as she allowed the towel to slip down her chest to reveal the two pert globes. "The swimsuit inserts are surprisingly realistic. I probably went a little too big, but at this point, I figured, why the hell not?"

Chrissie burst into tears. She wished she could concentrate her anger and use that as a shield, or at least ride the wave of her fury long enough to get a few answers, but this was who she was.

When anger came for her, she cried. And when her best friend of twenty-seven years had been diagnosed with cancer and undergone a double mastectomy all by herself, she cried even harder.

She couldn't contain an audible sob at that last thought, all the interactions of the past week pinging her like a hailstorm. It was all so obvious now—the oversized clothes and the way Scarlett refused to sleep one minute longer than she had to, the water she'd ordered at a swanky cocktail bar.

I should have noticed earlier. I should have made her tell me the truth.

"Chrissie, please don't cry." Scarlett was on her knees by Chrissie's side in an instant.

Somewhere in the back of Chrissie's mind, she knew this was backwards, and that she was the one who was supposed to be comforting Scarlett, but the hot tears kept scoring her cheeks.

"I'm a monster for waiting this long to tell you. A horrible friend. I just didn't want to worry you or add to your burdens more than I already have."

"My burdens?" Chrissie echoed. Nothing Scarlett was saying was making her feel any better about this. "You mean Kat? That's what this whole thing is about?"

"That's what everything between us is about, and you know it. Since the day she was born, she's been a wedge between us." Scarlett hesitated in a way that made Chrissie's entire body grow cold. Or maybe that was just the sun slipping behind a cloud and taking the warm temperature with it. "It was always my intention to tell you as soon as the trip got underway, but then we were having such a good time and you started inviting stray teenagers to join us, so—"

Chrissie stood up so abruptly that her head spun. Scarlett tried to rise with her, but Chrissie pushed her down with a hand on her shoulder. The ease with which she was able to do this—Scarlett's body weakened by her cancer and surgery and god-knew-what-other treatments she was currently undergoing—should have made her feel ashamed of herself, and she did, but more than that, she was *furious*.

Trust Scarlett Sanderson to make a diagnosis of cancer about more than just the uncontrolled growth and spread of abnormal cells. With her, it was a production worthy of the Broadway stage—and Chrissie was once again relegated to the audience.

"I'm going to join River for that walk," she announced.

"Chrissie, don't. I'm sorry, okay? I should have told you about this a long time ago. I just hoped… I thought… Oh, hell. You already know what I hoped and thought. You always have."

"Don't you dare. You're not turning this around and putting the burden of discovery on me. This is about you and the fact that you think my life is too small to handle any of the things you deal with on a daily basis. Poor little Chrissie Thomas, stuck in Medford raising a child all on her own. She'd never understand what it's like to travel the world and fall in love a dozen different times. She's too busy being a drudge to help me in my hour of need."

Her voice shook with each additional word—not because of her anger, but because of the truth that lay underneath. In all honesty, Chrissie's life *was* small. In the past sixteen years, it had shrunk to the size of exactly two people and one cat, and most days, even that was more than she could handle.

But she wasn't weak. And she didn't deserve to be treated like an afterthought in a big, glamorous life she'd only ever applauded and supported from afar.

"I'm going to the drugstore," Chrissie announced suddenly.

"The drugstore?"

"Yes. I'm going to see if they have any of those tiny emergency bottles of vodka, and I'm going to drink them in the parking lot until I can breathe again. Do you need anything while I'm there?"

Scarlett's only response to this was a long, hard stare that Chrissie had no difficulty in interpreting.

"I'm not asking because I'm a pushover. I'm asking because taking care of other people is what you're supposed to do in situations like these." Chrissie's legs were starting to grow numb, but they held her up just fine. They always had. When everyone around her got sick and struggled and fell, she was the one who kept putting one foot in front of the other. "It's who I am, Scarlett. It's who I've *always* been. You're just too busy thinking of yourself to see it."

Chapter Sixteen

PORTLAND, OR

2009

SCARLETT HAD ALWAYS PLANNED TO GO to Cabo for her eighteenth birthday.

The financial difficulties of this plan were secondary only to the problem of Chrissie being two months, fourteen days, and six hours younger than her and therefore unable to drink. This, however, had been neatly circumvented by a fake ID that Scarlett had ordered from a twelve-year-old hacker she'd found on 4chan.

That ID now sat untouched in her underwear drawer, nestled beneath the Victoria's Secret thongs she'd bought in every color of the rainbow. And there, unfortunately, it would stay. A trip to celebrate her transition to adulthood was out of the question—an *international* trip even more so.

"Morning, Grandma." Scarlett kissed her grandmother on the cheek as she padded out of her bedroom and made her way to the kitchen. In birthdays past, there had always been a tray of hot cinnamon rolls waiting on the counter for her, dripping with cream cheese frosting that her grandmother put on too soon so it melted everywhere.

This time, all she saw was the package of bread she'd left open last night. An army of ants swarmed inside the clear plastic, making the most of their good fortune while it lasted.

"Morning, child," her grandmother responded. She was wrapped in a hideous crocheted blanket on her usual recliner, her feet up on the ottoman and covered in a pair of even more hideous crocheted socks—both of which had been made by Chrissie, who'd recently taken to needlework like she lived in a little house on the prairie. "What time are you leaving for school today?"

"I'm not." Scarlett tossed the bread into the garbage and tried to scoop a handful of ants in there with it, but she only managed to corral about half. "And please don't make that face at me. I don't have any big tests today, so no one will notice. I was thinking about going to a movie or something instead."

Her grandmother didn't respond, her face still wearing that disappointed look. Despite the six months that had passed since her stroke—or perhaps *because* of them—her grandmother had a tendency to wear that frown from the moment she woke up in the morning until she went to bed at night. In fact, the only time she wasn't wearing it was when—

"Good morning, my lovelies!"

The front door swung open with a clang. Scarlett was so surprised that her heart leaped to her throat—and then she was so happy by what she saw that it stayed there.

"Sorry I'm late. I meant to have these babies hot and waiting for you when you woke up this morning, but traffic was a witch-with-a-capital-B." Chrissie set a tray of cinnamon rolls on the counter, squishing the last of the ants, and turned to pull Scarlett into a fierce hug. "They're not homemade, but I did make them add twelve extra tubs of frosting, so I figure it still counts."

Scarlett's heart-lodged throat rendered speech impossible, so Chrissie moved on to the living room next.

"And how are you feeling today, Nan? Please tell me you made it to your bed last night. You know it's not good for you to sit propped up for so many hours."

Scarlett watched as her grandmother's frown transformed itself into a tremulous smile. Chrissie fussed and clucked over her like a mother hen, tucking in the blanket and whisking away the empty mugs of tea that had a tendency to build up around her grandmother like a fortress.

"I'm just fine, as always. You know me. I can't complain."

Scarlett's mood, which had been starting to buoy, sank like a rock. Her grandmother *could* complain. In fact, Scarlett very much wished that she would. Anything would be better than the grim determination with which she went through each day.

In fact, now that she was thinking about it, she wished Chrissie would complain, too. Ever since that fateful day when her grandmother had been found collapsed at the foot of the apartment steps, nonresponsive and with a bleeding gash on her temple caused by the fall, not a single person had voiced any of the emotions that roiled inside Scarlett's own breast.

It's not fair. How many medical crises can one person be expected to undergo in one lifetime? Why can't I just go to Mexico with my best friend like I always planned?

"Well, I stopped by Redbox and got a whole bunch of movies for us to watch together, so complaining wouldn't do you any good anyway. The medical van should be here around noon to pick you up for your appointment, and I have all the ingredients we need to make bagel pizzas for dinner." Chrissie tossed a grin over her shoulder at Scarlett. "*And* I have a surprise for you, so go put on something cute. It'll be here any minute."

Her grandmother furrowed her brow in the slow, heavy way that seemed to precede most of her conversations. Ever since the stroke, her thoughts dragged a few steps behind the rest of her, a weight she couldn't quite shake.

"Are you skipping school today, too?" Grandma asked. "I'm not sure your parents would like that."

"What they don't know won't hurt them," Chrissie said with the same broad smile, though Scarlett could tell it was starting to fray around the edges. "Now, I'm starting *Mamma Mia* and making you a cup of your good chamomile tea, and I won't hear any arguments."

Scarlett had yet to move toward her bedroom to put on anything, cute or otherwise, so she watched as Chrissie set about fulfilling her promises—and in the quiet, efficient way that had become her habit.

For the first month after her grandma had been sent home from the hospital against medical advice, they'd had a full-time nurse to help them out. The doctors had wanted Grandma to stay under observation or, at the very least, go to a nursing home to recover, but she'd insisted on being home. Ostensibly, this had been because her grandma preferred the comforts of her familiar surroundings, but everyone had been quick to perceive the real reason. Leaving her seventeen-year-old granddaughter on her own would mean getting the state involved—and that, Grandma had determined, was a thing she'd never do.

Unfortunately, the home-health nurse they'd been assigned had been a loud, domineering woman who thumped through the apartment with such a heavy tread that six different complaints had been lodged against them from the other apartment tenants. She made every bath and bedtime routine seem like a feat of Olympic proportions, and with a martyred air that had made them all happy to see the last of her.

Chrissie was nothing like that. She coaxed and wheedled to get results, and with such relentless good cheer that no one could find fault in anything she did.

"I can make the tea," Scarlett offered now, both insulted that her friend felt the need to take the task upon herself and guilty that it hadn't occurred to her first. Why, oh why was it so hard for her to remember basic human decency? And why, oh why did it come so naturally to Chrissie?

"I've got this," Chrissie said. "Birthday girls don't have to do chores, remember?"

Tell that to the bread and ants she'd already cleaned up. "I don't mind. She likes it with an extra dash of honey."

Chrissie put her hands on Scarlett's shoulders and nudged her gently into her room. She waited until the door was closed behind them before saying softly, "I know how she takes her tea, Scarlett. This isn't my first rodeo."

She knew it wasn't. She also knew that even when it *had* been Chrissie's first rodeo, she'd charged out of the gate without the least hesitation. Unlike Scarlett—falling flat on her back, dazed and breathless before the crowd even had a chance to get on their feet.

"Like you'd ever go anywhere as cool as a rodeo," Scarlett muttered under her breath.

When Chrissie turned toward her with a puzzled look, she feared she'd been overheard. And when Chrissie forced a bright smile and said, "Well? Are you going to get dressed and eat your cinnamon rolls, or are you going to stand there like a block all day?" she *knew* she had.

Scarlett's lower lip started to tremble. She *hated* that her lower lip started to tremble. "She didn't remember, Chrissie. She forgot my eighteenth birthday."

In this, as in everything else, Chrissie refused to back down—or to acknowledge the truth of this situation: that life sucked and it wasn't fair and they'd both been dealt equally crappy hands.

"Or maybe she's planning you a killer surprise party for when you get back, and you're ruining it by taking so long to get ready," she said. Or *lied*, rather. In addition to the physical side effects of her grandmother's stroke, the mental ones had been chipping away at all three of them, one depressive episode at a time.

We often forget that a stroke is, at its core, a brain injury, the doctor had patiently explained to Scarlett and Chrissie when they'd voiced concerns—Scarlett sitting there picking at her nail polish; Chrissie with a notepad and a pen handy to jot down any notes or questions that arose. *Some patients experience permanent personality changes, and the best we can do is get to know and love this new version of them.*

"Chrissie, you don't have to do this," Scarlett began, but it was no use. Chrissie had already grabbed a pair of low-rise jeans and one of Scarlett's favorite layering tanks from the ever-growing pile of unfolded laundry on her bed.

"Just get dressed and pretend to have a good time with Grimshaw, okay?" Chrissie said, showing exasperation for the first time since she'd waltzed into the apartment. "He drove all the way down from Seattle to take you out so I can throw a semblance of a surprise party together. I know it's not Cabo, and that you don't feel much like celebrating this year, but—"

Scarlett pounced on Chrissie before she could finish, wrapping her arms around her in a whole-body hug. Chrissie wasn't a physically affectionate person as a general rule, but she always relaxed whenever Scarlett took her by surprise like this.

"You're the best," Scarlett said into Chrissie's hair. It was in its longest phase right now, a week or two out from being cut and shipped off—a glorious waterfall of silk and strawberry-scented shampoo. "You always have been. I'm gonna spend all day making Grimshaw miserable. I hope you warned him, Chrissie. All I want for my birthday is to reduce him to sad, emo tears. I bet his eyeliner won't even run."

Chrissie laughed and planted a kiss on Scarlett. "It's your day,

Scarlett. Do whatever you want. Just be back here at five so we can eat bagel pizzas and pretend we're on a beach in Mexico where we belong."

If anyone had told Scarlett that she might not hate eight hours spent in the company of a guy who was majoring in comparative history of ideas (how was that even a real thing?) at the University of Washington, she'd have laughed them right out of the room. *And* out of the arcade where they spent two hours in a cutthroat Ms. Pac-Man battle, *and* out of the frozen yogurt shop where Grimshaw had ironically insisted they eat lunch.

"Spill," she said, pointing her plastic spoon at Grimshaw as they sat across from each other at a sticky booth in the corner. She'd purposefully loaded up as many brownie and cookie dough chunks as she could to rack up the price tag, but even that didn't seem to have affected him. "What did Chrissie say to get you to be so nice to me?"

He touched an ironic hand to his heart, where the artfully faded image of Miles Davis was emblazoned across his T-shirt. "I'm hurt, Sanderson. What makes you think this wasn't my idea?"

"Because you're the most selfish person I've ever known," she replied without any need to think about it. "Except for myself, of course."

A lopsided grin touched the corners of his mouth in the manner of teenage heartthrobs everywhere. "Then what would Chrissie have to say to get *you* to be nice to *me*?"

Scarlett didn't have to think about this one, either.

"She wouldn't have to *say* anything. She'd just look at me with those big, soulful eyes, and I'd have no other choice. She sees the good in people even when it's hidden under layers of bullshit—both mine and yours—and we're powerless against it."

"Then there you go." His gaze caught hers in a wave of such

understanding that it left her feeling breathless. "It seems you and I were meant to be. Now hurry up and eat. We've got a few more stops on our road to redemption."

Scarlett wasn't sure what she expected their next stop to be, but it definitely wasn't a high school pickup line on the south side of Portland.

"No way." She sat bolt upright in the passenger seat of Grimshaw's ancient Honda Accord and watched as students poured out of the flat, sprawling building. "Is that Mitchell? Blue-vomit Mitchell? And is he cute now?"

"Grimmy Bear!" As soon as he spotted them, Mitchell loped across the parking lot, his long-legged stride making quick work of the pavement. "Mom said you'd be by to pick me up today, only I thought—" He stopped, his chiseled jaw dropping when he noticed Scarlett in the front seat. In the past six months, his jaw wasn't the only thing that had gained definition. He was almost as tall as Grimshaw now, his body honed and lean in the way that always happened when teenage boys hit a major growth spurt. He'd never be as good-looking as his older, more deliberately disheveled cousin, but there was something about his wide-eyed earnestness that worked.

"Get in, loser," she said, punctuating her statement with a smile so he knew she meant no harm. "It's my birthday, and Grimshaw is in charge of keeping me entertained until my surprise party. Only he keeps quoting *Catcher in the Rye* at me without any context, so I might not make it. If I hear 'Life is a game, boy' one more time, I'm tucking and rolling out of this car even if we're on the freeway."

Grimshaw laugh-grunted, a habit he must have picked up his first year at college. "You just quoted *Mean Girls* without any context. How is that better?"

Scarlett laugh-grunted right back. "It's not my fault you're, like, in love with me or something."

Mitchell piled into the back seat of the car. The door hadn't even closed behind him before Grimshaw was flooring it, tearing away from the school at a pace Scarlett felt pretty sure would earn him a speeding ticket from the traffic camera posted at the corner.

Which, good. Even though she knew that Chrissie had given her the ultimate gift in lending Scarlett her boyfriend for the day, she still didn't like the guy. Sure, he could be charming when he pulled out all the stops, and yeah, he was being way nicer than he'd ever been before, but he was still just a boy, when all was said and done.

He wasn't a best friend. He wasn't someone who *mattered.*

One of these days, Chrissie would be done with him, and then Scarlett could finally have her friend to herself again.

Of course Grimshaw took them to Powell's to finish out the day.

"Why does everything with you have to do with books?" Scarlett grumbled as she and Mitchell trailed him through the massive bookstore. Crowds of tourists were taking pictures in front of the doors; just as many of them shuffled down the aisles with the wide-eyed wonder of people who apparently had never been to a bookstore before. "Chrissie told you to entertain *me*, not yourself."

"I am entertaining you." He lifted a huge art book titled *Nudes Throughout History* from the shelf and flashed it at her. She didn't bother to hide her disgust. Beneath Grimshaw's academic, devil-may-care facade beat the most predictable heart in the world. "I didn't get you a birthday present, so you should pick one out. You can get anything you want."

Scarlett noticed the price sticker on the book—a whopping eighty-five dollars—and pointed at it. "Okay. You convinced me. I'll take it."

Grimshaw visibly blanched and hurried to slip it back on the shelf. Behind them, Mitchell laughed. "Scarlett's got your number, Grim.

You're honor bound to buy it now. For an extra fifteen, they'll probably even gift wrap it for you."

"No way. Chrissie only gave me a hundred bucks for the whole day. Pick a romance novel or something."

Scarlett swiveled to stare at Grimshaw. He'd recovered his color by this time, once again back to endlessly flopping his hair and stopping to catch the flash of his reflection in every passing window.

"I'm sorry. Say that again?"

"What? About getting a romance novel? I don't know what you like to read. You seem like the type to salivate over some duke rescuing damsels from the back of his horse."

Scarlett gave a *tsk* of annoyance. She did, in fact, enjoy dukes rescuing damsels, but she'd never admit it to Grimshaw. Especially since he was clearly trying to give those dukes a run for their money in the rakish asshole department.

"I meant about Chrissie giving you money to take me out. All those Ms. Pac-Man games and frozen yogurt and stuff—she paid for it? Not you?"

"I mean, yeah. I'm a college student. I don't have extra cash lying around to blow on my girlfriend's best friend's birthday. She paid for my gas down here, too." Grimshaw shrugged. "It's not like it means anything to her. Her parents are loaded."

Mitchell gave an uncomfortable cough. "What Grim means is that Chrissie would do anything for you—"

Scarlett cut off the younger cousin by flinging up her hand. "I don't need you to tell me what Chrissie would or wouldn't do for me. She was *my* friend long before she ever heard the name Grimshaw Pemberly." Tamping down the urge to grab the art book and bring it down on Grimshaw's head, she said, "Did she tell you to keep this a secret from me? To pretend like this was all done from the goodness of your heart?"

"Chill, Scarlett. What difference does it make where the money came from? It's not like anyone is asking you to pay it back."

"How much did she pay you for gas?" Scarlett demanded.

"I dunno. Another hundred, I think? It's a long drive from Seattle, and I had to blow off two classes to be here. Her parents gave her the cash, so it's not a big deal."

"Okay. Then I'd like to go home now."

She spoke the words without inflection—a rare thing for her, as if she was channeling her inner Chrissie. The sensation was uncomfortable, like wearing a skin that was three sizes too big. For that brief moment, she wasn't a useless granddaughter who was making her friend pick up all her slack. She wasn't a straight-C student with no real prospects for the future and dreams as wide as the sky. She was just the person who got things done, who quietly and carefully picked her way through life as though determined not to disturb anyone's peace.

"Of course you do," Mitchell said. He patted an awkward hand on her shoulder. "We'll take you back, won't we, Grim?"

Grimshaw, who would have benefited from his cousin's less polished but more authentic manner, merely smirked. "No can do, I'm afraid. I have my orders. You can go home at five o'clock and not a minute earlier."

"Fine." Scarlett turned on her heel and pushed past the crowds of tourists to the door. "I'll take the bus. You can pocket any leftover cash your girlfriend paid you to entertain me. Your services are no longer required."

"Scarlett, don't be like that." Grimshaw loped after her with his long, easy strides. "I'm sorry, okay?"

He didn't sound sorry—not even a little—but Scarlett stopped and waited for him to catch up anyway.

"Do you have any idea how much she hates asking her parents

for money?" Scarlett asked. "How much she hates asking them for *anything*?"

"Uh…no?"

Of course he didn't. Because he didn't know Chrissie the way Scarlett did—deeply, viscerally, like she was the twin she'd once absorbed inside her cell by cell.

"They don't deserve her, and neither do you," she snapped.

Somewhere in the back of her mind, she registered Mitchell touching her elbow in concern, someone else jostling her other elbow as they pushed out of the bookstore. Something fell to the pavement next to her—a bag of books, probably—but she wasn't aware of anything but her own seething whirl of emotion.

I don't deserve her, either. None of us do, but that doesn't stop us from taking what we can anyway.

"Is…everything okay?" Mitchell asked, looking back and forth between them. "Are we going to the party now?"

"It's up to Scarlett," Grimshaw said. He shrugged in a way that showed just how little he understood about this situation, his girlfriend, the whole freaking world. "If she wants to ruin all Chrissie's plans over a few hundred bucks that her parents can definitely afford, I'm not going to stop her."

In that moment, Scarlett desperately wished she was the kind of person who would get on that bus—who could stick to the force of her convictions and refuse to take anything else from the friend who'd already given her so much.

But she wasn't. She wasn't even close. In the end, she was just another greedy, self-important, boring-ass Grimshaw Pemberly.

"No, we can wait until Chrissie is ready." Scarlett's voice sounded defeated even to her own ears. "She's obviously put a lot of time and effort into this party. The least we can do is show up when she's asked us to."

"Thatta girl." Grimshaw slung his arm over Scarlett's shoulder and led her back into the bookstore. He squeezed as though to say he understood just how far she'd fallen—and just how willing she was to accept this state. "Now let's go get you a cheap, trashy romance novel—emphasis on the 'cheap.' If we don't at least *pretend* to make it look like I care enough about you to get you a birthday present, then we're both screwed."

Chapter Seventeen

BLACK RIVER FALLS, WISCONSIN

Present Day

THE THREE-HOUR DRIVE FROM THE CHAIN hotel to their first stop at Black River Falls—home of the Karner Blue Butterfly Festival—was one of the longest of Chrissie's life.

She wished she was a teenager like River, who could simply plug in a pair of headphones as a way to avoid interaction with her fellow passengers, or a professional talker like Scarlett, who could while away the time in an endless stream of chatter that conveyed both nothing and everything, but she wasn't.

She was a suburban single mom who'd spent the better part of the night crying into her pillow—and she both looked and felt the part.

"According to this, Black River Falls is the place to be if you want to go fishing or if you're in witness protection and want to make sure the Mafia never finds you to finish the job they started." Scarlett folded up her map and tossed it in the back seat, narrowly missing River in the process. "Personally, I'd choose somewhere like Florida if I had to go into hiding from the mob. Not only is it a hell of a lot warmer than this place, but you could easily get lost in the crowd. The best you could do here is slip on a black bear costume and hope a hunter takes you out before a hit man does."

Chrissie parked the car in a lot designated for daily ATV use and sat with her hands on the wheel. Long after the engine stopped purring, she found herself unable to move from that position, her hands locked in their ten and two positions.

"Sooo," Scarlett said, imbuing the word with enough syllables to make all three of them feel uncomfortable. "Did you need to use the restroom, or are we just here for the view? Because I gotta say—at the very least, I expect a water feature if we're going to do some local sightseeing."

"River, could you please give us a minute?" Chrissie said by way of answer. She didn't move her hands, but she did manage to toss a tight smile over her shoulder at the girl. "I know there's not much to do here, but—"

"Say no more." River had the door open and was halfway out before Chrissie could finish her sentence. "I saw some bored-looking guys over by the entrance. At this point, I figure I'm better off with them than stuck another minute between the two of you."

Chrissie felt an immediate sense of guilt and was about to protest, but Scarlett's rich chuckle stopped her short. "Sorry, River. We haven't been very good company, have we? We'll have a loud, cathartic airing of our grievances and be back to normal for the next leg of the trip."

Chrissie didn't share her friend's amusement. Loud catharsis had never been her way of dealing with problems, and Scarlett knew it.

Naturally, that didn't stop Scarlett from making the attempt.

"So much for being a caretaker," she said as she pushed her seat back and gave a languid stretch. In honor of her medical condition being outed, she'd opted to wear a formfitting tank top for the day. It highlighted not only her too-thin frame, but also the fact that she wasn't wearing one of her prosthetic bras.

And why would she? The cat was out of the bag, the lies exposed. And Scarlett, in true Scarlett fashion, now only wanted to put it behind her. Her past was a graveyard of all the skeletons that had been ripped unceremoniously from her closet and just as unceremoniously discarded once they'd been freed.

"It's not like this was unexpected," Scarlett added in a voice that was far too irreverent. "Mantle field irradiation is a bitch. They told me that when I was a kid, and they've continued telling me every year since. I should've had my stupid boobs removed years ago and saved myself the trouble, but you know how vain I am."

Chrissie was in no mood to be charmed. "It's not funny. When were you going to tell me? Why did you go through all that on your own?"

"I didn't. Mitchell was with me for most of it. He's been a real sweetheart during the whole process."

It was a good thing Chrissie was sitting down, because that bit of news—dropped like an anvil to the head—would have knocked her flat.

"You're talking to Mitchell again? Since when?"

"I wouldn't say that *talking* has been our primary activity." Scarlett laughed and slid a hand over to forestall Chrissie from jumping out of the car—a thing she hadn't even realized she was in danger of doing until she felt the press of her friend's palm. "I'm sorry. I shouldn't joke about that. If Mitchell hadn't been there to ferry me to doctor's appointments and force-feed me protein shakes, I probably would have broken down and called you. But he got a job at some tech company in San Jose last year, so he *was* there. And I hoped..."

She let her voice trail off and slid her hand from Chrissie's. For what was probably the first time since they'd started this trip, the insouciant mask slipped away and she looked exactly like what she was—a thirty-four-year old woman battling cancer for the second time. The pixie-short hair, which had looked so chic a few days ago, now spoke of a struggle to grow back what had likely been lost to chemo. The way she slept all of two hours a night said the same thing. Scarlett had never been able to close her eyes when there was even a slight chance it might be the last time.

"I'm glad you had someone," Chrissie said and meant it. She meant the next part, too. "I just wish that someone had been me."

"I've already burdened you enough for one lifetime." Scarlett spoke so quietly that Chrissie had to strain to hear her. "Especially since I—"

Chrissie's phone rang before Scarlett could finish her sentence. She was tempted to ignore the call, since it seemed like the two of them were *finally* getting somewhere, but one glance at the screen showed her that it was from her daughter.

Chrissie winced. "Sorry. It's Kat. I have to take it."

"Of course you do," Scarlett said in a voice that was difficult to interpret. Even though Scarlett knew Chrissie didn't have a choice—that Kat, of necessity, had to come first—she'd always harbored an affectionate resentment over their relationship.

"Hey, Kitty Kat. What's up? You caught me at a good time. We're stopped at this cute little town—"

"Don't you dare call me Kitty Kat right now."

Chrissie pinched the bridge of her nose to keep her sigh from escaping. She should have known that a call could only presage disaster. "Is everything okay?" she asked, already knowing what the answer would be. "Lily? The cat? Walsh?"

Kat's snort of derision was loud enough to fill the whole car. "I'm surprised you managed to list Coach last. That must have taken all your self-control—*Oh, wait. You don't have any.*"

Scarlett waggled her fingers as if to take the phone, but Chrissie didn't hand it over. Something in Kat's voice felt different than her usual angst. This was more controlled, somehow. More dangerous. In some deep, untouched part of Chrissie's brain, she registered the voice as an exact copy of her own when she was doing her best not to give herself away, but this wasn't the moment for self-reflection. Not until the bomb ticking inside her daughter was defused.

"I'm not a mind reader, Kat. Just tell me what I did so I can fix it."

It was the wrong thing to say. "Lily has her dad's phone password. Did you know that? She gets on there all the time to buy stuff from Amazon."

"O-kay… Do you want my password? It's pretty easy. It's your birth date, only backwards."

"Omigod, Mom. I've known that for like ten years." Something like a sob sounded. "Lily saw the picture. We both did. How *could* you?"

In that moment, Chrissie felt the earth open up from underneath her. In the grand scheme of things, her teenage daughter learning that she was a hot-blooded thirty-four-year-old woman who wore bikinis and took pictures of herself and sometimes accidentally sent them to hot-blooded forty-eight-year-old men wasn't important. Awkward, yes. Unfortunate, sure. But Chrissie was literally sitting inside a car with her best friend in the whole world—a best friend who had scar tissue where her breasts used to be, and who may or may not be facing a long road of recovery ahead of her.

Friends got sick. Brothers died. Parents stopped caring. The world freaking *hurt*, and Chrissie was tired of tiptoeing around a girl who'd never experienced that truth for herself.

"For crying out loud, Kat, calm down. It's just a picture."

Out of the corner of her eye, she could see Scarlett clapping her hands in support of this response, but Kat literally howled into the phone.

"It's not just anything!" Kat cried. "It's *everything*. Coach is the *one* adult who doesn't talk down to me, who isn't nice to me just because he, like, pushed me out of his vagina or whatever. And now you're trying to take that away from me, too?"

"I'm not—"

"What? Secretly pining after my volleyball coach? Dangling your naked body in front of him until it ruins everything?"

"Kat, don't—"

"It's fine. Whatever. You already drove my dad so far away that he wants nothing to do with me. Why not do it again with Coach? Or my science teacher who thinks I might have a chance of a scholarship to OSU? Heck—there's a super-nice old man who always smiles at me when I grab a breakfast sandwich at the gas station on the way to school. You might as well shove your tits at him and see what happens."

The bottom of the earth closed up again. Chrissie planted her feet so firmly against the gas that if the car had been on, they'd have shot through the parking lot back onto the freeway.

"Kathleen Genevieve Thomas, what did you just say to me?"

A scream sounded, so loud it could have belonged to a fire truck.

But it didn't. It was her daughter, her beating heart, the best thing she'd ever done.

"It's not fair," Kat wailed. "You'll ruin everything. You'll take him in and mother him and *smother* him. And when he can't take it another second, he'll disappear just like my dad and my grandparents and everyone else."

Chrissie didn't want to say it. She didn't want to ask.

She did anyway.

"And that's not enough for you? *I'm* not enough?"

Kat seemed to age a hundred years in the silence that followed. "You know what?" she said. "I hope you and Coach do get married. I hope things are so good between you that he formally adopts me. Then, when things fall apart, I can live with him instead. I'll cut you out of my life, the same way you did with your own parents, and you'll finally see what it's like."

Chrissie didn't want to ask the next part, either, but she was in too far to stop now. "What *what* is like?"

Kat was almost triumphant as she shot her parting words. "To be alone. To have no one in your life but *you*. To know that if I had a thousand different lives in a thousand different bodies, I wouldn't pick you to be my mom in a single one."

By the time Kat hung up the phone, Chrissie felt as though she'd been slapped so hard that her ears would never stop ringing. She could see Scarlett's mouth moving and feel her phone being lifted from her fingers, but no sound registered other than a strange, eerie whistling like wind through the Grand Canyon.

Which, now that she thought about it, was a sound she'd never heard before and probably never would. The Grand Canyon was just one of the several hundred places she hadn't visited. She'd been too busy trying to be the best mom in the world to the only person who mattered.

And too busy failing every step of the way.

Scarlett and River tried to cheer her up in a dozen different ways.

When highlighting their own teenage temper tantrums didn't work—*Don't you remember that time I told my grandma that if she fed me one more piece of kale I'd go on a hunger strike for the rest of my life? You wouldn't believe some of the things I threatened to do to my dad after he got remarried. At one point, I even considered framing him for murder.*—they moved on to dangling enticing pit stops in front of her.

"Look! This one is called Cave of the Mounds. That sounds almost as dirty as Knob Lick, Kentucky."

"Oooh, or what about the Museum of Historic Torture Devices? That'll help put things in perspective."

With each new attempt, Chrissie managed a smile, but each one seemed to cost her more and more.

"I'm sorry, you guys. I appreciate you trying, but all I want right now is to get to Chicago before nightfall." Her smile got even more strained at that, pulling at her scalp like a too-tight ponytail. "It would be nice if I manage to help at least *one* person in this lifetime. If Kat's out, I might as well do what I can for River."

Since Chrissie was in the back seat—ostensibly to nap but really just to lick her wounds in peace—she could see the very obvious look that Scarlett and River shared.

"I know, I know." She slumped down in her seat, rendering her seat belt ineffective. "I'm being more dramatic than Kat. Just let me sit in my misery for a few hours, okay? It's been a long time since I've thrown myself a truly rocking pity party. I'd hate to leave this one early."

With that, she slapped on a pair of headphones and turned up the volume on her phone. As this was set to an audiobook narrated by Juliet Stevenson, whose lilting upper-crust voice could soothe all the world's ills, and not the overly emotional lyrics favored by girls of Kat's and River's ilk, the end result wasn't the same, but Chrissie didn't care. The more distracted she was, the less likely she was to hear the memory of Kat's voice echoing around inside her head.

If I had a thousand lives in a thousand bodies, I wouldn't pick you to be my mom.

It was painfully similar to what she used to think back when she was a girl. On the rare occasions when she'd find herself at the dinner table with her mom, or her mom would pass through the music room where Chrissie sat tickling the ivories in an attempt to draw her out, she'd indulge in that very same fantasy—a world where she had literally any other parent on earth. Someone forthright but gentle like Scarlett's grandmother. Someone who screamed and stomped all over the floor like the people who lived in the apartment above them. Maybe even someone who was a combination of the two—loud and loving and *alive.*

As much as she'd enjoyed those thoughts, however, she'd never actually said them out loud. It would have been a cruel thing to do—and no matter how much she resented the way her parents protected themselves after the loss of Malcolm, she couldn't find it in her to hurt them.

Not when life—and death—had already done it for her.

She brushed at a wayward tear with the back of her hand and hoped that no one in the front seat had seen it. If they had, they were discreet enough not to mention it because the car continued flying down the highway at Scarlett's usual breakneck pace.

Despite Chrissie's reservations about letting Scarlett take the wheel when her health was in flux, she was glad for the reprieve. She wouldn't say she *regretted* the decision to take River to her great-aunt's house, but she'd be glad to shut the door on this part of the trip. She and Scarlett still had a lot of talking left to do, and it would be much easier once they were on their own again.

Thanks to Scarlett's lead foot and the fact that no one felt much like eating, they made it to Chicago well before darkness started to fall. Despite Chrissie's mood and the fact that Ms. Stevenson's voice was making her long for the rough moors of England instead of midwestern urban sprawl, she found herself growing interested in her surroundings. Large cities had never been a favorite of hers, as evidenced by the fact that she'd moved to Medford from Portland as soon as Kat was born, but there was something to be said for the bustling evidence of activity all around them. People honked and swerved as if they were on the way to the most important meeting of their lives, and she found herself getting caught up in anticipation as they wound closer to the neighborhoods near the south end of the lake.

She also managed to pull her head out of the clouds enough to realize that the car had become almost as tense as it had been during the phone call with Kat.

"What if she's not home?" River asked as they waited at a stoplight underneath the freeway. She chewed nervously on her fingernails. "What if she, like, moved and didn't tell me? Or she only offered to let me live with her because she knew I'd never take her up on it?"

The mom in Chrissie immediately pushed her own problems aside. She knew Scarlett would hate it—that this call to action was the only thing able to pull her out of her slump—but there was no stopping that particular train once it left the station.

To her surprise, Scarlett beat her to the punch.

"If she's not home, we'll go have a nice dinner somewhere and try again in a few hours," Scarlett said in a short, matter-of-fact voice that reminded Chrissie so much of Nan that her heart squeezed. "If she moved and didn't tell you, we'll get a hotel nearby and hunt down a forwarding address. And if she shuts the door in your face, we'll go in through a window and make her see reason. It's as easy as that."

River rallied under this approach. "Yeah. Okay. Thanks. I don't know why I'm getting so freaked out over this."

"I do," Scarlett said, and then she surprised Chrissie even more. "A similar loss happened to me when I was your age. I went from having a home and a family to being entirely on my own overnight. Believe me when I say that you're handling it a hell of a lot better than I did."

The speech, Chrissie knew, wasn't meant for River. But River was the one who spoke first.

"What did you do?" she asked. "When your world fell apart?"

Scarlett glanced at Chrissie then, but it was only a brief flicker in the rearview mirror as she pulled the car up in front of a two-story apartment building of dark red brick.

"I can't tell you that," she said as she turned the car off and plunged them all into silence. "I made a promise a long time ago to take that secret to my grave."

Chrissie liked Great-Aunt Rose on sight.

"Oh, finally. *Finally!*"

Those had been her only words when the door swung open to reveal three women standing on the landing—one of whom she recognized and two of whom could have been saleswomen peddling Avon through the portals of time, for all she knew. She hadn't hugged River or burst into tears—two things Chrissie felt sure she would have done in the same situation—but she did usher them inside without a moment's hesitation.

The house smelled strongly of cat and turpentine, but not in an unpleasant way, especially to one who had long since become inured to the power of ammonia-scented urine. Equally strange, but not necessarily in a bad way, were the stacks of half-finished canvases resting against every available wall.

"I wasn't expecting company, and I wouldn't have bothered cleaning if I had, so you'll just have to excuse the mess," Great-Aunt Rose said as she led them through a narrow, cluttered hallway to the kitchen. Three cats lay curled up on the table, each one taking a woven placemat for itself. "I don't have anything to drink but tea that went stale a good three years ago, and you'll have to drink it black. Alecto, Tisiphone, and Megaera got the last of the milk this morning."

Chrissie smiled at the names of the cats—the three Furies, if she wasn't mistaken—but politely accepted the offer of a beverage.

"We can't stay long," she said as she poked a tentative finger at one of the cats, a calico with half an ear bitten off. "We only came to drop River off before we continue on our way. We, uh, *can* leave her here with you, right? She said you invited her, but—"

"But I'm a cranky old recluse who looks like she cooks children in her oven and eats them for dinner?" Great-Aunt Rose suggested. Since she did, in fact, look exactly like this, with a paint-covered smock and her long, steely gray hair held up with a spatula shoved through it like a spear, Chrissie kept her mouth shut. "Don't worry. River doesn't have nearly enough meat on her bones to make a decent meal. It'll take me at least a year to fatten her up properly."

At this, River promptly burst into tears.

Chrissie's heart lurched at the sight of the heavy mascara starting to run down River's cheeks, but Great-Aunt Rose was already on top of things. With a short but maternal cluck, she handed the teenager a napkin.

"No need for waterworks, girl," she said. "I won't eat you unless things get really desperate. Why don't you get the table cleaned up while I finish this tea?"

Chrissie was forced to acknowledge the effectiveness of this approach in place of the comforting embrace and gentle nothings she'd have offered in this situation. River straightened and dabbed her eyes. "Thanks," she said, a little shy. "I'm not usually like this. It's been a rough few months."

"Of course it has," Great-Aunt Rose said as she turned back to her task.

This was also the right thing to do. Faced with nothing but this stringent, no-nonsense support, River drew a deep breath and immediately set to work. She gently lifted the cats from the table, cleared off the stacks of newspapers and other debris, and even managed to wipe a dish towel over the surface before the four of them sat down to enjoy their stale tea.

Chrissie was too busy marveling at the success of both Scarlett and River's aunt in handling the girl to pay much attention to River's competence, but Scarlett's soft chuckle soon pulled her back.

"I'd offer to help, but you seem to have a handle on things," Scarlett said as she lifted the cat that had resettled onto her seat. "How'd you get to be such a good little housewife?"

"Stepsisters, remember?" River said. "Before I left, I was on nanny duty every day after school. Most weekends, too. My stepmom said I had to do my part."

Great-Aunt Rose fell to her own seat with the full force of her weight, which was on the generous side. Unlike her great-niece, she'd have made a delicious meal for any witch craving fresh meat.

"*That woman*," she spat—as in, literally spat—before making the motion of a cross over her chest. "I told your father she only wanted to get married for the free labor, but he never listens to me—not even when he was a kid and I had some actual sway over him. I'd have given anything to see their faces the morning after you left, with no breakfast on the table and that pack of brats howling to be fed. A more selfish, self-involved, self-serving pair of—"

"It's okay." River reached across the table and touched her great-aunt's arm. "I'm with you now. I mean…I *am* with you, right? I know you always said I was welcome to visit, and that you'd come get me if it was at all possible, but—"

"But nothing." The older woman pushed out her jaw in a way that reminded Chrissie forcibly of Scarlett at her most determined. "You'll stay with me for as long as you need. I'm only sorry I couldn't do more to get you here. I'm sorry for a lot of things I can't change, but I was never one to cry over spilled milk. That's what the cats are for."

Scarlett had yet to sip her tea, but she sat blowing on it as though the movement of the steam across her lips was enough. "Amen to that," she murmured.

Great-Aunt Rose and Scarlett shared a knowing look. "You too, honey?"

"Like you wouldn't believe."

A pause settled over the table, but it didn't last long. Scarlett flashed a tight smile and pushed back from the table, her tea still largely untouched. "If everything is good here, should we hit the road,

Chrissie? We're ahead of schedule to reach Vermont, but there's still that other thing we need to take care of..."

There was no need to say more. *That other thing* could easily be code for Scarlett wanting to make a polite escape, but it could also mean any of the rest: the breast cancer, the mastectomy, the fight with Kat, the fact that Scarlett was seeing Mitchell again. There was enough fodder there for *three* cross-country road trips.

But "It's up to River" was what Chrissie said. She turned toward the girl with a determined smile. "If you'd like us to stick around, we're happy to park in Chicago for as long as you might need us. We won't leave until you're ready."

River leaped to her feet and threw her arms around Chrissie's neck. It was the fierce, ferocious kind of hug that could only happen after a long and complicated relationship—or after a young woman found a helping hand when she needed it most.

"Thanks for bringing me here. And for doing it without question. There aren't many people in the world who would do the same."

"That's not true." Chrissie hugged the girl back just as fiercely. "Most of us don't get the chance, that's all."

She had no idea how long they stood in the middle of that kitchen, hugging and delaying their goodbyes, but when they pulled apart again, it was to find that Great-Aunt Rose and Scarlett had discreetly left them to their privacy. Only the cats remained, two of which had returned to the table and were sniffing at the discarded cups of tea.

"Actually, there is one thing you can do for me before you leave." River gestured toward Chrissie's purse, which hung from the back of one of the chairs. "Is your list still in there?"

Chrissie blinked. She'd been so sure she was about to be asked for a small loan that it took her a moment to register the remark.

"The one Scarlett's making me keep? Of course." She fished out the crisscrossed slip of paper and handed it to the girl. "Did you want to keep it?"

"No. I want to add to it." River scrawled a brief sentence before handing the paper back. There, underneath the last item—*I don't have to explain myself to ANYONE*—she had added another line:

Your daughter is lucky to have you.

Chrissie felt the tears welling up in her eyes. "Thank you for saying that, but—"

"But nothing. It's the truth. She might not realize it right now, but she will someday, and she'll come to you with her heart wide open. I promise you that."

Chrissie nodded, wishing more than believing this to be true. While she hesitated, River took her lower lip between her teeth and started chewing on one of her piercings. "Can I say one more thing before you go?" she asked and then rushed on without waiting for an answer. "It's about those pills I saw in Scarlett's bag the other night."

Chrissie didn't realize how hard she'd gripped the back of the chair until she felt her fingernails starting to push back from their beds. "The pills?"

"I'm not a doctor, obviously, and I have no idea what her situation is, but I remember my mom taking a lot of different medications for a lot of different reasons. And those meds…well. Let's just say they weren't the ones she was taking when she was trying to get well again." She paused, and the whole world seemed to pause with her. "I'm so sorry, Chrissie."

"Sorry for what?"

"I think you should talk to Scarlett," was all River would say. Considering the way she choked off at the end, it was more than enough. "And the sooner, the better."

Chapter Eighteen

PORTLAND, OR

2009

LAUREL SANDERSON DIED THE SAME WAY she lived—quietly and without fuss, her final thoughts centered on the granddaughter she'd dedicated her life to.

"I know it's small consolation right now, but you won't have to worry about money for a while."

Grandma's estate lawyer, a slip of a woman with the most enormous pair of black-rimmed glasses Scarlett had ever seen, pushed a piece of paper across the dining room table at her. Since Scarlett's hands were clasped in her lap and seemed inclined to stay that way, Chrissie had to reach for it.

This past week, Chrissie had been doing a lot of things Scarlett couldn't. She cooked and she cleaned. She made funeral arrangements. She brushed Scarlett's hair and teeth and forced her into the shower at regular intervals. The first time her friend had made her shower, she'd forgotten to check in and entered the bathroom an hour later to find Scarlett balled up in the tub, shivering as ice-cold water cascaded down her naked body.

"But this is a check for half a million dollars," Chrissie said as she stared at it. "That can't be right."

"I assure you it is. Laurel took out a life insurance policy the same day she was granted custody of Scarlett. She wanted to make sure her granddaughter would be taken care of if anything happened to her."

Scarlett's hands remained clenched in her lap, as in stasis as the rest of her.

Grandma is gone. I'm all alone. There's no one left who's obligated to love me.

She still had Chrissie, of course. And somewhere out there, the mother who'd given her life. And Mitchell and Grimshaw, not to mention a host of school friends who'd been posting all over Facebook about how sorry they were for her loss. None of them mattered except for Chrissie. If she were to leave, if she were to decide that Scarlett was too much to handle on her own—

"Give half of the money to Chrissie," Scarlett said. They were the first words she'd spoken in over an hour, so it was understandable that both parties were taken aback.

"I'm sorry?" the lawyer said at the same time as Chrissie's vehement "Absolutely not."

"I mean it. She was as much your grandmother as mine. She would have wanted you to have it." She turned to the lawyer, pleased to find that her hands had unclenched and were now on top of the table like a normal person's. "I can do that, right? You can be in charge of splitting everything down the middle?"

"I can." The lawyer spoke slowly and looked between the two girls even slower still. "But I don't recommend it. You'll be surprised how quickly this gets eaten up by funeral costs and taxes and—"

"Do it. I don't care."

"Maybe not, but *I* do." Chrissie crossed her arms and set her beautiful face in her toughest, most determined mask.

Someday, that face would save the world, but for now, all Scarlett wanted was for it to promise never to leave her. A quarter of a million dollars seemed like a fair enough price tag for that.

"I'm sorry, Ms. Kahul, but I don't accept. If Scarlett insists on giving away half her inheritance, you can send my share to the kids' cancer center at OHSU."

"Chrissie!"

Chrissie's expression didn't change. "What? If you're going to throw money around like it doesn't matter, then I'm going to do it, too. What happened to Paris? To your dreams of getting out of Portland? Nan just gave you the ticket you needed to make that happen. You aren't throwing it away out of some stupid sense of personal justice. I won't let you."

The lawyer coughed and pushed back from the table. There wasn't enough room in the tiny apartment for her to do it properly, so her chair thunked against the wall.

"I'll just, ah, give you two a few days to discuss this, okay? I'll keep the check with me for now, but I'm ready to hand it over whenever you give me the green light."

The lawyer dropped a hand on Scarlett's shoulder and let it sit there. People had been touching her a lot ever since the ambulance had come to take Grandma away, lifting her gently from the chair where she'd spent so much of the last few months of her life. They'd accidentally taken the crocheted blanket with her, but Chrissie had spent hours on the phone to get it back.

It sat now, washed and folded, at the foot of Scarlett's bed. Chrissie had been the one to do that, too.

Scarlett fought the urge to shrug the woman's hand away and nodded. "Yeah. Sure. Whatever."

The door had barely clicked behind her when Chrissie turned on her—and she turned *hard*. "You know she held on just for you, right?"

There was so much anger in Chrissie's voice that Scarlett had to do a double take. Was that her best friend speaking to her like that? When her grandmother had just *died*?

"What are you talking about?"

Chrissie's chair went the same way as the lawyer's, clanging so hard against the wall that an answering thud sounded from the other side.

"You know exactly what I'm talking about. Your grandmother. The one who died two weeks to the day after you turned eighteen. The one who probably had to scrimp and save every single day for the past fifteen years to cover that life insurance payment."

Scarlett could feel all her blood draining away. "Why are you yelling at me?"

"Because you need it," Chrissie said—no, *yelled*. "These past six months were torture for her. She was in pain. She was disoriented. She suffered. For every single second of every single day, she suffered."

"She… Chrissie. *Chrissie*." Scarlett, who had not cried when she woke up to find her grandmother's dead body, who had not cried when the ambulance took her away for the last time, who had not cried even when the funeral home called to tell her the date of the last time she'd ever see her grandmother again, felt her eyes well up. "That's not true. She had good days as well as bad ones. You were here. You saw it."

The look Chrissie leveled on her turned her blood cold. "What I saw was her putting on a brave face for you. But I also saw her relief during your birthday party. She might not have remembered the day in time to make your cinnamon rolls, but she remembered when she saw you blow out the candles."

"I don't understand," Scarlett said, though she did. She understood everything.

And Chrissie, drat her, knew it. "You're a lot of things, Scarlett Sanderson, but stupid isn't one of them. If you give me one single penny of that money, I'll never forgive you. She bought that insurance policy for you. She *lived* for you. The least you can do is live for her in return."

Without missing a beat, Chrissie grabbed the handset of the landline that Scarlett's grandmother had insisted on keeping well into the twenty-first century.

"Yes, hello. This is Chrissie Thomas. I'm calling about the church for Laurel Sanderson's funeral service on Saturday. Could you please confirm that it's still available?"

She spoke with the ease of long practice for this and the dozen other calls to follow: to the county clerk offices to get copies of Grandma's death certificate, to the ladies from church who'd offered casseroles and baked goods en masse, to the funeral home and the headstone engraver and the other twenty thousand people it seemed were involved in the spectacle of loss.

Later, Scarlett would remember that Chrissie had done all this before. Later, she would sob fat, grateful tears for the seventeen-year-old girl who took the reins in her hands so Scarlett could have the space she needed to grieve.

Right now, however, she took one look at her composed, saintly best friend and stormed out the door.

There wasn't a dry eye in the house.

Thanks to Chrissie's careful planning, the house was a packed one. Grandma had been an active part of both her community and her church, but Scarlett had no idea how active until she was escorted to her seat in the front row. She'd have preferred to sit in the back, away from the casket and the flowers and the staring, sympathetic crowd, but that apparently wasn't a choice. She was Grandma's closest family, which meant she was the one everyone had come to see.

In typical Chrissie fashion, arrangements had been made to ensure that Scarlett wasn't alone throughout the ordeal. A somber, suited Grimshaw greeted her at the door to the church. A somber, suited Grimshaw walked her down the aisle to her reserved seat. And a not-quite-as-somber, suited Grimshaw passed her a flask and encouraged her to drink as much as she wanted while they waited for the service to begin.

"Chrissie's orders," he said as she accepted the flask.

"Chrissie told you to get me drunk?" Scarlett whispered as she slumped low in her seat and discreetly tipped back the contents. The strong, unpleasant burn of a college boy's idea of whiskey scored her throat.

"Not exactly." Grimshaw took the flask back and kicked back his own discreet tipple before grinning at her in a way that *no one* had grinned at her for weeks. People sighed and frowned, sometimes even ran away to avoid talking to her altogether, but they didn't smile. Scarlett thought she'd never seen anything so wonderful as that bright flash of teeth. "But she said to make sure you're taken care of, and this seemed like the best way to do it." His grin dimmed slightly. "My grandma died last year. She didn't raise me or anything the way yours did, but it still sucked."

For some reason, that brief summation of events coupled with the cheap alcohol was the exact combination Scarlett needed right now. Thanks to Grimshaw, she was able to sit through endless hymns and prayers, listen to a dozen eulogies that painted her grandmother into an unrecognizable character, and even watch with a semblance of serenity as Chrissie took her place at the piano and played Grandma's favorite song.

That was when the dry eyes really disappeared. Handkerchiefs were whipped out and tissues passed down the aisle, everyone sobbing as the repeated *hallelujahs* rose from the piano like a snake being charmed out of its basket.

"Oh wow." Even Grimshaw seemed touched by the tribute—though he might have just as easily been touched by the sight of Chrissie sitting ethereal and serene as her fingers flew over the keys, a decorous black dress hugging her body and an actual string of pearls at her neck. "Where did Chrissie learn to play like that?"

Despite the several people urging them to hush, Scarlett turned to face him. "You've never heard her practice?"

He shook his head, sipped, and passed Scarlett the flask. "No. Never."

"She didn't tell you about all the lessons she has to take?" Scarlett took a long sip in an attempt to rally her thoughts. Was he being serious? Had Chrissie really shut him out of this part of her life? "Or about her…brother?"

Grimshaw's brows rose into his swooped hairline. "She has a brother?"

Scarlett wasn't sure why those four words pleased her so much, but they did. She liked thinking of the vast difference between the Chrissie that Grimshaw knew and the Chrissie she did.

She doesn't love him. She never has. He's just some bookish yogurt boy she's practicing on until she finds the real deal, and he has no idea.

This feeling of satisfaction only grew when Grimshaw frowned and ran his fingers through his hair. "I'm not even sure why we're together," he whispered glumly.

Scarlett drank a toast to that and then, as the song ended and everyone gave in to their sobs, she drank a toast to that, too. "Tell me all about it," she soothed.

Grimshaw was only too happy to comply. "She says she's fine with the way we are, but I dunno. If that was true, wouldn't she be less… *distant*? It's like she's the Platonic ideal of a girlfriend instead of the real deal. Perfect but untouchable, like a chair I'll never get a chance to sit on."

Scarlett knew this was just Grimshaw's Introduction to Philosophy class talking, and that he didn't mean to imbue his words with such heavy sexual innuendo, but she laughed anyway. Since the flask was empty by this time, he laughed back, which set her off even more.

"If you want to sit on someone, all you have to do is ask," Scarlett said, avoiding the curious glances from the sobbing masses around her.

One of the nice things about losing the most important person in your life was that you could laugh at her funeral all you wanted, and the most that anyone could do about it was judge from their safe, lofty, no-dead-grandmother heights. No one would call her out for inappropriate behavior, even if she were to slip out of this nightmare and disappear into one of the dark hallways.

In fact…

As she tottered to her feet and pushed out of the pew, she caught a glimpse of Chrissie. Her friend had yet to get up from the piano, her hands at rest as they sat clasped in her lap. She looked for all the world as though she'd been born for this exact moment—dry-eyed, calm, prepared to face the worst that life had to offer without so much as a hair out of place. There wasn't even a change in her expression as she watched Grimshaw take Scarlett by the hand and lead her away, both of them tripping over their feet as they made good their escape.

The same could not be said of the person just inside the doorway to the church, standing awkwardly in a navy blue suit that was two sizes too small for his lanky frame and clutching a bouquet of drooping carnations that were somehow both too much and not enough for their intended purpose.

"Grim, what are you doing?" Mitchell hissed as he looked first at the flask clutched in one of Grimshaw's hands and then at the other, which tightly held Scarlett's own. "The service isn't over yet."

"It's over when I say it's over." Grimshaw proved himself worthy of every inch of his six-foot brooding perfection by looming over his cousin and leering, "Scarlett is upset, so I'm taking her somewhere different. Somewhere better."

"It's a funeral. *Everywhere* is better than this. That's not the point." Mitchell turned his hurt, puzzled expression on Scarlett. "C'mon. I'll take you back in. I'm sure no one will notice if we slip in through the side."

Scarlett recoiled from him and those sad, pathetic carnations as though they were both poised to attack.

"I don't want to go back in. I don't want anything to do with all those people crying their eyes out and telling stories about Grandma like any of it matters. Chrissie will take care of it for me. Chrissie takes care of everything."

"Yeah," Grimshaw added on a hiccup. "And what's more, Chrissie *likes* it."

Grimshaw pushed past his cousin easily, his larger bulk and alcohol-fueled belligerence making him the physical superior of the two. Mitchell staggered back, the petals of the flowers falling to the tiled floor in a flurry of faded colors.

"Why are you guys acting like this? I thought you loved Chrissie."

Scarlett would never be able to say for sure which of them Mitchell was talking to. His eyes were trained on his cousin, but the question belonged to Scarlett and Scarlett alone.

Because she did love Chrissie. She loved her more than any other person on the planet, more than the combination of every single attendee reciting psalms in the next room.

She also knew that if one more person sang her friend's praises today, Scarlett would scream. Just once, couldn't Chrissie drop the perfect facade and show how much she was hurting inside? For one day—the day of her grandmother's funeral—couldn't she be the hot mess so Scarlett could step up and be the heroine?

"Chrissie has nothing to do with this," Scarlett said as she and

Grimshaw stumbled-walked over the flowers and toward the exit. She didn't dare look over her shoulder at Mitchell for fear of what she'd find there.

Shock. Horror. Disappointment.

In other words, all the things she felt in herself and somehow couldn't contain.

Chapter Nineteen

CHICAGO, ILLINOIS

Present Day

"OKAY, SO THERE ARE A FEW things I think you'll really enjoy in Chicago." Scarlett sat across from Chrissie in a café that sold a much fancier brand of tea than what they'd been offered at Great-Aunt Rose's house—and with the price tag to match. A steaming pot of something called Apricot Amaretto sat between them, a timer on the table set to alert them when it had reached optimal stewing time. "The Museum of Contemporary Art is one of those things that everyone says you should go see, but it's supposed to be such good weather tomorrow that I don't think we should stay cooped up inside. Jackson Park has a ton of great outdoor spaces, and it's impossible to leave the city without doing the architecture river tour. I wouldn't mind driving you by the apartment where I used to live, and—"

The timer gave a cheerful chime, interrupting Scarlett in the middle of a flow of chatter that she was almost certainly using to avoid the real issue. Scarlett continued extolling the virtues of the Chicago tourist scene as she set about pouring the tea, either oblivious or uncaring of the fact that Chrissie hadn't yet tried to lodge a word in edgewise. There was nothing to say and even less to do, but that didn't stop Chrissie from gratefully sipping as she tried to marshal her thoughts into a semblance of order.

Without getting her hands on the pills inside Scarlett's purse, she had no way of knowing what made River so sure that Scarlett's condition was more serious than she was letting on. A teenager was hardly a trustworthy source of medical information, even if said teenager had witnessed the loss of a parent to a similar condition.

Then again, Chrissie had only been seventeen when she'd parceled out pills for Scarlett's grandmother, the colorful shapes filling the days of the week with depressing regularity. Even at that young age, she'd known *exactly* what each drug meant.

"Hello? Earth to Chrissie. Are you listening to a word I'm saying?"

Chrissie blinked, torn back to the present so suddenly that she almost dropped her cup. As her vision came into focus, she saw Scarlett with knit brows and dark shadows under her eyes.

The former made sense, given the strain between them; the latter if what River had said was true.

"Let me see the pills in your purse," Chrissie said suddenly. She reached for the bag dangling from the table hook, but no matter how sick Scarlett was, she still had the reflexes of a cat.

"What? Why? No." The bag was whisked behind Scarlett's back, but not before she added, "What did that wretched brat tell you? Dammit, I knew we should've left her back in Boise. Our trip was never supposed to include a third person. She's throwing everything off."

Chrissie's phone started ringing before she could respond.

"Oh, for Pete's sake. Kat is just as bad as River. That child has the worst timing known to mankind." Scarlett waved a hand at her. "Go ahead and answer it. I know you're dying to talk to her so she can make you cry again."

"In case you failed to notice, I haven't cried *once* since everyone started slinging insults and cancer diagnoses at me. I think I deserve some credit." Chrissie frowned down at the screen. The call wasn't from Kat, but Walsh—and it wasn't a voice call. He was videoing in. "But I'm going to take it outside, and if you follow me, I'll scream to everyone that you're trying to rob me."

"And everyone says *I'm* the dramatic one," Scarlett muttered. But she let Chrissie go outside without trying to follow.

"Oh, good. You're not on the road. I was afraid I might've caught you behind the wheel." Walsh's kind, smiling face was such a welcome sight that Chrissie almost made a liar out of herself and started bawling on the spot. She'd always felt a frisson of electricity when she looked at him—whether he was swishing through the gym in his track pants and matching jacket or coaxing her down for drinks in a hotel lobby in slacks and a button-down—but this was different. This was like coming home after a long, wearying journey and finding the one person you wanted most waiting behind the front door.

"We're stopping a few days in Chicago," she said as she sagged against the brick exterior of the café. Even that, a slight relaxation of her normally rigid posture, seemed to bring immeasurable relief. "At least I assume that's what we're doing. Scarlett won't tell me anything for sure. She's being…difficult."

Then she remembered who she was talking to.

"Sorry. I imagine you're not having too great of a time, either. How's the cleanup of Chernobyl going?"

"Oh, you know. Nuclear waste and mutant wildlife as far as the eye can see." He grimaced, the heavy lines of his face folding like an accordion. "I'm really sorry, Chrissie. I should've deleted that photo the second we finished texting. I don't know why I held on to it."

Chrissie felt like she was tiptoeing across a tight wire in a circus act, balancing a bar burdened on either side with heavy, oversized barbells. One of the barbells was Kat and one was Scarlett, and they were both doing their best to send her plummeting to her death.

She loved them both, she really did. And the right thing to do in this situation was to keep moving across the wire until all three of them were carried to safety. But the words on her stupid list kept flashing in her mind.

"I don't have to explain myself to anyone," she said aloud.

One of Walsh's brows rose. "What's that?"

"Nothing." Then, more forcefully. "*Nothing.* And I'm glad you kept that photo. In fact, I hope you have a secret copy of it stashed somewhere. I hope it haunts your dreams and keeps you lying awake long into the night."

"I…um…" On the screen, Walsh became a blur of movement. Footsteps pattered, a door closed shut, and he returned to stillness once again. The smile that had been on his face was now replaced by concern. "Have you and Scarlett been drinking? Are you somewhere safe? Are you close enough to your hotel to walk back?"

Chrissie laughed. She didn't know what strange magic about this man allowed her to laugh when her life was falling apart, but she wasn't about to question it. Not when the magic was weaving its spell tighter around her. "The only thing I've had to drink today is tea, although the first batch may have been laced with turpentine. Does that mean you haven't deleted the picture?"

The concern in his face transformed to what looked suspiciously like chagrin. "Am I allowed to plead the Fifth?"

A warm, liquid sensation replaced all of Chrissie's other emotions. All of a sudden, she wasn't standing next to a garbage-scented alleyway with the rumbling of the El one block over. She wasn't wearing yesterday's jeans and her favorite rainbow Crocs, her beautiful haircut now back to its regularly scheduled bundle on top of her head. She was just a woman talking to a man she liked, and who she was pretty sure liked her back.

"Good for you," she said. "I mean, *shame* on you, obviously, but I'm glad you kept it. If you want, I'll send you a few more to round out your collection."

"I…" On the screen, Walsh glanced nervously around before dropping his voice. Based on the glimpses of background she could see—dark blue wallpaper and a bookcase filled with wartime thrillers, the edge of a neatly made bed with a paisley quilt over the top—she was pretty sure he was in his bedroom. "Chrissie, are you sure you're not drunk? Or being held at gunpoint? Blink once for yes and twice for no."

Her laugh came a little less confidently this time. "Should I stop? Is this not okay?"

"Yes! I mean—no." He cleared his throat and fell to the bed. On one corner of the screen, Chrissie could just make out a patch of fake green grass. It was Rufio's pee carpet. *In Walsh's bedroom.* Any chance Chrissie had of making it out of this call with her whole heart disappeared in a flash.

"It's…amazing, actually," he said, his voice low. "You know how I feel about you—about you and Kat both."

Chrissie nodded, her throat too tight to allow words to escape.

"But this is the first time you've given *any* indication that you're willing to try this thing between us. That you want it, even. I might need a minute."

The tightness in her throat moved to her chest, where it remained. Walsh's kind and careful response—taking into account not just the two of them, but their two children—was as far from romance as possible. This was the point where passion was supposed to take the place of reason, when they stopped talking and thinking and planning and just, you know, *did* the thing.

But even in her youth, Chrissie had never been that girl. Where others acted, she stood back and watched. When they gave in, she smiled tightly and prepared to clean up the mess that was left behind.

Walsh Hampton, she was starting to realize, was very much the same. And instead of balking at the curveball she'd just tossed him, he'd caught it and was holding it patiently until he was ready to throw it back.

"Kat was right, you know," Chrissie said when Walsh's silence extended longer than even *she* could stand. "How much of our call did you overhear?"

He sighed and scrubbed a hand over his face. "I was outside mowing the lawn when it happened. I only got the story secondhand from Lily. Was it as bad as she made it out to be?"

Chrissie thought about the venom that had been in Kat's voice, the way all of her hatred had been angled directly at her head, and winced.

"Yeah, it was pretty brutal. But I don't think it would've bothered me nearly as much if there hadn't been an element of truth to what she said. Her world is small. *My* world is small. There are all of three adults in her life she can count on—me, you, and Scarlett—and I'm threatening her relationship with one of them. Of course she's worried."

"She has no need to be." Walsh's smile was so full of warmth and understanding that she felt her breath catch. "You could tear my heart out of my chest and eat it with your bare hands, and I'd still want to be in Kat's life. But that's not what this stuff between the two of you is really about, is it?"

Chrissie shook her head. She thought about sagging to the sidewalk and letting it absorb her weight, but the scattered cigarette butts and a greasy patch of unidentifiable goo stopped her.

So did Walsh's next words.

"Tell me about him. Her dad, I mean."

It was the first time anyone had asked her that question since Kat was a newborn. The hospital had wanted to know so they could fill out the birth certificate, but few people beyond those bureaucratic walls were interested in more. Or they *were* interested but too polite to ask. There was something about very young, very inexperienced mothers that made people shy away from pushing too hard. They knew, as almost everyone did, that the story wasn't one that painted the main characters in a good light.

"His name is Grimshaw Pemberly."

"No way. You're making that up."

Chrissie's laugh bubbled up and escaped so quickly that it could have been a sob. "That's what everyone says when they hear his name for the first time, but believe me when I say it suits him. He's an English lit professor somewhere down in California. I want to say Berkeley, but he tends to move around a lot."

"English lit, huh?"

"I know. The first time I ever saw him—when I was a giddy, inexperienced fifteen, mind you—he was intently reading a copy of Dante's *Inferno*. Naturally, it was all downhill from there."

"Naturally." Walsh grinned in a way that not only encouraged Chrissie to keep going, but actually made her *want* to. "If I could go back and give my teenaged self one piece of advice, it would be to start carrying around classic literature that I'm way too young to understand. That's how you get all the really worthwhile chicks."

Her heart gave a little hum at that word—*worthwhile*—but she didn't allow herself to dwell on it. Not *too* much, anyway.

"Yeah, well. Turns out that being well read and being a decent human don't go hand in hand. Grimshaw has never been interested in any kind of relationship with Kat. I offer every couple of years—a quick email update on how she's doing, an open line of communication so he knows he's welcome to reach out, but he never does. He just says I'm doing a great job without him and he doesn't want to do anything to upset that."

Although she spoke lightly, each word came at a cost. The last time she'd emailed Grimshaw had been the time Scarlett threatened to have him taken out by a hit man. Not only had he offered his two lines of usual garbage—*Nice to hear from you. Still not interested.*—but he'd actually asked her to stop emailing altogether.

I'm seeing someone, he'd written. *It's serious. I can't do right by her if you keep opening up this part of my past.*

"Does Kat know you do that?" Walsh asked.

"Of course not. It would break her heart." Chrissie fired the answer out like it came from a slingshot anchored to her rib cage. "I've gone back and forth about it inside my head a thousand different times, but I always end up in the same place. It's better for her to think that her father is out there somewhere, missing her as much she misses him, than to know how little he cares. I spent my entire childhood living with parents who didn't care, and it was torture."

"So…you're protecting her." It wasn't a question.

"Until the day I die." It was definitely an answer.

On the screen, a calico blur jumped up onto Walsh's lap. Rufus turned once, twice, three times, and then he did the unthinkable. He actually lay down and started purring as Walsh's hand began to move up and down his spine.

It was as good a segue as any.

"Walsh, what on earth have you done to my cat? Is he…? Is that…? Good god, are those purrs I'm hearing?"

Walsh chuckled, but his expression didn't lose any of the severity that had fallen over it when Chrissie started talking about Grimshaw. "He's not such a bad cat. We've reached an understanding, he and I. But for what it's worth, I think you're wrong about Kat."

"Walsh, please—"

He stopped petting the traitorous cat long enough to hold up a hand. "I know. I'm not her parent, and you're more than capable of handling your daughter on your own terms. I'm just saying. Although I make it a point never to say anything bad about Lily's mother, I am honest about why she left us—why she left *her*. Kat's reaction might surprise you."

Chrissie very much doubted it. Kat was a mercurial creature, so tied to her emotions that they dictated their life together like an atomic clock keeping impeccable time in the background. Chrissie had survived her childhood by learning to cut her emotions off at the source. She very much doubted whether Kat was capable of the same.

Or that she'd be the same laughing, high-spirited girl afterward.

"I'll bear your advice in mind, thanks."

Walsh chuckled. "That's the closest you're going to get to telling me to mind my own business, isn't it?"

Even that, a grain of discord lodging between them, seemed like nothing in the face of that smile. "While my mangy old cat is in your lap and my daughter is under your roof? Yes. I owe you too much already."

"You don't owe me a damn thing, Chrissie." He leaned closer to the phone. Chrissie had never been a big fan of video chats, but she could almost smell his volleyball tape scent from here. "I just wish I could do more."

Chrissie knew she shouldn't ask. She'd already left Scarlett alone inside the café for too long, had made so many demands on Walsh's time and energy that she was starting to feel like one of his athletes instead of his peer. But something about the way he spoke—as if he meant every word—loosened her tongue.

"Actually, are you near a computer right now?"

"No, but I can be." He set aside the cat and moved to a desk set in one corner of the room. "What do you need?"

To put her actual needs into words would have taken the rest of the day—if not the whole week—so she focused on the one thing that was bothering her more than all the rest.

"This village in Vermont we're going to… Would you google it real quick for me? I looked it up when Scarlett first started talking about the trip, but that was when I thought we were just going to be antiquing and taking in the sights. Now, however…" She let her voice trail off, hesitant to put her actual fear into words.

"What am I looking for?"

"I'm not sure. Anything unique about it. Especially if it's related to medical stuff. Specifically cancer."

"On it." He propped his phone against the monitor and started typing. Chrissie tried not to count the seconds, but she had to do something to keep the creeping anxiety at bay.

The results came quicker than she expected.

"Huh."

She wasn't sure what was worse—the way he said the word or the look on his face as he said it. "How bad is it?"

"I'm not sure 'bad' is the right word—and I don't even know if I'm looking at the right thing." Walsh slipped a pair of readers over his eyes to peer more intently at the screen. "But there's a place here called Tranquility Estates. A spa of sorts. A fancy one on a literal estate with horse stables and everything. Only—"

He cut himself off so quickly that Chrissie was afraid the call had been dropped. But the way he directed his full attention toward the screen told her that he was still very much present. "Chrissie, are you sure you want to hear this?"

Chrissie nodded—or rather, she *assumed* she did. In that moment, with Walsh's eyes widening behind the black plastic rims of his readers and her own thoughts rushing together in a confluence of conflicting emotions, she wasn't sure she'd moved at all.

"I think you and your friend need to sit down and have a chat," Walsh said. "According to this website, Tranquility Estates is a cancer care center."

"A cancer care center," Chrissie echoed.

"That's what I'm reading. Only according to their About page, it's more of a hospice than a hospital. I'm so sorry, but it kind of looks like—"

Chrissie didn't need to hear the rest. She already knew—*had* known for much longer than she was willing to admit. From the moment this road trip had started, there had been something different about Scarlett, something urgent.

Something final.

"It's a place where people go to die."

Chapter Twenty

PORTLAND, OR

2009

THE FIRST THING SCARLETT BOUGHT WITH the money from her grandmother's life insurance policy was a pair of first-class plane tickets to Paris.

The second thing she bought was a pregnancy test.

"Omigod, Scarlett. Please tell me you didn't actually spend five thousand dollars of your inheritance on a senior trip for us to France." Chrissie's voice, caught somewhere between a scold and a squeal, reached the bathroom from the living room with a soft echo. Every conversation inside the apartment these days sounded like that, thanks in large part to the growing pile of boxes that contained the entirety of Scarlett's childhood.

Bit by bit, Chrissie was packing up the pieces of Grandma that remained. Bit by bit, she was forcing Scarlett to move on with her life.

Scarlett hastily shoved the pregnancy test underneath a pile of towels on the back of the toilet. The requisite three minutes hadn't passed, but there was no way she was risking Chrissie popping her head inside and catching Scarlett in the act.

"They're nonrefundable, so you have no choice but to go with me," Scarlett said brightly as she stepped into the living room. She tried not to wince at the sight of the cardboard stacks or at how bare and empty the apartment looked without her grandmother's knickknacks on every available surface, but she couldn't seem to help herself.

She *knew* the lease was up at the end of the month and she had no other choice but to find a new place to live. She *knew* all her grandmother's belongings were waiting for her inside those boxes, ready to decorate wherever she ended up next.

But that didn't make her resent them any less. *Or to resent Chrissie less, either.* How could her friend keep putting one foot in front of the other? Why was she so capable of carrying on when all Scarlett wanted to do was curl up in a ball and stay here forever?

"I know." Chrissie's arms were around her within seconds. "It's awful in here while everything is in flux. I'm sorry. I'll go to Paris with you to make up for it, and I won't complain a single time. I might even try escargots."

"And wine," Scarlett sniffled, wishing that instead of helping her every step of the way, Chrissie would be less amazing of a friend. She needed that so much more than she was willing to admit. "And frog legs. And you have to have a scandalous love affair with at least two Frenchmen, but if you wear a beret even once, so help me..."

Chrissie laughed and let her go, which had been Scarlett's objective from the start.

"I don't think Grimshaw would appreciate me having *two* love affairs. I can probably get him down to one, but that's as far as I'm willing to push it."

A wave of nausea came over Scarlett, so strong it was impossible to chalk up to the mild bouts of sickness she'd been having on and off the past few weeks. Chrissie had never used the L-word with regards to Grimshaw before, even as a joke. Whatever that stupid pregnancy test in the bathroom ended up saying, she couldn't carry on like this.

"Chrissie, I—"

A knock sounded before she could make the confession that would ruin them both. Scarlett reared back, but Chrissie's pleased look indicated that she'd been expecting someone—had even, possibly, planned yet another surprise to try and lift Scarlett's spirits.

"That'll be Mitchell," she said as she went to answer the door. "I hope you don't mind, but I convinced him to borrow his dad's truck to help us haul some of this stuff to the storage facility."

"Oh. Mitchell. *Goody.*"

Chrissie turned and pulled a face at Scarlett. "Be nice, Scarlett. He only wants to help. It's not his fault he's head over heels in love with you. If you want guys to stop doing that, you should try being less gorgeous."

That made Scarlett snort. "I hate to break it to you, Chrissie, but it's not my looks boys are after. Not when they have you for that."

Chrissie shot her a puzzled look, but there was no time to explain herself before the door opened and Mitchell bounded in. Which was probably for the best because what could she say to make Chrissie understand?

You're the gorgeous one, both inside and out. I'm the walking disaster. The good time. The bad mistake.

"My dad says we have until five o'clock, and then he needs to pick up my sister from band practice." Mitchell strode into the apartment with his long-legged gait, his brow puckering as he took in the empty shelves and even emptier walls. "Oh, wow. You guys made a lot of progress in here."

"*Chrissie* made a lot of progress in here," Scarlett corrected him. "All I've been doing is playing Doodle Jump and eating two-month-old pie."

"Two-month-old pie?" Mitchell's face showed his horror. "Is that…safe?"

"Have some and see for yourself. There's peach and strawberry rhubarb. Or, if you're feeling really brave, coconut cream."

Chrissie rolled her eyes as she grabbed the dolly Mitchell had brought with him and dragged it through the apartment. "Don't listen to her. They've been in the freezer since the funeral. I don't know why, but everyone seemed to think pie was the one thing that would make all of this bearable."

"Since the funeral, huh?" Mitchell eyed Scarlett askance. She wished Chrissie could see that look. Far from showing the lovelorn signs of a boy infatuated with her, he looked like a judgmental little prick.

"Yes, since the funeral." Scarlett swung open the refrigerator door and started slamming pies onto the counter. "Is that a problem, Mitchell? Is there anything you'd like to add?"

"I'll take a slice of the strawberry rhubarb, thanks."

This was said with such a calm, good-natured air that Scarlett immediately started to deflate. She didn't know *what* was wrong with her. Two incredibly generous people were standing in her apartment, helping her to pack up her old life so she could start a new one. There was more money in her bank account than she'd ever seen in one place before, and her best friend had just agreed to accompany her on the trip to Paris that she'd been planning since the day they'd met.

She was living the life she wanted. She was living the life her grandmother had given her.

Tears sprang to her eyes before she could stop them. They fell in fat, heavy splotches all over the freezer-burned pie.

"Oh god. I'm such a mess. You can't possibly eat this now."

The plate was lifted from her hands before she could add her dripping snot to the rest. Mitchell's hand fell to her shoulder and forced her onto a stool while Chrissie poured her a glass of water and slid it across the counter.

"I'm sorry," Chrissie said. "We don't have to do this today if you aren't feeling up to it. Or you and Mitchell can go to a movie or something, while I—"

"Stop."

Instead of stopping, Chrissie started to rub slow, comforting circles on Scarlett's back.

"Don't, Chrissie." Scarlett shrugged her off with a twitch. "It's fine. I'm fine."

She could hear rather than see Mitchell and Chrissie share a concerned look over her head. She sprang to her feet, ignoring her sudden whirl of dizziness, and turned on them. "Omigod, you guys. *Enough.*"

They both moved toward her at the same time but she flung up her hands, holding them back like an exorcist keeping the demons at bay. Only…that wasn't right. *She* was the demon in this scenario, not them.

"Scarlett, what's going on?" Chrissie's voice started to take on a concerned vibrato. "What's gotten into you?"

She would forever regret the way she responded to that question—not with the gratitude she should have shown her best friend of eleven years, and not with the calm, self-assured grace of a woman facing an inevitable dead end, but with a laugh.

Granted, it was a laugh that went on for a few seconds too long, as unhinged at the jaw as she felt all over, but that didn't make it any more appropriate. Nor did it explain the words that next left her lips.

"Your perfect college boyfriend, Chrissie. That's what got into me."

When her confession was met with a shocked stare from one side—Chrissie's—and a pain that seemed to extend into eternity—Mitchell's—she dropped her head to the counter with another one of those eerie laughs.

"It was Grimshaw Pemberly. At the funeral. With the statue of

Mary Magdalene looking on." Each sentence was recited like a game of Clue. "There. I confessed. Are you happy now? Can I cry into the rest of this pie in peace now?"

She had no idea how she made it to the couch or how an actual cup of chamomile tea—the last of her grandmother's stash—was placed in her hand. Or why there was suddenly a blanket over her shoulders, which were shaking, shaking, shaking in a way that looked like crying but felt like worse. If she had to guess, she'd have said that Chrissie had clicked into full-on martyr mode. Her saccharine soul had been prepping for this moment for years—for her whole life, in fact.

She was wrong.

"Drink that, Scarlett." Mitchell spoke softly but gruffly, his voice belonging to a man twice his age. "It has an obscene amount of sugar in it, but you look like you're about to pass out. In fact, I think you *did* pass out for a second there."

"Where's Chrissie?"

Scarlett used the lengthy pause that ensued to sip the tea, which was hot enough to burn her tongue. Instead of spitting it out, she let the burning water swirl around her mouth, scalding everything until it felt almost as numb as the rest of her.

"She, uh, went outside," Mitchell said. He jerked his head toward the double doors on the far end of the apartment, which opened up onto a minuscule balcony overlooking the parking lot. From her position on the couch, Scarlett could make out a flash of Chrissie's hair but little else. "She said she needed some air."

"That's right. A little oxygen, a moment to reflect, and she'll be back to her usual self." Scarlett was unable to hide the bitterness in her tone, but that might have been because of the first-degree mouth burns. "I can't wait to see how she blames herself for this."

"Scarlett, that's not fair."

She knew it wasn't. That was the whole point. *None* of this was fair.

"Do you think maybe we should post someone below to catch her in case she jumps?" Scarlett asked. "I don't think I have the emotional capacity to attend another funeral so soon after the last one. I bet Grimshaw wouldn't mind, though. He keeps texting me, wanting to know when we can hook up like that again."

Mitchell gave her a disgusted look before snatching the tea away from her, hissing sharply as the hot water scalded the backs of his hands. "Look at her shoulders, Scarlett. She's out there sobbing. *Sobbing*."

She didn't want to look. She didn't want to know. But there was such an aura of command around Mitchell—annoying little Mitchell—that she had no choice but to do as he said. And the moment she saw the way Chrissie's whole body heaved, as if every breath came at a cost, she wished she hadn't given in.

She'd *never* seen Chrissie cry like that before. Not one tear had she shed for her dead brother. Not a single streak of mascara had darkened her eyes after Grandma had been laid to rest. When calamity struck, there was a stoicism to Chrissie that seemed to strengthen her from within.

But Scarlett had done the unthinkable. Scarlett had done the one thing that broke her.

"I don't know what I'm supposed to do," Scarlett whispered. Her own eyes started to fill again. "Mitchell, I don't know how to fix this."

"I don't think you *can* fix it," he said, his voice as cold as the blood running through Scarlett's veins. "What the hell is wrong with you, Scarlett? It's bad enough that you left the funeral with my stupid cousin. Why did you have to go and tell Chrissie about it? And in such a way?"

That, at least, she had an answer for. She got to her feet, surprised to find that her legs held her weight without a single tremor.

"Don't go out there," Mitchell warned. "Give the poor girl a minute to herself."

"I wasn't planning on it." She strode to the bathroom and pulled the pregnancy test out from under the towel. She was tempted to squeeze her eyes shut or shove the plastic under a cascade of running water to render the results null and void, but she didn't. She needed to see those two pink lines for herself—to realize the full enormity of what she'd done.

Her legs continued not shaking as she reentered the living room and placed the evidence on the coffee table next to the still-steaming tea. It was her voice that did that instead.

"I'm pregnant," she said. "And as I'm sure you can guess, the baby is Grimshaw's."

Chapter Twenty-One

CHICAGO, ILLINOIS

Present Day

CHRISSIE KNEW SHE'D BEEN FOUND OUT the moment they walked into the lobby of the St. Regis Hotel.

Luxury accommodations had never been her thing. The sleek marble and shining gold accents, the upholstery that was too expensive to sit on, the way everyone talked in hushed, muted tones—it all reminded her too much of her childhood. If she wanted a sterile mausoleum where sincerity went to die, she knew exactly where to get it and not pay five hundred bucks a night for the privilege, thank you very much.

"Don't get mad, but I booked us a suite. After the past few days, I figured we've earned it." Scarlett's arms wound around Chrissie from behind. Since the breast cancer disclosure, Scarlett had eschewed the molded bras she'd been wearing the entire trip. The flat of her chest pressed against Chrissie's back in a way that felt achingly real. "According to the lady I talked to, the bathtub in there is like something out of an Icelandic architecture magazine. I plan to get you just drunk enough to let me do a photo shoot we can send to Walsh. Is he more of a leg man or a breast man, do you think?"

Chrissie let herself back in the warmth of Scarlett's hug for exactly ten seconds before detaching herself. "He's a personality man."

Scarlett snorted. "Of course he is. I bet he used to read his dad's old *Playboys* for the articles, too. Do you want to head up straightaway, or should we grab a bite to eat first?"

The moment of truth had arrived.

"What I want is for you to stop trying to buy me off with expensive hotels. And to tell me why we're heading to a mystery destination in one of the only states in the country that allows nonresidents to access death-with-dignity services." Chrissie paused just long enough to clock the way all the blood drained from Scarlett's face. "Whether we have this conversation in the privacy of a suite I neither want nor need, or if we hold it in a crowded hotel bar with witnesses around is up to you."

To give Scarlett credit, she didn't try to deflect. She might have been devious, sneaky, and wholly untrustworthy, but she'd never been the sort to run and hide when things came to a head.

"I pick witnesses. Lots and lots of witnesses."

Chrissie tilted her head in the direction of the bar. "Then lead the way. I hope they have the good kind of fries here. I'm craving carbs and salt like you wouldn't believe."

"That's the shock," Scarlett said. "When I found out my cancer had come back, I ate nothing but potato chips for a whole week."

"With Mitchell." It wasn't a question.

"He mostly eats chicken and steamed broccoli these days, but yeah."

There was something surreal about the way they continued chatting as they were led to a corner booth with a view of the busy street outside. To look at them, they were just two travel-stained women enjoying a late dinner at a five-star hotel. They could have been old college friends meeting up for a girls' weekend or sisters taking a vacation from the hectic whirlwind of their middle class lives.

Or, Chrissie reflected wryly, lifelong best friends on their way to a fancy estate that only one of them would leave.

"It was River, wasn't it?" Scarlett said as they placed their orders and settled into the plush booth seats. "Knowing about the pills, I mean? I wish she'd just been a drug addict and stolen them like a normal hitchhiker."

Chrissie accepted this cavalier statement with equal calm. For whatever reason, Scarlett had decided to treat this whole thing like a blip in an otherwise ordinary day, which meant that she would, too.

Chrissie wouldn't be the first to give in. She wouldn't be the first to crack.

"She hinted as much, yes. But I had Walsh look up the village while we were on the phone. That was the real tip-off. You should have lied about where we were going."

"I considered it." Scarlett pursed her lips and toyed with the lid on the bottle of sparkling water the waiter had brought out. "But there was no need. I always planned on telling you the truth long before we got there."

Chrissie could only stare across the table at her.

"I'm not lying," Scarlett said, her defensive armor sliding into place and clicking between her brows. "I was working my way up to it, but then we got to Boise and you went all white knight on me. I *told* you not to invite River to come with us. I *begged* you to leave her well enough alone. I could hardly spill my secrets with some teenage runaway on our hands."

Chrissie didn't point out the obvious—that the time to disclose the truth would have been during the planning stages of the trip or, better yet, the moment Scarlett had gotten the call from her doctor.

There was no need. The longer they sat there, casually discussing the end of the world as she knew it, the fewer excuses she wanted to hear.

She's not denying it. She's not even trying.

That, more than anything else, spoke to the severity of this situation. Scarlett denied *everything*—it was her preferred state of being. If you asked her, she'd never had any real feelings for Mitchell Pemberly. She was more than happy traveling the world all by herself, always searching for the next big adventure. And of course her cancer would never come back. That was for other people, *boring* people.

"How bad is it?" Chrissie folded her hands on the table to keep them still. "And no more bullshit, please."

"Then free of bullshit, we're talking DEFCON 1." Scarlett turned to look out the window. The lower lip she drew between her teeth was the only evidence she gave of feeling anything at all. "I'm afraid this is it, Chrissie. The final countdown. Judgment day. The end."

At some point in the following ten minutes, a silver basket of fries appeared in front of Chrissie. She must have eaten a few of them, because the ramekin of aioli had a healthy dent in it, and there were sprinklings of salt all over her fingers. Her sparkling water was half-empty. But if someone offered her a million dollars to recollect even *one* memory from those ten minutes, she'd have walked away with a wallet as empty as her heart.

"Aren't you going to say anything? Ask questions?" Scarlett held one of the fries between her two fingers, toying with it the way she might a cigarette. "I know you've always been good at this part, but I figured you'd want a few more details."

Chrissie's senses came crashing back all at once—the slightly garlicky taste in her mouth, the hum of voices in the background, the sickening lurch in her stomach she feared would never go away.

"I'm sorry. Did you just say I'm good at this part?"

Scarlett dropped the fry with a shrug. "Well, yeah. You forget that I've seen you lose two people close to you already. I used to joke about it on the radio, actually—never naming names, of course, but about how everyone should find that one person who rises to disaster like Lea Michele finally getting the call from Broadway. For some reason, a lot of my listeners are obsessed with musical theater. I've never understood why."

Chrissie recognized this insouciant prattle for what it was and cut right through it. "No one is *good* at handling death, Scarlett."

"Morticians are. Coroners, too. And don't even get me started on necrophiliacs. They rise in a totally different way, if you get what I'm saying."

In the entirety of her life, Chrissie had never slapped another human being, but in that moment, she came damn near to it. Her hands itched not just to force Scarlett to stop joking, but to say *anything* other than what was coming out of her mouth.

"Stop it. Stop it right now." She spoke through teeth clenched tight enough to crack her fillings.

"It's not an insult, Chrissie. In fact, it's a compliment—the highest compliment I could possibly give. You were so poised when your brother died. Grandma, too. At the time, it made me furious—that you could be so cool and collected while the world was burning—but I get it now. Someone has to be there to hold things together. It's not a glamorous job, and I doubt it's a very thankful one, but it has to get done." Scarlett paused and slipped her hands over Chrissie's clutched palms. "I'm asking you to do it again, one last time, for me."

"For you," Chrissie echoed blankly.

Scarlett nodded, the familiar lines of her face as serene as if she'd just asked for directions to the bathroom.

"I won't die in a hospital. I promised myself that a long time ago. This place we're going—Tranquility Estates—is designed to make the process as comfortable as possible. It's basically a hospice that feels nothing like hospice. We get a private cabin, full access to all their services, and then…you know."

Chrissie *did* know, but oh, how she wished she didn't.

"I've already coordinated everything with my doctor back home. They have a pharmacist on staff to give me the medication I need, and then I take it at my own leisure and under my own recognizance. And while we wait for me to get up the nerve, we can ride horses or go for nature walks or even just sit and hang out by the firepit, chatting long into the night."

For the first time, Scarlett showed signs of strain. Her grip on Chrissie's hands tightened so much that it pushed her fingernails through the skin of her palm.

"You *will* come with me, right? We can finish the road trip? Ride horses together?"

Chrissie almost said yes. Just like that. Just yes. As if the thing Scarlett was asking for was a simple favor, one of the thousands of give-and-take transactions that defined twenty-seven years of friendship. But nothing with Scarlett was simple—especially not her favors. When Scarlett asked for something, she didn't want just a small piece of your soul.

She wanted the whole thing.

"Fuck you." Chrissie got to her feet so fast that her head swam. Some of the salt from her fingertips touched the open cut on her palm, but she barely felt the sting of it. "I can't believe you'd do this to me… Only, wait. You know what? I *can* believe it. I should've known the moment you called me and dangled a free cross-country trip in my face. Everything involving you comes with strings attached."

"Strings?" Scarlett was on her feet next to Chrissie. "You think me asking you to sit by my side so I don't have to be alone when I kill myself is a *string*?"

Chrissie almost reached out to steady Scarlett as she swayed first left and then right before clutching the table to catch herself. Every instinct she had urged her to follow the same path she always had where Scarlett was concerned: to protect and to serve, to go along for the ride because, let's face it, who else was going to invite her anywhere?

Chrissie tucked her hands in her armpits instead—and, sure enough, Scarlett managed to catch herself just fine on her own.

That, more than anything else, fueled her next words.

"You tricked me. You knew that once this trip was underway, I'd have no choice but to agree to every single one of your plans—the visits to random roadside attractions, the hotels I could never afford on my own, the haircuts and flirtatious photos like we're just two ordinary women enjoying a getaway." Chrissie's eyes felt hot with emotion as she considered how wonderful all that had sounded a few days ago—how wonderful it *still* sounded, even now. "Even the list you're making me write to show all the ways my life is lacking is part of it, isn't it? You're paving the way. You're saying goodbye. Only you didn't have the guts to say it to my face, so I had to find out the truth from a stranger."

"You invited her, not me."

"And *you* had plenty of opportunities to come clean before we stumbled across her. Our first night, you wore a swimsuit literally designed to throw the dust in my eyes. You were waiting until it was too late to turn back."

"Or I was trying to hold onto my dignity while I still could." Scarlett continued clutching the table as though it was the only thing keeping her upright—the only thing, short of Chrissie, standing between her and death. "Cut me a little slack here. You forget that I've been down this road before. Once cancer is added to the picture, it changes the shape and color of everything. You'd have been worried about me every single second, making sure I took my medication and got plenty of rest, taking over all of the driving while I sat curled up in a useless heap next to you."

"I never treated you like that before. Not once."

"Then say you won't do it," Scarlett ordered, her voice softer now and all the more dangerous because of it. That silky, seductive purr had been the ruin of many a woman—and even more men. "Tell me you won't finish the road trip with me, that you won't walk through the doors of Tranquility Estates and immediately demand to speak to the manager on my behalf."

Chrissie's sharp, sudden laugh dislodged a lone tear, which she wiped away before it could snake a traitorous path down her cheek. "Don't make me laugh. None of this is funny."

"I know it's not. Believe me. *I know.*"

It was, at once, everything and nothing that Chrissie needed to hear. "There's really nothing more you can do? Medically speaking, I mean?"

Scarlett shook her head. The gold hoops in her ears swayed gently. "If I went in for another round of chemo, I might buy myself a few more months, but they'd be the kind of months you wouldn't wish on your worst enemy." She paused, and the uncertain tremor that followed broke something inside Chrissie. "I'm not that, right, Chrissie? After everything I've done to you, all the ways I've let you down, we're still on the same side?"

Chrissie didn't answer. Not because she wanted her friend to suffer any more than she had to, and not because her anger had stopped simmering in the pit of her stomach, but because reality slammed into her with so much force that all the air left her lungs.

We're on the same side. We've always been on the same side.

From the moment Scarlett called to her from that first hospital bed, a scrap of a girl in a wasted body that somehow—*always*—vibrated with vitality, Chrissie had come equally alive. She hadn't been able to save her brother or her parents. She'd been on the cusp of being entombed in that house along with them.

But Scarlett had saved her. She'd held out a tiny hand and yanked Chrissie onto the lifeboat with her.

Only now the lifeboat was deflating around them, and Chrissie didn't know what to do. Whether she sank or swam, the end result was going to be the same.

The waves were going to pull Scarlett under, and there was nothing she could do to stop them.

Chapter Twenty-Two

PORTLAND, OR

2009

CHRISSIE WENT WITH SCARLETT TO EVERY single one of her prenatal appointments.

Not surprisingly, Chrissie was a huge hit with the medical staff, all of whom were *way* more emotionally invested in this baby than Scarlett understood.

Or, if she was being honest, appreciated.

Scarlett could be lying there in her uncomfortable paper gown for hours without eliciting anything so much as "And how are you *feeling*, dear?" but the moment the nurses and ultrasound techs caught sight of Chrissie sitting in a plastic chair with her annotated copy of *What to Expect When You're Expecting* in her lap, they went all googly-eyed.

"Aren't you just the sweetest friend in the world?"

"Have you gotten to the chapter on mucus plugs yet? Never underestimate the horrors of the bloody show."

"Can I get you anything, Chrissie? A pillow, maybe? Or a sandwich from the cafeteria? We're gonna be another hour or so, and you're looking a little pale."

"I could use a sandwich," Scarlett said, her hands clasped around the growing lump of her six-months-pregnant belly. That belly was too big for the doctor's comfort, which was why they were here in the first place. "I'm starving to death."

The nurse, a lithe, twentysomething man who seemed to have the energy of a dozen overfed hyenas, only laughed and wagged a finger at Scarlett. "Now, now. You know the glucose test won't give us accurate results unless you're fasting. Just sit tight a little bit longer, and we'll make sure we get you a pudding cup for your troubles."

Scarlett waited until he walked out of the room before turning to Chrissie. "A pudding cup? I'm growing a whole freaking human being over here, and that's the best he can offer? You should take him up on the sandwich offer and feed it to me in little bites. I won't tell anyone if you don't."

Chrissie laughed in the same way the nurse had, as if she knew down to her very bones that Scarlett wouldn't do anything to jeopardize the glucose test—and, by extension, her baby.

Scarlett wished she knew how they could all be so certain. They had no idea how many times she fantasized about doing all the things she wasn't supposed to. Drinking and smoking and eating her body weight in sushi and soft cheeses. Sitting in a sauna until she was so hot that her skin started to peel off or riding a horse across the country, her hair freshly bleached and trailing in the wind behind her.

You know, totally normal teenage activities.

"I know it sucks. I promise not to eat anything until they give you the all clear. That way we can suffer together." Chrissie set the book aside and gave Scarlett her full attention. "Wanna play tic-tac-toe to pass the time? Or we can fuck-marry-kill the medical staff again. There's a new resident with really soft hands who might mix things up."

Scarlett relaxed and lay back against her paper pillow, her eyes closed. "You're just saying that to cheer me up."

"Well, yeah." Scarlett felt a different soft hand—the one belonging to Chrissie—brush hair off her forehead. "We can also talk, if you want. I know how hard today is for you. We were supposed to be on our flight to Paris."

Scarlett felt a familiar tightness seize hold of her belly. The first time it had happened, she'd been so afraid she'd done something to hurt the baby that she'd had Chrissie run her to the emergency room. The second time, a late-night call to her doctor had sufficed. Now she recognized the sensation for what it was: plain old ordinary anxiety.

It was so strange. Her whole life, she'd lived on a precipice of sorts—straddling the line between life and death, her future not guaranteed so much as beckoning. She'd never had much money, wasn't particularly good at school, and rarely made the kind of choices a guidance counselor would approve of. Yet she'd never felt any fears about what would be become of her. For good or bad, better or worse, she was going to *live* her life, and that was enough.

It was only now that she had a bank account six figures in the black and the next eighteen years of her life mapped out that she felt a swirling, all-consuming worry so powerful that it took a physical form.

"Hey. Forget I said anything. It's supposed to be one of the hottest summers on record over there anyway. We're better off in the good ol' marine west coast climate zone."

Scarlett popped her eyes open again. As expected, Chrissie was looking down on her with a pucker of worry drawing the delicate arches of her brows together.

"I don't deserve you," Scarlett said suddenly. "I never have."

The line down Chrissie's forehead deepened. "Stop that. I thought we decided not to give the sperm donor any more real estate inside our heads. He's *definitely* not thinking about us, so why should we bother with him?"

Scarlett couldn't help but smile at Chrissie's use of the term they'd adopted whenever discussing Grimshaw Pemberly—ex-boyfriend, intercourse denier, and master in the art of disappearance. In many ways, Scarlett had a lot to thank him for. If he'd risen to the occasion and taken ownership of his actions, stepping up as the other responsible half in this debacle of biology and hormones, there was a good chance Chrissie would have walked out the door and out of Scarlett's life forever. To say that she'd been hurt by Scarlett's confession would be an understatement.

But when Grimshaw coldly denied any part in what had happened the day of her grandmother's funeral—even in the face of Mitchell's confirmation of the facts—Chrissie had done all the rising for him. In the face of adversity, she would always, *always* have Scarlett's back.

And even though Chrissie would never admit it out loud, an unexpected pregnancy in an eighteen-year-old body that everyone had proclaimed unable to support life was adversity. It was adversity as only Chrissie and Scarlett could understand.

"It's not just him," Scarlett said. "I mean, it *is* him, but—"

"Hey." Chrissie covered Scarlett's hand with her own. "Paris will still be there in a few years, and so will I. As long as we have each other, nothing else matters, remember?"

Scarlett nodded, but she also felt a well of frustration starting to bubble up in her throat. Chrissie was and always would be the rock in her life. She was the parent neither of them had ever had, the one constant she could count on no matter what. But she was also *happy* about what the next few years held. The baby blankets she'd crocheted and the bassinet they'd refurbished, the new apartment in Medford they were moving into together—all of it held charm for her, a chance to build a life perfectly suited to her tastes.

But Scarlett didn't want to live in stupid Medford, where the good schools and low cost of living made life as a single unwed mother feasible. She didn't want to raise a baby she'd never planned on having, a baby belonging to a man whose very name made her blood curdle with shame.

As if on cue, the staff social worker popped into the room, looking as bright and chipper as the earlier nurse. Scarlett tried to shoo the woman away, but for someone whose job it was to navigate tricky personal issues, she remained obstinately myopic.

"Good to see you again, Scarlett," the woman said as she took a seat and pulled out a bag of carrot sticks. Scarlett hadn't eaten a carrot stick in years, and would have stared down anyone who suggested she might want to chomp down on a dirt-flavored piece of chalk, but the injustice of the midmorning snack only served to enrage her. "Is this a good time to chat about that thing we were discussing on your last visit?"

"What thing?" Chrissie asked as she waved away the offer of a carrot stick. "Is there something I should know about?"

The social worker—Tammy Twaddle, according to the business card Scarlett was carrying around in her purse—blinked expectantly. Scarlett wouldn't have chosen this moment for disclosure and did, in fact, resent everything about it, but the conversation was going to have to happen one way or another. Best to do it under the bright lights of the doctor's office, where a full medical staff was on hand.

"Sure. Now is fine."

Tammy snapped down on her carrot stick and opened the file in her lap. "Excellent! I know this has been a difficult time for you, and that your mind isn't made up yet, but I'm here to reassure you that you *do* have options. At your age, it's completely normal to feel like the whole world is crumbling around you, but that doesn't have to be the case."

Scarlett snorted. It seemed as good a response as any.

"And I know you said that your upbringing—your grandmother's faith—meant you weren't interested in abortion, but that doesn't leave you with nothing," she continued as though Scarlett hadn't made a sound. "We work with several great adoption agencies, some of which are located here in Portland and others that—"

"I'm sorry. *Adoption agencies*?" Chrissie's voice registered a full octave higher than usual. "Scarlett, what's going on?"

Scarlett closed her eyes again, but she felt none of the earlier peace of the action. She didn't have to see Chrissie to picture the expression of complete and utter betrayal she wore.

"Uh-oh. She didn't tell you? Should I come back?"

"No, she didn't tell me. Is this for real? Scarlett, are you seriously considering adoption?"

Even though it was the coward's way out, Scarlett didn't open her eyes. Better to let the social worker handle this. After all, that was her job, right? The reason she'd gotten into this career in the first place?

"It was just a conversation," Scarlett murmured.

"That's right," Tammy said so brightly that Scarlett could hear the smile being injected into her voice. "No need to make a decision right now. The best thing you can do at this stage is get lots of rest and make sure you follow your doctor's orders. Although if you *did* want to pursue the open adoption course, I'd suggest starting to vet the prospective parents early. Since you'll be connected to them for the rest of your life, it's important to find the right social and emotional fit. Plus, a lot of them get really excited about the delivery."

"Open adoption," Chrissie echoed. She sounded less shocked now and more resigned. As if this was just one more in a long line of disappointments Scarlett had in store for her.

"Yep. That's when the parents and Scarlett keep a line of communication open—updates and pictures, sometimes even visits. It all depends on what your friend wants."

"Thank you. I know what it is."

A hand slipped into Scarlett's, the gentle fingers of her best friend intertwining with her own. Scarlett was so surprised by this gesture that she allowed herself to look at Chrissie—and then immediately regretted it. So far from the bitter disappointment she'd shown when Scarlett confessed her liaison with Grimshaw or the heart-wrenching shock of the positive pregnancy test, Chrissie looked…seriously pissed.

Chrissie squeezed Scarlett's hand so hard that she felt some of the joints crack, but when she spoke, it was with the same detached resignation as before.

"You can leave the paperwork with me," Chrissie said. "We'll look over it and get back to you with any questions."

"Are you sure?" Tammy turned to Scarlett with the careful look of a woman accustomed to reading between the lines. "This is a decision only *you* can make."

"It's fine," Scarlett reassured her. She even managed a wan smile. "I trust Chrissie more than anyone else on the planet."

"Okay, then." Tammy got up and gently placed the folder on the seat she vacated. Scarlett could tell she wasn't fully convinced that Chrissie wasn't some evil, manipulative bestie who would strong-arm Scarlett into doing her own bidding, but short of manually hauling her out of the room, there was little she could do. "That baby girl of yours is lucky to have so many people who care about her. Remember that. No matter what else happens, she's loved—and it's my job to make sure she stays that way."

Scarlett expected Chrissie to attack the moment the door closed behind the social worker, but she didn't. All she did was stare down at where their hands linked—Chrissie's perfectly glossed nails next to Scarlett's chewed ones, the way her long fingers remained strong and supple despite the fact that she hadn't touched a piano in months.

"She said 'that baby girl of yours,'" Chrissie eventually said. "Is that true? You opened the envelope they gave us? It's a girl?"

Scarlett nodded, unable to trust herself to speak. She hadn't told Chrissie for fear of this exact reaction.

"A daughter," Chrissie breathed.

Scarlett braced herself for the rest—the oohs and ahhs, the declaration that a daughter was all that was needed to make Scarlett happy about her pregnancy—but it never came.

Instead, Chrissie asked a question that cut right to the bone. "Did you decide what you want to name her?"

"Kathleen, I think. It was my grandma's middle name." Scarlett tried not to dwell on what Grandma would say if she was in this room with them right now. Something true, probably. Something that would make her feel as guilty as she deserved. "Unless they won't let me. *Do* they let you name your baby before it's adopted out?"

That did the trick. Chrissie snatched her hand away and shoved it in her lap, her gaze fixed downward.

"Scarlett, you aren't really thinking about adoption, are you?" Her voice was smaller than it had been in years—smaller, even, than it had been during those first few days after the pregnancy test came back positive. "Even if you pick out the family, there's no saying what will happen ten years from now—what they'll do if life gets hard for them. People don't... They don't always get things right."

Scarlett felt each word like a stab to the back. "Not everyone is like your parents, Chrissie."

Chrissie lifted her gaze to Scarlett's, which moved the stab wounds directly to her heart. But when she spoke, she didn't touch on her pain. In true Chrissie fashion, she moved right on to business instead.

"We signed the lease on the apartment already," she insisted. "We have the bassinet. I even ordered the baby shower invitations. They're supposed to get here tomorrow."

Scarlett wasn't sure why that last part felt worse than all the rest, but it did.

"Who's going to come to that? Who even cares? Not Grimshaw. Not your parents. Certainly not mine." With her grandmother gone, she wasn't even sure *how* to contact her mother—if it was even a choice in the first place. Frustrated, self-pitying tears started to spring to her eyes. "The moment this baby is born, it's all over. It'll just be me and her, and the rest of the world will move on."

Scarlett could tell by the way Chrissie's cheeks flooded with splotches of red that her friend was rapidly reaching her limit.

"*Me*, Scarlett. I care. I'm not going anywhere without you."

"Fine. Then you can have her."

Scarlett had no idea where the words came from, but there was no taking them back once they were out.

"Scarlett!" Chrissie's eyes widened until Scarlett could see the full circle of her irises. "That's not funny. Don't joke about something like that. I'm not going to take your baby."

"You mean *our* baby. That's what you keep saying, isn't it? That we'll do this together? That this diaper-filled future belongs as much to you as me?" Scarlett had the distinct impression that her voice was too loud—yelling, almost—but that didn't seem right. She wasn't angry. She wasn't even upset. In fact, for the first time in six long months, she finally saw a glimmer of hope on the horizon. "I'll give you money. Half of what my grandma left me, just like I always wanted to. You could take care of her. Raise her. We wouldn't even have to tell her who her real mom is."

Scarlett knew that she had no right to keep going. With every word, her own burden felt lighter and lighter—and she knew exactly why.

It was because she was heaping it onto Chrissie instead.

"I'd much rather she be with you than some stranger picked out of a file." Scarlett nodded toward the folder sitting on the vacated chair. The hunger she'd been feeling since she woke up that morning disappeared under the sensation of something different—something that tasted an awful lot like brimstone.

Contrary to what most of her life choices indicated, Scarlett *did* possess a conscience. It didn't prick often, but when it did, it was because she was doing the one thing she'd promised herself not to do.

I'm using her again. I'm putting my own needs before hers.

But she couldn't stop. Now that the idea was out there and freedom was beckoning on the horizon, Scarlett had never wanted anything as much. So she gave in to the worst part of her nature—not with a whimper, but with a bang.

"Can't you see?" she asked. "We have to do it. It's the only way to make sure she doesn't get parents like ours."

Chrissie's whole being went still. If it weren't for the rush of blood through her head and the steady beeping of the monitor next to her, Scarlett might have thought that time had literally stopped.

But time, like life, found a way. Chrissie had barely started to blanch to the color of marble before the nurse popped back into the room.

"All right, Ms. Sanderson. Your hour's up. Time to draw that blood of yours and see how we're doing." He snapped a pair of latex gloves on and approached the bed. If he was aware of the tension in the room, he didn't show it. "Chrissie can come around to the other side and hold your hand, if you want. This might be a little uncomfortable."

Scarlett winced. Things were already was uncomfortable and only likely to get worse. But Chrissie reached for Scarlett's hand without hesitation.

"I'm here," she said. "You can relax. I've got you."

"I know you do," Scarlett said and closed her eyes once again. Not because she was especially scared of the needle and not because she was tired, but because she didn't want her best friend to see her relief. Because if Chrissie had her—if Chrissie was still willing to hold her hand, even after all this—she *could* relax. That was the one thing in the world she'd always been able to count on.

Chapter Twenty-Three

BUFFALO, NEW YORK

Present Day

IF IT HAD BEEN UP TO Chrissie, she'd have pushed through the last leg of the road trip in one long day.

The second half of the journey was always meant to be the more exciting part. Where the Dakotas and Midwest offered long stretches of open skies and isolation, the East Coast had cities and cultural outposts. All the places Chrissie had never been before and had hoped to see on this trip—Detroit and Cleveland, Niagara Falls and maybe even Toronto—passed in a blur as she drove with her foot heavy on the gas.

"I think we should stop here in Buffalo," she said as she pulled up in front of a fifties-style motel that had been recently revamped and painted electric pink. The flamingo-shaped neon sign out front was just kitschy enough to appeal to Scarlett's quest for eccentricity, while the modern updates appealed to Chrissie's quest for comfort.

Not for herself, obviously, but for Scarlett. Ever since the truth about where they were going—and why—had come out, Scarlett seemed to have relinquished the ironlike grip she'd held on herself.

She'd still woken up well before the sun that morning, but she was no longer attempting to cover it up with jokes about sleeping when she was dead or by pretending she was a carefree tourist making the most of her time away from work.

She was just a woman appreciating her final days on this planet, staving off the inevitable for as long as she possibly could.

"Is there something here you wanted to see?" Scarlett flipped her sunglasses to the top of her head and frowned at their surroundings. "Because I'm not gonna lie... Buffalo is kind of a drag. I was here for a work conference once, and we got buried in our hotel after a freak blizzard hit. We ran out of booze after the first day."

Chrissie allowed herself to be diverted by this. "Out of how many total days?"

"Well, only three. But two days trapped in a hotel with radio personalities and no alcohol is its own circle of hell. You know how loud and obnoxious I get once I start in on a subject. Imagine a hundred of me all talking at once and then remove anything harder than a handful of antihistamines to take the edge off."

"Well, I've never been here before, so we're staying." Chrissie turned off the car and stretched as she exited, fighting every urge she had to bustle over to the passenger side and help Scarlett out. "And if I get too loud and obnoxious for you, just say the word. I can be quiet for as long as you need."

"Not for all the booze in the world." Scarlett linked her arm with Chrissie's and started walking toward the lobby. To all outward appearances, they were just two women stepping into a neon pink hotel, but Chrissie felt the pull of Scarlett's body weight, sensed how each step was wearing on her. "I don't want you to be quiet. I want you to stay up all night talking with me like we used to when we were kids."

"When we were kids, I used to pray that you'd wear yourself out so

I could finally close my eyes, but you never did. I think I sleepwalked through our entire eighth-grade year."

"Don't worry. You should get plenty of sleep after next week. I promise not to haunt you after ten o'clock on weeknights."

Not unsurprisingly, this joke made neither one of them laugh. Instead, it robbed the entire pink hotel of its charm. Rather than appreciating the cheeky decor or the way their room boasted a photo of a pinup girl who looked *exactly* like Marilyn Monroe with brown hair, Chrissie felt the enormity of what this place signified.

This is the last bed Scarlett will sleep in that isn't also her deathbed. After tonight, we'll be heading into the final chapter of her life.

Even though neither one of them spoke the words aloud, they seemed to echo off the gingham-papered walls. It had been Chrissie's intention to make it through the rest of the trip without enacting any big dramas, but she suddenly felt so exhausted that all she could do was sink to the mattress and stare out the window, where cars zipped by the freeway as though the world contained nothing more than a series of starting points and destinations.

"It was a bad joke," Scarlett said as she sank to the mattress next to her. "I'm sorry. I promised myself I wouldn't reduce our trip to that, but you know how I get. Excessive emotions make me seasick."

"They don't make you seasick. They make you confront reality. *That's* the thing you hate about them."

Scarlett rested her head on Chrissie's shoulder. Her short hair tickled Chrissie's cheek, but she didn't brush it away. That living, itchy reminder of Scarlett's existence suddenly seemed like the most precious thing in the world.

"I know," Scarlett said. "I used to think it was the childhood cancer that did that to me—gave me a chip on the shoulder and an inability to appropriately process human emotions—but I'm pretty sure I just used it as an excuse. It's easier to be a selfish bitch if you pretend like normal things don't affect you."

"If you're waiting for me to contradict you, I'm not going to do it."

Scarlett slipped her fingers through Chrissie's. "I know you aren't. It's always been my favorite thing about you. I can be my worst self around you, and you'll still love me with every fiber of your being." She hesitated. "Do you know how many people find that? Let alone when they're seven years old?"

"I mean, I would have *preferred* you to be your best self all those years, but I was willing to take what I could get."

Scarlett gave a watery chuckle, her grip suddenly talon-tight. "Can we go out tonight? Somewhere entirely inappropriate for a woman with stage-four breast cancer? I know I should be taking things easy, but I can't. I just *can't*."

The last thing Chrissie wanted right now was to put on anything other than her volleyball mom sweatshirt. She wanted to curl up under the blankets, put on a low-stakes rom-com, and fall asleep next to her best friend in the whole world. But the truth was, Scarlett *was* selfish. She'd always put her own needs above those of the other people in her life, forcing everyone around her to match her in energy and pitch or risk getting left behind.

Even now, on her determined march to death, she was doing it. Instead of accepting the inevitability of her diagnosis—playing by the rules that forced everyone else into their proverbial lives of quiet desperation—Scarlett was pushing fast forward. She was skipping the messy bits, the painful bits. She was forcing Chrissie to keep up so she could stand by and watch as Scarlett leaped into the great and final unknown without her.

"Okay," Chrissie said.

Scarlett did a legitimate double take. "Wait. Really? You're not going to fight me? Or sigh and drag your feet every step of the way?"

"Of course not."

Chrissie smiled then, a slow, creeping thing that both looked and felt genuine. To Scarlett, *fighting* meant the obvious—pitched battles and raised voices, adrenaline pumping every step of the way. But Chrissie had been fighting more insidious battles her whole life.

That was the one thing Scarlett had never been able to understand about her. Where she saw Chrissie bending and twisting to make way for the winds that tried to knock her down, Chrissie saw only the strength it took to stay rooted where life had planted her.

"Okay. So, walk me through your expectations for Tranquility Estates. I need to take a few notes."

Chrissie sat perched on a barstool, a martini in front of her left hand and a pad of paper on her right. Scarlett had made an annoyed *tsk* when Chrissie had pulled both it and a pen out of her oversized purse, but she'd known better than to put up more than a nominal protest.

"Define what you mean by 'expectations,'" Scarlett asked as she twirled an olive on the end of a swizzle stick.

"The usual. What kind of staff will be there? What's my exact role? Will I be in your cabin with you, or are there rules about who can sleep where? After it's all over, am I responsible for getting your remains back to Oregon? Do you even *want* to go back to Oregon?"

Chrissie sipped her drink and grimaced at the powerful, pine-needle punch of gin on an empty stomach.

Scarlett, naturally, pounced on that rather than any of the other things Chrissie had just said. "You hate gin, Chrissie. You always have. Why did you order a martini if you don't even want one? Have we learned nothing these past few weeks?"

Chrissie fought the urge to toss the rest of the glass's contents in Scarlett's face.

"You brought us to a martini bar, Scarlett. The waitress asked what I wanted before we even sat down. Forgive me for panicking and ordering *a martini*."

Scarlett rolled her eyes and lifted a hand. Right on cue, their waitress, a fiftysomething woman who looked as harassed as Chrissie felt, came bustling back. "Is everything okay?"

"I'm so sorry, but my friend here doesn't actually want this martini. She panic-ordered it. Her first instinct is to always say what she thinks people want to hear rather than what's in her heart. Is there any way we can get you to replace it?"

The waitress smiled as though people routinely came into this bar and mistakenly ordered twenty-dollar drinks. "No problem. What would you rather have, hon?"

"It's not a crime to consider other people's feelings," Chrissie said.

The waitress blinked down at her. "Um...we have a few specials, if you'd like to hear them. Otherwise I can leave you with the menu and—"

"It's not a crime to order something you want, either," Scarlett returned.

The waitress took a step backwards. "I feel like maybe you two could use a minute."

"Don't go anywhere," Scarlett warned in a dangerous voice. "My friend's going to order exactly what she wants and only what she wants. And we'll sit here for as long as it takes for her to come up with it."

"Actually, I have a few other things I need to do before—"

"See, Scarlett? She has other things to do. Other customers to serve. She can't stand around at my beck and call all night just because I want her to." Chrissie turned to the waitress with a determined smile. "The martini I ordered is just fine, thank you. Please tell the bartender I appreciate the twist of lime."

The waitress would have scuttled gratefully away, but Scarlett wasn't done yet.

"I couldn't help noticing that you have a piano in the corner," she said. "Would it be okay if my friend played a few songs? She went viral recently. Maybe you've seen the videos? It could be a real boost to your business."

Chrissie didn't give the waitress a chance to recognize her. She also didn't give her a chance to take the drink away. Barely suppressing a grunt of rage, she kicked back the entire martini at once, letting the powerful wave of alcohol light her up from the inside.

"I don't want to play the stupid piano, Scarlett, and I don't want a different drink. I want you to stop acting like my whole life has been a waste just because I dared to live it differently than you."

Instead of reeling back at the sudden venom in Chrissie's voice, Scarlett leaned forward and clasped her hands on the table.

"Excellent. *Now* we're getting somewhere. Tell me what else you're feeling. Shout it from the rooftops if you have to."

"Yeeeaah, I'm going to come back later." The waitress snatched the empty glass as she dashed to safety on the other side of the bar. "And I'm taking all the projectiles with me. I'm getting way too old for this."

Chrissie barely registered the woman's absence. Despite the dim lighting and the general buzz of conversation in the background—or maybe because of it—the entire world reduced to just the two of them.

"You're pissed at me, aren't you?" Scarlett asked. For the briefest moment, Chrissie could have sworn she looked pleased by this—*happy*, even. "You want to scream and shout and tell me exactly how awful I am for putting you in this position. What kind of a best friend springs an assisted suicide on someone at the last possible second? Who would be awful enough to do that?"

Instead of answering, Chrissie dug into her purse and pulled out another piece of paper—this one with the name of the Royal Mills Motel emblazoned across the top. Scarlett looked delighted at that, too—that Chrissie, in her fury, would resort to the same tactics that

Scarlett had been using all along—but she didn't care. She was too busy writing underneath River's line about Kat being lucky to have her.

Stand by your best friend even when she doesn't deserve it.

"Oooh, nice." Scarlett nodded at the page. "What else have you got for me?"

Tell her how much you sometimes hate her.

"Hurtful, but fair."

Be true to yourself even if Scarlett refuses to accept it.

That gave Scarlett a moment's pause. "What don't I accept, Chrissie? How much I'm asking of you? How much I've *always* asked of you?"

Chrissie felt her eyes flood with tears, but she dashed them away. Hot streaks clung to her cheeks, and she felt sure she'd ruined her mascara, but what did it matter? There weren't enough martinis in the world to wash away the feeling of despair that was starting to spread outward from her chest, weighing down every movement until she felt like she was swimming through wet cement.

"I *hate* playing the piano, Scarlett. Did you know that? I always have. I can't sit at the keyboard and not feel that other person inside of me—the twin who never was, the brother I only knew for seven years—taking over." She held up a hand before Scarlett could say anything. If she didn't get this out now, she wasn't sure when—or if—she ever would. "I know you think it's your fault I gave it up, that without your grandmother's death or Kat to take care of, I'd have become this world-famous classical pianist traveling the world with you, but it's not true. The moment I moved out of that house and away from my parents was always going to be the end of that musical road for me."

"But you were so good."

"Yeah, because I spent a literal *eight thousand hours* practicing. I did the math once. Two hours every single day for eleven years adds up. If my parents had given me a violin or a soccer ball instead, I'd have been just as technically proficient at those things. All I wanted was for them to see me the way they saw Malcolm, to open up again after he closed them down, but they either couldn't or wouldn't, and I was too young to try any other method. In the end, that's all I have, Scarlett. Technical proficiency. Without heart, it doesn't mean anything."

"Chrissie, that's awful."

Chrissie rolled her eyes. "Of course it's awful. I was a *child.* One who was hurting just as much as they were. But if you think me chaining myself to that same instrument for the next forty years will make up for what you did to me—for what you're doing to me right now—then you're just as bad as they are." She paused, considering. "You know what? It actually makes you worse. Because unlike them, you saw what their indifference did to me."

"You mean I *saved* you from it."

All of sudden, the waitress's removal of the empty glass seemed like a wise move. "I beg your pardon?"

Scarlett's strange, glinting delight in this conversation was back. "You heard me, Chrissie. I'm the one who saved you from them. I made it possible for you to come to my house after school every single day. I gave you half my grandmother. And then I gave you half my grandmother's money so you'd never have to go crawling back to them. Say what you want about what I've done to you since then, but that means something."

Chrissie laughed. There was no humor in it, no joy. Just sound and air and the further cracking of a heart that had never been whole to begin with. "You're a real piece of work, you know that, Scarlett Sanderson?"

"I do, actually. It's why you love me." Scarlett folded her hands smugly on the table. "Is the part where we *finally* talk about what's between us?"

Chrissie should have been prepared for this. From the second she'd discovered the truth about this trip, they'd been marching toward this exact conversation, this exact moment in time.

Still. Nothing could have prepared her for the way the chill started seeping through her veins.

"If you're about to tell me that giving me Kat makes up for all the rest, I'm going to get up from this table, walk out the door, and book the first flight home," she said in a voice as cold as her blood.

Scarlett's smirk deepened. "I know she's been a real pain in the ass lately, but she'll come around eventually. She'll break up with a boyfriend or bang her knee in volleyball and go running to her mother to kiss it and make it all better. You'll forgive her, just like you *always* forgave me, and then go on to repeat the cycle until you two are the old ladies boarding a steam packet and traveling across all four oceans. You guys can even take my trunk if you want. I'll leave it to you in my will."

Chrissie almost did it. She almost pushed back from the table and left her terminally ill friend to find her own way the last four hundred miles to her destination. But one of the ironclad tenets of their relationship was that Scarlett was the one who left.

Chrissie was the one who stayed behind and held things together with every ounce of strength she had.

"That's the last joke I'll stand by and listen to you make about dying, so be very careful how you proceed," Chrissie said in the same tone of voice she used when Kat was being particularly difficult—a thing she often was, because she was very much her mother's daughter, and because Chrissie loved them both so much that she never tried to quash the indomitable spirit that beat its wings inside them. "I'm going to go with you to Vermont. I'm going to stand by and hold your hand while you do whatever it is you need to do to make peace with your decision. I'll love you and carry your remains home and inter them next to your grandmother's—"

But here she had to stop to draw a deep, shuddering breath. Her hands gripped the edge of the table so tightly that she could no longer feel her fingers, but Scarlett sat in shocked silence until she was able to finish.

"I'll lay you to rest next to that beautiful, kind woman who gave us both so much," she managed through a throat thick with tears. "And then I'm going to go home and take care of *our* daughter until she no longer needs me. Maybe that'll only be for a few more years, or maybe it'll be for the next sixty, but I made a promise and I intend to keep it. If you have a problem with *any* of that, that's too damn bad. My life will never be as big or as glamorous as you want it to be. I won't become a world-famous pianist. I might never get married. There's not some secret superpower lurking in my jacked-up, half-twin DNA waiting to be awakened from dormancy. I'm a boring, basic nobody who's learned to find joy in the simple things, and that's exactly how I intend to stay. Do you understand all of that?"

"Chrissie, I—"

Chrissie leaned across the table, her fingers still clutching the table. "It's a yes or no question, Scarlett, and those are the only responses I want to hear. Do. You. Understand?"

Chrissie could see the struggle taking place inside her friend. Scarlett ate one olive. Then another. She fidgeted and squirmed like a toddler trying to stave off naptime. When none of this failed to move Chrissie in the slightest, then and only then did she crash.

"Yes."

All of the air seemed to escape Chrissie at once. She leaned back against her chair, her adrenaline ebbing away only to leave an aching emptiness behind. With shaking hands, she dug her phone out of her purse and pulled up the website she'd bookmarked the night before. The time had come to start putting that list to good use. Not for

Scarlett to absolve herself of the guilt she was trying to unload before she died, and not because Chrissie was feeling particularly brave, but because it was time. It had been time for several years now.

Scarlett, never one to stay down for long, noticed what she was doing almost immediately.

"What are you doing? Is that an airline website?" Panic robbed Scarlett's voice of its usual rich timbre. "You aren't buying a ticket home, are you? You already said you'd stay with me. You promised!"

"And it's a promise I intend to keep, just as I've kept all the others," she said as she grabbed her credit card and started entering the information into the website. She didn't tell Scarlett what she was doing. Her friend would learn for herself soon enough.

"But for once in your goddamned life, Scarlett—even now, at the very end—I need you to realize that not everything in the world is about you."

Chapter Twenty-Four

PORTLAND, OR

2009

CHILDBIRTH WAS EVERY BIT AS HORRIBLE as Scarlett knew it would be.

"Get it out, please. I don't want to do this anymore. It hurts."

No matter how many times Scarlett said the words, no one seemed to be in a hurry to comply. Her delivery nurse—*not* Nurse Penny, alas, but a humorless block of a woman—and the bored-looking doctor who popped in every couple of hours just patted her on the knee and told her that she was doing great.

"But I'm not great. I'm not even good. Why won't anyone help me?"

Chrissie waited until the contraction passed before wiping Scarlett's forehead with the cool, jasmine-scented washcloth she'd somehow procured from the supply closet.

"It won't be much longer now, Scarlett. You've been through worse."

"I'm gonna *kill* Grimshaw."

"Not if I beat you to it."

"Then I'm gonna dance on his grave."

"I'll bring the playlist."

"I'll even pee on it."

"Why stop there? We should light the whole graveyard on fire."

Scarlett bit back a sudden sob—though whether it was a sob of physical or emotional pain, she couldn't say. Thanks to the birthing plan Chrissie had been vigilantly upholding, the room was set the exact way Scarlett had wanted it to be. Bright lights, the TV blaring, no sign of a mirror anywhere. She'd decided early on that she would avoid everything that had been suggested in the stupid pregnancy books. She didn't want to feel calm and one with nature. She didn't want to bond with her baby by watching its enormous head push through a hole that *definitely* wasn't big enough for all this. The less of the magic miracle oxytocin her body produced, the sooner she could put this whole horrible chapter behind her.

"Would you really light Grimshaw's grave on fire for me?" Scarlett asked. She barely had the energy to turn her head to look at her friend, but she was glad when she did. Chrissie's was a face she'd never get tired of looking at. "Really, truly?"

"Really, truly." Chrissie spoke in a tone that Scarlett knew she could trust. "I've got your back, Scarlett. For now and for always."

Scarlett nodded gratefully. The doctors could pump her full of drugs and jasmine-scented manna could fall from the heavens, and none of it would be half as effective as her best friend pressing a kiss on her sweaty forehead and promising to wreak vengeance on her enemies.

"And you still want this?" Scarlett asked. She could feel her stomach starting to clench like the jaws of a rabid animal were tearing her apart from the inside, but she kept talking. Talking was the only thing she'd ever really been good at. "You're sure you don't mind? You aren't going to think I'm a horrible person and stop talking to me forever when I move to Paris next month?"

The pain took over then, but Scarlett wasn't done. Even though she and Chrissie had sat down with a lawyer already—the most grown-up thing she'd ever done and, with any luck, the most grown-up thing she'd *ever* do—a part of her was still terrified that their plans would fall through.

That Chrissie would take one look at the baby about to become her sole responsibility and run screaming for the hills. That the money already transferred to Chrissie's account would prove insufficient to cover the first few years until Scarlett managed to find a well-paying job.

Or, most terrifying of all, that the doctors would put the baby in Scarlett's arms and one tiny glimpse of her daughter would make her change her mind about this whole thing.

"I could never think you're a horrible person, Scarlett." Chrissie leaned close and pressed her cool, soft forehead to Scarlett's sweaty one. "You're the love of my life, and you always will be."

Words became impossible as the contraction hit her in full. She breathed when Chrissie told her to. Screamed when breathing became too hard. By the time this one was over, she was so tired that all she could do was cling to her best friend's hand and croak one final command.

"And you won't tell her, right? Not ever? No matter what?"

Of all the rules Scarlett had attached to the upcoming adoption, that was the one Chrissie had caviled about the hardest. In almost every other regard, she and Chrissie were on the same page. The name Kathleen—to honor her grandmother—had been an easy one. The apartment in Medford and the funds from the life insurance payout had been transferred with just a few quick phone calls. Even Scarlett's plan to go to Paris, albeit on her own, had been surprisingly drama-free. Instead of balking at being left to care for a newborn baby all by herself, Chrissie had voiced her wholehearted approval.

"The entire point of this is so you can live your life, Scarlett," she'd said as they'd shopped together for all the things the two of them would need—diapers and baby bottles for Chrissie, luggage and a French translation guide for Scarlett. "If your life requires exotic world travel and endless adventure for the next fifty years, then I'm all in. Just don't forget to call sometimes."

Which was why it had been such a surprise when the one thing Chrissie couldn't understand—the thing she *wouldn't* understand—was Scarlett's need to cut all ties to this child.

"The moment I put her in your arms, she's yours," Scarlett said now. She was desperate—not just to get this baby out of her, but to hear Chrissie confirm one more time that she could walk away after all this was done.

Guiltless. Untethered. *Free.*

"Please, Chrissie. I can't tell her. I'd never want her to think that I—"

She screamed then, but not from the pain. This was frustration, pure and simple.

"You don't have to say anything more," Chrissie said when the sound finally ebbed away. "I promise. If that's what you need to get through this, then I'll do it. I'll never tell her anything about her real birth mom."

That moment marked the first true rift in their friendship. Chrissie didn't feel it, since she was busy scooping ice chips and holding them to Scarlett's lips, but Scarlett felt it twinge inside of her, so deep that she knew the baby must have felt it, too.

What she couldn't seem to put into words, no matter how many times she tried, was that she knew exactly how this baby would feel if Chrissie told her the truth about her parentage. To grow up knowing that her mother didn't want her, that her mother had *never* wanted her, would ruin any chance the poor little scrap had of real happiness.

She knew because she'd lived that feeling every day of her life. Chrissie might be able to forgive and forget, to somehow become a better person despite her upbringing, but this child had Scarlett's blood. She'd resent the woman who gave her away and spend her whole life wondering what it was that had made her so difficult to love.

"Let's see how things are progressing, shall we?" asked the nurse as she stepped into the room. Scarlett tried not to react as her legs were pried open and an intrusive hand shoved between then, but when these actions were accompanied by an excited "I do believe we're ready to get this show on the road," she cried.

She continued crying for the next twenty minutes as people shouted at her to push and told her how brave she was being. She cried as her insides were ripped out of her body, followed by a gushing sensation that felt like a waterslide pouring through her. She cried even more when a warm, wet, squirming bundle was mistakenly placed on her chest instead of being handed to Chrissie.

The nurse must have realized her mistake because she immediately snatched the baby away.

"No—wait," Scarlett cried. "Give her back for a second."

Even though the most important and highly underlined part of the birth plan had directed every staff member to give the baby to Chrissie, to defer to Chrissie's wishes, to treat Chrissie as the most important person in the room at every turn, Scarlett tossed all of that aside the moment she caught sight of that red, squished, angry little face.

Nothing about what had just happened to her was a miracle. There were still people doing unmentionable things to her body, and her baby was covered in a slimy substance that smelled just as unmentionable. So far from being an angelic vision, the baby looked like she wanted nothing more than to tell the people in the room exactly what she thought about the horrible treatment she'd just undergone.

It was that look that halted Scarlett in her tracks.

"I feel the exact same way, kid," Scarlett said, unable to stop herself. "What did either of us do to deserve *that*?"

"You can change your mind, you know." Chrissie flicked a finger to touch the baby's wet cheek. In the back of her mind, Scarlett realized that Chrissie's face was equally wet, streaked with tears that none of them had heard fall, but the way she smiled down at them indicated nothing but complete joy. "Women do sometimes. I read about it, and I'm not going to hold you to any promises except the ones you choose to keep."

"I don't want to keep her," Scarlett said quickly—too quickly, her voice harsh enough to cause the baby to let out a protesting squall. "I just want a second to tell her something."

The baby squirmed awkwardly in her arms, as if aware that the person holding her had no idea what she was doing. But then she blinked and looked up at Scarlett, and everything shifted.

The amount of love—of trust—in that gaze was almost more than she could bear.

"I wasn't going to do this," she told the baby in a low voice. She was dimly aware of the medical staff stepping out of the room to leave her with Chrissie and the baby, but it didn't matter. Privacy had gone out the window the moment she'd put her feet in the stirrups, and any respect the nurses had for her had disappeared once they realized she was really and truly going to hand her baby off to her eighteen-year-old best friend to raise on her own. "I was going to give you to your mom without a word so you wouldn't get attached to my voice. It seemed safer that way...for us both."

Chrissie made a motion to follow the rest of the staff into the hallway but Scarlett gave a slight shake of her head. What she had to say was for Chrissie's benefit almost as much as the baby's—Kathleen Genevieve Thomas, a big name for a small person, and the only thing Scarlett planned to give her before she ran away as fast and as far as her legs would take her.

"I'm sorry I can't do better than this," she said, still in the low voice that sounded strange to her own ears. "And I'm sorry that you'll never get to meet the great-grandma you're named for. You'd have liked her—and she, I know, would have adored you."

But not me. She'd have been so *disappointed in me.*

She started crying then, and was annoyed with herself for indulging in tears. She didn't deserve them. Not from herself, and not from anyone. As if recognizing her distress, the baby began crying, too.

"I know, kid. It's awful. *I'm* awful. But I'm doing you a favor in the long run, I promise. A week from now, you're going to wake up in your beautiful bassinet to the sight of your beautiful mother, and you'll realize that you've got the best possible life ahead of you." The baby stopped crying long enough to blink up at her. Scarlett leaned down to press a kiss on her puckered little forehead and then drew a deep breath. "The next time I kiss you, it will be as your cool, worldly Aunt Scarlett and nothing more. I'll buy you all the candy you want and teach you about Paris and tell you stories about all the ways your mom pulled me out of trouble when we were kids."

With a strength she didn't know she had, Scarlett lifted the baby and put her into Chrissie's waiting arms.

"Scarlett..." Chrissie began, but there was nothing she could say. This was what they'd decided on. This was what Scarlett wanted.

The moment her arms were empty, Scarlett felt the absence of the baby as a physical ache so deep that she wondered if it was a wound that would ever heal. Almost—*almost*—she asked for her back. But when she saw the way Chrissie's whole body went soft, the way the two of them looked at each other, she knew she'd made the right choice.

"I'm sorry, Kitty Kat," she said again, this time with her normal voice. She waited until Chrissie's gaze caught hers before saying the one thing that meant more than all the rest—the one thing that had haunted her ever since her own mom had walked out on her and never looked back.

It was a mother's abandonment, an escape. An act of cruelty and love so intertwined that Scarlett finally found a way to forgive.

"I don't have it in me to take care of you, so I'm doing the next best thing. I'm giving you to someone who can."

Chapter Twenty-Five

TRANQUILITY ESTATES, VERMONT

Present Day

"I HAD NO IDEA YOU WERE such a horse girl. Your parents missed a serious opportunity when they put you in piano instead of dressage."

Chrissie pulled on the reins and gently murmured "whoa," as she'd been instructed. The horse she was sitting atop—a brown, silken creature with a glorious mane and the even more glorious name of Shadowfox—immediately came to a halt and whinnied.

"I didn't know I was a horse girl, either," she confessed as she took the hand being offered her and slid down from the horse. The stable hand, a gruff, grizzled man who walked with a limp and could have been anywhere from forty to eighty years old, grunted and began leading the animal away before Chrissie could book another appointment to ride the animal.

She suspected that the horses were actually supposed to be for the patients of the facility, part of the entire line of therapeutic relaxation offerings that included a spa, hot baths, sunrise yoga, group talk sessions, and art classes, but Scarlett had taken one look at the massive, heaving animal and decided to watch from a comfortable Adirondack chair overlooking the corral.

"Well, I think you should take up riding when you get back home," Scarlett said. Before Chrissie could say anything, she added, "And no, that's not me trying to order your life from beyond the grave. It's just a suggestion. Medford probably has lots of good stables to choose from. You know how people in small towns get about horses. They're all one step removed from going full Wyatt Earp."

Chrissie nodded, unable to voice the protest that was bubbling up inside her throat. For some reason, setting foot at this place had deflated any and all of the arguments that had sprung up between them over the past few days.

Maybe it was how warmly they'd been greeted at the gates and shown to their private cabin, or perhaps it was the way they'd immediately been visited by a hospice nurse who had a full working knowledge of Scarlett's medical history, prognosis, and end-of-life plans, but for the first time since Chicago, Chrissie felt as if she was standing on solid ground again.

"I might just do that," she agreed. "Well? What's next? A dip in the pool? A tour of the grounds? A nap?"

Scarlett pulled a face at that last one. "I've never taken a nap that wasn't medically enforced, and I'm not about to start now." Her frown deepened. "And I wish you'd stop agreeing with everything I say. If you don't want to ride horses, then don't. I'm not holding a gun to your head."

Chrissie tried not to react to that, either, but considering where they were, it wasn't easy.

"Ha!" Scarlett pounced—in a purely metaphorical way, of course. Thanks to the prescription she'd picked up from the on-site pharmacy, which included not only the drugs she would eventually take in the quiet of her cabin but also a host of other things designed to ease her discomfort, she was more languid and relaxed than Chrissie had ever seen her. "See? You *are* still mad at me. I think we should go to the soundproof room and scream for a while. The intake specialist said it can be very helpful."

Chrissie busied herself with brushing the horse hairs from her jeans. She didn't make much progress, but at least she was able to buy herself a few seconds to gain her bearings.

"If you'd like to scream, I'm more than happy to go with you. But I do all of my screaming on the inside like a lady, thank you."

Scarlett laughed and allowed Chrissie to help her to her feet. She was oncc again wearing her beige cashmere sweat suit and oversized sunglasses, looking so much like a waifish and chic millionaire that it *almost* felt like they were staying at some upscale rehab facility instead of a place where majestic horses and scream rooms gently ushered you to your death.

"That's the most accurate description of you I've ever heard," Scarlett said as she linked her arm in Chrissie's. She rested her head on Chrissie's shoulder with a sigh. "It's nice here, right? You don't hate it? You don't want to leave?"

"I hate it with every cell in my body," Chrissie said. "But no, I don't want to leave."

There wasn't much more to say after that. According to the hospice nurse, they were free to use the facilities as much or as little as they wanted. Their cabin was private and entirely their own for the duration of their stay. Room service was included whenever they wanted it, the doctor could be visited at any time, and therapy sessions were offered around the clock. The only thing that differentiated it from an all-inclusive resort was that when the time came to check out, only Chrissie would be leaving through the front door.

"Oh! Ms. Thomas. There you are. I thought I might find you out in the stables. Everyone always seems to want to start here." One of the staff members, a short, ponytailed woman in a blue polo shirt bearing the Tranquility Estates logo, came bustling up to them with a clipboard in her hand. "I was able to book the extra cabin, as you requested. We're also happy to move you to one of the bigger rentals, if you'd all prefer to stay under one roof. It's entirely up to you, of course. I just need two signatures here and here."

Chrissie took the pen being offered her and braced for the incoming storm. When it didn't come, she took a few extra seconds pretending to read through the fine print on the form. When it *still* didn't come, she plastered a bright smile on her face and handed the pen back.

"And you're sure about the pet policy?" she asked.

"Oh, yes. Lots of our guests prefer to have their four-legged friends with them at the end. One man even brought his eight-legged friend. I can't say I *enjoyed* catching grasshoppers and crickets for a tarantula's dinner, but it's all part of what we do here." She checked and nodded at Scarlett. Some of the false brightness dimmed to be replaced with a genuine smile. "If you need anything, Ms. Sanderson, just say the word. No request is off-limits."

The woman took herself off then, pausing only to share a few words with the grizzled stable hand. Scarlett waited until she disappeared from view before turning toward Chrissie. She looked so much like her grandmother, what with the purse of her lips and annoyed crinkles around her eyes, that Chrissie felt all the unfairness of the situation rushing back to her.

Scarlett would never get a chance to grow into the woman her grandmother had been—full of warmth and beloved of everyone she met, fiercely protective of those she called her own. She'd been handed a ticking clock from almost the moment of her birth, and even though they'd all done their best to push the hands back, there was no reversing them now.

Unfortunately, the softening of Chrissie's heart couldn't have come at a worse time. She was going to need all the armor she could get if she wanted out of this part alive.

"Chrissie, please tell me you bought me a puppy somewhere on the road and have been hiding it from me this whole time." Scarlett's voice was almost as rough as the stable hand's. "Or that you've ordered an exotic bird online and are having it delivered here as a final gift to me."

"Yeeeaah. About that—"

Scarlett shoved her—as in, actually lifted a hand and pushed it against Chrissie's shoulder. She wasn't strong enough to do much damage, but Chrissie was forced to take a step back to avoid falling flat on her ass.

"At the very most, I'll allow Rufio to be shipped here in a crate—but only if you've officially decided to do away with him and want to make sure he goes out in comfort." Scarlett shoved again. Again, Chrissie had to keep moving backwards if she wanted to stay standing. "Is Rufio being shipped here in a crate? Is that what this is?"

Chrissie ducked out of the way to avoid the next attack.

"Scarlett, don't. You'll wear yourself out."

"Maybe you should've thought of that before you invited complete strangers to my deathbed. That's why you were on that airline website, isn't it?" Scarlett's voice suddenly turned sharp. This time, it wasn't her grandmother that peeked through, but Kat—angry, frustrated, *heartsick* Kat. "Chrissie, how could you? I wanted it to be just the two of us for a reason. I know I haven't handled this whole thing the way you'd have liked, but it's my decision. My body, my life, my goodbye."

"And it still will be your decision. You don't have to see or talk to anyone you don't want to." Honesty compelled Chrissie to pause and add, "Actually, that's not true. If you'd prefer to keep Walsh and Lily and the dratted cat away, then I promise you won't even catch a whiff of them. I completely respect your privacy in that regard. But that's where I draw the line."

All of the color drained from Scarlett's face.

"What did you do?" she demanded. "What did you tell her?"

"I haven't told Kat anything…yet. But if you thought you could just up and die without telling that girl goodbye, you underestimated me." Chrissie crossed her arms, aware that she was treading a fine line and determined to move forward anyway.

The truth was, Scarlett wasn't wrong about her. Chrissie would never be the type of woman who made a lasting impression. She could write out all the lists in the world and make all the viral videos she wanted, but there was no denying that she was happiest in her cat-pee-scented home with a home-cooked meal on one end of the table and her daughter busy doing homework on the other. People would continue taking advantage of her good nature. Stray teenagers in piano bars would continue to beg her to drive them across the country. She'd grow and cut her hair in an endless cycle as a self-imposed penance for her brother's death, and that was okay with her.

But no one—not even Scarlett—was going to hurt her baby.

"Their flight gets in tomorrow morning, so you'd better start planning what you want to say—and I can tell you right now that if it doesn't include the words *I*, *am*, *your*, and *mother*, then you'll be finishing your stay here without me."

The color came rushing back to Scarlett's face at such a rapid pace that Chrissie had to reach out and steady her.

"You can't be serious, Chrissie. Why would I tell her that here? *Now?* We had a deal. You made a promise!"

"Yeah, well. I'm breaking it. Sue me."

Scarlett was startled into a harsh laugh. "You can't make me do anything."

"No, I can't. But I'm telling her the truth one way or another, so I'm giving you a chance to come clean first." Chrissie blew out a long breath. She'd known she had a battle on her hands, but she hadn't realized how much it would cost to strike the killing blow against a woman who only had a few days left to live. "You heard the things she said, Scarlett. About how her father and grandparents want nothing to do with her, about how the only person she has in her life is me. To her, that's the reality she lives every day, but you and I both know that's not true. Whether you admit it or not, you've been there for her every step of the way."

"Please, Chrissie. I can't."

"You can, and you will. The last time you begged me like this was when you were giving birth to that child, and you managed to push her out just fine." Chrissie had to bite down on her tongue to keep the sympathy from rising. She needed to get through this while she still had enough anger in her heart to successfully pull it off. "You made me write that stupid list for a reason, remember? You want me to learn to stand up for myself and put my own needs before other people's, so I am. It just so happens that the person I'm putting them in front of is *you*."

Scarlett opened her mouth and closed it again, her eyes so wide that Chrissie could see the map of red veins traveling across them. "Well, I'll be damned."

"I hope not. I'd very much like to see you again someday."

Scarlett staggered back as though struck. For the longest moment, Chrissie was afraid she'd overstepped some unknown boundary between them. She stood by her decision to tell Kat the truth, and she refused to regret this new foray into self-assertion, but she desperately hoped it wouldn't come at the cost of her best friend. That was the one price she'd never been asked to pay before.

Which was why it came as such a surprise when Scarlett rushed into Chrissie's arms.

"I don't want to die," she said on a sob. Her whole body heaved as she gave herself over to the emotions flooding through her. Even though

Scarlett's head was buried in her shoulder, Chrissie could hear each word as clearly as a bell being rung against her heart. "I'm not finished yet. There's so much I haven't seen. So many things I haven't done."

Any remaining anger Chrissie might have felt toward her friend disappeared in that instant. She ran her hand over the short strands of Scarlett's hair, the oversized sunglasses hitting the ground with the shatter of plastic.

"I know, sweetie. Shh. It's okay. I know."

Scarlett's petite, emaciated body shook in her arms, the tears flowing so hot and fast that there was no containing them. That, more than anything else, spoke to the despair that had so far remained unspoken between them. In all their years of friendship—in good times and bad, in sickness and health—Scarlett had never cried like this before. According to her, life was too short to waste on tears, and there was always something new and shiny around the corner.

She was right about that first part, but not the second. Once Scarlett turned that corner, there would be no going back again.

"It's not fair," Scarlett added, still clutching Chrissie as though she was the only thing keeping her standing. Chrissie continued murmuring into Scarlett's hair—nonsense words and maternal nothings, the same kind of thing she used to say to Kat when she fell down and scraped her knees on the playground—but then Scarlett spoke again. "You've had to bury so many people already. We keep leaving you behind to hold the pieces together without us. And I'm so afraid that we'll keep doing it until you finally shatter."

For the longest moment, Chrissie didn't speak. She couldn't. Her whole life, she'd operated under the belief that Scarlett's love for her—though deep—was selfish. To love Scarlett Sanderson was to stand in her shadow. Something bigger and brighter always loomed on her horizon, and the best you could hope for was to be standing in the right place when she moved enough to let the sunshine through.

But she'd been wrong. Scarlett wasn't the gatekeeper of the sunshine. She *was* the sunshine.

"I'll tell her anything you want," Scarlett sobbed. She was too absorbed in her own grief to notice that Chrissie had gone perfectly still. "I'll tell her everything. If it's what you really want, I'll move heaven and earth to make it happen."

Chapter Twenty-Six

TRANQUILITY ESTATES, VERMONT

Present Day

CHRISSIE STOOD ALONE AT THE GATES to Tranquility Estates, her hand raised to shield her eyes as the rideshare she'd ordered pulled up to deposit two bewildered teenagers, one exhausted man, and a howling cat in a carrier.

"You have no idea how happy I am to see you." Walsh was the first to speak. Since he was the one holding Rufio, who rattled inside his carrier the way Chrissie imagined a rabid raccoon might, she was pretty sure she understood why.

"Was he awful on the plane? Did he pee on everything? Are you banned from that airline forever?" She rushed forward to relieve Walsh of his burden, but by the time she reached him, he'd already set the carrier down. He'd also opened his arms and pulled her into a bear hug that knocked the breath right out of her body.

"How are you holding up?" He didn't relax his hold on her by so much as an inch. "We've been worried sick about you. When we got delayed in Denver, I thought Kat was going to hijack one of the planes and start flying it herself." He chuckled, the rumbling of his warm, solid body so thorough that she was forced to move with him. "She probably could, too. I wouldn't put anything past that girl."

Kat snorted. "It's not like it's hard. Planes are almost all automated these days anyway."

Contrary to Chrissie's expectations, Walsh didn't relinquish his position right away. He lingered long enough to step back and put his hands on Chrissie's shoulders, his face inches from hers as he examined every line of her swollen-eyed exhaustion. She could smell the mint on his breath and the tang of his aftershave, feel the warmth pulsing from his palms into her skin.

"Do you need anything? A bag of pretzels? A tiny bottle of alcohol? Hand sanitizer? We raided the airline supplies while the flight attendant's back was turned."

Chrissie shook her head, unable to speak around the sudden lump in her throat. Until this exact moment, she hadn't realized just how much she'd needed a friend—*this* friend in particular. Walsh's calm, easy affability was so far removed from this place that it almost felt wrong.

"Okay. But if you change your mind, I'm pretty sure Kat and Lily are hoarding a few illicit bottles in their backpacks. I'm planning on grounding Lily later, but Kat's punishment is on you."

Instead of laughing, as her daughter normally did whenever Walsh teased her, Kat pushed herself forward.

"If I *did* steal alcohol, I'm pretty sure it's justified." She swept an anxious look at the gate, with its elegantly scrolling script and high-tech security camera mounted up high, the rolling hills extending behind it. Like Chrissie, she seemed to have a difficult time reconciling the gorgeous grounds with what they signified. "Mom, Scarlett's not *really* dying, is she?"

Chrissie's chest squeezed so tightly that she couldn't breathe for a full twenty seconds. A few weeks ago, she'd have given anything to hear that particular note in Kat's voice. It had been a long time since her daughter felt safe—and vulnerable—enough to let her guard down, especially in front of someone like Lily. But although the other girl looked uncomfortable, her tall, lean body shifting from one foot to the other as she chewed nervously on the end of one of her box braids, she didn't seem to feel any urge to rake Kat down.

"I'm afraid she is, Kitty Kat." Even that—her use of Kat's despised nickname—didn't have its usual reaction.

Risking everything, or perhaps nothing at all, Chrissie reached out to pull her daughter into her arms.

"I'm so sorry, sweetie. I'd have never dragged you across the country unless it was for real."

Like the hug with Walsh, the tight grip of her daughter's embrace seemed to unlock all of the tension that had been holding Chrissie together. She'd promised herself that she wouldn't cry, that she'd be the strong, stoic mother Kat would need to get through this, but it was all too much. The familiar scent of Kat's shampoo, the way her breath whooshed over her skin… It was like coming home after a long, painful absence.

"But I don't understand." Kat's voice was muffled where it pressed into Chrissie's neck. "Was Aunt Scarlett going to leave without telling me? Without saying goodbye?"

Thankfully, Chrissie and Scarlett had already discussed this part last night. They'd discussed *a lot* of things last night, and even though none of it had been pleasant, it had been necessary.

"Do you remember that time Rufio disappeared for a few days and we couldn't find him anywhere?" Chrissie asked gently. She pulled away just enough to search her daughter's face—that sweet, heart-shaped face that was so similar to Scarlett's, but with the long-lashed, dark eyes that belonged to Grimshaw. Kat was so much a part of both of them that Chrissie could see it in every expression. "We were worried he'd run off to find his previous owners, but the vet said it was more likely that he was dying and wanted to do it somewhere private."

Kat sniffled. "You spent two whole nights searching the neighborhood for him. I was worried he'd change his mind and not be able to make it back to us on his own."

Chrissie nodded and smiled at this oversimplification of what had been, at the time, a harrowing experience. Kat had been eleven years old and so enamored of that dratted cat that Chrissie would have spent every night outside for a year if Kat had asked it of her. But Rufio had eventually dragged himself back, having decided that the life he lost was only one of nine.

"It's a bit like that," Chrissie said. "Scarlett didn't want to hurt you, that's all. She was trying to save you the heartache by making sure your last memory of her was a good one."

"But not you? She didn't care how much *you* hurt?"

The question almost laid Chrissie out flat. Trust a child to cut straight to the heart of a matter and then stand by watching as the bleeding started.

Walsh's hand came crashing down on Kat's shoulder.

"I expect it's a little more complicated than that. When you've been friends with someone as long as your mom and Scarlett have, there's a lot of baggage that doesn't get unpacked in time. Or at all." He drew a deep breath and smiled down on them both. "Speaking of baggage, what do you say we find our room and get this poor cat settled in? We're all a little worse for wear right now."

"Yes. Yes of course." Chrissie felt her cheeks flame as she realized her lapse. These three—four, if she counted Rufio—had been traveling for almost sixteen hours, and it showed. "I'm staying with Scarlett, but I booked you guys a separate cabin. It's got a really pretty view of the Green Mountains, and you can walk to the stables from there. I asked, and they said you're welcome to use as many of the amenities as you want. All they ask is that you respect the privacy of the other guests."

Walsh nodded and started hoisting the suitcases. Kat looked far from happy to leave the conversation there, but she picked up Rufio and prepared to follow suit. Only Lily hesitated, one of her braids still dangling from her lips.

"I don't like this place," she announced. Like Kat, she was dressed in black leggings and a crop top—the chosen outfit of almost every volleyball player under the age of twenty—her expression one of mingled distaste and fear. "It's weird. This whole thing is weird."

Chrissie braced herself for Kat's inevitable explosion, but her daughter only rolled her eyes and handed Lily the cat carrier.

"Yeah, well. I told you already. My family is weird. Wait until you meet my aunt Scarlett. She's the only person I know who could throw a destination funeral and make it seem like the most natural thing in the world."

Chrissie grimaced as she watched the two girls head up the gravel drive. Walsh made no move to follow them, his own expression heavier than she was used to seeing on him.

"I don't think Kat's fully processed what's about to happen," he said in a voice soft enough for only her to hear. "To be honest, I don't know that Lily and I have, either. Far be it from me to critique your parenting choices, Chrissie, but are you sure you want her here for this? Or any of us? Your friend—"

"Is dying to meet you," Chrissie said and gave a bitter laugh. "Sorry. Bad joke. But if you left now, I'm not sure I could get through this on my own, and she knows it. She won't turn you away."

"Chrissie..."

Chrissie shook her head and flung up a hand to keep Walsh from throwing aside the suitcases and pulling her into another of those warm, friendly hugs. She wanted one so much that it was a physical ache, but that kind of proximity was too dangerous. Until she talked to Kat, until *Scarlett* talked to Kat…

Well, it was too risky, that was all.

"Please don't, Walsh. I know what you want to say—that Kat's just a kid, that Scarlett should be allowed to die on her own terms, that there's a good chance I'm ruining everything that's left of my relationship with my daughter by dragging her here to be a part of this." There was so much truth in what she said that she had to fight a wave of nausea before continuing. "The truth is, the situation is a little more complicated than I told you over the phone."

Walsh hesitated, anxious lines starting to form behind the lenses of his plastic-rimmed glasses. "Complicated *how*?"

Chrissie drew a deep breath. This would be the first of many such confessions, and she wasn't looking forward to any of them.

"Kat doesn't know this yet, but I'm not her biological mother."

She didn't say the rest. There was no need. The puzzled anxiety that made Walsh look so endearing transformed first to surprise and then to understanding.

And then, as the full meaning sank in, pity.

"Oh," he said. "*Oh*."

"Yeah," she agreed. "*Oh*."

Walsh took his time formulating his response, his mouth working as though testing the weight of his words ahead of time. "To be honest, I *did* wonder after I saw Scarlett on one of our video calls. There's something about the shape of her face and the way she carries herself. It's almost like—"

"She's never questioned her place in the world or what she wants out of it? Confidence oozes out of her pores and makes everyone around her feel inadequate?"

"I was going to say that she seems like a woman who's used to getting her own way, but that works, too." His lips twisted in a wry grimace. "Kat's going to be none too pleased when she finds out you've been hiding this from her. She's putting up a brave front, but I think this news will hit her a lot harder than either of you anticipate."

Chrissie believed it. "If you and Lily want to get out of here before the fireworks start, I won't blame you one bit. Things are going to get worse before they get, well, even worse."

Walsh glanced toward the retreating forms of the two girls before fixing his whole attention on her. Basking in it felt like basking in the full glory of the sun, but not in the same way she felt around Scarlett. Scarlett's light was all-consuming and dangerous to the touch; Walsh's was a beacon she could follow to any safe shore.

"You haven't scared me away yet, Chrissie," he said gently. "What makes you think I'm going to run now?"

The moment Chrissie and Scarlett stepped into the cabin rented for Walsh, Kat, Lily, and Rufio, she knew she was in trouble.

"Oh, he's *tall.* And good-looking. And—wait—is that salmon I smell? Good for you, Chrissie. No one has ever cooked me salmon before."

Scarlett uttered each of these sentences at top volume to ensure that no innuendo was missed. The cabins at Tranquility Estates were spacious, with fully equipped open kitchens, two to four bedrooms depending on need, and a back patio angled to give the appearance that they were all alone in the most beautiful corner of the earth, but when Scarlett wanted to be heard, Scarlett was heard.

Chrissie was tempted to flee right then and there, but Walsh dispelled the mounting tension with his low chuckle.

"Don't get too excited. The salmon is for Rufio. The rest of us are having burgers." He paused in the act of basting the filet of salmon on the stove to offer Scarlett his hand. "You must be Scarlett. Come on in and have a seat. Can I pour you a glass of something? Beer? Wine? Hemlock?"

It was the exact right thing to say. Scarlett, who'd been looking particularly wilted on the walk over, perked up and flashed Walsh her most flirtatious smile.

"The hemlock will have to wait. I'm not due to meet my maker for another forty-eight hours. The wine sounds good, though."

He winked at her and poured out two generous glasses of pinot grigio—a wine that happened to be Chrissie's preferred choice, and that Scarlett immediately understood the significance of.

"*And* he buys your favorite kind of suburban mom wine?" Scarlett tsked as she settled onto a stool propped next to the kitchen counter. Chrissie would have vastly preferred to see her on the couch—or, if possible, one of the chaise longues outside—but she knew better than to make the suggestion. "No wonder you get all blushing and giggly when you talk about him. I officially approve."

Walsh merely waggled his eyebrows as he returned to the salmon, but Kat bounded out of one of the bedrooms with a scowl turning down the corners of her mouth.

"Gross. Don't encourage them."

Scarlett started a slow blink at Kat as she took a leisurely sip of her wine. "Don't encourage two grown people who've been good friends for years? Who clearly respect and admire each other? Whose daughters are almost all grown up and will be going away to college in a few short years?" She blinked even slower. "You're right. What could I possibly be thinking?"

Kat flushed an angry pink. The color matched her bicycling shorts and flip-flops almost to the exact shade. "It's not fair. You're just taking Mom's side because you know I can't start a fight with you."

"Sure you can. What's stopping you?"

Chrissie's whole body flinched. Her whole *being* flinched, actually, and she had to lock her muscles to keep from jumping into the conversation—though whether she wanted to support her daughter or support her friend, she had no idea.

In the next ten seconds, Kat's face went through almost every imaginable emotion like the spinning of a slot machine, but it landed on a pinched determination not to cry.

"That's not funny, Aunt Scarlett."

Scarlett took another calm sip of her wine. "I mean, it's a little bit funny. I could say anything I want to you right now, and you can't do anything about it. For the next two days, you're basically my emotional hostage." She pursed her lips and tapped them thoughtfully. "Hmm. I wonder where I should start. With the fact that your eyeliner is lopsided on one side? Or that you're single-handedly ruining your mother's chances at happiness because you refuse to consider anyone's needs but your own?"

All the mounting color drained out of Kat's face. Chrissie gasped and almost dropped her wine. Even Walsh coughed uncomfortably, the salmon starting to burn.

Chrissie opened her mouth to defend her daughter, but Lily stepped into the room then, Rufio carried in her arms like a baby. The cat looked none the worse for his cross-country journey and actually seemed to be enjoying his captivity in the lanky teenager's arms. He even mewled a protest when Lily set him down on the floor and turned to face the three adults, her arms akimbo.

"You guys are being serious jerks right now." Lily snatched the plate of salmon her dad held out and put it on the floor for the cat. Rufio pounced on the pink square of fish in a way that Chrissie had never seen before.

She'd also never seen Lily willingly put an arm around Kat's shoulders before, but she did that, too, offering Kat a quick squeeze before letting go.

"You're not the only people this is happening to, you know," Lily said. "If all you're gonna do is make jokes like any of this is normal, then you're the ones only thinking about yourselves."

Chrissie stared, trying not to let her shock show as Kat threw Lily a grateful glance. "Thanks, Lily. That means a lot."

"Yeah, well. I know injustice when I see it." Lily shrugged as though uncomfortable with the new role being assigned to her. "You three can eat your stupid burgers and drink your stupid wine and laugh your stupid laughs. We're heading down to the stables to see the horses."

Kat visibly brightened. Chrissie wouldn't have gone so far as to say that she looked *happy*, but she no longer looked like she was going to cry.

"Do you think they'll let us ride them this late in the day?" Kat asked.

"I don't see why not. And if they don't, we'll just take them out on our own and make our parents pay for the damages."

With that, Lily turned on her heel and stalked out of the room. Kat paused just long enough to glance back at Chrissie—seeking permission, maybe? or a refusal?—but when all Chrissie did was shrug, she took herself off without another word.

"Well, really," Scarlett said as soon as the door slammed shut behind the girls. "They don't honestly think they can steal a pair of horses in flip-flops, do they?"

Chrissie almost spat out her wine. Kat was right, and there was very little about this situation that was funny, but she couldn't help it. "Scarlett!"

"What?" Scarlett shrugged. "I'm just saying. If you're going to storm off in a huff, it's better to do it in a pair of tennis shoes—or better yet, Doc Martens. They'll learn the hard way, I suppose. As did we all."

"I'll drink to that," Walsh said as he raised his glass.

"Here, here!" Scarlett raised hers in return.

As they both turned the toast on Chrissie, a whirling mix of emotions flooded through her. This moment in time was everything she'd never known she wanted: Scarlett and Walsh in the same room together, getting along as though they'd known each other their whole lives; her daughter and her daughter's nemesis banding together to fight against the imagined tyranny of youth. Even Rufio was content as he finished his meal, his furry little paws busy as he wiped away the crumbs from his whiskers.

Tears started falling before she could stop them.

"Oh, geez." Scarlett made a motion as if to rush to her, but Walsh was the first to reach Chrissie's side.

"Shh, Chrissie. It's okay. They won't get into any real trouble." He pressed a napkin into her hand and fell into a squat in front of her, his eyes gently probing as he scanned her face. It was a position she'd seen him adopt hundreds of times before, a way of putting himself on a level with whatever teenage volleyball player was falling apart in front of him at the time.

"No, I know." She dabbed the napkin ineffectively at her eyes. "It's not that. At least, not entirely."

Scarlett spoke up from her position on the stool. "It's me she's upset with, Walsh. Well, me and fate."

"Mostly fate." Chrissie sniffled. "And I'm not sad—at least, not about the girls."

Walsh took her hands and lightly chafed them, his gaze still tender as he continued watching her for signs of distress. She'd never admit it to Scarlett, but that small intimacy meant more to her than a thousand romantic kisses on top of the Eiffel Tower or weeks of passion on the Amalfi Coast.

"I'm okay, Walsh. Really." She managed a smile. "In fact, I can't believe we didn't think of doing this before. Nothing unites people like a common enemy."

"A reverse *Parent Trap*." His thumbs brushed over the backs of her hands as he rose to his full height and pulled her into a hug. "All we have to do is be as cringey in public as possible, and they'll be so busy hating us that they'll forget they ever had a rivalry between them."

The image these words conjured up—of a future where she and Walsh were an "us," where Kat and Lily had the support of each other to draw from—was so agreeable that she almost started crying again. But Walsh still had his arm around her waist and Scarlett was beaming so hard that she couldn't eke out a single tear.

This is okay. I'm okay.

As if echoing the words inside her own head, Scarlett nodded. She also set down the wineglass, which, despite the sips she'd been taking, remained full.

"Well, that's one loose end tied up," Scarlett said. "A few more, and I think I can finally set the seal on this thing."

Chrissie didn't trust Scarlett's tone for an instant. "What do you mean? What other loose ends are you dangling around?"

"You mean, other than playing matchmaker between you two and gathering up the nerve to reveal my deep, dark past to a teenage girl who's going to hate me for the rest of her life?" Scarlett shrugged. "Don't make me reveal *all* my secrets, Chrissie. A little mystery is the only thing I have left."

Walsh's arm slid away from Chrissie's waist. Her first instinct at losing that warm, solid support was to cry out in protest, but he coughed and scooped up the cat before she could make a sound.

"I'll just take Rufio to his patch of fake grass and start the grill for dinner." He winked. "And maybe call down to the stables to make sure all their horses are accounted for. Just to be on the safe side."

Chrissie waited only until he ducked out of view before settling onto the stool next to Scarlett. She slid her hand over her friend's.

"She's not going to hate you for the rest of her life, Scarlett. She might be a little upset at first, but she'll come around. She loves you more than almost anyone else on the planet. She always has."

Scarlett toyed with Chrissie's fingers the way she used to when they were kids, when Chrissie's ability to sit at a piano and force music to flow from them was a source of wonder to Scarlett. She'd always said there was something supernatural about Chrissie's skill, as though it had been the product of magic rather than the hard, boring, laborious work of reality.

"Is it awful that I never really considered what life must be like for her?" Scarlett asked as she started picking at a hangnail on Chrissie's thumb. "Not knowing her dad or having grandparents or aunts and uncles and cousins, I mean. I always assumed that giving her you was enough."

Chrissie had to smile. "Don't you mean giving her *to* me?"

"No." Scarlett's hands grew still. "I know you love that girl more than anything, and that you think about her every minute of every day, but I've never been the least bit worried about her." When she glanced up, it was through eyes wet with tears. "That day in the hospital was the only time in my life I've done an unselfish act. I knew, even before I put Kat in your arms, that you were going to love her more than me—that you would *always* love her more than me."

Chrissie wished she could find it in her to protest, but one of the nice things—the *only* nice thing—about this situation was how bare it stripped them both.

"I think that's why it never occurred to me that her life might be lacking. You were the only person I ever needed, so why should she be any different?" Scarlett drew a deep breath and slid her hand back to her lap. "Once I gave her my best friend in the whole world, what else could she possibly need?"

This time, Chrissie *did* protest. "We're still best friends, Scarlett. We've never stopped being that."

"Yeah, but it's never been the same since she was born. Every decision you've made has taken her into consideration first. Just think about how long it took us to finally go on this road trip together—and how much I had to coerce you to make it happen."

Chrissie didn't say anything. There was no need. Every word Scarlett spoke was the truth.

"Even now, even here, you're putting her before me." Scarlett flashed Chrissie a sad smile. "Don't get me wrong—I'm not complaining. She *should* be your first concern, and I'm glad you're going to have each other to lean on. It's not how I expected things to go, that's all."

In that moment, Chrissie realized Scarlett wasn't just drawing physically back—she was also making an emotional retreat. This was the beginning of the end, the separation that would cover so much more than just distance and time. And just like Scarlett letting her daughter and best friend go on that crisp fall day back in 2009, Chrissie had no choice but to do the same now.

"I'll fix this, Chrissie, I promise. I don't have a lot of time left to me, but that much I can do."

Chapter Twenty-Seven

TRANQUILITY ESTATES, VERMONT

Present Day

THE NEXT MORNING, SCARLETT TOOK A drastic turn for the worse.

"This happens a lot more often than you'd think. In fact, I'd have been very surprised to see her up and about for too much longer." The end-of-life doula, a doe-eyed sixtysomething retired hospice nurse who seemed like a grandmother, mother, and confessor wrapped up in one, patted Chrissie on the shoulder. "She's probably been holding it together for your sake—for you and that sweet little family of yours. But now that she's here and the end is in sight, she can finally let her mind accept what her body has known for months." Her smile turned sad. "For most of our guests, it's honestly more of a relief than anything else. Like coming home after a long, exhausting day."

Chrissie nodded, feeling dazed as the doula issued further instructions about what she could do to make Scarlett comfortable and who she should call if the need arose.

"Not that I think it will. She has her pills and knows what she wants. All we can do now is give her all our love and support."

The doula offered Chrissie a hug—which she gratefully accepted—before quietly stepping out of the cabin. The hour was early enough that Chrissie would have appreciated a cup of coffee and the chance to take in the pink and orange streaks of the sunrise, but she paused only to take a deep breath before pushing her way into Scarlett's bedroom.

"Hey, you."

"Hey back."

Scarlett was sitting up in bed, propped up by so many pillows that a few were already in danger of slipping to the floor. Chrissie fought the urge to start fluffing them and organizing the bedside table, where pill bottles, a lipstick-rimmed teacup, and a framed photo of the two of them with Scarlett's grandma smiled across the room.

Instead, she picked up the photo and slipped under the covers next to Scarlett.

"I remember this day," she said as she dropped her head to Scarlett's shoulder and let it rest there. She had no idea how, but it felt as though Scarlett had lost half of her body weight overnight—a return to the seven-year-old girl she'd once walked past in a hospital bed that was both nothing and everything like this one. Her fingers traced lightly over the image of their faces, just a few years younger than Kat. "Your grandma took us to Broughton Beach to go swimming, but it was only like sixty degrees, so she bought us a cheap kite and we spent hours flying it up and down the riverbank instead."

Scarlett tilted her head on top of Chrissie's. The steady, even pace of her breathing and warmth of her body felt so natural that she found it almost impossible to believe they wouldn't continue that way forever.

"I still would've gone swimming even though the water was freezing," Scarlett said. "In fact, I dared you to go in. I offered you my best butterfly hair clips and everything."

"Did you? I don't remember that part."

"You never do," Scarlett agreed. She burrowed deeper into

Chrissie's side. "You were always doing stuff like that—putting your foot down in that quiet, deceptive way of yours—so it never meant much to you. It did to me, though. I loved you more and more each time you did that. If I'm being honest, I hated you a little more each time, too."

Chrissie let the picture fall to her lap. "What are you talking about? When I was doing *what* stuff?"

"Being right. Being good." Scarlett pressed her lips against Chrissie's temple. "You'd better bring Kat to me. I thought we'd have more time than this—to chat and hang out and eat Walsh's amazing cheeseburgers, but I'm just so *tired*."

Chrissie was seized by a sudden panic. What had seemed so imperative back in Chicago and Buffalo now felt like an unnecessarily cruel trick to play on a woman who had no tricks left to play back.

"You don't have to tell her if you don't want to. We can just snuggle here and watch some Mary Kate and Ashley Olsen like we used to in the old days."

"You mean back when all I wanted in life was the same glamour and intrigue as a pair of twelve-year-old millionaires?" The smile in Scarlett's voice was unmistakable. "I like to think I've done a decent job of living up to the Olsen twin legacy. I visited every city with a living pulse. I slept with just as many living, pulse-bearing men. I got to spend hours of every working day talking to anyone who cared to listen to me. And anytime I felt even the tiniest bit lonely, I could call you up and you'd be waiting for me on the other end of the line."

"That's not an answer."

"Yes, it is. Thanks to you and my grandmother, I was able to live my life exactly the way I wanted to. And now I'm going to die on my own terms, too. There aren't a whole lot of people who get to say the same."

Scarlett pulled away so that Chrissie could examine her face. She looked wan and exhausted, but she also looked at peace. In all the years Chrissie had known Scarlett, she'd never looked peaceful before.

"Let me do this for you, Chrissie. For you...and for her."

Chrissie nodded and slipped out from under the covers. She didn't trust herself to speak, but as she headed for the door to get dressed and introduce her daughter to her birth mother for both the first and last time, she did sneak a peek back at the bed.

Scarlett held the photo in her hand, a smile hovering on the corner of her lips as she traced the shape of the three of them. Chrissie couldn't help thinking that it was just like her to be the first to see what the next world had to offer. Scarlett had always been the ringleader, the trailblazer, the one who forced Chrissie to confront a world that terrified her more often than it didn't.

Of course she'd be the first to leave, to return to her grandmother's arms. To step into the unknown and make sure there was something amazing waiting when Chrissie finally joined her.

"I don't understand. Why are you being so weird?"

Chrissie had been striving to be as *un*-weird as possible as she led Kat into the cabin and directed her toward Scarlett's room, but she'd clearly missed a step somewhere.

"I'm not being weird. I'm being honest. Aunt Scarlett isn't doing well today, and she has a few things she wants to talk to you about before she... You know. Before tomorrow."

Kat reared to a halt in the middle of the living room. She was dressed in jeans and close-toed shoes, her hair pulled back in a long ponytail. Both she and Lily had been awake and sipping energy drinks when Chrissie had arrived, the pair of them looking surprisingly spry for the hour of morning—a circumstance she soon learned was due to their determination to reach the stables for a morning's ride before the horses got too tired.

"What kind of things?" Kat asked. "Is she going to yell at me some more about you and Coach? Because I'm not changing my mind. I think it's wrong on every possible level."

"Kat."

Her daughter flushed. "What? I'm allowed to have my own opinions. You guys being old doesn't make you right about everything."

"No, but Scarlett dying does give her a perspective that neither you nor I could possibly understand. So maybe give her the benefit of the doubt, yeah?"

The flush seeped to Kat's ears, and she lost some of the belligerence in her bearing. "It's not fair. I love Scarlett, but she's basically weaponized her cancer. She's holding us hostage here."

Chrissie laughed—not because what Kat said was funny, but because it was the most selfish and Scarlett-like thing she could possibly say.

"How do you think *I* feel? She's been holding me hostage my whole life."

Kat slumped her shoulders and started to head to the bedroom, but Chrissie called out before she made it more than a few steps. "No—wait."

Kat stopped and turned, her eyebrows lifted in surprise. Chrissie ached with the urge to pull her daughter into her arms one last time before the bomb dropped, but she wasn't sure if it was a good idea. The Kat who was entering the bedroom wasn't the same Kat who would walk out of it, and she was terrified of the results.

In her own girlhood, she'd often dreamed of what it would be like to learn that her parents weren't really her parents—that she'd been switched at birth or dropped off by a poor but loving mother who'd seen the big house and assumed the people inside would take good care of her. Kat wasn't wrong when she said her life was worse because of the isolation of it.

She needed to know that more than just one person loved her. She *deserved* more.

"What?" Kat demanded. She crossed her arms over her chest. "What did I do now?"

"Nothing. I just..." Chrissie tried not to let her voice wobble, but wobble it did. "I love you, honey. No matter what happens, I want you to remember that. You're the best thing that's ever happened to me, and nothing can change that."

Kat looked understandably confused—and concerned—by this, but all she did was roll her eyes.

"Whatever. Don't let Lily go to the stables without me, okay? If I don't keep an eye on her, she'll take Shadowfox out before I have a chance to call dibs."

Chrissie nodded, not trusting herself to speak. As the door snicked open and closed again, Kat's soft voice calling, "Aunt Scarlett?" before it was cut off entirely, she wasn't sure she'd ever be able to speak again.

But first thirty seconds ticked by...then thirty seconds more. Just when she was considering pacing the floor like a caged animal or at least finding a dust rag and working out her anxiety that way, a knock sounded at the front door. She practically ran to answer it.

"Hey, Ms. Thomas." Lily stood on the other side, looking even more ready for the stables in a flannel shirt and dark wash jeans, her braids pulled back underneath a baseball cap. She held a wax-paper bundle in one hand that smelled suspiciously like sausage. "My dad wanted me to bring this over for you. He made breakfast burritos. He was afraid you'd be too preoccupied this morning to remember to eat."

"Oh." Chrissie blinked down at the bundle. "That's really sweet, but he didn't have to do that."

Lily rolled her eyes in an exact imitation of Kat. "He can't help himself. Cooking is his way of showing he cares. He's like an old-timey grandma who thinks everyone around him is about to collapse from hunger. It used to drive my mom crazy. Every time they had a fight, he'd spend like six hours making her favorite dinner to apologize."

Chrissie couldn't help but smile as she accepted the gift.

"My nan—Scarlett's grandmother, that is—was the same way. Only she never made anything delicious like breakfast burritos. In times of stress, she turned to quinoa."

"Ew."

"Agreed. But thank your dad for me. He's done too much already."

Lily rolled one shoulder in a shrug, looking embarrassed. "It's a lot to take in at first, but you get used to it. You should see some of the things he's cooked for your cat. He even puts parsley on the plates like in those canned cat food commercials."

She made no move to leave. Chrissie was loath to invite her inside, knowing Kat might not appreciate an audience when she eventually emerged from Scarlett's room, but the girl seemed inclined to linger.

"Did you want to come in for a bit?"

Lily peeked over Chrissie's shoulder as she shifted from one foot to the other. "No, thanks. I don't think Kat would want me here. She, uh, doesn't really like me."

It was on the tip of Chrissie's tongue to deny this claim, but she had the feeling that wouldn't go over well. Tranquility Estates was a place of truth, even more than a church or court of law.

"Don't give up on her yet. I know she can be a lot, but she's worth it." Chrissie felt the truth of her words reverberate down to her very bones. If there was one thing this life had taught her, it was that the Kats and Scarletts of the world were *always* worth the effort. "If it helps, I think you're getting closer."

Lily brightened to such a degree that Chrissie wished there was some way to capture the image and save it for her daughter. That wasn't the face of an enemy; that was a girl who desperately wanted in.

"It has been pretty cool having her around the house. Her and Rufio both. It can get pretty quiet with just me and Dad all the time."

"Don't forget the burritos."

Lily rolled her eyes again, but it was different this time. Less like an annoyed teen and more like someone who was trying her hardest not to show her pleasure. "Are you guys like...dating now? You and my dad?"

Chrissie had no idea how to answer, so she stuck to the theme of the day: honesty.

"It's under discussion, yes. But nothing is official yet, and if you and Kat genuinely hate the idea—"

"We don't." Lily looked startled at her own interruption, but she pushed through. "At least, *I* don't. You're not nearly as bad as some of the other volleyball moms, and he's been really happy these past few weeks. Like, singing in the shower and buying new aftershave and stuff." She wrinkled her nose. "It smells kinda gross, but don't tell him I said that. And don't—"

But here she stopped, as if suddenly aware that she was a sixteen-year-old girl discussing her father's love life with the woman responsible for it.

"I won't," Chrissie promised. Their eyes met in a moment of understanding that made Chrissie both happy and sad for the girl. Happy, because Lily was obviously a kid with a good head on her shoulders, and sad, because that kind of responsibility could only come from a childhood fraught with heavy emotions. "And can I ask you for a small favor in return?"

"I guess so."

"Kat is about to get some pretty big news—bigger, even, than Scarlett's cancer." It was a strange thing to say, to assume that anything could be bigger than the loss of a woman who'd cheered Kat on through almost every childhood milestone, but Chrissie knew her daughter.

She also knew herself. Pushing back the rush of nausea that threatened to overtake her, she forced herself to keep going.

"There's also a good chance that she's not going to want anything to do with me after this. Will you—you and your dad both—be there if she needs you? I'd feel a lot better knowing she has you there to catch her."

Lily eyed her with a strange glint. "She'll still want you."

Chrissie wished she was the adult in this conversation, the one with all the answers, but she felt very much like a lost seven-year-old wandering the halls of a hospital in search of someone to love. "You don't know that."

"Yeah, I do. I hate my mom for leaving us, hate her even more for how she broke my dad's heart, but if she walked in the door right now, I'd hug her so hard." Lily pushed the brim of her hat down as if to shield the sudden spring of tears that welled to her eyes. "I miss her, even after all these years. Sometimes, I think I always will."

Chrissie watched as the girl turned away and trotted down the steps. She stayed there, watching her retreating form and then watching the wind push through the trees and then watching not much of anything at all. She had no idea how much time passed, the breakfast burrito long grown cold in her hand before the sound of the bedroom door clicking open caused her to whirl around.

The burrito fell to the floor with a heavy *splat*. She braced herself for the inevitable—the tears, the recriminations, the stone-cold silence—but nothing could have prepared her for Kat's small, tear-streaked face or the hesitant way she searched the room, as if uncertain whether or not Chrissie would be there waiting for her.

"Mom?" a tentative voice called, and there was something more than just a question in the word. It contained so much doubt…and even more hope. "Mommy? Are you still here?"

Chrissie crossed the room in three massive strides and yanked her daughter into her arms, so rough that it startled a grunt out of Kat. That grunt turned to a sob as Kat burrowed into her, clinging to her waist as though her every heartbeat depended on it.

"Of course I'm here, honey," Chrissie said into that soft, smooth hair—hair that she'd washed times past counting, hair that she used to braid while Kat's small, restless body squirmed between her knees, hair that smelled, even now, of the childhood bubble bath that had been Kat's favorite. "For you, I'll always be here."

Chapter Twenty-Eight

TRANQUILITY ESTATES, VERMONT

Present Day

ONCE UPON A TIME, CHRISSIE HAD read a relationship article that stated the best way to hold difficult conversations was while taking a walk. There was something in the act of moving in the same direction, side by side, both parties heading to the future together, that made it easier to tackle subjects that were too much to take on head-to-head.

That it also gave her a chance to hold her daughter's hand hadn't been mentioned in the article, but it probably should have been. She couldn't remember the last time she and Kat had held hands, let alone in a sylvan setting like this one.

"Are you sure Aunt Scarlett will be okay alone at the cabin this long?" Kat asked as they headed along a path marked with signs promising a lake at the end. Her fingers squeezed against Chrissie's. "She said she wanted to rest for a while, but—"

"She'll be fine," Chrissie promised. "And if she's not… Honey, you know that her plans haven't changed, right? You and I never talked much about the cancer she had as a kid or the way her grandmother died or even my brother, Malcolm, but she and I have experienced a lot of death in our lives. This is her decision, and it's one she didn't make lightly."

"Oh. Okay." She hesitated, her voice sounding so small that it made Chrissie's chest clench. "What was he like, your brother?"

Chrissie hesitated, too. Of all the loss she'd experienced in her life, that one didn't hurt nearly as much as it used to, but to say so felt wrong somehow. Like promising that with time, this pain would dissipate the same way.

"He was quiet," she said. "Smart. Gentle. I don't remember much else, to be honest. I was very young at the time, and so much of his life had been spent in and out of hospitals, that we barely got a chance to know each other."

"Is that why you never talk about him?"

Chrissie took her time stepping over a fallen tree covered with moss. All of her parenting instincts urged her to gloss over this bit, to shove through to the real heart of the matter, but she pushed those instincts aside. Kat was no longer the small, vulnerable child she'd sworn to protect. She was a strong and beautiful young woman who'd just had her world turned upside down—and who was navigating her way through it with a surprising amount of grace.

"That's part of it, yes. But I also don't like talking about him because I've spent my whole life feeling responsible for his death."

This made Kat halt in her tracks. "Wait—why?"

They weren't anywhere near the lake yet, or even in a comfortable clearing, but Chrissie allowed them to pause next to a spindly birch grove.

"They wanted to give him a bone marrow transplant, and as his sister, I was his best chance at a match. But I wasn't, and he died before they could find a different donor." She paused, surprised at how readily the story fell from her tongue to her daughter's understanding ears. "Even though my parents never expressly blamed me for not being able to help Malcolm, I always felt the accusation simmering under the surface. They pulled away from me after his death—mostly to protect themselves from feeling that kind of pain again—but I had no way of knowing it at the time. I just assumed they were done with me."

"Is that..." Kat hesitated, her lower lip between her teeth as she struggled to find the words. She drew a deep breath and tried again. "Is that why you don't talk to them? Or let me talk to them, either?"

"Yes and no." Chrissie had never spoken the words aloud before, but she was done trying to shield Kat from the worst the world had to offer—mostly because she was coming to learn that the worst and the best often went hand in hand. "Yes, my relationship with them suffered because of Malcolm. And no, that's not the entire reason why I have nothing to do with them now. The truth is, they never approved of me adopting you the way I did. They couldn't understand why I'd give up college and a career and dedicate myself to a child who didn't share my blood."

"Oh."

The way Kat said this was so bewildered that Chrissie felt all the anger and frustration of her childhood come rushing to the surface.

"Don't think for one second that I regret their loss. I *did* share their blood, but they still never gave up anything for me. I'll introduce them to you if you want, but Scarlett's grandmother was the one who raised me, not them. Everything I am today is thanks to her."

"Oh." This time, the word felt less bleak and more like a growing acceptance. "So you and Scarlett were like sisters."

"We *are* sisters. We always have been and always will be."

Kat nodded, accepting this statement as well as the ferocity with which it was uttered. "And my dad was your high school boyfriend."

Chrissie nodded.

"But he and Scarlett hooked up one time."

She nodded again.

"At her grandmother's funeral."

A laugh escaped Chrissie before she could stop herself. It seemed Scarlett had held nothing back. How incredibly typical of her.

"You have to remember that we were only a few years older than you at the time. Alone, grieving, with no idea what to do or how we were going to do it. I don't blame Aunt Scarlett at all. You know what she's like. Wild and impulsive and—"

"A lot like me," Kat finished with a wry smile.

Chrissie nodded and started moving along the path again. This time, it was more for her own benefit than Kat's.

"If Grimshaw had done the decent thing and stepped up—or even acknowledged his part in all this—I'd have found a way to involve him in your life. But he was just as young as we were, when all is said and done. Kat, this part might be hard for you to hear, but he's made it very clear over the years that he's not interested in having a relationship with you. Maybe that will change someday, but I don't want you getting your hopes up. He's not the man I wanted him to be."

For the next few minutes, the crunch of their feet was the only sound between them. Which was why Chrissie was so surprised when Kat suddenly broke it.

"Why didn't you tell me any of this before?"

"About your father? Or about your…mother?"

Kat stumbled over this last bit, but she caught herself just as quickly. "About any of it. Aunt Scarlett—Scarlett—my birth mother—said that it was her rule that I never know the truth about my parents, and that she'd have gone to her grave without telling me, only you made her. You said you wouldn't be here in Vermont with her unless she told me everything."

Chrissie nodded. "I did."

"But *why*? Why now? Why like this?"

Each question came out harsher and more gratingly, sloughing away the last of Chrissie's reserve. She forced the two of them to halt again, this time so she could look her daughter squarely in the eyes. It was a thing she should have done years ago, only she'd been too scared—of changing what they had, of changing who they were.

Unfortunately, things changed anyway. People were born. People left. People died. And all they had to hold onto in the meantime were those they continued to love.

"My parents forced me to grow up way too fast," she said without bitterness or rancor—without any emotion at all, really. "So did Scarlett's. Between the people who created us and the amount of time we both spent in hospitals growing up, we didn't have much of a childhood. I think we both, in our own ways, were determined that you'd never suffer the same way. Only somewhere along the line, we forgot that you're a responsible, well-adjusted, *amazing* human being who deserves the chance to form her own opinion about things."

Now her voice cracked. *Now* she started to break.

"I wanted you to have a chance to say goodbye to Scarlett properly—knowing her for who she really is, and understanding the sacrifices she made in loving you so much." She dashed a hand at her eyes, but the tears were already starting to fall. "And I wanted you to realize that you're not nearly as alone as you think you are. I've always known that there would come a time when you won't need me anymore—when you won't *want* me—but I was hoping we wouldn't get here so soon."

"*Mom*."

Chrissie held up a hand to stop Kat from saying anything more. She needed to get this out before she lost the courage—or, worse, the words.

"I *am* your mother. I will *always* be your mother. From the moment you were put into my arms, I knew I'd do anything in this world to keep you safe and happy and loved. None of that has changed." She swallowed around the lump in her throat. "But you've been my whole life for so long—and I've been yours—that I forgot there's a big world out there waiting for us both. Scarlett made me realize that on this trip. And so did you."

"Me? What did I do?"

"Easy. You asked for more—no. You *demanded* more." And just like that, the lump in her throat dissolved to nothing. "We'll find you a family, Kat. We'll make one if we have to. We'll surround you with so many people who love you and want what's best for you that you'll long for the days when the only person whose back you had to sneak around behind was mine."

She paused, thinking of Walsh cooking to show how much he cared. Of Lily, dreaming of her mother's hug. Of River, gratefully accepting the gruff affection of a great-aunt she barely knew. Of Scarlett, lying in her deathbed and confessing everything for no reason other than because Chrissie asked her to.

Then she started walking again, her almost-grown daughter's footsteps keeping time with her own.

"If it's all right with you, Kitty Kat, we'll find me a family, too. I think that sounds awfully nice right about now."

Chapter Twenty-Nine

TRANQUILITY ESTATES, VERMONT

Present Day

"YOU'LL FIND THE AFGHAN YOU CROCHETED Grandma in the bottom of the steamer trunk. There's also a stack of legal papers and a bottle of Jack Daniels. That last one's for you, by the way. You and Walsh both. Drink a toast to me when you rush into his arms later, okay? And then let him kiss all your sorrows away. Preferably with tongue."

Chrissie didn't want to laugh. She *tried* not to. But as she located the oversized 1.75 liter bottle complete with a handle, a laugh escaped anyway.

"Just how depressed are you expecting me to get? There's enough whiskey here to get me drunk twenty times over."

Scarlett leaned back on the chaise longue, a smile playing about the corners of her mouth, which was made up in a shade of red that would have given Dita Von Teese a run for her money. She'd wanted to do Chrissie's makeup, as well, the pair of them sobbing their way through layers of false eyelashes and no-run mascara, but Chrissie had declined the honor. She was willing to do a lot to make her friend more comfortable, but dressing up for her deathbed wasn't one of them. The fact that she'd even brushed her hair this morning spoke to the enormity of what she was willing to endure.

"You can douse my body with the rest of the alcohol and light me on fire. That's how the Vikings did it, right?" Even though Scarlett's words were uttered playfully, she immediately dropped the act. "Actually, I made the arrangements already. I'll be cremated here and sent back to Oregon. I took your suggestion and asked the funeral home to make space for me to be interred next to Grandma. I hope that's okay."

Chrissie lifted the afghan out of the trunk and busied herself arranging it over Scarlett's feet. They were sitting on the back porch of the little cabin, their view of the mountains unimpeded. It seemed strange that city-loving, life-of-the-party Scarlett Sanderson would have chosen nothing but nature and Chrissie in her final moments, but Chrissie wasn't about to question her.

Scarlett had done a lot of things in this life that Chrissie would likely never experience. Travel and glamour and a high-profile career. Lovers and foreign languages and parties that didn't involve latex balloons and homemade birthday cakes. If a quiet, intimate goodbye was how she wanted to punctuate a life lived large in every interpretation of the word, then Chrissie would support her every step of the way.

"I think that's nice," Chrissie said as she smoothed the ragged ends of the blankets over Scarlett's lap. "Nan would have liked that."

She was trying her best not to fuss over Scarlett—at her request—so as soon as her friend was comfortable, she slid onto the longue next to her. There was barely room for the pair of them, but they managed to shift and snuggle until they felt like girls again, hunkering down in a blanket fort barely big enough to hold them both.

"Everything else is arranged already, too," Scarlett said as she pulled Chrissie's head down to her chest and started running her fingers through her hair. "My house and my bank accounts, I mean. I doubt I need to say this, but you and Kat are getting everything. That's what's in the stack of papers."

Chrissie didn't respond. Underneath her ear, Scarlett's heartbeat felt steady and strong in a way that felt totally wrong for the time and place. How could a heart that still had that much strength, that much determination to keep going, be so close to stopping forever?

"You aren't going to argue about the bank accounts? That's a new one." Scarlett laughed lightly. "You usually kick and scream any time I transfer money to you."

"I'm saving my kicking and screaming for after," Chrissie said. "I'm determined to get through this without a single disagreement."

"Is that a challenge?" Scarlett laughed again, this time with real humor. "Because I have a few other things I'm planning on saying before I take the pills. There's no way you'll last that long."

Her fingers kept moving in long, slow strokes through Chrissie's hair. In the back of Chrissie's mind, she felt that this was backwards somehow—that she should have been the one comforting Scarlett, soothing and petting her way through this, but the familiar sensation felt too good to pull away.

"You can say whatever you want. After what you did for me yesterday, I owe you big time. Telling Kat the truth couldn't have been easy."

Scarlett's fingers faltered. "She's a good egg, isn't she?"

Chrissie nodded and burrowed deeper into Scarlett's embrace. "The *best* egg. Thank you for her." She twisted her head to look up at her friend. "I mean that. She's the greatest thing that's ever happened to me—present company excepted, of course."

Scarlett's lips drooped at the corners. "Don't lie to me, Chrissie. Not today."

Chrissie's heart gave an odd lurch in her chest.

"I'm glad you love her more than me," Scarlett added before

Chrissie could decide on what she wanted to say—if, indeed, she wanted to say anything at all. "That wasn't always the case, obviously. That first year, when I ran away to Paris… I never did apologize for that, did I? Going radio silent for as long as I did, not even calling to check in on how you two were doing—I don't have a lot of regrets in my life, but that's one of them. I shouldn't have abandoned you like that."

"Honestly?" Chrissie sniffled, but the tears had yet to fall. "It was probably for the best. I had to learn to stand on my own two feet eventually. Better to toss me in the water and make me swim. You know how reluctant I am to get wet any other way."

Scarlett's hand stilled on her head. "Do you really mean that?"

Chrissie gave herself time to consider her answer. Time was the one thing they didn't have much of, but this was too important to rush.

"I do, actually. At first, I was furious and heartbroken, but in retrospect, I think it was the best thing you could have done. You gave me and Kat a chance to be a family—a *real* family."

"I'm not sure she'll ever forgive me. The way she looked at me yesterday, how quick she was to run out of the room and into your arms—"

Chrissie cut her off before Scarlett could travel too far down that path. Nothing but pain lay at the end of it. "That was you giving us a chance to be a family, too. I'm serious, Scarlett. For the first time in months, we're talking—*really* talking. I'm starting to suspect we might actually make it through these teen years alive."

She blanched as soon as realized what she'd just said. "Oh god. I'm sorry. I—"

But Scarlett chuckled, breaking the tension and wrapping her arms around Chrissie's shoulders. "No, don't apologize. Never apologize—especially when you're right."

"Is that another item for my list? Should I grab a pen?"

Scarlett's hold on her tightened, though whether out of affection or to keep her from reaching for a writing utensil, Chrissie couldn't say.

"Yeah, sorry about that whole thing," Scarlett said. "I was being kind of an asshole."

"It's okay. You were just trying to help me get my life back on track."

Instead of accepting this olive branch, Scarlett grew pensive, her steady breathing matching the light breeze swirling onto the porch around them. "I don't think that's true," she eventually said. "I mean, I *do* want you to be happy, but that list was less about you and more about me. It's just that...none of the other kids at the hospital told me, you know? Grandma either."

"Told you what?"

Scarlett's fingers stopped weaving through her hair. "How desperate you get, right at the end, to leave something of yourself behind."

"Oh." Chrissie wished she had something more articulate to say, but words had always been Scarlett's forte, not hers.

"Grandma told me once that you were the strongest person she knew. Did I ever tell you about that? It was right before I pulled that fake cancer scare to get you to spend more time with me. She knew, long before I did, that you'd be the one to carry us through life—that your strength would be the one thing I could count on." She sighed. "She was right, of course. She always was."

"For what it's worth, I forgave you for that about five minutes later."

Scarlett released a light scoff. "I don't know why. I didn't deserve it. Our whole lives, I've always been jealous of how well you know yourself, and how easy you made it seem to stick to your principles—that's why I made you write the list. Not because you need to learn from me, but because I wanted, in my own desperate, clawing way, to inject a little bit of me into your DNA." She laughed, and that contained a scoff, too. "But that's not fair, is it? You're already carrying more than one person in there. The last thing you need is to scrunch yourself smaller to make room for me."

"Why are you still so obsessed with my twin? I've never understood it." As soon as Chrissie said the words aloud, she heard the lie—not about Scarlett's obsession, but about her own lack of understanding.

Because the truth was, she *did* understand Scarlett. She always had. Her bright, funny, exuberant friend was the sort of person who loved outwardly. Scarlett's affection was unwavering, her joie de vivre the stuff of legends. She could brighten a whole room with just a laugh and, once she claimed you as her own, would fight endless battles to keep you close.

But Scarlett couldn't imagine a world where love took an inward path. Where you made room inside your heart, pushed a part of yourself down in order to ensure someone else had the space they needed to grow. *That* was what it meant to be a mother.

That was what it meant to be her.

So, with a deep breath and her head nestled against the best friend she'd ever have, Chrissie pushed down one last time.

"You don't have to worry about being forgotten, and you don't have to be afraid there isn't room in my heart to carry you. Half of it has always belonged to you anyway."

Scarlett sniffled. "You're not just saying that?"

"Never. I gave it to you the day you called me into your hospital room. And in return, you gave me more happiness than I ever thought I'd see in this lifetime. Thank you, Scarlett. For loving me. For sharing your grandmother with me. For giving me our daughter and trusting me to take care of her for both of us. I won't let you down."

She felt Scarlett's nod brush against the top of her head before they both fell silent. Time passed, but neither one of them marked it in any discernible way. They just lay curled up together on the chaise longue, the rhythm of their breathing and heartbeats in sync, the world continuing to revolve in the same way it always would.

Scarlett was the first to break the comfortable silence. "I think I'm ready now."

Even though Chrissie had known this moment was coming, every part of her cried out in protest—so much so that it was a physical ache, a hard knot inside her chest that felt cemented in place.

"You think, or you know?"

"I know." Scarlett kissed the top of her head. "And you do, too. It's time."

Chrissie's eyes grew hot with tears as she sat up and handed Scarlett the medication she'd been prescribed. The rules stated that Scarlett had to be the one to take them, and that she had to do so with her own two hands, but that didn't mean Chrissie couldn't hold the glass to Scarlett's lips as she swallowed or pull her into her arms, her whole body rocking back and forth as Scarlett slipped into a time and place where Chrissie couldn't follow.

In her thirty-four years of life on this planet, Chrissie had watched too many people go down that same path without her. The twin she never met. The brother she barely knew. The honorary grandmother who had taught her how to love. The best friend who'd given her the greatest gift she'd ever receive.

It hurt—always it hurt, the wound cutting deeper each time it was reopened—but Scarlett had been right.

Chrissie had gotten through this before. She would get through it again. She was the strongest person she knew, and even though she'd never asked to be the person who carried the memories of the dead in her heart, she would do it.

"I'll do it because you asked me to," Chrissie whispered as she leaned down to kiss her friend for the final time. "And because carrying everyone in my heart is what makes me strong. Stay safe in there, Scarlett. You and I still have so much living left to do."

Chapter Thirty

MEDFORD, OREGON

One Year Later

"WALSH, THERE'S ENOUGH FOOD HERE TO feed a small army. You know this memorial is just for us, right?"

Chrissie strode into her backyard, a heaping platter of uncooked meat in her arms. It had been her intention to slide it precariously onto the picnic table, but Walsh was ready and waiting for her. He lifted the platter and ducked to brush a soft kiss across her lips.

"I know, but Kat challenged me to make steakburgendogs. I didn't want to let her down. We'll need at least four of everything—with a little extra for the margin of error." As soon as he caught sight of his daughter's expression, he threw his hands up. "And that's the last time I'll make a math reference, I swear. After last night's SAT prep, Lily refuses to have anything to do with integers, exponential decay or, god forbid, the Bernoulli distribution."

"I'm with Lily on this one," Kat said as she joined them to inspect the meats. "Absolutely no more math."

Kat cast Lily a look of such understanding that Chrissie was hard put not to set up a rallying cheer. A year of navigating a new relationship with two strong-willed teenagers watching their every move had been no easy task. One week, the girls were the best of friends. The next, they wanted nothing to do with each other. The past few had been especially rough thanks to the looming SATs, a volleyball recruiter who'd flown out from California to watch them both, and the fact that Lily had been asked to prom but Kat hadn't.

It was only today, a day they all carried differently, that they'd reached a kind of truce. Today was for eating ridiculous meat concoctions, for remembering a trip that had taken them all by surprise, for letting their defenses down and turning the music up.

Today was for celebrating life.

"By the way, it's our turn to have Rufio," Lily said as she flopped down onto the seat of the picnic table and started picking at a tray of olives. She cast Kat a glare from underneath a lopsided row of bangs. They were all trying very politely to pretend they liked them, but Chrissie couldn't look at the girl's hair without wincing. She'd sported that particularly terrible page-boy fringe for too many years to look on it with any admiration.

Scarlett had been right about that. Chrissie could—and did—still donate her hair, but that didn't mean she had to suffer at the hands of a butcher in order to do it.

"But we just got him!" Kat protested. She yanked the tray of olives closer to her side. "You had an extra week last month."

"Yeah, but only because you went to that sleepaway camp. Fair's fair. Check the custody agreement if you don't believe me."

Over the top of the girls' heads, Chrissie and Walsh shared a knowing look. The remedy to their shared ownership of a cat who still peed on the carpet more than any of them cared for was an easy one—and one that they'd have both gladly adopted—if not for the girls. No matter how many times they very rationally pointed out that they could *all* enjoy Rufio's dubious company if they lived under one shared roof, neither girl was willing to uproot her life to move in with the other.

Which was fine, really. Scarlett would have been at the front lines of battle, determined to put Chrissie and Walsh's relationship above all else, but the two of them were more than happy to wait. In a year's time, both girls would be heading off to college, and none of this would matter anymore. To youth, or to a woman who knew her life was coming to an end, a year sounded like an eternity.

To them, it was just twelve months of romantic date nights and talking on the phone late into the evening. It was a chance to take their relationship one step at a time, enjoying the slow, natural pace of a courtship both of them treasured all the more because of how carefully they were taking it.

"While we're on the subject of shared custody, don't think I didn't see you wearing my favorite Taylor Swift tour shirt the other day," Lily said before Chrissie and Walsh's gaze could grow any deeper.

"That's *my* shirt, thank you very much, and it fits my vibe better, anyway. Especially since your bangs look like—"

Fortunately for the peace of the afternoon, the sound of footsteps came through the side yard. The creaking of the gate and the sight of a tall, dark-haired man stopped the argument short—only to be replaced by Kat's sudden squeal of delight.

"You came! You're here!"

Chrissie felt Walsh approach her side as they watched Kat run into the man's arms, his strong grip twirling her in an ecstatic circle. The sight of him, all grown up but still as sweet as he'd always been, warmed Chrissie to her core.

"Uncle Mitchell, you should have seen me at last night's volleyball game! A recruiter came to watch me—well, me and Lily, technically—and I didn't miss a single serve. I was on fire." In a voice carefully crafted to carry to Lily, she added, "Lily missed two of her serves. Foot faults both times."

"That ref had it out for me from the very start!" Lily called back.

Walsh chuckled and reached over to ruffle his daughter's hair. "Let her have this one, Lil. You know how hard today must be for her."

It spoke volumes about Walsh's kind but firm parenting style that Lily accepted this with grace. The fact that he led her away to start assembling the steakburgendogs spoke just as loudly about his good heart.

Chrissie made her way over to where Kat was enthusiastically giving Mitchell a play-by-play of the night before, happy to stand back and watch as her daughter chattered away. Seeing Kat standing next to Mitchell—dark-eyed, rangy Mitchell—always gave her heart a slight shock. Her daughter looked so much like the Pemberly side of her bloodline that the link was undeniable.

But the talking, the enthusiasm, the vibrant, beating heart that Chrissie gave thanks for every day—those were a hundred percent Scarlett and always would be.

"Hey, Chrissie." As soon as Kat paused for breath, Mitchell flashed her his shy, lopsided smile. "Thanks for inviting me today. I didn't realize how much I needed it until I pulled up in front of your house to the smell of roasting meat."

"That's Walsh's doing. And Kat's. She's been looking forward to seeing you all week."

"Ugh, Mom. Make me sound like a pathetic wreck, why don't you?" Even though Kat rolled her eyes, the light shining in them was impossible to hide. "Tell me all about your trip to New York. Did they make you sit in meetings the whole time, or did you get to do all the tourist stuff? Broadway, Times Square, MoMA? If I get into Princeton, I'm totally gonna visit Manhattan as much as I can."

"I'll tell you everything," Mitchell promised as he squeezed her arm. "But first, let me catch up with your mom for a sec, okay? I've got something I'm supposed to give her. From Scarlett."

Chrissie wasn't sure how to take this. Scarlett had already done so much for them, not only in leaving behind enough money for Kat to go to Princeton three times over, but in giving them Mitchell, a gift so unexpected and welcome that it shamed Chrissie for not thinking of it before. A letter from him had been waiting when they'd returned home from Vermont—the first overture of many to follow, and one of the only bright spots in those difficult first months.

I know I can't replace Kat's real dad, but I'd like to be in her life. For you and for her. And for Scarlett.

Thinking of it—and of her friend—she bit back a sob. "I'm not sure I'm ready for anything like that. Not today."

Kat pressed a quick kiss on her cheek, her own voice tight. "Sure you can, Mom. *Especially* today. It's what she would have wanted."

And that was it. With those simple words, Chrissie let someone else call the shots. She was doing that a lot more lately, letting Walsh shower her with his easy affection, indulging Lily's determination to keep Rufio half the time, giving Kat the space she needed to grow into the strong and capable young woman she was rapidly becoming. Life was a lot easier when you weren't the only one shouldering all the burdens.

"Yeah. Okay. I'd like that."

Mitchell ran a hand through his already disheveled locks and grimaced. "You're only saying that because you haven't seen what she's bequeathed you yet. She gave it to me right before we… Right before I… Well, you know. Before we said our goodbyes." He reached into the bag and pulled out a flat, rectangular parcel. "She wouldn't tell me what it meant or why it was important. She just said you'd understand."

The moment Chrissie tore the brown paper from the package,

she laughed. That the laugh was mixed with tears was nothing new—almost all of her joy these days was wrapped up in at least a little sorrow. Her therapist said that it would go away with time, and that one day, she'd wake up and just laugh without feeling like she was sacrificing her friend with the act, but that day hadn't yet arrived.

Especially since the gift was a paint-by-numbers kit of a bunch of puppies spilling out—not from a basket—but an oversized rain boot.

"So she was right," Mitchell said. "You *do* understand."

Chrissie nodded, unable to speak around the lump in her throat. A Post-it note affixed to the front of the package, written in Scarlett's handwriting, provided one last message to add to the list now framed and sitting on her bedside table.

Just paint the damn painting. Always paint the damn painting.

"Of course. It's Scarlett reminding me that life goes on."

"Yeah," he said simply. "She keeps doing that to me, too."

They paused a moment, letting the silence take over as they shared a moment in Scarlett's memory. Chrissie had no idea how long they might have stayed like that, each of them lost in reflection of the beautiful whirlwind of a girl they both missed, if not for a sudden burst of music from over by the barbecue.

"Oh! It's on again! Turn it up."

"I love this song!"

Mitchell immediately turned to join the group, beaming as the sounds of a rich, dulcet voice crooned through the outdoor speaker, but Chrissie hung back, the canvas clutched against her chest. Lily and Kat joined hands and started dancing while Walsh tapped his feet in time to the beat. Even Rufio poked his head out the cat door to see what all the fuss was about.

Through her slightly blurred eyes, Chrissie watched as her family—her dysfunctional, perfect, always-expanding family—sang along to the hottest hit of the summer by a new artist out of the indie Chicago music scene who went only by the name of River.

Family is an open road with no destination in sight.
Family is whoever you have to hold you tight.
My family doesn't look the same as yours, and I think
that's all right.

AUTHOR'S NOTE

At the time of writing this novel, Oregon and Vermont are the only states in the United States that allow nonresidents to access assisted suicide and death-with-dignity services. Although many states have adopted policies that allow their own citizens to make these kinds of deeply personal medical decisions, they come with residency requirements that make it difficult (if not impossible) for those who live in other states to have the same rights.

If you or someone you know is struggling with thoughts of suicide, please call or text 988 to reach the Suicide & Crisis Hotline. You can also visit them online at https://988lifeline.org/.

1

THE DAY I MET ARTHUR MCLACHLAN was perfectly ordinary.

I woke up at my usual hour. I ate my usual bowl of oatmeal while hunched over the last few pages of my library copy of *Parable of the Sower*. I can't remember what I wore, but I'm pretty sure it was both machine washable and designed for comfort.

Everything in my closet was machine washable and designed for comfort, but not by choice. Rule number one of being a librarian: You'll leave work every day looking like you waged battle with a league of ancient scribes. Adapt early and adapt often, or your dry-cleaning bills will bury you.

When Arthur first came barreling into my life, I was in the Fiction section restocking a bunch of titles someone had moved for the sake of internet kudos. There was a new TikTok trend going around where people descended on bookstores and public libraries in order to write out sentences using titles. If you ignored the part where *I* was the one who had to put everything back where it belonged, it was kind of clever.

Looking for Alaska Where the Sidewalk Ends

We Were Liars Under the Never Sky

Are You Anybody? I Am No One

I was still chuckling over that last one when I heard the sound of an annoyed cough behind me.

"Young lady, you are blocking the way to Roman History."

Years of practice had me immediately stepping back, an apology on my lips. As I pushed my cart aside, I noticed the man was elderly, his wire glasses perched on the end of his nose and his tweed jacket sporting a pair of suede elbow patches. He walked with the aid of a gold-tipped cane that looked as though it might conceal a sword stick inside.

"Do you want me to look up a specific title for you?" I asked, since he had some way to go to reach the nonfiction shelves. "Anything by Tom Holland is good, but I find I prefer to get my history from Mary Beard. Her approach is wonderfully emotional."

He snorted. "Typical sentimental claptrap."

I blinked at him, wondering what I could have said to cause offense. "I'm…sorry?"

He tapped his cane sharply. "Emotion doesn't belong in history. Emotion belongs in maudlin childhood literature. You should know that, *Pollyanna*."

I was taken aback but not dismayed by the belligerence in his tone. Strange though it seemed, we had actual library rules about patrons like this. Soothe and disarm, that was the order of the day. Leave them in a better frame of mind than when they arrived. And never, under any circumstances, engage.

"You don't have to read anything you don't want to," I said with a careful smile. "But my name isn't Pollyanna. It's Sloane."

Instead of accepting my peace offering, Arthur tilted his head and appraised me. Something about the intelligent gray eyes behind his rims caught my attention.

"You know what I meant," he said, stabbing a finger at my cart. Sure enough, a copy of Eleanor Porter's beloved childhood tale sat on the top. One of the teens had had the audacity to pair it with John Grisham's *A Time to Kill.*

I held both books up with a laugh. "Don't blame me," I said. "It's *A Time to Kill Pollyanna.*"

He looked pained.

"It's a joke," I explained. "Kids trying to make sentences out of book titles. Some of them are actually pretty good. Maybe I should try my hand at it next time I run into a patron." In an attempt to defuse the tension, I said the first title that came to mind. "*Pollyanna* is *Pleased to Meet You.*"

"Those kids are a plague on the public library system," he said, glaring. "And so, I'm starting to think, are you."

I had no response for this. Well, to be fair, I *had* one, but I knew better than to voice it aloud. One of my greatest skills in this world—some might say it was my only skill—was how good I was at being inoffensive. The trick was to look bland, act blander, and voice no opinions whatsoever. The looking bland part I had down pat, my frizzy brown hair and lightly freckled skin blending into the background so easily that I sometimes felt like a potted ficus. The acting part was easy, too. I could go for days at a time without opening my mouth to say anything but "Yes, of course" and "No, you're right," and no one seemed to think there was anything odd about it.

The opinions part was harder, but working in a public space like the Coeur d'Alene library had taught me the value of tact.

"Well?" he demanded. "Don't you have anything else to say?"

I shrugged, wishing—not for the first time—that I was more like my sister Emily. She'd have known *exactly* how to wrap a grouchy old man like this around her finger. I don't know if it was all the doctors she grew up around or just her natural charm, but she'd had a way of making even the meanest grumps do her bidding. Before she'd gotten too sick to roam the neighborhood with me, we used to visit an ice cream shop a few blocks away from our house. No matter how many fingerprints we left on the glass or how exasperated the shopkeeper got with all our requests for free samples, she always walked out of there with at least one extra scoop.

What would Emily do?

"We could probably incorporate some Roman history, if it helps," I said, thinking of the towering ice cream cones Emily used to carry home with her. She'd never been able to eat the whole thing, but that hadn't been the point. It had been the *triumph* of it she'd enjoyed. In all the years since I'd lost her, I hadn't triumphed over anything.

Or anyone. Not even myself.

Before I could think better of it, I reached for a copy of Toni Morrison's *Beloved* and held it up. "How about *Beloved Pagans and Christians*? You have to admit it's catchy."

I could have almost sworn that Arthur's nostrils flared to twice their size. "So that's how you want to play this, huh?"

I wasn't sure I wanted to play much of *anything*, but I was already in too deep at that point. There was no ice cream at the end of this particular rainbow, but I couldn't help feeling that Emily would have been proud of me all the same.

"*The Roman Triumph Of Mice and Men*?" I suggested, thinking up Roman history titles as quickly as I could. Inspiration struck, and I snapped my fingers. "Oh! I know. *I, Claudius, Journey to the End of the Night*. These are good. I should probably write them down."

Something almost like respect was starting to spark in Arthur's eyes. "You seem to know an awful lot about books on ancient Rome," he said grudgingly. "Why? Are you planning to stab someone in the back?"

This time, I didn't hesitate over my reply. "Only if he deserves it."

A sound somewhere between a bark and a laugh escaped him. "Is that your way of telling me that Caesar got what was coming to him? Is that what it says in your precious Mary Beard?"

"Not exactly," I was forced to admit.

If this conversation kept going along these lines, I was going to have to admit a lot more: namely, that I wasn't nearly as conversant with Roman history as I was letting on. As far as librarians went, I was more of a jill-of-all-trades than a deep scholar. I knew lots of random book titles and could recite the first line from almost every classic piece of literature, but I could only talk intelligently on a subject for about three minutes before my storehouse of knowledge petered out.

"Ha!" he practically shouted. "That's what I thought. You don't know anything about Caesar that isn't written in the back-cover copy somewhere."

This was the point where I should have bowed gracefully out of the conversation. I'd already broken all the rules about not antagonizing the patrons, disorganized my own library cart, and said unthinkable things to a man who was old enough to be my grandfather.

For the first time in my life, however, I didn't bow out. Strangely enough, it didn't even occur to me to try.

"That's not true," I said as I pushed the copy of *Pollyanna* back on the shelf where it belonged. "I just think that anyone who had as many enemies as Caesar did should've been more careful. If he didn't see that knife coming, that's on him. My only enemy is the copier by the south window, and even I know better than to believe it when it says the toner levels are totally fine."

That was when it happened. I wasn't a good enough writer to describe it, but it was as if Arthur decided, right then and there, that I was an adversary worth having.

"I've forgotten more about Roman history than you'll ever know," he said, pointing his cane at me.

"That's probably true," I admitted.

"And I've already read every word Mary Beard has ever written."

"That's...impressive," I said.

He didn't appear to find my return to meekness to his taste. With suddenly narrowed eyes, he added, "And when I want book recommendations from a second-rate Pollyanna who wouldn't know a good book if it landed in her lap, I'll ask for it."

This barb stung more than he realized. Finding pleasure in reading—*losing* myself in a story—was the one thing I did know.

"*The Art of Racing in the Rain*," I said.

He blinked and took a step back, as if even the title of such—what had he called it? *sentimental claptrap?*—had the power to harm him. "What did you just say to me?"

I wore a smile that was only partially faked. He couldn't have been more outraged if I'd told him we were holding a book-burning party down by the lake that made our little city famous.

"If you're looking for a book recommendation, I think you should pick up *The Art of Racing in the Rain*. It's what I suggest to all our regular patrons. I know it has a reputation for being sad, but—"

The spark in his eyes grew almost martial. "Not now. Not ever. Not if it was the only book left in the world. If I want to immerse myself in someone else's pointlessly self-indulgent drivel, I'd give in and listen to podcasts."

I kept my mouth shut. It just so happened that I loved that book. I loved podcasts, too, though that was mostly because I never cared for sitting alone in a silent apartment. There are these really fun ones of people reading classic books in a flat monotone to help you go to sleep. You haven't known true peace until you've drifted off to Proust read aloud in B-flat.

Arthur took himself off after that, muttering under his breath about Roman conquests and literary abominations and librarians who should know when to keep their uninformed opinions to themselves.

And all I could do was smile after him, feeling like I'd eaten a *dozen* scoops of ice cream.

"I can't believe you just tackled Arthur McLachlan and lived to tell the tale," a deep, rich voice said from behind me. I turned to find Mateo, my fellow librarian, watching me with a detached look of awe.

I'd always liked Mateo. Everyone did. His voice made him seem like he should be seven feet tall, but he was as slight of build and limb as I was. Add to that a boy-band swoop of inky-black hair and a willingness to laugh at everything including himself—and it was impossible *not* to enjoy his company.

"You know who that guy is, right?" Mateo asked.

"No," I said, my brow furrowed as I watched the gold-tipped cane and elbow patches disappear into the German Philosophy section. "Should I? I've never seen him here before."

"That's because he comes first thing in the morning and only lets Octavia help him. He says everyone else here drains his brain cells by proximity." Mateo clucked his tongue. "You never open, so you've never seen him reduce the staff to terrified goo. We usually have to keep a mop handy."

I thought about that spark in the old man's eyes that only intensified when I started to push back, and shook my head. "He's not that bad. A little curmudgeonly, maybe, but—"

"Yeah, right," Mateo interrupted. "Mark Twain was a curmudgeon. Ebenezer Scrooge is a curmudgeon. Arthur McLachlan is Satan's grandfather. One time, he even managed to eke a tear or two out of Octavia. He's that bad."

"Really?"

This was a more sinister warning than Mateo realized. Of all of us on staff at the Coeur d'Alene Public Library, Octavia was the best—and the fiercest. Mateo found himself here because this was as far from working in a hospital as he could physically get, and I was here because reading was my only real life skill, but Octavia was hard-core. She'd been a librarian for more years than I'd been on this earth, and I was pretty sure she had the Dewey decimal system memorized. As in *all* of it.

You know that thing when people come into a library and ask for a blue book with weird writing on the cover? She always knew the exact book they were talking about. Without fail. Someday, I was going to grow up and *be* her.

"Take it from me, Sloane," Mateo said. He eyed me up and down, sympathy in every sweep of that gaze. "If you want to keep this job, you'll stay far away from him. He'll tear you to pieces…and worse, he'll enjoy every second of it."

READING GROUP GUIDE

1. This story is told through two different points of view in two different timelines. What is the impact of only seeing Scarlett and Chrissie's childhood through Scarlett's eyes? And of only seeing their final journey through Chrissie's?

2. The theme of motherhood anchors this story. How did the different relationships (Chrissie/her parents, Scarlett/her mother and grandmother, Chrissie/Scarlett/Kat, River/her mother) help shape the book?

3. Do you think Chrissie changes and grows stronger as the story progresses, or was her character already formed from the first page?

4. Do you agree that Chrissie's life was "small" while Scarlett's was "big"? Why or why not?

5. Was Scarlett's decision to give her daughter to Chrissie more of a selfish act or a selfless one?

6. The idea of *deserving* things—love, respect, a stranger's kindness—is brought up several times throughout the course

of the book. Do you believe that some good things should be earned first?

7. Why do you think Scarlett chose to hide her cancer diagnosis and the real reason for the road trip from Chrissie for as long as she did?

8. Critics of death-with-dignity policies in places like Vermont and Oregon fear that allowing outside residents to access their services will turn them into "death tourism" locations. Do you agree with this concern? Why or why not?

9. The two-headed calf tourist site mentioned in the book is fictional, but Crane Hot Springs, Devils Tower, and the giant ball of twine in Minnesota are real. What must-see Americana sites are on your road-trip wish list?

10. What significance do you think the title has? What were some of the key goodbyes said by characters along the way?

ABOUT THE AUTHOR

Lucy Gilmore is a celebrated novelist in a wide range of genres, including literary fiction, contemporary romance, and cozy mystery. She began her reading (and writing) career as an English literature major and ended as a booklover without all those pesky academic papers attached.

She lives in Spokane, Washington, with her family.

Website: LucyGilmore.com
Facebook: AuthorLucyGilmore
Instagram: tamaratamaralucy

COMING SOON
FROM LUCY GILMORE

THE BOOK OF FORGOTTEN THINGS

When the gruff hermit who saved them from a forest fire lies dying, a group of former childhood friends reunite, only to discover that the stories they've built their lives around are finally ready to be rewritten.